PENGUIN BOOKS

CORPSING

Toby Litt was born in 1968. His first two books are a short-story collection, *Adventures in Capitalism*, and a novel, *Beatniks*.

Corpsing

TOBY LITT

PENGUIN BOOKS

To Mum and Dad

✦ ✦ ✦

PENGUIN BOOKS

Published by the Penguin Group
Penguin Books Ltd, 27 Wrights Lane, London W8 5TZ, England
Penguin Putnam Inc., 375 Hudson Street, New York, New York 10014, USA
Penguin Books Australia Ltd, Ringwood, Victoria, Australia
Penguin Books Canada Ltd, 10 Alcorn Avenue, Toronto, Ontario, Canada M4V 3B2
Penguin Books India (P) Ltd, 11 Community Centre, Panchsheel Park,
New Delhi – 110 017, India
Penguin Books (NZ) Ltd, Cnr Rosedale and Airborne Roads, Albany,
Auckland, New Zealand
Penguin Books (South Africa) (Pty) Ltd, 5 Watkins Street, Denver Ext 4,
Johannesburg 2094, South Africa

Penguin Books Ltd, Registered Offices: Harmondsworth, Middlesex, England

First published by Hamish Hamilton Ltd 2000
Published in Penguin Books 2000
1

Lyrics from 'Violence' (Sparhawk/Micheletti/Parker/Nichols) © 1995 by kind
permission of Universal Music Publishing Ltd

The moral right of the author has been asserted

Set in Monotype Garamond
Printed in Great Britain by Clays Ltd, St Ives plc

Corpse (korps), v. slang. 1874.
1. To kill (*vulgar*) 1884. **2.** *Actors' slang.* To confuse or put out (an actor), or spoil (a piece of acting), by some blunder.

The Shorter Oxford English Dictionary

No, you can't trust violence
— Low, 'Violence'

1

'Conrad? It's Lily. Hi. Yes. Glad I got the number right. How are you? Really? That's – *encouraging*. Look, someone's just blown me out. I've got this table at a restaurant, Le Corbusier, Soho. D'you know it? Uh-huh. Yeah, but the food's really wonderful – and we do need to meet up sometime, you know. There are things we need to talk about. Like you said. So why don't we make it this evening and keep it in a public place – try and make it *pleasant*, at least. Well, it's y'know a difficult situation. And I promise I won't cry if you won't. Conrad, that was a *joke*. Christ! Eight, yeah. You don't want to meet up for a drink beforehand? You never. Hey. It was a jo. Mmmm. Touch-eee. Okay, yeah-oh. Yeah, there's some. I'll bring it along. God. Mm-'kay. Yeah-bye.'

Lily has caught me in the edit suite at the Discovery Channel, so the VT Editor, Chris – all VT Editors are called Chris – is sitting next to me with a big I'm-not-listening smirk on his face.

We are putting together the sixth of seven scarifying trailers for Shark Week. A Great White is freeze-framed on the screen in front of us, having just taken a watermelon-huge slice out of a scuba-diver's right thigh.

No way can we cut this particular shark-attack footage into what is intended to be a heavy-rotation trail. But Chris and I enjoy watching it – forwards and backwards, in ultraslow motion, frame by bloody frame.

At the moment Lily calls, we are using the Great White's gaping

1

mouth as a sort of pseudo-screensaver. We are planning what we'll do next – more company coffee or going for a take-out.

I don't even pretend to Lily that I might have something better to do that evening.

2

On the walk to the restaurant I try very hard not to think of what is about to take place: my first meeting with Lily since she dumped me.

As I turn down Frith Street I am still relatively okay.

I think: I am going to have to sit at a table with her. I am going to have to choose what to eat. As if I *cared* what I ate. As if I *cared* about food or restaurants or anything.

Anything but her. And us.

Lily is there already – standing at the downstairs bar, flirting with the barman. She looks great, as always. I haven't seen her wearing this dress before – it must be new: I know all her dresses, even the ones that never made it out of the wardrobe.

I think she may have changed her perfume as well.

'Hello, Suit,' Lily says.

It is an old joke – a couple-joke, now and in this context particularly painful: I have only one suit, and when Lily used to meet me in town, before some smart party to which she'd been invited and at which I'd be barely tolerated, Lily used to greet the suit rather than me. Sometimes, she used to say, she thought she was actually going out with the suit, and not me – I just came along to animate the suit (not particularly well, others would have done it better).

As I realize what Lily has just said, I begin to feel bad: Lily has forfeited the right to make the suit joke. If she wants to regain that right, she will first have to take me back. Which she may, of course, do. That may be why she wanted to see me.

'Hello, Frock.'

'Oh, do you like it? It's new – from ghost.'

The maître d' approaches us. The maître d' addresses Lily. 'I'm afraid you'll have a couple of minutes' wait before your table comes free.'

'Fine,' she says, smiling.

3

Lily is an actress. At this, the time of our last meeting, she is best known for her rôle in a series of TV advertisements.

In each ad Lily's character (*Bran*-dy) dresses up in one of a variety of mainstream-kinky outfits – flirty French maid, saucy schoolgirl, nympho ski-instructress, whip-cracking dominatrix – in a renewed attempt to persuade her hunky-but-chunky husband (Cyril) to sample a particularly bran-heavy breakfast cereal. The pay-off – which never ever varies – is that, as soon as Brandy has given her trademark *humph* and slammed the kitchen door behind her, hunky-but-chunky Cyril will slyly produce a large bowl of the bran-heavy cereal from beneath his trademark newspaper. He will then cheekily turn to the camera, wink endearingly and start ecstatically chomping.

Buh-boom.

All of Lily's cereal ads take place in that strange parallel universe, the Cosmos of Commercials – where colours are primary, perspectives neo-Expressionist, gestures cartoonish and pain non-existent.

And for most people this is the universe that Brandy-Lily will for ever inhabit. Blissfully married to a husband who cynically deceives her; endlessly propositioning him, eternally rebuffed; constantly crashing from blazing optimism to fiery pique. For most people Brandy-Lily is in Hell eternal.

A year or so before I met her, Lily spent six months at EuroDisney – playing Snow White in a black wig and a crushingly uncomfortable bodice. She could still flip into Snow White's cutesy, high-pitched accent at will. If anything marked Lily out as a natural actress, it was her wonderful way with voices. The smile-lines she'd acquired from all that corporate grinning in Mauschwitz never quite left the sides of her mouth – the way she told it, she'd practically been in muscle-spasm by the end of each and every shift. One sure way I'd always had of driving Lily crazy was to whistle while I worked.

After Snow White there'd been a few months' gap before she was cast in a made-for-TV murder mystery. Her part was simple enough: she took her clothes off, had a shower and was violently murdered. Her big break.

At the time of the meal, I still have this episode on video. Since she dumped me, the tape has become quite worn. I am intending, one day soon, to take it in to work and make a copy of it.

Being Brandy pays Lily well enough to think of Le Corbusier as reasonably affordable.

While we are waiting for the table to come free, Lily has been telling me her good news. She has just got the lead in a likely-to-be-controversial new play at the Royal Court. It is called 'deathsex' and is about women and necrophilia. She is about to quit the ads.

Really, Lily is going to make it very big, very quickly.

She has It.

4

'So,' Lily is saying to me.

My life is very different to hers – a slow and painful coming-to-terms with first the possibility, then the suspicion, and finally the utter certainty that I don't have It.

Instead, I am working in television, as a Promotions Producer – editing trails for whichever of the satellite channels happens to need me that month.

I have always wanted to make films. Even at school I was constantly thinking of cheapo special effects that could be used in a low-budget movie. (If you want a sink to look like someone's been sick in it, slosh a Pot Noodle in there. If you want something that looks exactly like spunk, use shampoo.) Needless to say, I have never come anywhere close to needing cheapo vomit or low-budget spunk. (A shame I never came up with placebo blood – tomato ketchup isn't anywhere realistic enough.)

It is my ultimate ambition to write and direct a serious full-length feature film and win two Oscars (Best Original Screenplay, Best Director) and be world famous and rich and loved.

Instead I am being fucked around by a series of decreasingly talented and increasingly stroppy writers.

As enthusiastic film-buffs, these writers and I have sat together in bars and pubs discussing Tarkovsky and Tarantino, Huston and Hitchcock. As a pitch-making mean machine, we have approached producers and have received much encouragement but no cash. As a writer-director team, we have entered a hundred BBC short-film competitions and never even got past the first round.

I am thirty, and I know things just aren't going to happen for me like they're happening for Lily.

I just don't have It.

Lily knows this.

It – or my lack of It – may be one of the reasons she left me. We still need to talk about It (or just it).

'This is ridiculous,' Lily says, meaning my long silences.

'Your table is ready,' says the maître d'.

5

It is a balmy, bare-fleshed Friday evening, late in August. Lily and I are seated opposite each other upstairs at Le Corbusier, a Modern French restaurant half-way along Frith Street.

The interior designer has won several international awards for creating this innovative-yet-functional space.

The upstairs room is clinical. The tables are a frosty-looking brushed aluminium. The walls are half mirror, half stainless steel. The floor is hard, pale, unpolished wood. The lighting comes from fluorescent strip-lights part-concealed behind the edges of the mirrors. The food is served on white porcelain plates. The cutlery is stainless steel. The napkins are white cotton. The napkin holders are rings of shiny stainless steel. The waiters wear white cotton jackets with stainless-steel buttons. French bread is served on a napkin of white cotton in a bowl of latticed aluminium with a rim of stainless steel.

The waiter – with close-shaven head and a thick goatee-beard – is taking our orders: for me, the puffball and the grilled plaice, for Lily, the asparagus and the veal escalope.

Already, we have compromised on a 1992 Chardonnay – which has turned out aromatic and endearing, the little of it we have so far drunk.

All of this – the restaurant, the mere idea of the restaurant – is much more expensive than I can afford.

But I can afford even less to let Lily know that.

'Fine,' I say, handing the menu back to the waiter.

It is far from fine.

6

It is six-weeks-three-days since Lily and I split up, unamicably, at her insistence. Before then we had been going out for two years, and living together for one. The top-floor Notting Hill flat which we shared belonged to her (and before her to her parents), so I was the one forced to move out. I found myself a ground-floor flat in Mortlake, grotty but cheap.

The moment Lily said she didn't love me or fancy me any more, pop songs started to play in my head – and not just any pop songs: really crappy, supposedly forgettable ones: 'Can't Smile Without You', 'Leaving on a Jet Plane', 'All By Myself', 'You're an Uptown Uptempo Woman (I'm a Downtown Down-beat Guy)'. I sat on the edge of what was now *her* sofa, weeping. She told me not to be so silly. I was out of there within a fort-night. I remember walking away from the flat for what I thought was the last time – the keys to the front door no longer in my pocket.

And yet here I am with Lily again, facing her over a frosty-looking brushed-aluminium table in Le Corbusier.

Lily's body is something I am so familiar with – yet there it is, sitting across from me, become a forbidden thing.

I know and can remember the minutest things about her: the squeak her fingernails made against the pillows under my head; the little clattering clicks her teeth made in the few slow moments after she fell asleep, always before me; the eggy smell of her early morning yawns.

Never again will my fingertips tap down upon her hard flat

stomach. Never again will my tongue make tiny circles around her salty-sweet clitoris.

This is outrageous, I am thinking. *This is almost obscene.*

I remember her habits, her ways: how she used to steal my pillow the moment I got out of bed to go to work, cradling its warmth to her belly as she had so rarely cradled me; how she would suck me off, and would swallow, but had to brush her teeth immediately afterwards, couldn't not.

As I sit there opposite her, I feel that her body is something that I have almost a *right* to be intimately involved with.

What I really want to do, I am thinking, as I look across at Lily, gazing out over the widening gap of success and down into the chasm of indifference, *what I want most of all in the world is to make you pregnant: I want to put a cut in your life so deep that the scar will be the first thing people mention when they mention you, think of when they think of you. And, even more, I want you to* want *me to make you pregnant.*

I am still in love with her.

All that happened, all she said, and I am still in love with her.

She is saying something now.

'Bastard,' I hear Lily say.

Bullet #1

The first bullet (there are to be six: evenly distributed – three for her, three for me – though not equally destructive) enters Lily's body approximately two inches beneath her left breast. Slowly, or if not slowly then gradually, or if not gradually then at least moment by moment, leaving no gap in actual proceeding time, jumping no millimetre completely, the bullet begins its inevitable passage into Lily's thorax. A small brown mole taking the shape of a capsized figure-of-eight which she bears approximately two inches beneath her left breast, stark against her blue-white and otherwise unblemished skin, will be nowhere accounted for at the autopsy – and so instantly must be vaporized: pouff! Already, before it accomplishes even this minor initial slaughter, that first bullet has traversed ten feet of air-conditioned air, has clipped through the floating grey viscose of Lily's ghost frock, has slit the slick black silk of her camisole. Now, however, that almost-perfect skin of hers begins slowly to stretch – resisting the onwardness of the bullet's metal apex, denting inwards above her delicate ribcage, tightening momentarily from shoulder to hip: but then – after this false, hopeless opposition – punctures easily enough. An anticlockwise spin has been imparted to the bullet by spiral grooves – called rifles – back inside the barrel of the guilty gun. This spinning motion maximizes flight-stability and therefore increases terminal accuracy. But it is the skin-stretch of kinetic energy not the drill of missile-spin that takes the bullet through into first flesh.

Entrance wounds are notoriously sexy. And although I will not get to see Lily's wounds while they are fresh, I will study photographs of other penetrations: the abrasion ring that encircles an entrance wound, caused by the bullet rubbing the skin, turning it raw, looks like bright pink lipstick under slick lipgloss.

The bullet, during the long moment of entry, is not only spinning but also yawing slightly – like a fish, swimming, seen from above.

Despite refinements in weapon design over the past twenty-five years (particularly in higher quality barrelling and improved systems of rifling) some instability is always likely to occur in the flight paths of physical objects. However, this yawing only begins to play a major rôle in trajectorization once this first bullet has passed out of the air and into the denser material of the human body.

Lily's body.

After the skin and a thin layer of fat (forgive me, Lily), some thoracic vessels, nerves and membranes, the bullet next enters the red cross-hatching of Lily's ribcage muscles: external oblique, external intercostal, internal intercostal, innermost intercostal.

As the bullet passes through the cohesive but elastic tissue of the muscles, a cavity of greater diameter than the bullet's own is temporarily created – around and behind it. For all of five to ten milliseconds after the bullet passes, this ripping-rippling emptiness pulsates – in and out, in and out – spreading damage laterally, through to tissues the bullet itself hasn't even touched. This phenomenon is technically known as cavitation.

Next, the bullet breaks both Lily's fifth and sixth ribs. The thudding force of this impact sends off a number of bone-splinters to do further peripheral damage.

These secondary missiles are a well-known feature of gunshot wounds, and often – as in Lily's case – do as much damage as the primary missile.

One particularly sharp rib-fragment slides up in a smooth parabola of harm towards the apex of Lily's heart. Another, broader and less bladelike, plunges down in the direction of her liver. A third – almost circular in shape – stops millimetres short of puncturing her spleen.

It is bone-spray and not bullet-bluntness that slits the gauzy sheet of Lily's pleura.

By now the bullet has lost some but not much of its forward impetus, its kinetic energy. The fifth and sixth ribs – as it smashes through them – have rocked it a little, exaggerating its fishlike yawing, its ongoing wobble.

One of the ballistic laws governing the motion of a projectile through a *body states: the greatest damage will occur neither at the point of initial entry, nor at some arbitrary mid-point, but at exactly the point where there is the greatest loss of kinetic energy. In other words, the more the moving bullet starts to yaw, to wobble, to tumble, the more harm its passage will cause.*

Next, the bullet carves into the inferior lobe of her left lung, a greater and more passable space – less dense, less damageable.

The bullet passes out of Lily's left lung between the sixth and seventh ribs, severing the intercostal nerve, vein and artery. The sixth rib itself is only cracked, but the seventh shatters – spewing dusty bone-fragments off in the direction of the bullet.

When the bullet has passed a sufficient distance onwards, these bone-fragments will start to be sucked back inwards again by the contraction and resettlement of the muscle tissues.

At the moment the bullet meets the muscles of Lily's back, it is travelling sideways. Harsh contact with her posterior ribcage has finally converted its wobble into a fully developed tumble. The bone-resistance has also slightly deformed the front end of the bullet. Tissue damage to the internal oblique, erector spinae and latissimus dorsi muscles is therefore exaggerated.

Next, through fat, dermis, epidermis, dead skin, hairs.

Because Lily – at the moment the shooting takes place – is leaning against a metal chair-back, the exit wound of the first bullet is not quite as simple as it might otherwise have been.

Exit wounds commonly look like stars, slits, circles or crescents.

In Lily's case, the wound – because of the presence of the chair-back – becomes what is known as shored.

As the sideways bullet pops from her back, the skin is stretching outwards – and pressing, hard, against the firm stopping surface of the chair.

This pressure, which is exerted also through the fabric of Lily's camisole and Lily's frock, turns her exit wound from a clean, simple shape into a smeared, succulent, minutely latticed, clitoris-like thing.

7

'Bastard,' she is saying.

The hitman – at this point – is a brightly coloured blur across the extreme right of my peripheral vision.

But after the first bullet has gone through Lily, shattering the mirror behind her, I glance round to look at him.

Lily is being executed by a bike courier. He is dressed in a Day-Glo-orange cycle top. He is wearing skin-tight bicycling shorts and has a dispatch rider's bag by his side. He is wearing a safety helmet. His eyes are hidden behind splat-shaped mirror-lensed glasses. His mouth and nose are covered by a pollution-exclusion mask. His calves are sinewy-powerful. He has a two-way radio on his left shoulder. In his right hand is a black and metallic-silver gun.

He looks like a vision of the future – a future where everyone is concerned solely with keeping their bodies fit and dodging between fast new technologies of danger, a future of which I want no part.

Somehow, I can't believe that someone prepared to wear a Day-Glo-orange cycle top would also be prepared to kill. (Or vice versa.)

This man isn't shooting Lily properly. He should be coached in the etiquette of it, by respectful professionals of the old school. The business should be done by men dressed in black suits (impeccably tailored by their honest uncles) and white shirts (freshly laundered by their devoted mothers). As they go gliding past the waiters, these men should share a wisecrack about the lobsters outliving the clientele. 'It's a job of work,' that should be the attitude – not 'Come out and play' or 'Let's stop off for a burger.' This guy has stepped out of the traffic and he will step back into the traffic. It is like being killed by his bicycle, not by him. That someone wearing this techno-fibred get-up can shoot someone seems to undermine the seriousness of the act. Lily's death – I am certain she is going to die – is being made into a joke. He should go away and change and then come back and apologize, and do it properly, with the full decorum it deserves.

As I look back at Lily, the second bullet hits her.

It is a headshot.

A plume of bloody spray whips back into the broken mirror behind her.

Her scalp is flipping up, still connected to the back of her head by a flap of skin.

I start to giggle.

As Lily leans slowly forwards, she catches my eye. I am sure she is looking out at me. From death.

'Bastard,' she is saying.

Lily's head tilts further. Her eyes go up into the back of her head. As if at orgasm. As if a dying saint.

The third bullet hits her, biting through the edge of the table and lodging in her belly.

She lolls.

I am giggling and giggling and giggling and I don't know why.

(The very last thing Lily saw in this life was – most likely, most terribly – me, my face, my open mouth, my inexplicable giggling. I don't think I could frame an expression for her to look at at such a time that would have been adequate – but I am not an actor. And, anyway, we're all meant to be able to perform our own lives. Only, there was no rehearsal time scheduled for this – or maybe there was. Maybe that's why I felt so bad. I'd practised a thousand times – at the movies, in front of a video. Bang.)

16

Then the hitman turns and aims at me. He is about ten feet away.

I lean back in my chair, without pushing it backwards. I want to get up. I want to hide.

But I can't. I am starting to lose my balance.

The fourth bullet, my first, skids diagonally across my chest and mashes into my left arm.

I am shouting the usual victim-things.

My head falls backwards as I lose balance.

I flinch away from the hitman.

The fifth bullet misses me completely.

The hitman moves a step closer.

I am now stuck in a ridiculous position, my chair tipping far far back, my feet supported by the underside of the table, almost horizontal, almost flying.

The sixth shot goes through my lower right side, my bowels.

People are now moving around in the edges of what I can see.

The hitman fires a shot into the ceiling.

The people stop moving.

My eyes close.

No further shots come.

I am opening my eyes.

The hitman has gone.

I am looking down.

I see that I have a white-cotton napkin in my hands and that I have folded it up several times, in halves.

As I bleed, I continue folding the napkin until it is as tight as it will go.

I look up to the ceiling and see blood dripping down.

I look down at the table.

Blood. Lots of blood. Blood everywhere. Blood all over. Blood pooling in Lily's lap. Blood in a fine misty spray on the mirror shattered behind her. Blood jumping from her chest-wound, like a heavy red frog. Blood seeping between my fingers. Blood

17

staining the pale wood of the floor. Blood in the hair of the screaming woman at the table next to ours. Blood on her quiet husband's white shirt. Blood on our food. Blood on blood. Her blood. My blood. My blood on hers. Her blood on mine. Our blood together. Blood-in-blood. Arterial blood. Venous blood. Dripping blood and blood smearing. Flowing blood and blood coagulating. Blood exiting from my body. Blood pulsing with my pulse. My blood. Life-blood. Bloody fucking. Fucking bloody.

Blessedly, I lose consciousness.

I don't get it back for six weeks.

Hospital Admission Report

Name: (Alun Grey – deleted) Conrad Redman
DOB: ?
Address: ?
Occupation: ?
Smoker: ?
Blood type: AB
Estimated length of stay: 9 months

Report:
Severe internal haemorrhaging caused by gunshot wound
– lower left abdomen, kidneys damaged. Massive trauma.

Patient lost consciousness at site of shooting. Con-
cussion – fell off chair on to floor.

CPR. Blood transfusion. Lost four to five pints of
blood. Adrenalin drip infused.

Surgery, straight into. Requires immediate intervention.

Summary:
Critical but stable.

Signed:

EMERGENCY

BRANDY SHOT DEAD

by SHEILA BURROUGHS

Actress Lilian Irish, 26, best known as 'Brandy', was yesterday brutally shot and killed whilst dining in London's exclusive Le Corbusier restaurant.

After a chase through the crowded backstreets of Soho, the hitman was himself shot and wounded by police.

Eye-witnesses report the hitman was dressed as a bicycle courier.

Members of Scotland Yard's specialist firearms unit SO16 are understood to have been involved in the pursuit.

Cont. p. 2 col. 6

Brandy's companion, a man of around 30, whose identity is not at this time known, was also shot.

He was taken to University College Hospital, where his condition is reported to be 'critical but stable'.

The shootings bears all the hallmarks of a contract-killing. Scotland Yard has refused to comment on this possibility. A police spokesman was quoted as saying, 'The inquiry is at too early a stage to indulge in such speculation.'

MIRROR GROUP NEWSPAPERS

.40 ESP

Manufactured from high-strength corrosion-free polymers, the .40 ESP (European Self-loading Pistol) is the most technologically advanced pistol Gruber & Litvak have ever created.

Available in three finishes (matt black, blue or stainless), the .40 ESP will take all the punishment you can throw at it.

Our engineers and scientists have immersed the .40 ESP for extended periods in salt water, have fired it at temperatures of −44°F (−42°C) and 153°F (67°C) and have subjected it to NATO Mil-Spec mud and rain tests.

The result?

As this catalogue goes to press, the .40 ESP has test-fired over 37,000 Smith & Wesson rounds without malfunction: no failures to feed, no stovepipes, no jams whatsoever!

The specially designed Smooth-barrelling System (patent pending) reduces wear and tear, to enhance and prolong the .40 ESP's service life.

In the .40 ESP, we at Gruber & Litvak have created a mid-size defensive pistol with all the stopping power that the discerning shooter will ever require.

As well as setting new standards for the future, our scientists have also learnt from the successes of the past. The .40 ESP therefore operates with a modified Browning-type action – as based upon the classic and much-loved Government Model 1911.

In addition to which, the .40 ESP – thanks to our Recoil Disenhancement System (RDS™) – produces far less felt recoil and muzzle flip than equivalent pistols.

Finally, the .40 ESP is a remarkably *safe* pistol. It has an ergonomically efficient mixture of five separate safeties – some passive, some active.

Gruber & Litvak have a world-wide reputation for creating quality firearms, a reputation that the launch of the .40 ESP can only serve to enhance.

The .40 ESP is yet another step on our long road 'towards the perfect pistol'.

8

There's not much you can say about being in a coma.

For six weeks I was less a human being, more a terribly unproductive drain upon the National Grid. I owe my life to the men and women of Southern Electric. Six weeks. Their power breathed for me, regulated my pulse, kept me warm, fed me, made quietly eloquent beeps on my behalf, and monitored almost every aspect of my physical and mental existence.

This was the dream-illness: the one you're not around for.

The best analogy I've managed to come up with is this: Being in a coma is like being a perfectly functioning, top-of-the-range television transported to a completely uninhabited moon. With no TV signals to receive, my mind was the clearest cleanest static. In static, just as in flames, you soon start to imagine patterns – and to see pictures. These pictures are the much-debated topic of coma-dreams. My chief terror was the wolf, who appeared in my mind periodically – though I had no real sense of time. The wolf would eat my legs. Other people in my Internet coma-recovery group claimed also to have encountered the wolf – but only after I had mentioned him first.

When I came round I was inexplicably bruised all over, particularly on my upper arms. My foreskin appeared to have been pierced by a sharp object, possibly a scalpel.

My legs were slightly wasted away, making walking an issue of rehabilitation and encouragement.

The only period in my entire adult life that I've had a full set of fingernails was the first few hours after I came out of my coma.

My room in the ITU was dim. Anglepoise lamps rained their light down on to desks. LCDs glowed green and red.

Mother was there at my bedside – as she had been for most of the previous month and a half. The first thing I saw when I opened my eyes was her smiling face.

My first thought was *I need to have a piss*; my second, *There is someone out there who it is now my obligation to kill.*

Yes, even the word *obligation* was there in my mind.

They removed my respirator a few hours afterwards. I indulged myself with a marathon choking and gasping session.

There was a great deal of mother-love.

Still, I started biting my fingernails before I started talking. (As soon as I realized it really *was* my mother who was there.)

'Granny sends her love,' she said.

This was a lie: Granny had Parkinson's and couldn't remember whether she took sugar in her tea, let alone the existence of some abstract grandson. (She took two.)

Doctors and nurses came and went.

I began to recover.

Waking was often a trauma, and it was best I did it alone. I attacked people – that's how it seemed to them. Really, I was trying to fight them off – them and their whole physicality.

I was terrified of bunches of flowers. They made me cower. Yet I felt compelled to count all the grapes in any bunch I received, in order to control them.

People were too much: giant beings with pancake-sized pores, football-bulging zits and spearlike nostril hairs. Doctors leaning in to my face with penlights always made me scream.

'This won't hurt.'

It already does.

If I could, I would have tried to encourage the nurses to wear even more make-up, to be as artificial as they could possibly be. My ultimate wish was for them to become medical geisha.

It felt as if I had popped up into the world like an *écorché* – a flayed man, peeled of all protection, experiencing breeze as hurricane, cough as cataclysm, smell as orgasm (if nice) or disembowelment (if nasty), touch as torture. I didn't want to be so beyond-human. I wanted the muffled dullness of my old-self. The hippies thought that the doors of perception could be cleansed with one sort of acid. But when it happened to me, it felt more like the other sort. Hydrochloric. An acid bath. Everything outside dissolving until the inner is exposed to forces it was never meant to face.

There is too much world.

That was the only sentence I could come up with.

There is too much world.

(Remember the playground joke: What goes plink-plink fizz? Two babies dropped in an acid bath.)

I refused to be prodigal of my perceptions. I closed my eyes and listened to the ticking of the floor, the walls.

I got a reputation for being mildly eccentric.

Why couldn't they credit me with surviving? That's all I wanted. My badge and go home.

It was music that lassooed me and pulled me back in towards humanity. Hospital Radio – like a downer, slowing the world up and shooting it through a filter of hazy rippling golden nostalgia. I would sit there with the disability-grey headphones in my ears, blissing out. Hospital Radio is audio heroin. I heard rumours that some of the porters took bootleg tapes along with them when they went to visit their dealers – swapping a stack of C90s and some legal storeroom drugs (Valium, methadone, Mogadon) for a 10 per cent discount on their few twists of coke. Hospital Radio – it brought me close to a sad ecstasy. This was music for another generation, a generation of which I was temporarily a member. Frank Sinatra, Bing Crosby, Dean Martin, Doris Day – these people knew about pain and suffering, they understood the need for mollification and nullity. These were the Saints in the Church

25

of Our Lady of Nice'n'Easy. Bless them, bless each and every one of them.

My recovery was progressing well.

Then, all at once, they started telling me the news – the good news and the bad news.

9

First there was my doctor.

'Umm, listen . . .'

He pulled up a chair and sat down at my bedside. (This meant news.) He spoke quietly and quickly. (This meant the news was not good.) And he used my first name. (This meant Lily was dead.) He spoke for a while in a comforting tone. (This meant Lily had died very slowly, in an agony so extreme that it took her beyond being Lily, being female, almost beyond being human.)

I counted the square tiles in the ceiling.

When I started listening again, the doctor was talking about my legs. Apparently I was going to have to do physiotherapy.

'How long did she take to die?' I asked.

The doctor looked at me, realizing a lot of things all at once. He knew he shouldn't lose his temper with me, so he went back to the beginning.

'We estimate the time of her death to be approximately twenty minutes after the shooting.'

'In the ambulance?'

'We didn't try moving her – she died in the restaurant.'

'Were you there?'

'No, I wasn't.'

'Have you ever been there?'

'Um, no.'

'Well, I wouldn't recommend it as a dining experience.'

He obviously didn't feel this was a gag he had any right to laugh at.

'After she died, she was brought here – to UCH. Then she was buried. It was a nice funeral, I hear.'

'Did you ever see her?'

'No. I didn't. By the time she got here it was a matter for the pathologist.'

'Mmm,' I said, 'brain matter.'

'Perhaps we should discuss this later.'

'Do you know if she said anything? If she said anything about me?'

'To be honest, the injuries she sustained were so severe –'

'You mean her head?'

'Principally.'

I smiled, I believe for the first time.

'I like that – *principally*.'

He went on.

'The areas of her brain that dealt with speech were still physically intact. However, the shock must have been so great that I doubt she would have been capable of using them.'

'Is that your professional opinion?'

'It is.'

'How long have you been a doctor?'

'Twelve years.'

'It would probably be a good idea to take you seriously, then.'

'I'll leave that up to you.'

'You know, it's funny. I'm sure I heard her saying *bastard-bastard-bastard* as I was dying.'

'Given that you were in a room full of people who'd just seen a hitman shoot you, I'd say it's quite likely one of them was calling *him* a bastard. You probably heard that.'

'Lily was my girlfriend for two years. I know her voice.'

'Well, maybe you weren't in quite the best state –'

'I did die, didn't I?'

'For about half a minute, yes. In the operating theatre.'
'Tell me about the guy who shot us.'
'I think I'd better leave that to the police.'

10

The police came next. They asked me question after question. My questions back to them went unanswered.

Eventually, I found out that the hitman was now in jail. The way he had been caught, putting it together from what I'd read in the newspapers (my mother kept all the cuttings) and from what the police let slip, was actually quite stupid.

Apparently, he'd arranged for some kid to stand outside Le Corbusier holding his bike while he went inside to do the job. This, he'd thought, would save him valuable getaway time afterwards. No need to unlock the bike, just take it from the kid who he'd paid to hold it. Of course, the boy wasn't to know what was about to happen inside the restaurant. It seemed a sensible plan. However, this particular boy thought that the money the hitman was paying him wasn't enough – so he decided to nick the bike instead. Unfortunately, his feet didn't really reach the pedals. So when the hitman emerged, fresh from his crime, he found the boy and the bike gone. But when he looked fifty yards along the road, he saw the boy wobbling up to, then crashing into, the side of a black cab. The hitman sprinted down the street, becoming more conspicuous with every step. The police would have no shortage of witnesses to his mad run. He started shouting. More witnesses. The cab-driver got out of his vehicle to see if the bike had done any damage to his paintwork. The bike – a Cannondale Super-V Raven 4000 – was worth a couple of months of most people's wages: including the cab-driver's. This was the simple reason for the hitman's pursuit. When the police later asked him whatever he was thinking of, running away from the commission of a serious crime and straight into a confrontation that would draw the attention of half the street, the hitman replied: 'My bike is a Cannondale Super-V Raven 4000. You don't just let some kid steal one of those. The kid was going to die, especially if it was damaged.' 'But you'd just shot someone,' the police said. 'To be honest,' the bike-crazed hitman replied, 'I forgot all about that the moment I saw my bike was gone.' The damage to the black cab was minor but unmissable: the pedal had removed paint, leaving behind a silver-grey slash on the left rear wheel-arch, the handlebars had skidded along the side of the door. The bike itself was unharmed. The kid, though, was in the way of getting himself killed – if not by the hitman then by the cab-driver. By this time, traffic was building up behind the incident. Horns were being honk-HONKED. Heads were snaking out of driver's-side windows. Expletives were escalating. As soon as the boy saw the hitman running towards him, he dropped the bike and took off. Again the handlebars slammed into the paintwork.

'It's mine,' shouted the hitman as he arrived, hardly out of breath. 'The bike is mine.'

He tore it from the cab-driver's hands.

'That little cunt was stealing it,' the hitman said.

'Well, someone's going to have to pay for this.'

The cabbie's thick finger touched the grey gash.

'Yeah,' said the hitman, mounting up. 'You will.'

Two of the drivers trapped in the cars behind had got out to give the cabbie some up-close-and-personal grief.

'Come back!' shouted the cab-driver.

The hitman was riding rapidly along the pavement, the bike rocking from side to side between his legs.

The cabbie swore, and didn't bother chasing him.

'Alright! Alright!' he said to the two irate drivers.

It was then that they heard the sirens, shortly followed by the gunfire.

The hitman was now in Wandsworth Prison.

I imagined him in his grey cell: doing squats and press-ups to keep those pecs and calves toned up, reading bike magazines and fantasizing about gear ratios, waking up from a nightmare about not having killed me – of having failed to do his job well enough.

11

Then there were two young women: Vicky, not her real name, and Anne-Marie.

Vicky was the Victim Support Counsellor sent along by the police.

She was a sweet, long-haired girl with a crumbly grandmother's chin and brown-stained teeth. When she spoke it came out as half comic-cockney and half joke-yokel.

'Any time you want to call me up – day or night, please do. We want to look after you, ahead of the trial.'

You could tell that she hated her job, hated her clients and most of all hated herself – for not having whatever it took (guts, imagination, ambition) to get herself somewhere else.

'Here's my office number. And my mobile.'

Altogether now – ahhhhh, for poor Vicky.

I gave her a line about me wanting to confront the perpetrator of the crime of which I'd been the victim. In other words, when I finally got out of hospital, was there any way she could get me in to see the hitman. She said she thought it wouldn't be possible. The police were still proceeding towards a prosecution. He would be the accused. I would be the chief witness. We weren't exactly going to be allowed to get together and compare notes. I would have to wait until after he was convicted – 'Are you sure of that?' I said. 'Convicted? We're talking about the police here.' – before I would be able to do any prison-visiting. But I wasn't going to get anything out of him the police hadn't already. What was he going to do? See me in a wheelchair and break down in contrite sobs, confess all and name names? Not outside of a very bad movie. I did want to see him, though. I wanted to see what kind of person he was, how he spoke, how he moved, whether I'd've liked him if he hadn't shot me.

Anne-Marie was much more of a surprise.

As far as I could remember, we'd been out for a couple of drinks together – and that was all. Yet here she was.

Anne-Marie worked as a booker in Lily's modelling agency, Select. She had the sad allure of a woman who spends her entire life assisting other women in the pursuit of a beauty she herself will never attain. Anne-Marie was nearly thirty. There were work-bags under her eyes, the corners of which were beginning to admit lines. Her teeth were the dull colour that Diet Coke stains ice cubes. She *was* beautiful, but not in the right way. If she'd been an actress, she'd have been perfect for young-and-damaged. As it was, damaged (really damaged) had yet to hit *Cosmopolitan*. If any harm was to be done to a model's appearance, then it was to be done by the make-up artist – and was to be temporary.

She seemed to be suffering from the fashion industry's love of tragedy-by-association. She'd brought flowers and grapes and magazines, as if she couldn't decide which.

'How are you?' she asked.

Then went on to talk about nothing but Lily for half an hour.

'I'll give you a call when I get out,' I said as she was going.

'Mmm,' she said, blushing. 'That'd be lovely.'

And another motive for her visit suddenly became apparent.

In between, for light relief, bringing neither good nor bad news, there were the the nurses.

'Aren't I supposed to find you attractive?' I said to the most lissome of all. 'Isn't that your job?'

She gave me an article to read about masculine sexualization of neutrally designed female work-uniforms.

'But I used to fancy schoolgirls, too,' I said, when I'd let enough time go by to pretend I'd read the article.

She gave me a pitying look.

'That's good,' I said. 'Could you do that again, but this time with your uniform off?'

She gave me the finger, smilingly – on the cusp of offence.

I rolled over on to my front and hiked down my pyjamas.

'Anything you say, nurse,' I said. 'But don't forget the lubrication.'

By the time I looked round again, she'd left the room.

I started crying.

12

Finally, there was Lily's solicitor.

He was a businesslike man in grey, obviously embarrassed by having to invent a bedside manner for himself.

The fact that I was recovering evidently caused him no small discomfort: if his errand had been a mercenary raid in search of a death-bed signature he would have been far more sanguine.

As it was, he gave me the news with a matter-of-factness that matched the cut of his hair, his suit, his fingernails.

'In the weeks before she died, following what I understand was your permanent separation, Lily neither made a new will nor altered the conditions of the old. Therefore, according to the terms of the latest will she made, about a year and a half before she died, you are named as sole beneficiary. You will therefore inherit all her assets, moveables and property. That includes the flat in Notting Hill which firstly belonged to Lily's parents and latterly to her mother alone. Lily's mother, I must warn you, is particularly distressed about this. I foresee some small trouble on that issue. There is also in existence a small life-insurance policy on a pension she had recently taken out.' Very unLily, I thought; then remembered I had persuaded her into it. He named some figures. 'However, I have consulted with Lily's parents – and they have indicated to me that among Lily's possessions there are a number of items – photographs and the like – which would be of some considerable sentimental value to them. They have therefore asked me to intercede with you on their behalf, and to ask if you would allow them to take these items from her flat.'

'I'll think about it,' I said.

'Also, I think you should know, for the sake of accuracy, or perhaps I should say conscience, that I did receive a phonecall from Lily on the very day of her death indicating that she fully intended to alter her will – urgently, in fact. Unfortunately, I wasn't able to meet her that day – and we all know the rest. But, in the knowledge of this, you might consider how Miss Irish might have wanted things.'

'How do you think she'd have wanted them?'

'She gave me some indication that she had a preference as to which of her parents was to receive the legacy.'

Her mother: Josephine.

'And Lily was going to make a new will giving everything to her?'

'That is what she led me to believe.'

'Including the flat,' I said.

'Including the flat,' he replied.

'I'll bear it in mind. Give Josephine the keys to the flat. Tell her she can take what she wants.'

13

Six months they gave me.

For a set number of hours a day, the State told me it valued and loved me.

However, I will spare you the tales of hospital-ward *bonhomie*; the horror stories and the at-the-time-hilarious jokes; the tributes to individual doctors and nurses; the deaths from trivial complaints and the recoveries from life-threatening illnesses; most of all, I'll spare you the unremitting devotion of my mother.

Count yourself lucky.

Walking my first few faltering steps was every bit as schmaltzy as you'd expect. Like a complete girl, I cried. But I'm not going to get all TV movie on you. My motivational methods were a little unconventional. (The physio disapproved.) I thought that if I hated myself enough, I would probably be able to shunt myself around. And so, to encourage movement, I used to chant with each step: Cri Pple Cri Pple. I walked.

My doctors bored me back to a semblance of a semblance of normality.

Six months since I recovered consciousness. Six months, and then I and my hardly-needed-any-more wheelchair were sitting in the back of a black London cab.

An interconnected group of strange-shaped metal objects were placed in my hands – these, I eventually recognized, were the keys to my flat.

The driver had already been given my address.

14

Turn the key in the Yale. I remember being a child and not being tall enough to reach the sink to wash my hands. Push open the door. I remember going to a wedding and falling off the churchyard wall and being winded and thinking I was dying – in a graveyard beneath yew trees. Step into the dead air, untickled by recent speech, unwarmed by skin or cooking, unloved by presence. I remember the month before I went to primary school, kneeling in front of a full-length mirror as my mother taught me to tie my shoelaces. Pick up the stack of letters on the sideboard in the hall. (There are no messages on my answerphone.) I remember the last day of term, the mystical boredom which I thought I'd never recapture – until I got my first job. Stagger into the toilet. I remember tripping over while I was running towards my mother holding my school report and smiling. *It looks like a spider has crawled across Conrad's page.* Vomit. Heave. Gag.

Cue my parents, a little late because of the traffic on the M40. My mother had already been into the flat to prepare it for my return.

'I've thrown away those magazines,' she'd said.

I didn't need to ask which. They'd been in the bottom drawer of my desk, along with my diary.

My mother knew me better than ever and liked me less and loved me more.

I opened the door for them.

'Oh, aren't you well? Let's get you to bed, then. Would you like a cup of tea? Herbal tea? Coffee? Hot milk? There's food in the fridge, frozen food in the freezer. There's fruit in the fruitbowl. I bought you a fruitbowl – it didn't look like you'd got one. You needed a fruitbowl. The rent's been paid. I've darned your socks. Please don't buy any more acrylic ones. There's a list of the people who left messages by the phone. Are you feeling better now? We had an awful journey. You're looking terrible. What time is it? Now, you know we both love you.' Beat. 'Very much.' Beat. 'You know. Dad is going to drive home now. I'm going to be staying in a little B&B round the corner. I've left their number for when you want to get in touch with me. They said they'd have you back at your work, whenever you feel like it. Everything's going to be all right. But you must be tired. Why don't you go to bed. I'll bring you some hot milk. Hug and kiss. Hug and kiss. There's no need to use that language.'

After that first year and a half of intensive ga-ga goo-goo, your parents can never address you sensibly again.

In the evening my mother brought me scrambled eggs – just like on the days I faked illness to get off going in to school. But I wasn't able to eat them.

'Why didn't you take the embryos out?' I bleated.

'There weren't any there.'

'Look, there's one. And another. They look like babies.'

I scraped them – crimson-flecked jelly – to the edge of the plate.

'I can't eat that.' Blood trailed across the yellow-white surface of the egg, blood swirled around the gelatinous not-yet-chick.

'I'll make you some more.'

'Please, no.'

'Baked beans on toast?'

'Okay.'

But the baked beans reminded me of the time my new pet lizard had a miscarriage, giving birth to the entirety of its womb.

'Weetabix and hot milk?'

'If you scrunch them up for me.'

She put her hand on my forehead. Even though I was obviously unwell, she wanted me to know how patient she was being. I would be expected to repay her – in kind – when I recovered: phonecalls, visits, Christmas.

I didn't sleep very well.

After being driven half mad by the deathly groaning and murderous snoring of the various terminal oldsters in my ward, I now found that I missed them.

The stereo was in reach of the bed. I put on Radio 2, which helped a little. But it was too harsh. It wasn't Hospital Radio.

I flicked the dial to one of the message stations – bleeping out inexplicable bursts of non-Morse. This was the sound of the Cold War, echoing past its use. I closed my eyes in a world still divided up between the Russian Bear and the American Eagle, Leonid Brezhnev and Ronald Reagan. Jets boomed over, descending towards Heathrow. I imagined them to be B-52s carrying atomic bombs – and I felt safe and warm and protected. Nuclear anxiety was merely another nostalgia.

Sleep came.

15

In the morning I got up before my mother arrived.

From around the flat I gathered together everything I could find that had any connection whatsoever with Lily.

I made a bonfire in the garden: an aerosol of Photo Mount, aftershave, an alarm clock, bank statements, books, CDs, a clockwork mouse, cutlery, diaries, dope, eau de cologne, a framed photograph of Francis Ford Coppola pointing a revolver into his head during the shooting of *Apocalypse Now*, Ikea things, letters, LPs, maps of our two holiday destinations (Dublin, Manhattan), medicines, newspaper cuttings, my NFT membership card, notebooks, pencils, pens, the photo album, Polaroids, postcards, Rizla papers, shampoo, the green Swatch she gave me, tapes, a toothbrush (special, for precoital brushings), a teddy-bear called 'Pinter' whom we'd always used as a prop to get past awkward silences, underwear (Calvins, not boxers), videos ('Brandy: The Complete Humphs'), a wastepaper basket in aluminium from Habitat, 3½″ diskettes.

I didn't have any paraffin or meths, so I poured a whole bottle of vodka over the pile.

Then I started to pick things off, thinking *not this, not this*.

First a Polaroid of Lily dressed as a Playboy Bunny. Next a tape of Nick Drake. Then Pinter. And the Nurofen. And another Polaroid, of Lily standing like a pale-yellow already-ghost in a friend's summer house. And the clockwork mouse.

~

Lily and I almost-met at a funeral. Highgate Cemetery. She was family – Malcolm (the deceased) had been her second cousin: childhood holidays in Cornwall, a crush. I was friends – I'd done work experience with Malcolm on a short film for which he was DP. Malcolm and I kept in touch afterwards, me always hoping I could use him for my directorial début. He was due to start on an adaptation of Henry James's *What Maisie Knew* two weeks after he died. The car mounted the pavement. Malcolm was killed instantly. If he hadn't been listening to his Walkman (*A Clockwork Orange* soundtrack), then maybe. For a fortnight, flowers and polythene marked the spot. Speed-bumps were put on the local council agenda, again. There was a five-line obituary in *Sight and Sound*. Malcolm 'possessed a rare visual acuity'.

After the funeral, family went to the reception in cars, friends walked to the nearest pub. I watched Lily get into the Mercedes-Benz and thought she was lovely, even though black didn't suit her. But she was one of those drastically gorgeous girls who are single for about five minutes every five years, so . . .

Several times – enough to make a worrying pattern – I have fallen in love with a woman because she reminded me of someone else, someone that I hadn't fallen in love with but felt I really should have. In Lily's case it was her voice: she had the exact same voice as someone in my tutorial group at university – someone I idolized intellectually but found in no way sexually attractive. I used to think *If only I were blind, then the fact I don't fancy her wouldn't matter. I could, I think, fall in love with the mere touch of her – but the sight of her, no*. Lily was the voice of this her, in just the most beautiful body imaginable.

The next time Lily and I met was in a kitchen, six months later, at a house party – totally unconnected to Malcolm. She was an actress, I was a film-person: we would have met, eventually – when old and married and bitter, maybe.

'It's Lily, isn't it?' I began. 'You were at Malcolm's funeral, weren't you?'

'Yes.'

I introduced myself, and we talked about Malcolm for five minutes. Then her boyfriend came in from the living room. Lily introduced us.

'We hardly know anyone here,' he said. 'We've been trying to guess what everyone does.'

'Him, for example,' said Lily, pointing out a man pouring a bottle of lemonade into the punch-bowl. 'He invented those blue fizzy things they have in chip shops to kill flies.'

'No,' said the boyfriend. 'He's actually a lumberjack.'

The lemonade-pourer was wearing a big black and red tartan shirt.

'What do *you* think he does?' asked Lily.

'Him?' I said. 'He's the Stannah-Stairlift test pilot.'

Lily snorted.

'And her?' said the boyfriend, indicating a very tall girl with a huge fuzz of hair. 'I thought she was an air hostess.'

The very tall girl was wearing navy blue.

'I thought she darned the Archbishop of Canterbury's wool-knit jockstrap,' said Lily.

'No,' I said. 'You're both wrong. She's actually an ex-Muppet. At the moment she's suing Jim Henson for sexual harassment. He claims he was only putting his hand up inside her to make her eyes move. She says he was doing a whole lot more. The jury is comprised of six conventional humans and six foam-rubber-based entities.'

(I'd played this game before.)

Lily leant forwards as she laughed. She was wearing a tight baby-blue T-shirt with sporty white trim at the sleeves and collar. It suited her.

'This guy's good,' she said to her boyfriend.

'What do *you* do?' he asked.

'Me? I repair clockwork mice.'

'Really?' he said.

'I've been thinking of diversifying into cats, but the market is dominated by an extended Swiss family who've been in the business for four hundred years.'

'What are they called?' asked Lily.

'The Von Mends,' I said.

Lily liked this a lot.

'I'm going to get a drink,' said the boyfriend, defeated. 'Do you want one?'

'No, I'm okay,' said Lily.

His eyes already on other women's bodies, he walked away.

Two hours later, I had Lily's phone number, a date for Friday and a smile so wide I thought it would permanently disfigure my face.

Harrods. Hamleys. Selfridges. It seemed there wasn't a clock-work mouse to be had anywhere in London. Camden Market. Carnaby Street. Covent Garden.

Eventually I saw a thing called a Go-Go Rat. It ran on batteries and didn't have a key in its back – which I'd wanted for full comic effect. But the Go-Go Rat would have to do.

I bought a big gold-papered box, stuffed it with cotton wool, placed the rat-mouse inside, tied it up with a silver ribbon – and on Friday, at the end of the meal, I presented it to Lily.

As we walked from the station to her Notting Hill flat, we let the rat-mouse chase us down the road.

After we got in through the door, we sat on her sofa and kissed through the whole first side of her tape of David Bowie's *Station to Station*.

(We were setting the first of our patterns. During those early days which followed, we kissed endlessly and did some epic smiling. We could just gaze at each other, perfectly amused, smiles widening until they cracked into laughter and we asked *What?* – each knowing already what *What?* was, and that it was us, and that it was also love, and that we were very glad it was so.)

Lily had dumped her boyfriend by phone that afternoon. He

45

was a lawyer, and had only ever given her presents of flowers and perfume.

We lay in bed laughing about him – making up ridiculous jobs for him. Procurer of grey paint for the Royal Navy. John Major's gag-writer.

But I really shouldn't have been laughing. Not if I'd understood anything at all.

And as it turned out I was – in movie-making terms – about as employable as a clockwork-mouse mender.

The bonfire didn't burn very well, but it *did* burn. Everything I'd thought about saving, I chucked back on.

Gestures like this are the sort of thing I've always hated in others. In films, I cringe when something is destroyed which is old and has a history of love. It's like when the stupid monster has its little doll taken away from it, and cries. I find these moments unbearable.

The death of Cordelia, as far as I'm concerned, is as nothing compared to the bursting of Eeyore's balloon.

The bonfire didn't make me cry – though I looked at it so hard and long through the black plastic-burning smoke that my eyes started to smart.

I watched as the surface of the Polaroids bubbled, turned black and peeled upwards. I watched as the deep-blue see-thru plastic handles of the knives, forks and spoons dripped off in flaming gouts. I watched as the clockwork mouse's synthetic fur turned to thick black smoke and its cheap inner workings of aluminium were exposed.

When little was left that was recognizable, I pissed on the fire to put it out.

'Is catharsis always this disappointing?' I wondered.

Bullet #2

The second bullet takes the top off Lily's head. It mashes through the gold-red hair on her white forehead. It passes into her right frontal lobe, about an inch and a half above her right eye. Due to the angle at which her skull presents itself at the moment of impact, the parietal bone is split from side to side in a horizontal line. As the bullet comes through the scalp it leaves behind a comma-shaped shard of metal. This will be clearly visible in X-rays during the autopsy. A trail of small lead fragments will evidence an internal ricochet, as the bullet strikes the back of Lily's head and rebounds. The entrance wound it creates is what is known as an explosive wound. This means that a great number of secondary fractures occur. The paper-thin temples crack. The top of her skull appears to flip open. Lily is wearing baby-blue contact lenses. The force of the second bullet's impact causes one lens to fly off the moist surface of her left eyeball. It is later recovered from the crime scene, fished out of Lily's glass of Chardonnay. Her head is snapped backwards, though her eyes remain focused on me. Because of the peculiar aerodynamic effects of the bullet, what happens when the missile enters the cavity of Lily's cranium is something like this – a temporary vacuum is created (cavitation occurring), around and behind the bullet, as it makes its way through the right frontal lobe. Because of the strength of this vacuum, Lily's brain tissue is sucked in towards the bullet – pulling away from the skull wall, sucked inwards, pulling away. The tissue of Lily's cerebrum is floppy, grey, not really like the conventionally imagined cauliflower or sponge. It is more like a sponge-cauliflower created out of a mixture of muddy jelly (neatly sliceable) and muffins. Lifted out, removed, it would wobble on a stainless-steel weighing tray. It would juice off in your hands, a little like a half-set treacle pudding. If you dropped it, it would slide sideways on its

47

various seeping liquids. The bullet continues. Lily's thalamus is distorted, elongated, pulled out of shape by the created skull-vacuum. (Lily will face no more jokes about being an airhead.) The hypothalamus, deep hippopotamus in the lowest mud of consciousness, is obliterated. The pineal body suffers passing damage.

Gunshot wounds come in two main categories: penetrating (which enter but do not exit the body) and perforating (which pass completely through). Skin is a remarkably tough material to puncture. Much harder to go through than muscle. Tests have been carried out on the lower extremities of human cadavers in order to determine whether or not skin was more resistant to projectiles than muscle.

However, something very unusual happens to the bullet after it enters Lily's cranial cavity: a vascular embolism. After the bullet ricochets off the inner table of the skull, it penetrates down into the right straight sinus. Following which, it is carried through the venous system, down the jugular vein, through the right atrium and ventricle, and into the pulmonary artery. It eventually comes to rest lodged in a major branch of the left pulmonary artery.

All this happens during the twenty or so minutes after Lily has been shot but whilst her heart is still pumping.

During the autopsy they will take over four hours to find the bullet.

At first, when Lily's head exploded, the gesture appeared so extravagant and party-trickish that it seemed no less likely, unlikely, that she'd be able to do it just as well backwards as she'd done it forwards – unexploding her head into talking wholeness. It was impossible for me to accept what I was seeing. That was when I began to giggle.

The damage the second bullet caused was enough to render her technically brain-dead from very shortly after the moment of impact. But I was convinced, sitting watching her from across the table, that her eyes were looking into mine.

One thing I have not been able to decide: what was going through her mind – what was in her mind – what was her mind still capable of thinking – when that second shot, the headshot, crested her, pluming red into everywhere?

I guess that, cognitively, there was probably just enough of her left to apprehend me and recognize me and remember who I was and assign me an emotional place in her past (passing) life and to see what I was doing, what my expression was. But that still doesn't explain how I heard her say bastard bastard bastard.

16

Two weeks after coming out of hospital, I'd got myself into some kind of a routine: I stayed home all day, spending equal amounts of time reading (books on anatomy, firearms and bullet wounds) and playing very violent computer games. There were certain games they hadn't allowed me in the hospital – mainly the ones featuring gunplay and gore. Many happy hours were spent in the zombie-infested sewers of *Resident Evil 2*. I was just executing a particularly troublesome biomutation when the telephone rang. As always, I didn't pick up. Call-screening, or so it sometimes seemed, was my only power over the outside world. I hadn't returned any old friends' inquiring calls.

My outgoing message played – it was digital, so made me sound as if I were drowning. In a sense, I was – I hadn't redone the recording since before the shooting. The voice that spoke was that of Conrad two days after moving in to a bedsit, on his own, having been dumped by The Love Of. Recording my new single-person's message on my new single-person's answerphone was about the worst of my post-split moments. It took two plays of Carole King's *Music* before I was capable even of making a cup of tea. (The California sound was always my post-break-up therapy – an early warning sign of how badly Hospital Radio would take me.) My outgoing message ended. There were six and a half rough beeps, then:

'Hello, Conrad. Good to hear you. This is Robert, Lily's father – you remember, I'm sure. At least, I hope you do . . . Oh, dear. Well, what I wanted to say was that I've been thinking we ought to – I hope you don't mind me ringing like this – your parents gave me – Conrad, there are things I think we should discuss. Call me at work. My number is –'

I picked up.

'Oh, you're there, Conrad.'

I explained about the wheelchair, difficulty getting to the phone, et cetera.

We arranged for him to come round the following day, after work.

The only thing I could think of that Lily's father might want to discuss was Lily's last will. She'd written it about six months into our relationship. In it she'd made everything she owned over to me. At that point, her everything (apart from the flat) didn't amount to very much. The gesture was symbolic – I'd made my everything over to her as well. But in the time that had passed before her death, Lily's career had taken off. Her bank account was probably full enough to become an issue, even for someone as wealthy as her father.

I could never think of Robert without thinking of him in relation to Josephine, his ex-wife, Lily's mother. This was because, between Lily and myself, he'd always been referred to as The Mistake. Lily had thought of her father in this way ever since she was a child. But it was only after a particularly disastrous dinner party, at which her father and one of his interchangeable post-Josephine women had been present, that Lily (with my help) managed to nail him.

'Mum should never have married him.'

'But then you wouldn't have been born.'

'No,' she said. 'I would've – any child my mother had would've been me. I'm inevitable –'

'I hope so,' I said, and kissed her – feeling particularly accidental myself: especially so as she hadn't said anything to the contrary about me.

We were lying on top of her bed, fully clothed, TV on with the sound down.

51

'– and he's a mistake,' completed Lily.

'That's a bit harsh. It makes him sound like an abortion or an unwanted pregnancy or something.'

'Mum doesn't make many mistakes.' Lily sent a thin stream of cigarette smoke up to kiss the lucky ceiling. 'In fact, I think my father is the only one.'

'He's her only mistake?'

'Yes, he's the mistake.'

'*The* Mistake?' I said.

'*The Mistake*,' Lily said.

Here, I'm giving her the credit, but when she was alive we used to argue over which of us said the words first. (It's a nickname, and I'm always giving things nicknames. Whereas Lily's usual trick was to abbreviate words to the shortest form she could think of.) Whatever the real truth of the actual conversation, Robert became and remained The Mistake.

Lily had told me long before this how her mother and father had originally got it together. The year was 1967. The month September. In the aftermath of *Sergeant Pepper's*, everyone was wearing uniforms – bright red and gold Boer War jackets, dark blue Prussian marching-band outfits. That The Mistake's uniform was of a different mark only made him appear all the more original. He wore a pinstripe suit and carried a bowler hat. But not only that, on any given commuter train his were the shiniest black leather uppers, the most sharply creased pinstripe trousers, his was the most tightly rolled umbrella. He was of the generation that had once, secretly, found the newly crowned Queen Elizabeth the most erotic object of contemplation in the social galaxy. When The Mistake happened into Josephine's circle – a young auctioneer who met painters as a matter of course and who, by them, was introduced to photographers, minor pop stars and coming young opera singers – she actually mistook him for a dangerous revolutionary. Josephine thought The Mistake, by his dress, bearing and overt opinions, was satirizing the establishment.

Every reactionary comment he made, she took as immensely accurate caricature. Such a dreadful misrecognition could, perhaps, only have taken place at that exact moment of social incoherence. For a short time, graduations of class – lost in parody and parade – could no longer accurately be judged. People, people like Josephine, still believed that things were *really* changing. She envisaged him at that time as burying himself deep within 'straight' society only to explode it with colourful countercultural insurgency a few years later – when the revolution came, as it would, as it must.

They moved in together, buying at a bargain price the Notting Hill flat that would later be Lily's.

In 1968 they married. A full Catholic ceremony. Josephine had had to convert.

Things began to go wrong almost immediately. The Mistake refused to drop LSD during their San Francisco honeymoon. Josephine did anyway, and was seduced during a marathon session of luminous body-painting by the hippie who'd sold it to her. The Mistake had joined in for a while – drawing an upside-down Union Jack around his belly button. The end had already begun. Yet they stayed together for years after it had become clear they had nothing between them to prolong but disaster. Lily's conception was their big mistake of 1972. They were almost separated at that point – but alcohol and Josephine's desire to redeem The Mistake by in some way liberating Robert had brought them again to bed. Whatever else happened, they never stopped fancying each other.

In 1974, they divorced. Josephine kept Lily, uncontested.

In the years since, The Mistake had become a man one couldn't help but admire, even though he was never likely to gain one's respect. He had moved upwards from auctioneering into estate valuations, from insurance to equity. He knew how things (in his limited version of the world) *should* be. He went to the best bespoke tailor on Savile Row, entrusted him with all decisions relating to cloth, cut and cost; and came away a very well-dressed if never particularly stylish man. He knew the finest and obscurest brand of soap, where it was stocked, how much it had cost when he first bought it in 1965, and a couple of good – if slightly *risqué* – jokes concerning soap. When one visited his Kensington mews, one found – in the bathroom, on the window shelf – a complete set of first edition Hoffnungs. He himself was almost completely without humour – although if to incarnate the ludicrousness of an entire generation is to be without humour, then life is an unnecessarily harsh affair. (As you might say.)

He was the perfect host – with all the deficiencies that implies.

During the time I was going out with Lily, we met only rarely – hacking our way towards each other through a jungle of awkwardness and embarrassment. Yet somehow, however much conversational machete-work we put in, the jungle was always far too thick for us, and we never managed – or so I felt – to end up simply face to face.

All that passed between us were lost cries of 'Where are you?' and 'Over here.'

17

When I opened the door to him the day after his phonecall, The Mistake stood there utterly unchanged.

He was tall with a slight stoop, and had very large hands and feet. His hair was plastered down with some outdated lotion which retained the comb's every last tooth-mark in semi-solid form. His face was a lightly orangy-pink ball whose features seemed never to know where to put themselves unless, as now, they were expressing a conventional sentiment in a conventional way. He was wearing one of his navy blue pinstripe suits.

'Conrad,' he said, glancing down at my wheelchair, 'it's good to see you.'

Looking back, I think he may even have prepared a hug for this grief-shadowed reunion. But, when the moment arrived, he merely bent down, took my hand and shook it slowly.

Entering the living room, he looked around for something on which to compliment me – décorwise.

'Gosh,' he said, finding nothing. 'Lovely and warm in here. Central heating, I suppose.'

I offered him a seat.

The tea things were out ready on the coffee table. When I offered, he said, 'Oh yes please,' and I poured him a cup.

'You seem to be doing very well,' he said.

'It's not permanent,' I replied, meaning the wheelchair.

'No,' he said. 'I hope not.'

In the silence that followed, he tea-slurped rather loudly.

'How are the cats?' I asked.

Just before we split up, Lily had bought two black and white kittens. Perhaps I should have taken it as a pack-your-bags sign – and not the first. Lily had always loved cats and had wanted more than one. The kittens, when they first arrived, got into so many object-scrapes that we called them Snafu and Glitch. They seemed happiest only when at a point exactly half-way up the back of Lily's black leather sofa – chasing each other in mad ripping circles while Lily and I tried to concentrate on a video or sex. Snafu in particular liked to join in with sex. She wanted to rake her claws through our hairy bits. I think she thought they were unformed or shy kittens, in need of a bit of catty-coaxing to bring them out.

The Mistake placed his cup and saucer down on the brown glass of the coffee-table.

'Do you want them – the cats, I mean?'

'I don't think I could really cope with them at the moment,' I said. 'But maybe in future.'

'I'm sure Josephine would hand them over.'

'Didn't you have them?'

'Perhaps I'd better explain.'

He explained. It took a while – but listening past the euphemism and evasion, the story went something like this: Arrangements for Lily's burial had naturally brought The Mistake and Josephine into closer contact than usual. However, it was not until the morning of the funeral that they actually met. Although both had friends and lovers to support them, they (as the stricken parents) found themselves being pulled together by the gravity of their grief. Pretty soon they were in tears, next in each other's arms, and – by the end of that terrible day – in bed.

(Although I didn't interrupt to tell him, one of Lily's most frequently recurrent nightmares had been of her parents sentimen-tally reuniting while on the dance-floor at her wedding.)

The Mistake was still living in the mews house where Lily had spent the first two years of her life. A week after the funeral,

Josephine moved back in. The Mistake may have been Josephine's only mistake, but – though her daughter wasn't around to witness it – it was one she was quite capable of repeating. My interpretation was that, to compensate for her grief, Josephine wanted some solidity. The Mistake was nothing if not solid. And although his solidity was one of the main reasons she had left him in the first place, it made him no less attractive now.

The reunion lasted two months. Josephine moved out again, back to her old flat in Hampstead. She took the cats with her, although The Mistake insisted he'd become particularly fond of them. Since that day contact between them had been minimal.

'Glitch has put on a bit of weight. I think Josephine is feeding them too often.'

He looked down into the shine on his shoes.

It was time for me to find out what our subject really was.

'You had something to tell me?'

'Not really. More to ask you, really. Um, on the night you went to the restaurant with Lily – did she have anything, you think, in particular that she wanted to discuss?'

'Definitely.'

He picked up his cup and saucer again – and started adjusting the cup's handles through right angles: 12 o'clock, 9 o'clock, 3 o'clock, 6 o'clock.

'What was it?'

'Perhaps it was something private between Lily and myself.'

'Of course,' he said quickly.

He put the cup and saucer down. His tea was all drunk. He'd had no reason for picking it up again, apart from the imperative of guilty fiddling.

'But if you did feel in any way able to tell me, I would be very grateful.'

'She didn't say anything about *you* if that's what you're worrying about.'

It was obvious that he was worrying about something.

'No, no, no.'

'Or Josephine.'

'It was more about herself, actually. Whether she had anything to tell you about herself.'

'Perhaps you'd better tell me what you think she might have said, then I can tell you whether she said it or not.'

'It's not so much that I want to find out what it was. I think I know what it was. What I'd like to know is whether she thought it worth while telling you – whether she particularly wanted to tell you – whether you were particularly involved in any way.'

'Robert,' I said. 'You're not making yourself *particularly* clear. What do you mean?'

'So she didn't?' he said.

'Didn't what?'

'If she had, you'd know exactly what I've been talking about.'

He stood up.

'Thank you very much for the tea,' he said. 'I think you've answered my question. Don't worry, I'll show myself out. Nice to see you, Conrad.'

'Tell me,' I said.

'You'll find out soon enough,' he said. 'But I don't think it's quite my place to tell you.'

'Do you know what we called you?' I shouted. 'What Lily and I called you?'

'What?' he said, turning awkwardly in the doorway.

'We called you The Mistake.'

'Really?' he said, slowly. 'How . . .'

He turned away again.

'. . . original.'

58

18

After The Mistake left I had plenty of time to think about our conversation. There was something he knew, but didn't want me to know – or didn't want to be the one to tell me. And it was something to do with what Lily had wanted to discuss during our meal. I guessed that it was to do with changing her will – some kind of verbal contract. Perhaps he intended to contest?

There seemed only one thing to do. Divorcees always have one major weakness: their ex. If The Mistake didn't want to tell me what was going on, then – merely by being informed of his taciturnity – Josephine would almost certainly want to blab the whole thing. I would simply be providing yet another opportunity for her to vent her bitterness.

Josephine, having gracefully given up opera-singing, was now a writer. She had just two years before published her first novel, *Root Ginger*. One hundred and eighty pages, and not one of them without the long lilting cadence of forced pathos. Her moral was always and everywhere: Pity me, I have suffered. But she hadn't – she was pampered constantly by everyone around her. Even her reviewers (mostly female) pampered her. (I'm sure out of sheer relief that she hadn't forced upon them another set of diva-ish memoirs.) A second novel, *Brocade*, was said to be 'in the making'.

Josephine had been with The Mistake for two months after Lily's death. If what he knew was something he'd found out during that time, she would surely know it as well. More likely, Josephine had been first to learn it. The Mistake had always

59

received most of his information about Lily at second hand.

The last time I'd seen Josephine had been about two months before Lily and I split up. She had come round to collect Lily and whisk her off to lunch somewhere far more expensive than she'd ever have taken the both of us together. We were unspoken though unsworn enemies by that point: she (rightly, perhaps) believed that I wasn't good enough for Lily – wasn't manly or fatherly enough. In her eyes, Lily needed someone to guide her towards the success that should rightfully (genetically) be hers: Lily's place was on the stage, not the TV. I stood for TV.

Lily was very careful to pass off on to me her own strong desire to be famous first and a good actress second. To her mother, she would make the ritual complaints about lack of work, of really *satisfying* work. Then she would sophisticate on for a while about the high fees of the cereal ad, the freedom and time it would give her to find something really *worth while*. And Josephine would be taken in: Lily pulled the act off brilliantly. She was the struggling artist; I was the debaser of genius.

No doubt Josephine also part-blamed me for getting her lovely daughter shot, killed and posthumously notorious. And, if she didn't blame me for having survived whilst Lily died, then Josephine would hardly have been human.

When I phoned her, her response was typical.

'Oh, Conrad. I was going to get in touch just as soon as I knew you were recovered.'

I had decided not to mention The Mistake and his little visit until I'd had more time to think about the situation.

'I'm getting better every day, thank you. I was wondering if we could meet up some time to talk about Lily.'

'Oh,' she said.

'I need to talk.'

'Is there anything in particular?'

I didn't tell her how much like her ex-husband she was starting to sound.

'There are things I need to say.'

'Of course.' She paused. 'I'm not particularly busy at the moment. How about tomorrow morning?'

Josephine and I agreed to meet up at Lily's flat – that would give her a chance – 'perhaps a last chance,' she said, parenthetically, pathetically – to look round. It would also enable me to take possession of the keys and the flat at one and the same time.

'How are Snafu and Glitch?' I asked.

We talked about Glitch for five minutes and Snafu for two.

19

The flat had been renovated by a young architect so up-and-coming that, if Lily hadn't seized him exactly when she did, he would have been out of her price range by the end of the following month. He talked the builders into producing what he, and therefore she, wanted: whitewashed walls, polished pine floors, split bamboo blinds lined with muslin, concealed lighting, stainless steel ornaments. He had created for her – as one of the magazine articles said – 'an atmosphere of light and space – and, most importantly of all, calm'. That, at least, was how it must've appeared to those that didn't actually have to live there.

I turned up fifteen minutes early, knowing that Josephine would be there already. She couldn't resist the chance of one final check around Lily's flat, just to make sure there was nothing she'd overlooked. I felt sure that many little things ('of sentimental value') were going to be missing. Nothing important enough for me to accuse her of stealing. But just enough to let me know that although, legally, the flat now belonged to me, morally it was theirs – to divide between them, just as they'd attempted but failed to divide Lily.

I had to wait for a minute or so on the doorstep before Josephine deigned to buzz me in: this was the final gesture of possession, after this she could but capitulate to my oikish invasion.

I wondered how much time she'd spent in Lily's flat over the past six months. Was it her mourning place? Had it become the place where she brought her lovers? Could she bear to fuck them in the bed that Lily and I had shared?

Josephine was one of those unfortunate women who have been born out of the proper time of their best beauty. Her face and figure were those of a Forces Sweetheart, *circa* 1943.

Yet the Josephine who finally opened the door at the top of the stairs to me was a smaller, sadder, older woman than the one who'd taken Lily out to lunch that day. She was harder, as well – as if to say, Death has taught me a lesson which I must pass on to others; if, in doing so, I myself become a little deathly, a little creepy, then so be it: this is not a vocation that I would have chosen – black never suited me. However, all such questions and preferences are vanity now.

The hall smelt of something faintly disgusting.

Josephine had expected me to be early – not this early, though. I'd caught her ten minutes before I was due. Her first reaction was one of anger, and the only emotion she could find to disguise it was pity.

'Conrad, my God – you look terrible . . . Oh, I'm sorry. I shouldn't have said *anything*, should I? But it's just you've lost some weight. Sit down – you must sit down. I'm afraid I can't offer you tea or anything – the power's off, you see . . . and the gas. I bring it for myself. In a flask. When I come; when I *used* to come . . . I suppose that's all over now. Do you think you're going to move in?'

I didn't answer. I did not sit down. I hadn't passed more than a step over the threshold. I had just walked back into my old life – into a room I'd expected never to see again. Lily wouldn't have wanted me back in her flat – and I would have done anything to avoid a return that couldn't fail to hurt me by being merely temporary. Now that I was here, though, I felt as if I were doubly trespassing: I was back without Lily's permission, and her permission was something she was no longer around either to give or to withhold.

It was only on entering the flat that I realized quite how dead my old life was, and how dead Lily was, too.

The last thing I wanted was for Josephine to see me in my weakness. There was no way of avoiding it, however.

I walked very consciously over to the sofa. It felt as if my every step was leaving a deep footprint in the fresh wet earth of Lily's new-dug grave.

The living room was done out like the reception of a large corporation: black leather sofa and chairs, pale wooden floor, oblong glass coffee table – even down to the industrial stainless-steel ashtrays-on-stalks.

'Are you alright?' asked Josephine, glad to be able to assert herself.

'I'll be fine,' I said. 'I just need a couple of minutes. The stairs.'

'Perhaps we could go for a walk – get out.'

'No, really. I think maybe it was the stairs.'

Josephine gave me a look that showed quite clearly that her indulgence had a limit, and that I'd just brushed against it. If I was going to be weak, then I could be weak – but I could not lie about the causes of it.

'Let me at least get you a drink.'

She came back from the kitchen with a large bottle of Absolut vodka, blue label. After straining for a while to unscrew the cap, she was forced to hand the bottle over to me.

'I can't,' she said, sitting down.

She rubbed the palms of her hands.

For something to say, I said: 'I thought you only drank gin and tonic.'

'Oh, I didn't buy this,' she said. 'There were two huge bottles of it in the cupboard.'

Even at the time I thought this odd: Lily never drank spirits, and I'd always bought Stolichnaya – one bottle at a time.

I unscrewed the cap without too much difficultly.

The respite over, I'd started to feel better.

Josephine was speaking.

'I've tidied up a little – well, quite a lot, actually. Obviously, we had to come round – to sort things out. It was very difficult for us, as you can imagine. Particularly the first time. Everything was exactly as Lily left it. The kittens weren't doing too badly, though they'd fouled the hall carpet – and you know how *that* can smell. At first we thought there was something dead in there.'

'You came with Robert?'

'Yes,' she said. 'A day or so after – you know. We couldn't face coming separately.'

Or, I thought, you didn't trust each other not to nick stuff.

I wondered if they'd done anything perverse. Had the idea even occurred to them of a grief-stricken memorial fuck on Lily's (undoubtedly) unmade bed? Had Josephine dressed up for it in Lily's clothes? (They had always been the same size: 8.) What had the sex been like? There was no way I could ask, but perhaps I might find some evidence in the bedroom – when I finally got there.

'Quite,' I said.

'Are you going to move back in, do you think?'

'I may,' I replied. 'I'll just have to see how I feel when I've spent a bit of time here.'

'The flat should be ours, you know. She was about to cut you out of her will.'

'You have a great deal of money,' I said. 'I have very little. But that's not really the point.'

'It has important sentimental associations for me.'

(I wondered what these might be: Josephine, accompanied by the infant Lily, had moved back in here immediately after she and The Mistake got divorced.)

'No doubt you've already taken a few things of Lily's from here. Perhaps you've even gone through and removed anything *particularly* personal. I'm not expecting to find, for example, her diaries.'

Josephine looked defiant.

'We *are* her parents,' she said.

'I never stopped loving her,' I replied. 'We may have broken up, but it was Lily that wanted it – not me, never me.'

'Well . . .' said Josephine.

'If I ask, will you let me read her diaries?'

Josephine looked shocked.

'The police have everything,' she said.

We paused at the thought of this: what might be in the diaries, what the police might know about Lily and about us.

Josephine indicated the stainless-steel bowl on the hall table.

'The keys are in there,' she said.

'Look,' I said. 'I'm not trying to take revenge on you or anything. I haven't decided what I'm going to do, yet. I may even just give the whole thing back to you.'

There seemed nothing Josephine could say to this – no way she could permit herself to express a desire which I could in an instant thwart.

But then she managed to think of a way out: 'Well, you just do what you think is right.'

Instantly, this made it seem as though keeping the flat would be an act of pure selfishness.

I went back into the hall and took the keys out of the bowl. It would have been a nice touch to try them in the locks, but I knew they were the same old ones – and Josephine wasn't going to leave me without the means to dead-bolt her precious flat.

20

'The funeral was dire,' Josephine began, as I came back into the living room. 'If you'd been able to go, you'd have wished that you hadn't. The vicar didn't know a thing about Lily, except of course the breakfast cereal thing. He made it seem as if her whole life had been some ludicrous quest to improve the nation's bowel movements. Really! I couldn't stand it. Nor could anyone. But how are you? It must have been quite terrible for you.'

I remembered this from when Lily and I used to visit Josephine at home, confrontation followed by compassion.

'I'm over the worst of it now, I think,' I said, sitting down beside her on the sofa.

'Glad to hear it,' she said, and touched my knee. 'What did you want to talk about, my darling dear?'

'Robert came round yesterday.'

'He *did*.'

Josephine, I could tell, hated the idea that Robert, and not she, had been first to pay me a visit.

'Yes, he particularly wanted to know what Lily and I talked about at the restaurant.'

'Right.'

Josephine was never this taciturn.

'You know how annoying he can be sometimes –'

'Oh god, yes. I *was* married to the man, you know.'

'He told me what happened – you moving back in with him.'

I think this was the first time I'd ever seen Josephine embarrassed.

'We all make mistakes.'

'Lily said you only ever made one mistake.'

'It isn't hard to guess which that was.'

'No,' I agreed. 'But Robert already seemed to know most of what Lily and I talked about.'

'Well, of course. I told him about it after she died. When we were . . . together. There seemed no reason for him not to know.'

'The thing is, he didn't seem to want to say directly –'

'Robert always was squeamish. You should have seen him at Lily's birth. Not that I saw much of him, myself. He was on the floor for most of it. Out cold.'

'He did seem rather uncomfortable.'

'I mean, as Lily said, it's only an abortion, isn't it?'

I managed to say, 'Yes.'

Josephine looked across at me.

'Oh, dear,' she said. 'I didn't mean to be quite so brutal. But that's how Lily looked on it. Didn't you find she was quite offhand about the whole matter?'

I remembered how calm Lily had seemed during our short time together in the restaurant. She was calmer than I'd ever seen her before. Resigned, that was the word. Resigned in advance to how ugly my reaction was going to be. She had been sitting me down. She had been making sure I was relaxed. She had been preparing me for the shock.

'When did she tell you?' I asked.

'A week or so before.'

'Before what?'

'Before' – Josephine was off into pathos before I could stop her – 'she was murdered, of course.'

'I'm sorry.'

'We've managed to keep it out of the papers, you know. So far. Whatever else you say, it is pretty ucky. The police have been very good about it. At least, I think they have. It may be that

68

they're just saving it up for shock-value during the trial. You know – brutal slaying of pregnant actress.'

My act fell apart.

Josephine looked at me, aghast.

'You didn't know?'

'What?' I said, no longer caring how I appeared. 'That she was carrying a baby when she was shot?'

'Oh, it's very clever of you to trick me into telling you. Mentioning Robert –'

'Josephine, tell me, please. Was it my baby? What did Lily say?'

Josephine wanted an effect – and the one she chose was a long silence of unexpected calm.

We sat there for a ridiculous amount of time.

'Why didn't you just ask?' she finally said. 'Why did you feel the need to trick me?'

'Robert wouldn't tell me. I thought you wouldn't either.'

This was the worst thing I could have said.

'If you'd asked, I would have told you. How could I not tell you? But as you didn't ask, you'll just have to find the rest out somewhere else. You said there were things you needed to say. I assumed you meant love. That you still loved her. That you –'

'I did.'

'It's no good, now. You've entirely lost my sympathy. I feel very hurt. Oh, Conrad, why couldn't you have just trusted me?'

She stood up to go.

'Josephine,' I said. 'I want to talk about her – generally, in other ways. Please, sit down again.'

'No. I'm sorry. I can't. Goodbye.'

And just like her ex-husband, she showed herself out.

21

Something happened. At the moment Lily's mother left I was suddenly granted access to all my own old emotions again. Once more I realized what had actually been done to Lily – this realization coming through the realization of what had been done to the child unborn inside her. That this child might have been mine made the emotions all the more intense, but I would have had them anyway. A very terrible thing had been done, and half of it – the unsuccessful, botched half – had been done to me. I was a fluff, even in what was meant to be the full-stopping of my life – a kind of perfection of sorts; one that I had anticipated many times. Death. Full stop. But that my emotions came back to me didn't make them any the less confused. They fell upon me in a messy waterfall – full of solid objects, arms and heads that struck my own head, my own arms. The contents of the charnel-house were being dropped upon me, not one by one, but all at once. Lily's autopsied body – deconstituted – was part of this thick foul rain. This human sleet. The heaviest of all the blows came when the baby's head struck mine. Even if it wasn't my baby, I took responsibility for it. I remembered exactly how I'd felt during the six weeks, once, when Lily skipped a period. We had been on holiday (to New York) and Lily had been under a lot of stress. That was in retrospect probably the best explanation. But at the time my feeling could only be put into these words: *If she is pregnant, then, even if I don't believe the embryo to be in possession of a soul, it might, were it to grow up into an adult, itself believe itself to be possessed of such a thing. And so – even if I don't believe in souls, by this*

70

act I would be bringing into the world (or excluding from the world for ever, if Lily were to have an abortion) the possibility of the possibility of a soul. Never had I felt such massive responsibility. This wasn't just birth defect and money anxieties; this was a metaphysical gamble of such immensity . . . But Lily's next period came without herald. She waited two days before telling me – having forgotten, the moment it started, how extreme (though for more career-related reasons) her own anxiety had been. She sat on the toilet, finally telling me that everything was okay – and I cried.

I cried this time, too. Therapy, however good, is no match for bastard events. I cried torrentially, storming out my renewed emotions: grief, rage, hatred, self-disgust.

What I found hardest to deal with, though, was the sheer direct uncensored undeniable passion that I felt. This was something terrible which I'd never had to face before: passion – passion with no recourse to irony. If there was any irony in this situation (if! if there was anything, in some ways, but) – then the irony was on me: it was beyond my control. No expression that I could give my passion was adequate.

I was multiply aggrieved: the baby was dead, dead without me knowing it existed, dead in some abortion clinic bucket even if Lily hadn't been shot, dead to my grief until I could be certain it had been mine.

For fifteen minutes or so, it was as if Lily were alive again – capable of new and surprising actions.

(In a way, the feeling I discovered that afternoon in Lily's flat has never quite left me. Even after coming to what I think and hope is The End, I cannot quite believe that Lily has no more ways of hurting me. This whole experience has almost made me disbelieve in death – or what you might call personal extinction. Lily's actions in life have come upon me – months after the cease of her pulse – as freshly and abruptly as any moment of living impulse or anger. This so-called dead person seems as capable as anyone alive of vindictiveness and contempt. She retains her cruel sense of actorly timing – the inopportune moment is always when she chooses once again to knock me sideways. It is almost as if, I feel, her nervous system still operates. If I pain her, she flinches – then she pains me back.)

When I came out of my reverie, one thing was clear: I needed to find out more about the baby.

Bullet *#3*

The third bullet entered Lily's abdomen, but not until it had clipped the edge of the table close up to where she had been sitting. It passed through her dress, her camisole, through her skin, the fat of her belly. (Again forgive me, Lily.) It plunged down towards her pelvis – its entry point was to the right of her tummy button, and slightly further down.

Ilium, pubis, sacrum – it entered the Latinate language of her tenderest innards as if travelling back in time to Ancient Rome, passing through the Fall, the Decline, to Greece, the birth of medicine, the Hippocratic Oath . . . A classicism of harm. That things with such exact names should meet with something so rough in its destruction! This was sacrilege, pollution, violation. Yes, this was rape.

The table edge had caused the third bullet to spin – the entry-wound was therefore larger, the bullet was losing kinetic energy faster. This bullet would be penetrating, not perforating. Already it was finding a place to lodge itself – working its way in – aimed directly at Lily's sex. And, inside, there was another being. It was soft and was making its home within softness. It was jelly in amniotic fluid. At this stage it was tadpoley and upside down, eyeless and like the sprig of some plant – curled up like the frond-front of a fern around the deep future importance of its spine.

Perhaps here, already, was a laugh and a way of holding the hands in repose. Perhaps, ready to die, was a love of Italian cooking or a fear of spiders. Perhaps this was the winning goal in the last minute of the FA Cup. Perhaps this was a live recording of Tosca.

The third bullet did not hit the perhaps directly. It may have been an irony, I'm no longer sure about these things, that the embryo (the baby) and the bullet were of approximately the same size. Is that an irony? Or is it merely a coincidence? The two missiles coincided inside Lily – the one a time bomb that she was about to have surgically defused, the other a permanent explorer-exploder.

The baby – a piece of housework needing to be sorted out – the hoovering; the bullet – an interior redecoration from which the structure of the building would never recover.

The third bullet finally lodged in the muscles of Lily's back – sideways on, a cavity closing around it.

22

After a very few minutes, I found I could no longer stand to be in Lily's flat.

I went out into the street and caught a taxi. There was a place I felt compelled to go.

Lily had been buried in the graveyard where I first saw her: Highgate Cemetery. I wondered if anyone else in the world was aware of that particular irony. I wondered if anyone else would have been particularly interested to hear of it.

The day was bright and muggy as I crunched down the wide gravel path – repeating the directions that the man on the gate had given me.

Up the path. Past Marx's tomb. Carry on. Right.

There were ten or twelve as-yet-unfilled graves, covered over with rough boards. Beside each oblong hole was a pile of heavy clayey earth, waiting to be clodded down on to a coffin.

Lily's grave, when I found it, was half-way along a row of small, tasteful headstones. There was, as yet, no headstone for her. Instead, the entire six feet by three (Lily had been five foot ten and a quarter) was covered by heaped-up bunches of now-invisible flowers – lilies, white, inevitably, unbearably – their Cellophane wrappers silvered over with condensation.

The bleating sound of geese came across from the lake in the adjacent park. Through the black iron railings I saw a couple of women pushing their prams past.

There was an empty bottle of whiskey and a half-filled bottle of olive oil over by the next grave along.

I'd loved Lily until that love was no longer capable of return. I had nothing to blame myself for – I'd loved her as well and as long as I could.

Another realization that Lily was really dead and what Lily really being dead really meant came upon me.

I wanted to sink down on to my knees, down on to the earth that lay above her, but my embarrassment held me back. I'd watched that sinking too many times: my natural reaction had been taken away from me. My mourning had been disallowed by soap opera, by TV movies, by Hollywood. I felt myself too English ever to get over my grief: someone needed to tell me that I could allow myself the vulgarity of tears, the kitsch of distraction, the camp of complete prostration.

But no-one was around to do that.

23

In the taxi on the way back to Mortlake I tried to work things out in my head. There were, it seemed, certain immediate facts I could begin with. In her phonecall to me, Lily had said she'd been blown out by someone else for the Le Corbusier dinner date.

Certain other details of the evening recurred to confirm this: Lily's dress – she wouldn't have worn a new ghost frock just to meet me. I had never seen it before, and so it must have been a recent purchase, post-split. It screamed special occasion. It strongly hinted at romance – Lily wanting to look her absolute gorgeous best.

This was for the person she had hoped to be meeting.

She'd phoned me from her mobile. She'd probably been doing something up in town. Something to do with the new play. No time to go home and get a less special dress.

So who was it she had been intending to meet? Who had cancelled?

The main suspect was Cyril. He was always sniffing around. If Lily had been looking for something instant, he'd probably have been it. Then there was the possibility of someone new – someone I'd never heard of. If that were the case, then it was most likely someone from the new play she was about to start rehearsing: the producer, the director, or even the writer.

I would have to think some more about that.

The hitman had known who Lily was – probably having seen her on television. The fact that he shot her first suggested that she was the main target – the emotional focus of the crime. But the fact that I had been shot as well suggested that someone was jealous of whoever it was Lily would have been with, even if it hadn't been me.

There was another line of thought to pursue as well – less comfortably.

Lily and I had not been one of those couples who, when they are falling apart, stop having sex. In fact, we seemed – during those final months – to be having sex a lot more, and a lot more spontaneously, in odder places: lifts, alleys, toilets, cupboards. We had gone *al fresco* for the first time (on Hampstead Heath) only a month before the end. The last time we had sex before we split was conventional enough – at home, in bed, with candle-light and cocaine. That was ten days before she dumped me.

Lily was on the pill, but was often forgetful about taking it. We had agreed that, if one of us were to have unprotected sex with someone else, we would confess to it – and use condoms until we'd both had AIDS tests. During the split-up conversation (sofa, tears, bad pop songs), I asked Lily if she'd been sleeping with someone else. Her reply was devastating: 'That isn't the point.'

It was for me. If she had that kind of flippant attitude about it, I wasn't going to stick around.

And so, while it was quite possible that I was the baby's father, it was also quite possible that it was someone else.

As far as I could work out, Lily had decided to have the abortion about five weeks after we split up. The last time we had sex (ten days before we split) had been just after her period. If I were the father, she would have skipped about three weeks after we broke up. But it wasn't like Lily to be bothered with pregnancy tests. She'd have waited to see if she skipped another month – and only *then* started to worry.

So, the father was almost certainly me or someone she had been fucking whilst still going out with me. There simply hadn't been time for her to get pregnant and then get worried about being pregnant in the six weeks after we split.

Clearly, I had to find out some more about the baby.

24

When I got home, there was a message on my answerphone from Anne-Marie. She was suggesting we meet up for coffee. She'd left all her numbers, work, home and mobile.

I wanted distracting. I didn't want to be alone. Anne-Marie, or so I thought, was the right kind of person for that moment.

With Anne-Marie, I'd always got the feeling that we were standing on the foredecks of parallel-coursed ships, trying to send signals with brightly coloured flags, neither of us having any knowledge of semaphore. So there we'd always stood, making desperate jerking motions – motions which conveyed, if nothing else, a certain desperation to communicate.

I remembered one particular incident, which hardly counted as an incident proper at all.

We had been to see a film (I can't remember what) and then to have a meal (I can't remember where). We were sitting four-in-a-row in a Tube carriage: Lily, me, Anne-Marie, Anne-Marie's long-term boyfriend. Lily and the boyfriend were slouching, their feet braced against the floor. Anne-Marie and I were sitting up straight with our legs crossed in the same direction, right over left. We were relaxed. We were a bit drunk. We were talking. And I noticed, as the carriage jolted round tunnel bends and bumped over joints in the track, that our feet – Anne-Marie's and mine – were moving with perfect synchrony. It reminded me of when, as a child, I'd discovered that, if I strapped two pencils together with a rubber band, I could draw parallel lines – and so I had started drawing parallel lines everywhere. Watching our feet dip-lift-dip together was like watching some inhumanly perfect choreography – as if nothing else we could ever physically do would be as minute and exact and intimate. As soon as I noticed this, I became very embarrassed. I felt as if in some obscure way I'd been unfaithful to Lily by even noticing. Quickly, I uncrossed my legs – and crossed them the other way. But I didn't realize that Anne-Marie had been looking where I'd been looking – and had noticed what I had noticed. She uncrossed-recrossed her legs, too.

'It's funny the way they do that, isn't it?' she said.

Lily would never have perceived such a thing. Lily didn't operate on such a scale.

So, when the long-term boyfriend (Will, I think he was called) asked, 'What do what?' and Anne-Marie told him, Lily was a bit perplexed – until we demonstrated, and they both joined in.

(Anne-Marie obviously had a far less guilty mind than mine. I would have died rather than give such a secret away.)

For the rest of the journey, we sat there, four-in-a-row, Lily, me, Anne-Marie, Will, watching our feet jog-jog-jogging.

And I felt terrible: First, by creating this intimacy, I'd been unfaithful with Anne-Marie; then, she'd been happy to betray our intimacy to others; and then, finally, we'd both joined in with a crude parody of that intimacy – a parody which destroyed it.

I called Anne-Marie on her work number.

Delight greeted my voice and acceptance my suggestion. 'Tonight?'

'Um,' she said. 'Wow! Quick. Yes.'

When I told her I found getting into town a bit much, Anne-Marie said she was more than happy to go out locally for a curry.

'See ya,' she said.

My first date, post-Lily. Six months plus.

I wondered how long I would have waited before seeing someone else had Lily still been alive. Much longer, I suspected

– what with me not being able to watch TV for fear of her humph.

The breakfast cereal company had – I heard – shown the final Brandy and Cyril ad once, with a black border, out of respect for Lily – but after that the entire campaign had been shelved. Lily's death had had no discernible effect on the sales of the bran-heavy cereal.

Anne-Marie arrived just after seven.

She stepped forwards to give me a kiss, but when she spotted my wheelchair – just where I'd placed it to be seen – she changed the kiss to a long and protective hug.

'Are you sure you're alright?'

Wanting to get that kind of question out of the way before we went to the restaurant, I invited Anne-Marie in.

For a while we sat on the sofa – me telling my body's story for the last few months.

From what Anne-Marie said, a few urban myths seemed to have ex-nihiloed up around my name. Various different parts of my anatomy had allegedly been shot at or shot off. It was rumoured that I would never walk/fuck again. That I needed constant nursing from my mother. That I'd gone mental and been sectioned after attacking a doctor.

'Please,' I said. 'Go back and tell everyone the rumours are true – or that their own particular rumour is true.'

'Why? People are worried about you. I had no idea what I was going to find when I got here.'

'Is my phone voice that bad?'

'You seem very cheerful.'

'Don't be fooled. Others have.'

We walked along to the Taste of Raj, all you would expect and want it to be: formula curries served in faux opulent surroundings to the accompaniment of a crunchy community-radio sitar.

82

I seated myself so that I was facing the door. For a moment the rigidity of irrational fear began to creep into me. Perhaps Lily had been killed by the mere fact of sitting opposite me in a restaurant. Perhaps the whole thing was about to happen again – to Anne-Marie, to me.

We both asked for pints of Kingfisher. We shared poppadams, dipping them into the three different chutneys. We ordered: I had the brinjal bhajee, prawn dhansak and vegetable korma. Anne-Marie had chicken tikka masala and nan bread. We decided to halve a portion of basmati rice.

Then we got to the interesting bit.

'Actually, I split up with Will soon after you were –'

'– shot. You can say it. It sounds nicer coming from you than anyone else. You make it sound like I'm going to be on the cover of *Vogue* in three months' time.'

'Yes,' she said, cracking a poppadam. 'I think it was partly *that* – the shooting, not me – which broke us up. Will seemed to think that in some obscure way Lily was asking for it.' She paused. 'No, we really shouldn't talk about this. It's far too . . . much.'

'Anne-Marie,' I said. 'There's no-one I would prefer to talk about it with – and it's good that you feel that we can.'

The boyfriend was off the scene, that's what was good.

The moment this became clear, I'd forgotten everything of the reality of my own situation. I didn't care if Anne-Marie came to bed laughing or crying, as long as she came. This, I remembered, was how I always used to be when out on dates. Concentrating on one simple objective: sex. Everything else blocked out.

'Will thought Lily was asking for it by being beautiful, by being female, by being famous. He saw the whole thing as some sick kind of fashion statement – granting her a status she hadn't really earned.'

'I wonder what he said about me?'

'I can tell you. He said, "Hang around her type long enough and you're bound to get caught in the crossfire eventually."'

Anger like you wouldn't believe came over me.

'Please tell Will, if you see him again (which I sincerely hope you won't) that I had three bullets, all my very own, aimed and fired directly at me. Crossfire had nothing to do with it. Still, if it broke you up with a tosser like that, maybe it was worth taking the odd slug.'

Anne-Marie ignored the compliment.

'He was almost misogynistic about it. As if a real woman hadn't really died. As if he were just coming out of a cinema and saying that the violence wasn't realistic enough.'

'Believe me,' I said, 'the young man doesn't *want* to see realistic violence.'

'But that's the thing – I think he does. What really broke us up was that he became almost enthusiastic about the killing – taping the news – collecting cuttings –'

'My mother did too. Do you think I should disown her? It might be a good excuse.'

'And finally I asked him, "You wish you'd been there to see it, don't you?" And he knew I meant he would've liked to see Lily get shot, not you.'

She trailed off, omitting the punch-line.

'What did he say?'

Anne-Marie took a gulp of Kingfisher.

'Well, he lied – he denied it. But I could tell I'd caught him out. I've been pretty disgusted with men ever since. I can't imagine having that kind of blood-lust, that cruel voyeurism. That's why I wanted to see you.'

'Ah,' I said. 'Only that?'

'Oh, of course not, Conrad. I wanted to make sure you were alright. But, I mean, you went through it. If any man has lost that brutality, it must be you. Like you said, he really wouldn't want to have seen what you saw.'

'I never liked him,' I said.

'That wasn't hard to tell.'

'He made me very jealous.'

'Please, tell me you didn't enjoy it. Tell me all men aren't like that.'

For my own selfish reasons, and in necessary defence of my gender, I decided to lie. Nobody should *have* to see what I saw. But there had been a part of me that had enjoyed it – and not a small part. What is one meant to feel if, half-way through an argument with the person who dumped you, fucked up your life and looks really fabulous on it, that person is shot? Of course there's going to be a certain amount of pleasure. It's undeniable that the thing, in a way, couldn't have been better timed. We all have revenge fantasies, born of impotence. She had kicked me out. I didn't feel all that good about it. And I wouldn't have felt all that bad about it if she'd been made to suffer a little. That didn't mean I'd have put in a specific request to see her brain spattered all over the wall, the mirror, the tabletop, the floor. But things just aren't that simple. Not as far as men in general are concerned. Of course, if something is known to happen – to be possible – to be visible – then men *will* want to see it. All men.

'No,' I said. 'All men aren't like that at all.'

Anne-Marie smiled beatifically. Her world had lightened. There was now one good man in it.

The second half of her beer went down twice as fast as the first. She ordered a second. We ate, talked, laughed, flirted. We avoided the subject. She had another half. We two-spooned a mango kulfi. I paid. We strolled home. I invited her in.

She hesitated for a moment before saying yes, she'd love to.

25

A sofa-scenario was in danger of developing.

When I mentioned the four-in-a-row jog-jog-jogging feet incident, Anne-Marie remembered immediately. She confessed how badly she'd felt for blabbing our micro-secret to the others. (We were us; they were the others: that was good.) Something intimate and almost non-existent in its dancing delicacy had been debased into a vulgar chorus line. She apologized – and said she'd only spoken up because she felt guilty: guilty because it was obvious that she and I were operating on the same scale, were – in a word – compatible. Or would be, if only we had a chance to get it together. She'd wanted to minimize that chance – by showing fidelity to her boyfriend (though it was impossible he'd notice this – being too great a giant to receive hints on our sub-scale) and by showing a certain callousness to me (which she knew I would feel – being a creature of minutiae like herself). She apologized and apologized for what she'd done – and I began to gain kisses from it, one for every apology.

We moved through into the bedroom.

Once we started to have sex, I felt unable to go through with things (kisses, caresses, etc.) because they seemed to be so obvious. But when Anne-Marie took hold of my cock, she seemed to be saying, 'It's okay. We can be obvious. That's what sex is about. It's not about the variety, it's about the sameness. Let's do now with each other what we've done before with others. Flesh is flesh, touch is touch, kiss is kiss. Isn't that enough for you?'

And I touched her cunt so as to say, 'More than enough.' And for a while it was.

But sex is never that simple. Even though she was dead and could not be hurt by this, I still felt as though I were betraying Lily. Merely to touch another woman's body, to allow that (for me) other women's bodies existed, was betrayal. And although it was highly likely that Lily had been unfaithful to me, I got little satisfaction out of this posthumous revenge. I felt sad that the sex was so haunted for me by Lily's presence. But then I remembered how rarely it had been that, during sex with her, even my few previous experiences with other women had been totally obliterated.

One thing I did manage – not to be thinking of Lily at the exact moment I ejaculated. At that instant (to block out Lily's imminent image) I pictured this: anonymous anal rape and the woman screaming for it to stop and the man not stopping. It was better that way, I thought.

And then, afterwards, there were moments, lying there, when it was all I could do to touch her spine with my fingertips. To have stroked her with my palm or brushed her with the side of my arm would have been too much.

I was so grateful. I wanted to cry and for her to catch me crying. I wanted to be allowed to pity her. I wanted to offer her certain varieties of care. It was a terrible thing not to be able to tell her I loved her just because I didn't, yet. But I knew that if I were able to say it, I would. It would be created by the mere utterance of it.

We fell asleep.

I woke up again around four and lay there in the half-dark, curtains badly-hurriedly drawn, looking at the perfection of her back. It was, I thought, absolutely without blemish – smooth, white, soft. Like Lily's. But as the light of morning intruded, I began to see moles. It was like someone had spilled coffee grounds on her. Then freckles emerged. And discolourations. And hairs.

But her failure to be flawless in anything other than half-dark only made her the more poignant to me.

I remembered how, when I was living with Lily, I used to wake up in the night and go into the bathroom and find dark bruises on my upper arms and all down my legs. I couldn't believe it – out of love, I'd learnt to sleep through being beaten up. Just as Lily hit me, unconsciously, so I unconscious received her blows. She even, one night, broke one of my front teeth.

I fell asleep again.

I felt happier than I had, since.

26

When I woke up, I found a note on the bedside table – simple, affectionate. Soon afterwards, a call came through from Anne-Marie. She had gone in to work – muzzy, smiling, and wearing the exact same outfit as the day before. In a rampantly gossipy modelling agency office – crammed with style-conscious young women and ultra-camp gay men – this couldn't fail to be noticed. Our voices on the phone maintained, as far as possible, the timbre of the pillow talk. But Anne-Marie kept breaking off to try and shh the catty backchat.

Over coffee, I decided I was now strong enough to go back to Lily's flat. I needed somehow to repossess it, take it back from Josephine.

The air in the hall as I walked in was cold and dead. The carpet still smelt rankly of Snafu and Glitch's shit and piss. There was a pile of mail on the hall table. I flicked through it distractedly. Of the earlier-dated mail, I saw that all the letters (including those addressed to me) had been opened: bank statements, phone bills, airmails, even junk mail. It hurt me to think that Josephine knew the exact magnitude of my overdraft. I stuffed all of it into my rucksack – deal with it later.

I walked through into the kitchen, wondering what exactly I was looking for. The room was quieter than I'd ever known it. It took me a moment to realize that this was because the fridge-freezer was off. When Lily and I had lived here, the thing had rumbled so earth-shakingly that I nicknamed it Rick Scale.

Its two doors hung whitely open. There was no food inside, no ice, no cold.

I checked the kitchen cupboards. A few tins were left: tomato soup, syrup sponge. My foods – crap I allowed myself when Lily was out rehearsing or touring; stuff she would never have allowed herself to eat but hadn't got round to chucking away.

I was very relieved to find that Lily hadn't managed totally to expunge me from her life, her flat. What had terrified me most, before I came back, was the possibility that my love for her had left nothing behind. But I was still here – I *was* still here. And in some ways, I was more here than her: disorder had always been Lily's trademark. (In our relationship, she was the Mess Monster and I was Tidy Heidi.) By clearing up, Josephine had reduced the flat to the minimalist paradise I'd always striven for – but never, in the face of Lily's chuck-down mentality, come near achieving.

These were the framed film-posters that I had chosen, because Lily was too busy to be bothered (*Pandora's Box*, *L'Atalante*, *Les Enfants du Paradis*); this was the coffee-maker that I'd decided (after a weekend of consumer research) was the best on the market. This was the stainless-steel swing-bin that cost me a quarter of one month's salary. Lily hadn't let me take it when I moved out. She said I owed her so much money she'd just keep anything of mine she liked.

She'd also taken over my taste in music (the only thing she listened to of her own accord was Joy Division). Most of the books, except for Lily's mashed-up acting texts, were mine. I'd read dozens of interviews where Lily claimed to have discovered something – band or novel – which I'd handed to her the week before, with plaudits. When I objected to this, Lily said (so like her mother): 'But, Conrad, I discovered *you* . . .'

The two large bottles of blue-label Absolut stood on one of the work surfaces. I was still wondering about them.

Lily's mother had missed some digestive biscuits I'd stuck in the dark back of a high cupboard. I took them out, walked through into the living room. I opened the pack and started to crumble the biscuits on to the shiny pine floor. I didn't know why. It just seemed like the right kind of absurd thing to do.

So far, in all the flat, I'd found nothing to suggest that Lily was the kind of person who was likely to get shot. I don't know exactly what I was looking for. But I felt there should be at least something unusual here – something that was probably already gone. An immense amount of tidying had been done – this became even clearer as I moved through into the bedroom.

Lily's clothes had always made their home either on the floor or in the huge metal laundry-basket. I don't think I'd ever seen the floor without a single ringworm of pants or scab of flesh-tights upon it – that simply wasn't the ecosystem within which Lily thrived.

I guessed Josephine had put things away in closets and drawers. I opened a few and found that I'd been right – everything was washed, ironed, ordered, stacked.

A sudden image came to me: Lily's mother, standing at the sink, handwashing the grunky stains out of Lily's last six weeks' knickers. Lily's blood and urine and shit, perhaps even some of my run-out and dried morning semen, dissolving into the suddy water around Josephine's working fingers. This was grief.

I checked Lily's secret hiding-place, under a couple of floorboards in the bedroom. I'd glimpsed inside before, but never dared open it. That would have been the instant end. Her diaries – all her diaries – (as I'd expected) were gone. The police, if Josephine were to be trusted.

Lily wrote left-handed, the page turned so she didn't drag her palm over the wet ink of her Rollerball. She wrote a page-a-day every day. Her distinctive handwriting slanted backwards and further backwards until – towards the end – it was an almost unbroken flat line. I couldn't believe she could read it back to herself. But she could.

Often, when she was writing about me in particular, she would lock herself in the toilet – just like an adolescent hiding their sex-thoughts from their mother and father. (Though Lily, of course, had shared, it sometimes seemed, every one of her sex-thoughts with her mother: I'd caught them at it. Lily guiltily putting the phone down as I walked in the door; Josephine smiling oddly the next time we met. Lily's mother knew far better than I what was likely to be in those diaries.)

In the bathroom, the mirrored cabinet was totally empty – all Lily's drugs were gone: no Valium, Librium, Lithium, Prozac, Xanax. I ran my hands around, looking for one single pill of hers. There was something gunked on to the back of the top shelf. An easy place to miss things. It was a folded piece of paper. I peeled it off and sat down on the toilet to look it over.

It was the instructions for a pregnancy-test kit.

27

I strolled back into the bedroom and lay on the bed, trying to think of something useful to do for the rest of the day. Nothing occurred to me – I was becoming more and more useless to myself. Even the most basic functioning was getting harder.

After fifteen minutes or so, I got up and started to look through Lily's wall-closets.

I flicked the hangers along the clothes rail, going through a catalogue of memories: this, the launch party for her first advertisement, that, to her mother's for a dreadful dinner party; this, hitched up under a tree on Hampstead Heath, that, thrown into the wastepaper bin in disgust (rescued and washed by me); this, bought in New York and never worn, that, still – I sniffed it to check – smelling mysteriously of seaweed; this, bought whilst touring *The Ghost Sonata*, that, in the week immediately before she dumped me.

Listlessly, I lay back on the bed.

My eyes explored the upper half of the room.

Up in the top of one of the closets was an overlooked box – flat, grey, minimal, dust-gathering. A single word on the outside: ghost.

Immediately I remembered the frock that Lily had been wearing when we met at Le Corbusier – the floaty insubstantial thing that had so flaunted her accessibility (to others) and her inaccessibility (to me).

I lifted the lid off the top of the box, expecting to find another dress from the same shop – another post-split present from Lily to herself.

It was the same colour as the other ghost frock.

I grabbed it.

A receipt fell to the floor.

Without Lily inside, it had almost no shape. In fact, it hardly seemed a dress at all – it was merely a waterfall of soft feminine material, draping itself off my hand and down towards the floor.

I went over to the mirror and held the dress up in front of me. I was expecting to see some subtle variation in cut – it would be shorter than the original, or sleeveless.

Shockingly, though, I saw it was – for all I could make out – the exact same dress Lily had been wearing when . . .

Why had Lily bought two of the same dress? As far as I could recall, she'd never bought two of anything (clotheswise) – even her socks seemed to be purchased singly.

I turned the dress around and looked at it front on: there was a message here. Not one that Lily had necessarily been expecting anyone to receive. But a message, all the same. If it was a message to me, then I was missing it. If to someone else, then . . .

I picked up the receipt. The date was about a month before Lily's death.

I decided to visit ghost.

28

Taxi there.

The exterior of the shop, a few hundred yards above Oxford Street, was poised neatly between matter-of-fact and prim. White paintwork. Four steps up to the door. A neutral window-display: three headless mannequins. This season's more colourful designs (Purple and crimson. No more grey.)

Once inside, I asked to speak to the manager. After she came out from the back of the shop, I explained who I was and who Lily had been. She asked if I would like to sit down. I said I would. We went through into her office.

'This has been very difficult for us,' the manageress said.

I had some idea what she meant: a few weeks previously the *Face* had done a highly editorial Lily-inspired fashion-shoot. In a warehouse apartment made to look as much like Le Corbusier as possible, slasher-movie special-effects had been used to turn the latest ghost outfits into an unwearable post-bloodbath gorefest.

'As if your girlfriend's death were some kind of fashion – or anti-fashion – statement.' I didn't correct her by saying ex-girlfriend. 'That coverage is the last thing anybody wants.'

Which was obviously why she had the entire eight-page spread pinned up on the noticeboard behind her desk.

'Did the police ever contact you?'

'Yes,' she said.

'Did they say why?'

'I assumed they were trying to work out her movements the day she was shot.'

'And?'

'And she came into the shop that afternoon.'

'She did?'

'She bought the dress she wore that evening. I served her myself. I packed it all up for her into a box. She seemed very pleased. It was the last one. The only reason I noticed at the time was that it was the third of these dresses – the exact same one – that she'd bought.'

'The third?' I said. 'Really?'

Number one, the one she'd been shot in, was presumably in the police's possession; number two was back in its box in her flat; but where was number three?

'Yes. She bought one right after they came out. That would have been about a year ago.'

I tried to think back – I tried to remember her wearing such a frock.

'Then another one about a month before she died. Then one on the day itself. "I just keep spilling things on them," that's what she said. But how are you? Have you recovered? You used to come in with her, sometimes, didn't you?'

I remembered stalking around the shop, proudly useless, very male, while Lily tried on outfit after outfit. (She said I had no taste in clothes, and she was probably right.)

'Yes,' I said. 'Did anyone else come in with her?'

'Um . . .'

'I know she was being unfaithful, if that's what you're worried about.'

'There were a couple of men.'

'Did you recognize any of them?'

'One of them looked familiar. He was an older man. I recognized him from somewhere. He came with her once or twice. And there were some others. Friends. The man from her advertisement.'

'Cyril?'

'Yes.'

'Do you know whether Cyril or this older man was with her the time – I should say the *first* time she bought that dress?

'Hang on,' she said. 'That wasn't me.' She went out of the office door. I heard her walking away over the shop's hard wood floors – the sound bouncing back off the hard white walls, hardly absorbed by the clothes at all. There were female voices, reacting; an *oh*; and a discernible *don't*. She came back.

'I'm sorry – I can't really say. The person who I think served her that time's just left. But I can tell you the dress was from last spring. We had them in until September. After the incident they sold out pretty quickly. Not to our usual customers, you know. Some of *them* even brought their dresses back – just to check they wouldn't be wearing the one.'

'Thank you,' I said. 'You've been very helpful.'

'She was so beautiful, wasn't she? Such a terrible –'

29

An older man.

It made sense. The thing about me that most annoyed Lily was my lack of social adeptness. 'Oh, you're so unsophisticated!' she used to groan, as I mismatched yet another outfit or praised her in the wrong way.

But who?

Being a true actress, Lily was intense but shallow in all her relations. (Except those with her analyst and her agent.) She had worked with dozens of older men. Once, in Norwich, she had played Juliet to a Romeo clearly in his forties. Most of her romantic leads needed some form of wigging or corseting.

I could go back through the cast lists of the ten or twelve productions she'd been in. But those were only the ones that had taken place since we'd started going out. Perhaps she'd met him before then. And, even so, there was nothing to say the older man hadn't met her backstage, or at the stage door, or somewhere completely unconnected with the theatre.

If anyone knew – if Lily had told anyone – it was her mother. But I doubted that Josephine would be speaking to me for quite some time. I needed to have something to offer her first – the flat, perhaps. At the moment, though, the information wasn't worth that much. Particularly as I'd thought of another way I might get at it.

I went straight round to Cyril's. It was a huge warehouse conversion on Old Street, right above the offices of *Dazed and Confused.* Stripped pine floors. Windows the size of cinema screens. Enough wall space to hang his six faux-Rothkos. It was everything I'd ever aspired to, and I hated it.

Lily and I had been round a couple of times for dinner with Cyril and his partner, Utne. They were intense seminars in awkwardness. Cyril always seemed to spend the entire evening exposing how completely dull my life was by showing an exquisite interest in every single aspect of it.

Since then, Utne had left him for a 2nd 2nd Assistant Director. When she did her topless tell-all story in the tabloids, she complained that Cyril had treated her like 'a body without a brain'. And she added: 'I have a very good brain.' (The readers were given ample opportunity to draw their own conclusions as to the quality of her body.)

It was two in the afternoon. Cyril was an actor: therefore he was likely to be unemployed and at home and bored. He was.

He answered the door looking casually handsome in khaki shorts and a Ben Sherman shirt. I couldn't believe it: he actually had a bowl of breakfast cereal in his hands. Not the one he advertised, though. He was eating CoCo Pops.

'Conrad,' he said. 'It is Conrad, isn't it?'

He walked back into the vast stage that was his kitchen before I'd had a chance to reply.

'It was terrible about Lily, wasn't it?'

Terrible for your career, I thought.

I remembered the cuttings: Cyril's Grief for Co-Star: 'We were leaving behind a body of work that people respected us for. They were closely following the development of our relationship. Sadly, no-one now will ever know what could have happened.'

I could smell toast.

'How can I help?'

'I'd just like to know – sorry, this is a bit embarrassing, but were you having an affair with Lily before she died?'

'Um,' he looked into the chocolatey milk in his bowl. 'No.'

'You weren't?'

'No.'

'But you did, at one stage, have an affair with her, didn't you?'

'Look, don't get cut up about it –'

'I'm not. I just need to know.'

He looked at me closely, assessing if I was likely to try attacking him – and probably concluding that, even if I did, he could easily take me.

'Yes. We saw each other now and again. Not just for sex. We went out for coffee. We went shopping. We talked.'

I felt empty. This was the first confirmation I'd had of Lily's unfaithfulness.

The toast popped up out of the stainless-steel toaster.

'So the tabloids were right? You're saying it was an "on-screen off-screen romance".'

'Yeah,' he said. 'I miss her, you know.'

'You think I don't?'

'No, man. I can see you do. You look like shit.'

I was determined to hold myself together until I was out of his sight.

'Can you answer a few simple questions? It would help a lot.'

'Okay.'

'When did you stop seeing Lily?'

'I guess it must have been about a month after the last ad. When was that? Spring some time. Things would cool off after we'd worked together. But for a month or so they'd be – sorry.'

'It's okay. So, you didn't have sex with her after that?'

'Maybe once or twice. I was away in June and August – doing this TV series.'

I remembered it now: some rural idyll of fucking in haylofts and fighting local developers. Lily had been up for a part.

'How can I know whether that's the truth?'

'Because I'm telling you. I was seeing someone else down there. My co-star.'

'A bit of a habit, that,' I said.

He smiled to himself.

'Oh, yes.'

Someone came out of the door at the end of the room. A woman, wearing one of Cyril's shirts. She called his real name in a whiny voice.

'Coming,' he shouted.

'And I want lots of marmalade on it!' she cried, then turned back into the dark bedroom.

'One last question,' I said. 'Did you ever go shopping with Lily to a shop called ghost?'

'She wants marmalade,' Cyril smarmed.

'It's a clothes shop.'

'I know that. What, do you think I'm stupid or something? Of course I know that.'

'Did you?'

He thought seriously for a moment. I got ready to catch him, in case the unusual effort made him fall over.

'I can't remember. We went to a lot of places. I don't think so.'

Another whine from the bedroom.

'It'll be cold!'

Cyril and I nodded our goodbyes, walked to the door.

'How was it, you know – being shot?' Cyril asked.

I didn't answer.

When I got home, I called Le Corbusier and asked for a booking – at *the* table where . . .

They told me it wasn't free in the evening for the next fortnight, and then only on a Monday.

I couldn't wait that long – it would have to be lunch. I gave them a pseudonym – my given middle name and my mother's maiden name: Bartholomew Young. I also informed them that I might need some help with the stairs.

I spent the evening without Anne-Marie. She had something

she couldn't get out of – it involved, according to her vivid description, an opening party for a bar, and models and shouted gossip and smoking until she lost her voice.

'You can read about it in next month's *Tatler*,' she said, on the phone. 'Much the best way of doing things.'

'I'll miss you,' I said.

I meant it – sort of: it would be good to have someone solidly there for when the nightmares woke me up.

(One which particularly disturbed me: myself gone asymmetrical with flesh, a huge oblong growing down the right half of my chest.)

30

Thursday.

It was time to see my Victim Support Counsellor. Though not on call twenty-four hours a day, she was supposedly there for me whenever I might need her. From our previous interviews I'd come away with the impression that the seriousness of the crime against me, the glamour of my co-victim, the promise of a press-covered trial – that all these Lily-gildings had bought me (dearly oh so dearly) a certain prestige within the hierarchy of victimhood.

I'd come back from the verge of becoming the ultimate victim – the dead person – and therefore I was worth paying attention to.

Vicky had given me all the details of how to contact her whilst I was still in hospital, in case of emergency.

I did twenty press-ups, twenty squat-thrusts and twenty more press-ups, then dialled her mobile number.

This was an emergency, my heart was racing, I was panicking.

She picked up.

'Can you come round? Please, can you?'

'Conrad? Is that you?'

'Can you come?'

'Are you okay?'

'Please.'

'Take a couple of deep breaths and tell me about it.'

'Come to see me, please. I'm scared.'

'Hang on,' she said.

She put her hand over the mouthpiece. I heard a door, footsteps. The background ambience was different when she came back – more open, echoey: from room to corridor, maybe.

'Hang on. Relax. I'll be there as soon as I can.'

'Please,' I said, then clattered the phone down as roughly as I could.

She arrived in less than twenty minutes.

As I let her in – maintaining my distraught act – it secretly pleased me to think that, in order to get over to me so quickly, she must have broken the law (speeding).

Once into the sitting room, I closed my eyes and – in front of her – halted my emotions completely.

'I know about the baby,' I said.

Vicky sat down on the edge of the sofa, uninvited.

'The baby?'

'That Lily was carrying.'

There was a distant mental thud from Vicky as this penetrated, hitting a wall of thick Oops.

'How did you find out?' she asked.

'That isn't the point,' I said. 'Why didn't you tell me?'

On came Vicky's good-with-people voice: 'Many reasons – all of them to do with you and your current state of mind. We thought you might find it too distressing. We are doing our best right now to keep it out of the newspapers – partly out of compassion for Lily's parents. In many ways, it isn't actually relevant to the case. The hitman was only trying to kill Lily and you. It is highly unlikely that he knew that she was pregnant.'

'And when were you planning on telling me?'

'We were going to observe –'

'Does *we* mean you?'

She was reluctant to leave the shelter of third person plural.

'Mostly. To observe your progress – see how you were getting back to normal life – and then –'

'Come in and fucking destroy it.'

'Who *told* you?'

'You are here to answer *my* questions. Your job is to deal with *me*, not other people. I'm your victim.'

'Of course, Conrad. Of course.'

'Was DNA-testing done on the baby?'

A deep breath, preparatory to coping with my response to her saying: 'I'm sorry, Conrad, but I can't tell you that.'

'They have or they haven't? Not whether I'm the father or not.'

'Really, whoever it was shouldn't have told you. You've been set back weeks.'

'That's the most unprofessional thing you've ever said to me, Vicky.'

'Vicky?' she said. 'But my name's –'

'I call you Vicky, because you're a Victim-person. It's my nickname for you. And I'd prefer to use it rather than your real name.'

'Whatever you want.'

'What can you tell me now that you haven't told me before? Is there anything else that's going to leap out of the grave and bite me?'

'Conrad,' she said, disgusted by the image.

'I know, it didn't necessarily have teeth. Although I have no idea how old it was – anything between six weeks and twenty-six. I don't know if it had fingers or whether its skull had begun to seal over –'

'Please,' she said, looking very distressed.

'This aspect of the case obviously disturbs you, doesn't it? Personally. Autobiographically.'

I made an educated guess.

'When did you have *your* abortion, Vicky?'

She looked at me, stunned – all her jobness gone.

'We are telling you all that we can.'

'No, you are telling me all that you see fit to tell me. But you seem to be forgetting that the person you have in prison isn't actually the one who wanted Lily and me dead. That person is nowhere near caught. And you don't seem to be doing much to find them. What are you doing?'

'We're doing everything possible. Be patient. They're a lot closer to an arrest than you might think. Very senior officers are involved.'

'Do you know what sex it was?' I asked. 'Yours – was it a boy or a girl? Did that make a difference?'

'I think I should go. I think I should talk to the social services about getting you some intensive counselling.'

'I may not testify,' I said. 'Oh, I'm sure you can make me turn up in court, but I won't say anything useful. Not unless I'm satisfied that you *have* done everything you can to find out who the real killer was.'

Professional distress was added on top of personal.

'You seem to be quite happy to bang up some hired hand. Perhaps the baby does have something to do with the real motive. Have you thought about that?'

'Of course we have,' she snapped. 'What do you think we are?'

'I think you're a bunch of fucking plods who couldn't make it into the marines – or as *proper* psychologists.'

'I'm glad we inspire such trust.'

'You will keep me properly informed,' I said.

'We will tell you whatever we can.'

I sat down.

'I must ask you not to pursue your own investigation. That would complicate things terribly. The matter is in the hands of professional men and women.'

'One more thing – do I have the right to receive an inventory of the items these professional men and women have removed from Lily's flat?'

'Such as?' she asked.

'Her medicines. Her diaries.'

Vicky went all awkward.

'I am, you know, the beneficiary of her will,' I said. 'Anything you took, I own.'

'You have a right,' she said.

'Then why don't I have an inventory?'

'An oversight, I'm sure.'

'Rectify it, immediately, okay?'

'I'll see what I can do.'

'Good,' I said. 'Now you can go.'

Vicky took up her purse and left.

I felt a bit guilty about treating her so badly. But she wasn't family or friends: she was engaged by the State to bring me back to being a happy and fulfilled citizen – and to fob me off with any excuse she could come up with. If finding out the truth meant that I had to give her a hard time, then fine. She should be able to take it. If she couldn't, she was in the wrong job. I guess she knew *that* already.

31

Managing the stairs at Le Corbusier was easy but I made out it wasn't. I'd taken along my NHS crutches, intending to appear as feeble as possible. The ploy worked. I was gently guided up the two flights – pausing for breath, pausing to regain my strength. The help came from the waiter with the shaven head and goatee beard – the one who'd served us the evening we were shot.

'Mr Young,' he called me – using the pseudonym I'd given when making the booking.

That he didn't recognize me was hardly surprising: I was only a lunch-time customer, a sick man on his own, not someone to be worried about over-much.

Slowly, swingingly, I approached the table – the place which had made me slow, made me swing. Or had made it necessary that I pretend.

I felt calm, very calm.

The interior had obviously been renovated since the shooting. However, there had been no change in overall style. Whatever they'd done, it had been a matter of replacement not refurbishment. A new mirror. A new frame. It made me wonder about the other objects surrounding the incident – the cutlery, the tabletop, the chairs, the table. Had the police taken them *all* away? Did anything escape the taint of being evidence? And, if so, outside what radius? Where did the circle of involvement find its circumference? Surely there had been enough blood flying around to incriminate half the restaurant. Was the man at the next table's shirt residing – at that moment – in an Ezy-seal plastic wallet at

Scotland Yard? Weren't some of the blood-misted wine glasses merely returned to the kitchen, washed and used in the next sitting that went ahead? (The restaurant had reopened, so I heard, exactly one week after the shooting. Booked solid.)

Closer in, and I could still see no difference between the table I now approached and the table at which I had almost died.

I sat down in Lily's place, not my own; and, looking all around, looking up and then down, I saw the first indication that something, that anything had happened here.

The floor of the restaurant was pale wood. However, around the table where I now sat – *the* table – the wood was discernibly paler. Only a shade, but some serious scrubbing had been done – and an attempt to efface had only succeeded in inscribing a more eloquent (though legible probably to no-one but myself and the restaurant staff) *memento mori*.

Also, now I looked, I could see that the gaps between the planks were slightly darker in the blood-affected area.

A movement in my peripheral vision. I glanced up. A waiter was coming over to take my drinks order. It was not the original waiter, not the one who had helped me up the stairs. It was the wrong waiter.

'I'd rather I was dealt with by him,' I told the wrong waiter, indicating the right.

The wrong smiled to himself, assuming homosexuality, then smiled at me, assuring complicity.

He left. A word or two passed between them and, in a few moments, the right waiter was at my table – obviously not too dissatisfied with my special request (from a homosexual point of view).

I had decided, once in the place, once under control, to proceed as quickly as possible.

'Before I order, I would like to settle up for a previous meal, which I believe was left unpaid for.'

The waiter looked baffled, poor dear.

'Don't you recognize me?' I asked. 'Maybe looking a little healthier – without the crutches.'

He snorted in a kind of pre-vomit way.

'Shit,' he said. 'Shit.'

'Would you like to sit down?' I asked. 'You look a bit greenish.'

'I'm fine.'

'I think you should,' I said, indicating the chair opposite me. 'That's the lucky seat.'

The next table along was empty, and the waiter pulled away one of its chairs – placing it at right angles to my table. He sat down slowly, in his own temporary zone of zero gravity.

'You're very brave to keep working here,' I said. 'What's your name?'

'Michael,' he said.

The wrong waiter glanced over, archly. It looked as though he was fantasizing some unlikely scenario: that I was a millionaire, offering his colleague a lifetime tenure on my Biarritz-based yacht (uniform obligatory, though minimal).

'Michael, may I settle the bill I left unpaid?'

'Are *you* all right?' he asked, distracted.

'I'm fine,' I said. 'How are you?'

'You'd have to ask the maître d' about that,' he said.

'About you?'

'About the bill.'

'Alright, then. I'll do it when I've finished eating. You know what I'd like to have?'

Le Corbusier was one of those restaurants where the waiters are so professional that they remember rather than write the orders down.

'Yes?' said Michael.

'I would like exactly what we had before. I'm sure you know what that was, don't you?'

'Puffball and plaice, asparagus and veal.'

'And the wine?'

'Chardonnay 1992.'

'Very good.'

The wrong waiter was now getting impatient with having to deal with Michael's covers whilst Michael had a sit-down.

'Are they all still on the menu?' I asked, a little surprised.

'Yes,' he said. 'People want to know which table it was – and they want to have what they, I mean you, what you had.'

'Almost famous, really,' I said. 'Aren't I?'

He looked at me nervously.

'Don't worry, Michael,' I said. 'I'm not going to do anything weird.'

Not yet, anyway.

He stood up.

'And a bottle of still mineral water,' I said.

'We've changed our brand,' he snapped back.

'From the blue bottles?' I asked. 'What a shame. Sure you don't have one lying around somewhere? Just fill it up with tap. I'll pay the same price.'

'I'll have a look,' he said.

'Thank you, Michael.'

As he walked away, I thought, *This will be difficult, but good for him.*

Mineral water came, blue as it should be, and then the starters, bringing back memories.

32

I sat in Lily's chair. I ate the food she had eaten. I looked in the direction she had been looking. And as I did so, I remembered our conversation – going through it again in my head, verbatim. But I could hear nothing new in it – no further hints as to what Lily would have told me had she lived a few minutes more.

It was unlikely she would have known for definite that I (or Cyril or the older man or another man altogether) was the baby's father. She wasn't likely to have had amniocentesis on something she was intending to abort. Nor, I doubted, would there have been time to organize one – unless she'd gone private. And that was something which Lily, trying to retain some vestige of her natural actorly leftism, had always been passionately against. Whatever Lily was intending to tell me it wasn't 'I'm carrying *your* baby, but I'm going to have an abortion.' Not unless she was prepared to lie – to cover up the fact she'd been sleeping with another man, or more than one other man. (And why do that? Hadn't the whole thing – last-minute call, expensive restaurant, new frock – been a demonstration of how totally in the past I was for her?) If there was a confusion as to who the baby's father was, Lily was unlikely to want to argue about it over asparagus and veal.

Veal, I thought, as I sliced into the pale flat flesh, *what a cruel thing to order*.

(When we met I was a conscience- and Lily a health-vegetarian. Her downfall, when it came, was not the archetypal bacon sarnie but a touring production of *The Ghost Sonata*. It had been Lily's

112

first really serious rôle: The Colonel's Daughter, in reality the Old Man's Daughter. Half-way through, Lily began to have fainting fits. The assistant director spotted her proto-anaemia and thought it very good for Strindberg but very bad for insurance. He therefore ordered her to eat steak and eggs. When she came back from tour, she corrupted me as well.)

A little undue attention came my way, as the other diners noticed I – sitting on my own – had ordered two meals but was only eating one. Michael had obviously told the other waiter, whilst out of sight in the kitchen, who I was and what I was doing there. Slowly, as he buzzed around, the other waiter began to pollinate the further off tables with this golden information. Cutlery clinked, heads turned, eyes narrowed then widened. More stamens of curiosity were tickled. The buzzing came closer. I heard the word *shot*.

The maître d' came and stood for a minute or two near the head of the stairs. To his right were the double doors to the kitchen. This was the point at which Lily might have seen the man who was about to kill her, *if* she'd been looking – but she hadn't.

Michael served me impeccably throughout the meal. I think he was trying to prove something to himself about his own professionalism. Today, for him, was well on its way from being a torture to becoming a good story; and maybe that in turn would rehabilitate the earlier and unmentionable day. Was Michael an actor, I wondered. Was he trained? Any more than serving the general public in *any* capacity is a training for disguised megalomania and moderated contempt. Speaking of which, the maître d' approached me after I'd asked for the bill.

'Mr Redman,' he said. 'What can I say? You are a very brave man. It is a privilege to have you as a customer.'

And all the time his body language was screaming – *Get out, low-life scum!*

'I hope you are making a swift and full recovery. And, as an expression of the esteem in which you are held by all at Le Corbusier, please accept this meal – and your tragic last meal – on the house.'

'Thank you for your generosity, but I am determined to pay for both meals. It's something I need to do for myself – and for Lily.'

'Well,' he said, hands flying apart like well-choreographed doves. 'Next time, perhaps.'

'Thank you,' I said. 'But this has all been rather traumatic for me. However, I may at some point want to book this particular table for some friends. I have strange friends. Curious people. It would be good to know that you would make it available for them – as a favour to me.'

'Of course,' he said, undisconcerted.

'But there is one thing you could do for me today.'

I could tell that the maître d' wanted to say *Anything* but was holding back. If he said that, I *could* ask for anything: I was a potential madman back from the dead. No-one could predict what obscenity I might want.

'What can we do for you?' he asked.

'Could I please have a look at your reservations book for August last year?'

'If we had it, Mr Redman, of course. But unfortunately the police have taken it away.'

Interesting.

'Ah, I don't suppose you can remember under what name the table for us was booked.'

The maître d' hesitated. Here was a chance for him to demonstrate his double power: the power of knowledge and the power of knowledge withheld. Both, in different ways, were a temptation – but he settled for disclosure, as it was most likely to send me away quietly and to keep me away once sent.

'Yes, I was with the Detective Inspector when he examined the reservation book. The name was Alun Grey. When the waiter

– Michael – called for the ambulance, he gave that as your name. Some confusion may have resulted.'

I made more of getting to my feet than was absolutely necessary, but not much.

'Thank you for clearing that up,' I said.

'A pleasure, Mr Redman.'

We began to move towards the door, eyes following us.

'I hope the *incident* hasn't affected your business.'

'On the contrary, Mr Redman. It may be a sad comment upon human nature, but our bookings have actually increased.'

'Really?' I asked.

'By over 10 per cent.'

There – I had discovered the greedy shopkeeper in him. He realized his mistake and was ashamed. A figure should never have been mentioned. Not to a customer, and particularly not to *this* customer. Attempting to cover up, he babbled.

'They are constantly asking for *that table* and they say *You know the one I mean*. Perhaps you experienced some difficulty in booking?'

'I would have preferred to come in the evening.'

'Unfortunately, Mr Redman, the ghouls are particularly fond of the evening.'

I turned to him at the top of the stairs.

'But you'll clear the table for me, if I ask.'

Only his eyelids moved, but it still conveyed a nod.

'Certainly.'

I made him shake hands on this and on our goodbye.

'Could Michael help me down the stairs again?' I asked.

The maître d' retreated – off to fetch him.

33

Half-way down the stairs I turned to Michael and said: 'Your maître d' just told me the name under which the table was booked – you know, the night I was shot.'

Michael halted.

'Yes,' he said.

'Do you remember what it was?' I asked.

He looked back up the stairs.

'Alun Grey,' he said.

'And did you take the booking?' I asked.

He nodded, quickly.

I looked at him. Did I really have to *ask* the next question? It seemed I did.

'Who made the booking?'

'The police already know this,' he said.

'But I don't,' I said. I lifted up one of my crutches – casually, as if I was so used to them they were merely a useful extension of my arms.

'Mr Grey actually made the booking.'

'On what day of the week.'

'Monday or Tuesday.'

He seemed to have something else to say, if only I asked the right question.

'And?' I asked.

'I think it was Monday,' he said. But that wasn't the answer he'd been meaning to give.

We turned our attention back to the stairs.

Once outside again on the street, I said to him, 'Thank you for your help.'

He smiled.

'Take care of yourself,' he said.

'And you,' I replied.

Really, we had much more in common with each other than either of us had with the maître d'. We were the same kind: strugglers-after-something-we-aren't-going-to-get.

'See you again, maybe,' he said.

He put his hand on my shoulder before jogging back up the stairs.

As I walked away from Le Corbusier I felt exhausted, but I had the name – an unexpected name – and I had my next task: Alun Grey.

34

Alun Grey was an actor. A large man with a resonant voice and eyebrows that grew bushier with each passing season in Stratford. In Sunday-magazine features he was always photographed standing in a greatcoat somewhere desolate – usually the Welsh Valleys, where he (and his resonance) originally hailed from. For years, because of this, he'd had to put up with tag of 'the new Richard Burton'. He had the requisites: voice, face, thirst, birds. Back in the early 1960s, he'd played lovable rogues – usually Cockney. His film career had really been taking off. There was talk of Hollywood. But something had halted his slide towards an interesting and vastly successful life – and that something had been his wife, the actress Dorothy Pale.

Dorothy had recently reached that age many actresses reach, where a combination of hormonal changes and the exercise of certain professional muscles had rendered her almost completely uncastable. Her throat had widened into a trunk of resonance, capable of rattling dentures in the gods. Her voice was now a blasted-out husk of cracks, creaks and virtuosic but unnatural octave leaps. Her mouth and eyes were so wide that any camera found them painful to look at. Skin aged by make-up and make-up removal, dried by the lights, wrinkled by the repeated-repeated-repeated emotions: again and again, grief. So much so, that her only plausible rôles nowadays were grief-stricken or aggrieved. But because she could no longer credibly carry off before-grief as well as after-grief, she rarely got the chance. Dorothy, you see, had ceased to be a believable human being. She was now a monster of the theatre – a creature whose only viable existence was on the stage of the Royal Shakespeare Company, shuddering and gesticulating, whispering and strutting, croaking out the pentameter, leaping into unscripted clutches with any actor that happened to be passing (much in contrast to her famously monogamous off-stage life).

Posters advertising Alun and Dorothy's modern dress production of *Macbeth* were all over London.

The whole thing was ridiculous – a last kiss-off by the RSC to a dedicated old stager. Dorothy was far too old to play a convincing Lady Macbeth. 'Bring forth men children only,' would be a hoot. (Dorothy was forty-eight and had a fifteen-year-old son, named Laurence after Olivier.) It was a vanity production, and all the critics knew that it was Dorothy's farewell. (Whether Dorothy knew was another matter.) After this it would be witches all the way.

Lily and Alun had toured together in *The Ghost Sonata*. But I hadn't been aware that they'd done anything else after that, other than keep in professional touch the way actors do – just in case they ever have to work with any particular co-actor again, perhaps for many performances, perhaps for many productions.

This secrecy suggested an affair – always assuming that they'd been seeing each other whilst she and I were still living together.

If they hadn't, then Lily's frock might still suggest an affair – maybe not in process, but definitely in the offing. Designer, as far as Lily was concerned, had always meant sex.

(During our last episode of fuckings, we'd done it on the floor of the women's changing rooms at Harvey Nichols – Lily flicking V-signs at the security camera over my shoulder. Well, it was a lot better than sitting outside with the other partners, exchanging shrugs and grimaces.)

Maybe the Le Corbusier date had been intended as their reunion – finally, we can be together, etc. But Alun wasn't going to leave his wife. *The* Dorothy Pale. Not for Lilian Irish. Mere Lilian Irish.

I had met Alun three times. Once when I picked Lily up after a *Ghost Sonata* rehearsal. Once drunkenly, at that production's first-night party. And once in the classical music section of the Virgin Megastore – where he apologized for his behaviour during and after the first-night party. On each of the three occasions I'd been impressed by his masculinity, his nostril hair and his aftershave – all of which were pronounced.

In a nearby newsagent I bought a copy of the *Standard*. Then I sat down at one of the pavement tables outside Bar Italia and looked through the theatre listings. There it was:

Sub Overdale's

MACBETH

starring

Alun Grey and Dorothy Pale

Barbican, Main Stage

Perfs 7.00, Thursday Matinee

After finishing my cappuccino, I went to one of the booking offices on Leicester Square. I bought myself a stalls ticket for the following evening. I let them know I'd be coming in a wheelchair.

After all that, I felt I had done enough for one day – I was beginning to get tired. Leg-weary and heart-sore, I let a taxi take me home.

35

On Friday morning, after Anne-Marie had left to go to work, I finally faced the pile of post I'd brought back with me from Lily's flat.

After being kicked out, I deliberately hadn't bothered to have my mail redirected – hoping that this would give me an excuse for some minimal contact with Lily. (I could think of her touching my forwarded post.) In fact, she'd been supposed to bring along my letters to our dinner date.

Josephine hadn't left very much personal stuff. There were letters and postcards from Lily's friends. I read a few of them. *Thailand is still totally wicked . . . And then he dumped me, just like that . . . Can't wait till this fucking shoot's over . . .* I'd never really liked Lily's friends.

Most of the envelopes were junk mail, continuing for months after Lily's death: credit cards, health insurance. There were also bills for her utilities: gas, electricity, water, phone.

A vague idea forming, I looked through the phone bill – it just gave totals. But turning to the bill for her mobile phone, I saw that it was fully itemized.

There were several pages of computer printout detailing the numbers which Lily had called, the length of those calls and how much she'd been charged for them. It covered the month before she died. I became excited. There would be plenty of useful stuff here, surely – Alunwise. But even before I'd started looking through properly, something struck me: I flicked to the last page – knowing that Lily's last hours would be there. She had made quite a few calls the day she was shot – which was all as expected. But what shocked me was what I saw at the very bottom of the page.

Date	Time	Destination	Duration (hrs:mins:secs)	Cost before discount (£)
30 Aug	21.52	(residential number)	0:02:01	0.042
30 Aug	21.54	(residential number)	0:01:37	0.042

The last two calls had been made *after* Lily was shot.

Someone had used her mobile, after she died – within an hour of her death.

As no further calls had been made since then, I had no reason for suspecting the phone had been stolen – not unless it had been assigned another number.

Obviously, now, the police would have the mobile somewhere in a plastic evidence bag. But just to check, I dialled Lily's number – having first shielded my own. All I got was *This mobile phone has been disconnected.*

I looked at the time of the calls again: 21.52 and 21.54. I remembered what the doctor had told me, back when I'd just come out of my coma. Lily had died in the restaurant. She'd then been taken, like me, to University College Hospital. Whoever it was that had used the phone had probably done so from there. That suggested two groups of people: police and hospital staff. Of the two, I immediately suspected the latter. Somehow the blaséness of using a dead person's mobile recalled the sick humour of medical students – tales of locking fellow students up in crates full of detached arms or dressing up real corpses and taking them down to the college bar . . .

Lily always kept her mobile in her handbag – and she'd had her handbag with her when she was shot, hung over the back of the chair.

Assuming that Lily's stuff had been taken along with her to the hospital, the likeliest maker-of-the-call seemed to be some cash-strapped assistant nurse left alone with the bag for five minutes.

Again, shielding my own, I phoned up the first of the two posthumous numbers.

A young woman answered.

'Who is that?' I asked.

'Who are you?' she said.

'Is that Anne-Marie?'

'No, you've got a wrong number.'

'Who are you?'

'Fuck off, creep.'

She put the phone down.

That hadn't gone very well. Before calling the second number, I formulated a plan. It was only very rough, but as things turned out, I didn't need anything more elaborate.

'Hello-yes?'

It was a woman's voice. Middle-aged.

'I'm phoning from the hospital.'

'Asif's on his way. He left all of fifteen minutes ago.'

Asian.

'Ah,' I said, assuming an authority I didn't have. 'Well, that's good.'

'I'm sorry,' the woman said.

'You're Asif's mother, I take it.'

'I am.'

'Can't you do anything about getting him here on time?'

'I'm very sorry. And I had promised Doctor Calcutt it wouldn't happen again.'

'Asif does *have* an alarm clock, doesn't he?'

I was enjoying this.

'But he falls asleep before he remembers to set it. He's so tired.'

'Wonderful.'

'Do you work in the pathology department, too?'

'No, I'm just a faceless manager, trying efficiently to deploy very limited resources. Asif's resources seem more limited than most, I must say.'

'Please don't be too hard on him.'

'Don't worry, I won't.'

'He's been trying his best, ever since the police spoke to him . . .'

'Ah, yes . . .'

'He works very hard.'

'I'm sure he does.'

36

Of course, it was hardly likely that the police *hadn't* checked up on Lily's phonecalls, as well. Asif must have already been in serious trouble for what he'd done.

An approach suggested itself – and I decided to pursue it immediately. Shielded, I phoned University College Hospital. When I got the switchboard, I asked for Pathology. When I got Pathology, I tricked Asif's surname – Prakash – out of them. (They also told me that he was an Assistant Pathologist.) Then I called up a second time and asked for him by name. He'd just arrived, and came to the phone guilty and out of breath.

'Yes?'

'Asif Prakash?'

'Yes?'

'Is it standard Hospital Trust procedure for pathologists to use the mobile phones of –'

'Shit.'

'– recently deceased persons?'

'Who are you?'

'I'm a freelance journalist. I work for the tabloids.'

Words he must have been dreading ever since.

'What do you want?'

'Do you have any comment?'

'No, I don't.'

'Do you deny using Lilian Irish's mobile phone to make two phonecalls, the first to a young woman, the second to your mother?'

I could hear his breath wheezing across the receiver, although he didn't speak.

'Asif?'

'No comment.'

'People who say *No comment* always come across as guilty, Asif. Take my advice – say something. Deny it if you want, but I know you did it. The police have spoken to you about it. You've already been disciplined by the hospital. I'll bet they don't want the story to get out. It won't look good for the police or for you. But it's going to get out – and you're going to look bad if you don't help me.'

'What's your name?'

'Look, it's probably not a good time for you, right now. I know you were late again for work today. Talking on the phone too long isn't a good idea. Let's say I call in a couple of days, then –'

Then I had a thought.

'Or maybe I'll just drop in at the hospital and see you. This story isn't exactly hot at the moment. But they'll run it whenever it's ready. The news desk's keen. If you want to talk, fine. But I've got more than enough already. See you, Asif.'

He spluttered something but the phone went down anyway.

After this obvious breakthrough, I decided to try and see if I could get a copy of Lily's mobile-phone bill – right from the day she bought it. The joint account for the flat phone – as I already knew – had been paid off and closed by Lily's parents.

I called the mobile-phone company. I said that I thought Lily had been overcharged for a number of calls. They asked why I hadn't taken the matter up earlier. I told them the truth: shooting, coma, threat of paralysis, therapy. They fetched their manager. I demanded a fully itemized bill. They promised it by return of post.

~

Next, I decided to go through the bill I already had – starting on the day she died and working back through it.

The best thing, I thought, would be to get really nerdy on it with some colour-coded fluourescent marker-pens: identify as many of the numbers as possible (paying special attention to Alun's), then trace them all back – in yellow, pink, blue and green.

First off, I fetched my address book and made a list of the numbers we might both have called. Quite a few I recognized immediately: Lily's mother, her agent, her analyst. The others I dialled, pretending to be a telemarketer.

'Hello,' I'd say. 'I'm Marcus Fishbourne from Direct Telesales International. Am I speaking to Made-Up Name?'

With many, I recognized their voices the moment they answered. With most of the rest, Marcus Fishbourne from Direct Telesales eventually extracted their real name from them.

Lily, as it turned out, had made the kind of calls you'd expect from anyone – to girlfriends, acquaintances, family. Then she'd made the calls of an actress – to her agent, to casting directors, to theatres. There were even some of her calls to me – at home and at work.

However, a few numbers continued to baffle me – there was a mobile number which Lily had called twice on her final day (once at 11.00 and once at 19.55)

I thought this might be important. Particularly as the printout revealed she'd never phoned this number before – at least, not during the month before she died.

I was about to put the phone bill aside when I noticed another couple of slightly odd things – near the end of the bill. It was hardly surprising I hadn't noticed them first time though. They were numbers I'd seen so often. The two calls came together:

| 30 Aug | 16.47 | Lily's home number | 0:04:44 | 0.158 |
| 30 Aug | 19.51 | My home number | 0:01:07 | 0.042 |

The first was to the number of Lily's flat in Notting Hill. Probably, she'd been checking her answerphone to see if there were any messages. What I found odd was that she'd spent over four minutes doing this. But then, maybe, she'd just had a lot of messages. It was possible.

The second call was to my flat in Mortlake – a number which she'd also called earlier in the day (16.25). When she hadn't found me there, she'd immediately called the Discovery Channel (16.27). She knew I'd be working there – when I *was* working – for at least three months after we split. I'd only just started on the temporary contract. So she hadn't had to try the other cable places.

(This is how dead relationships continue for a while, in zombie form – each knowing the other's movements and being able to anticipate them. Slowly, though, the zombie-knowledge becomes out-of-date and the relationship becomes rancid and clumsy. Mine and Lily's zombie, at the time of her death, was still fairly fresh – its face had yet to fall off, its eyes still worked.)

The question now was: why had Lily bothered to phone me at my house when she knew I definitely wasn't going to be there?

For the first time in a long while I was grateful for my mother's meticulous attention to detail. From a drawer in the hall, I pulled out her list of Messages Left On Your Machine While You Were Away.

As I'd guessed, the first message dated not from the last time I set the answerphone (Thursday evening) but from the following Monday, a couple of days after I'd been shot.

Now, although I wasn't exactly Mr Popular, I knew that I would have received at least one call during that time. Sunday evening was the most acceptable time of the week for people to appear to be at home with nothing better to do than phone other people they didn't really give a shit about. As lots of people didn't really give a shit about me, someone would almost certainly have called me on Sunday evening.

Checking further down the list, I saw that a couple of my genuine friends were missing completely. These were friends I spoke to almost every day, and they didn't appear to have called once. This might be because they didn't phone on Friday and, by Saturday afternoon, had heard of my condition. But even after Monday some friends were still calling my answerphone to speak to it, as if to me. One message my mum had noted down read: 'Distraught sobbing, female, one minute, no name left.' I wished I knew who that had been. Anne-Marie, maybe? Or some other secret admirer, regretting a romantic opportunity perhaps for ever missed.

These calls, according to my mum, had only started to arrive on Tuesday afternoon – which was hardly likely.

It seemed there was only one conclusion to draw. I went to my answerphone and confirmed it: the police had taken away my original answerphone and replaced it with an identical one.

One thing was certain: the police knew what it was that Lily had wanted to say to me only minutes before we met up for real.

I could make a few guesses at what this might be. She would have known that what she was about to tell me (the pregnancy, the abortion) was more than likely to make me very upset – in which case, it was quite possible that she'd phoned to leave a placatory message on my phone.

But why do that before the meeting even took place? There would surely have been time afterwards to call up and deal with a specific situation.

Another guess was that it was something she found too embarrassing to discuss in public, but needed to convey to me somehow. Also unlikely.

Another that she was phoning to cancel, but, when she found I hadn't gone home to change, she gave up and accepted that our dinner was fated to go ahead. Maybe not.

And there another possibility occurred to me – perhaps she hadn't, after all, been intending to break the news about the baby in person. It seemed rather cowardly for Lily, but this was an unprecedentedly awful situation. Perhaps she would just have said, 'I've left a message on your answerphone. It explains everything.'

In one minute seven seconds? Everything?

I dismissed this theory, as well as all the others.

The truth was, it was a mystery. I really didn't know, and the police really did.

In the end, Lily's mobile-phone bill looked something like this:

Date	Time	Destination	Duration (hrs:mins:secs)	Cost before discount (£)
30 Aug	09.15	Disconnected number	0:06:26	0.314
30 Aug	11.00	Unknown mobile	0:09:59	0.314
30 Aug	11.12	Lily's mother's mobile	0:09:23	0.314
30 Aug	11.41	Lily's solicitor	0:07:43	0.314
30 Aug	11.55	Vidal Sassoon	0:03:33	0.042
30 Aug	16.25	My home number	0:00:13	0.042
30 Aug	16.27	Discovery Channel Edit Suite	0:02:59	0.042
30 Aug	16.47	Lily's home number	0:04:44	0.158
30 Aug	19.51	My home number	0:01:07	0.042
30 Aug	19.55	Unknown mobile	0:03:01	0.042
30 Aug	21.52	Asif's girlfriend	0:02:01	0.042
30 Aug	21.54	Asif's mum	0:01:37	0.042

By the time I finished, it was almost six o'clock. I was exhausted.

Perhaps it was this that made me act so stupidly when I dialled the mobile Lily had called twice on her last day. No-one had answered the five times I'd tried it before. This time, though, a rough voice answered.

'Who's this?' it said. 'Where'd you get this number?'

In my confusion, I completely forgot my pseudonym and said, 'This is Conrad Redman from Direct Telesales International –'

'What do you want?'

'I'm sorry. It must be a bad time. I'll call back later.'

I put the phone down.

Something about the voice made me very afraid.

This wasn't helped by the fact that mistakenly I'd given out my real name.

37

Going to the theatre in a wheelchair was an interesting experience. Slight lulls in conversation announced and followed me wherever I went. When I rolled up to pre-order an interval drink at the bar, people got out of my way rather faster than they would a Sherman tank. (I was a Sherman tank armed with pathos – and they didn't want to catch a round of that full in the heart.) But the most interesting thing was the fact that there was no difference in my posture and attitude whilst watching the play and milling around beforehand and during the interval. Other people were able to mark their periods of (relative) concentration and relaxation by the difference between sitting and standing. For me, it was all the same performance – unbroken from beginning to end – and the beginning had been when the taxi-driver rang the doorbell and I sat down in the wheelchair and opened the front door; and the end would be when the taxi-driver (another taxi-driver) dropped me off back home.

The play itself was much as I'd expected. All in graffitoed concrete, the stage set was intended to re-create the reccie on a Glasgow council estate. The Scottish thanes were kitted out in garish tartan sportswear and last year's trainers. Macbeth and Lady Macbeth wore too much gold jewellery and wiped their noses on their acrylic sleeves. The Drunken Porter was an incoherent street-person who knew the combination lock numbers to every building. Videocameras on tall posts made a statement about surveillance – watching the actors and the audience from all four corners of the stage. On large television screens we could see ourselves – rows of heads in the reflected stage lights. The director, Sub Overdale, had obviously had a problem with updating the Shakespearean swordplay – so everyone on the estate was armed with machetes. ('MacBetty with a Machete', one of the reviews had been headed.) All in all, as is usual with the Royal Shakespeare Company, there was far far too much acting going on. The actors attempted to liven up 'the boring bits' by unnecessary pieces of business – acting out and literalizing every figure of speech. Their accents wandered all around the highlands and lowlands, occasionally taking a short holiday in Brooklyn or Bavaria. Every one of the usual RSC trademarks was on display: the men doing their stamping-stomping big-balled walks, the women about as feminine as drag queens, the overfussy crowd scenes (each crowd member trying to catch the audience's eye with some little bit of business), the far-past-pensionable actors who think verse speaking means e-nun-ci-ay-TTT, the young actors who think it means treat it all like slangy prose and the messianic middle-agers who, whenever a line comes through as if written in modern English, plant it in the audience like a flagpole: this is why Shakespeare is still relevant, why he still speaks to *you*, why we need more funding.

If I hadn't had ulterior motives for staying, I'd have wheeled my way out of there before the end of the first act.

Instead, I played my usual theatre-tedium games: Spot the members of the cast who . . .

    a. are sleeping together?
    b. have slept together but don't any more?
    c. will sleep together before the end of the run?
    d. will sleep together after the last-night party?
    e. hate each other's guts?
    f. hate the director's guts?
    g. hate themselves? (easy, they all do)
    h. hate the audience?

All that remained, finally, was the ultimate ordeal: the curtain call. How many hours – not in actual physical rehearsal, but in mental anticipation – do the actors secretly spend on this minute or two? How many times have they envisaged themselves stepping back to applaud a co-actor, smiling in admiration – behaviour which only says to the audience, 'Wasn't she *marvellous*? And doesn't she just know it?'? Or how often stood in front of the mirror perfecting that businesslike dip, upper body still curtly to obedience, which says, 'I'm a down-to-earth fellow, just like you – I have no airs. (But I *was* good, wasn't I?) Or how frequently practised that exhausted flop, hands dangling, which says, 'To you, my audience, in this my bravura performance, I have given my absolute all'?

I coped in the only way I could think of, by closing my eyes, listening to the clapping. I tried to imagine that it was an inhuman sound – a distant waterfall or a motorway heard across flat fields.

38

When it finally finished, I trundled round to the stage door and announced myself. Two years of Lily had been more than enough for me to learn the various techniques of blagging my way backstage. (What you must realize is that most security men would be profoundly grateful if someone were to execute the entire cast of any given play. Looking really suspicious is often all that's required for green-room passage to be granted.) With the added prop of the wheelchair, I could hardly fail.

I'd never been behind-the-scenes at the Barbican before, though I'd endured many thesp anecdotes about its legendary unpleasantness. Every cast that ever worked here became ill, through the lack of natural light and the constantly recycled air. They had a name for it: Barbicanitis.

I got into the lift and pushed the button for the dressing rooms, conveniently placed six floors above the stage.

The backstage décor was a curious mixture of office block and primary school – yellow walls and fuchsia trim.

And this was where these people wanted to spend their time, apart from the time they spent doing the atrocious things they'd just done to Shakespeare, the English language, my patience and over a thousand pairs of buttocks?

I only had to ask one passing person (the Drunken Porter, as it happened) where the star dressing-room was. Alun and Dorothy were famous for sharing, despite their exalted and senior status. Here it was that they were always photographed when interviewed as a couple – sitting side-by-side in front of a mirror with bulbs around it. (Dorothy, solo, specialized in looking winsome whilst leaning on trees; Alun, left to his own, did the far-gazing windswept-hilltop thing). These were proper actors, the Sunday supplement readers were meant to think: surrounded by make-up, costumes and cards from well-wishers.

It was Alun who said, after I knocked, 'Who's there i' the name of Beelzebub?' I went in anyway.

As I had taken my time wheeling round, they were both of them out of their costumes, showered and ready for home.

They had no other visitors – and the lines on their faces relaxed as they saw my wheelchair. (Though they cannot have been delighted to see the unlucky-coloured green shirt I was wearing. I knew it would discomfort them: Alun had once put his name to a ghost-written book about theatre superstitions.) They instantly expected me to deliver some banality of thanks, on behalf of the Variety Club, for the much-needed new minibus.

I'd decided to go all out for shock value, and their smug faces only encouraged me in this.

'Alun,' I said. 'Don't you remember me?'

He was used to this, but not as used to it from cripples – cripples are meant to be unforgettable. Like hospital visits to girls in comas and whispered chats with autistic boys who really understand Shakespeare better than all the critics, don't they?

'Ah,' he said, buying for . . .

'Conrad,' I said. 'I used to go out with Lily.'

The effect was so startling that (if I could) I would have repeated it straight away. Alun jumped out of his seat, at first as if he wanted to shy away from me and then – checking, as I thought, his first impulse – stepping up to the side of my chair and putting his huge hand on mine.

'Conrad, forgive me. How could I not recognize you?' he said.

Dorothy now joined him, bending down over my other side, touching my other hand. Not a situation I wanted to stay in very long – they both smelt rankly of animal exertion, and of expensive fragrances trying to refute animal exertion. I jerked the wheelchair into a wheelie and did one of those double pirouettes that pedestrians find so impressive.

'Quite simple, I'd've thought,' I said as I touched down. 'Last time we met I didn't have this.'

Alun looked at Dorothy, his contracted brow telegraphing her the message *Possibly disturbed.*

Dorothy knelt at my side and put her arms around me – this wasn't so much a hug as a black hole of perfume and female flesh felt through fabric.

'Oh, Conrad,' she said, going straight into a copeable-with recognition scene. 'How are you – after that terrible, terrible –'

The hug continued. I tried speaking, but my voice was muffled by muliebrity, baffled by breasts.

I felt Dorothy's body jerk slightly to one side – she had moved her head. While I was blinded, messages were passing between her and Alun – I wondered what they could be, apart from guilty.

My strongest desire was to bite one of Dorothy's nipples (they wouldn't have been hard to locate, dangling as they were) and force her to give me slightly less 'love' and slightly more room. But I compromised, and began faking a monster coughing-fit.

On cue, she stood up and stepped back.

'I'm sorry,' I gasped – cough, cough. 'Allergies.'

'Oh dear,' said Dorothy, and looked down at herself as if it were her very flesh that I was allergic to.

'A glass of water?' asked Alun, who (while I was engulfed) had moved over to stand by the mirror – rather further away than seemed truthful, particularly after the kneeling and the touching.

The mirror was plastered with photographs, mostly of Laurence, their son. In the early shots he was posed on beaches or in parks, holding some prop (a primary-coloured ball, a tennis racket) and smiling widely; in the later snaps he'd been caught, scowling and black-wearing, either at his computer or on his bed.

'I'll be fine,' I said.

Dorothy seemed to have something to say, but thought the better of it and retreated to her interview chair.

I did a final few pantomime coughs – not without enjoying the irony of putting on such a bacon-rind performance for two such monstrously huge Harrods hams.

Alun joined his wife in front of the mirror.

When I next looked at them, through cough-misted eyes, Alun and Dorothy were sitting, holding hands and waiting patiently – impregnably back in Sunday-supplement mode. For all their emotional involvement with me, I might have been a first-time interviewer fiddling with the batteries of my Dictaphone.

'How did you enjoy the production?' asked Dorothy.

'Oh,' I said – enjoying this scene much more than anything I'd seen on the stage – 'it was just the usual RSC crap, wasn't it? I expect the Japanese enjoyed it.'

Dorothy looked mortified. Alun maintained a stoic deadpan.

'But I thought the central performances . . .' Oh, how I love a dramatic pause '. . . towering.'

They glanced at each other, unable to resist dipping into even such a pathetically small goodie-bag of superlatives as I'd brought with me.

As in Inferno, I thought.

'Thank you,' said Dorothy, in a manner that said, *I have been much praised before, of course, but I accept with genuine pleasure all genuine praise.*

'You should have come on Saturday,' said Alun.

Dorothy looked at him, going slightly misty with the memory of Saturday.

This was getting too much: I was being dragged into some grotesque RSC production called *Backstage*.

'Tell me, Alun, when I was shot I was sitting at a table that had been booked under your name. Why?'

Alun sat deadpan still, but one of his hands did a Parkinson's-type twitch.

'Why don't we go and have a drink?' said Dorothy.

'Please tell me,' I said. 'As you'll understand, I'm quite interested in finding out.'

Still Alun didn't speak.

'You booked the table,' I said. 'I checked at Le Corbusier. You were meant to be sitting where I sat.'

'Yes,' said Alun. 'Shall we have a drink?'

He dipped his hand under the dressing table, reached into a cardboard box and came up holding a large bottle of Absolut vodka, blue label.

'I have no idea what you're trying to suggest,' he said.

'You've already spoken about this to the police. What did you tell them?'

Dorothy stood up.

'We've already told them everything we know.'

'Then tell me,' I said.

'It's very difficult for Alun,' Dorothy said, taking over. 'I've forgiven him, but he had a short affair with Lily. When I found out about it, I told him not to see her any more. He had to cancel at the restaurant. I have no way of knowing but I expect Lily phoned you as a last-minute replacement.'

'That's right,' said Alun. 'That's what we told the police.'

Dorothy stood to one side, ready to intervene in defence of her husband if I gave her a chance.

'Could I speak to you on your own?' I asked Alun.

Dorothy said, 'Really –'

'I have some private questions – about Lily.'

'Dorothy can stay,' said Alun. 'She knows all about it, anyway.'

I waited.

'Please go,' I said to Dorothy.

'No,' she said – the first honest syllable she'd uttered all evening.

'Okay,' I said. 'How long had you been seeing Lily?'

Alun glanced guiltily up at his wife.

'A couple of months.'

'Two months?' I asked.

'Three-ish.'

'You realize I was still living with her?'

'She told me she was going to finish with you, and – in the event – she did. I'm sorry –'

'You had sex with her.'

'I did.'

'Right from the beginning?'

'Yes.' He nodded.

'Unprotected sex?'

'Why does he have to answer that?' shrieked Dorothy.

'Because,' I said, calmly, 'Lily was pregnant when she died.'

'Oh-my-god,' said Dorothy.

'Christ Jesus,' said Alun.

Were they acting? I couldn't tell.

I turned to Alun.

'I take it that means it could have been yours.'

Alun turned pleadingly to Dorothy. 'I didn't know – really, I didn't. Why didn't the police tell me?' Then to me: 'Haven't they done any tests? Can't they tell whose it was?'

'Why were you meeting Lily that evening?'

'It was just . . . just dinner,' Alun said.

'Who wanted to meet up, you or her?'

'I think she suggested it. I can't remember.'

'And when did you decide not to go? When did Dorothy make you cancel?'

'Dorothy and I talked about it a couple of nights before. Wednesday. It was the best thing all round – that's what we decided. We are really very happily married, you know. We have a lovely son.'

Dorothy said, 'Alun was being foolish. He knows now.'

'So, how did you cancel? Did you phone? Or did you go and

see her at home? Or up in town? I take it you were breaking up at the same time, not just blowing her off over one date.'

Alun tried to sneak a sideways glance at Dorothy.

'I phoned from home late that evening. Thursday. We'd both been in rehearsal all day. I was in *Titus Andronicus*. Dorothy was in – what were you in?'

'*Three Sisters.*'

'Oh, yes. Anyway, it was late when I called – say, eleven-fifteen.'

'Were you with him when he phoned?'

Dorothy gave me a single nod – tight-mouthed. The very follicles of her hair seemed to pull tighter, about to go ping.

'And you said that you couldn't ever see her again – that your wife had found out – that you were sorry.'

'I think she understood. It wasn't spelt out. I told her it was over, for reasons that she –'

'Was she in love with you?'

Alun was now sitting with his feet apart, his elbows on his knees, his fingers in his hair, talking directly into the carpet, beginning to cry.

'I hope not,' he said.

'When I saw her on Friday, she seemed perfectly okay,' I said, remembering even as I spoke the special-occasion frock, the new perfume, the unusual calmness.

At what point, exactly, had Lily become attracted to this huge sobbing creature?

'Did you sleep with her during the Strindberg tour?'

'Surely that's enough,' said Dorothy.

'No,' said Alun. 'But the possibility was there. It seemed to hover between us, like –'

I didn't need his rehearsal-room similes.

'Last question: did *you* love *her*?'

'No, he did not,' intervened Dorothy once more. 'He was besotted for a time – even I saw that – but that was all.'

Alun drew himself up.

'Do you know,' he said, 'I think I probably was.'

Dorothy flounced over to him and slapped him, hard. Alun seemed to take this as a matter of course.

'What's the point in lying?' he said. 'The girl's dead.'

'I am not dead,' sobbed Dorothy, finally in tears. 'Not yet, anyway.'

'How about that drink?' I suggested.

They ignored me, slowly beginning to work their way towards touch, apology, reconciliation.

Not bothering with goodbye, I opened the door and backed the chair out of the room.

39

Taxi home.

Some of what Alun had said might even be true. After I'd told him about the baby, he might have forgotten himself and spoken honestly. But the whole conversation had been so heavily policed by Dorothy that between them they obviously had something to hide.

What seemed clear was that Alun had been seeing Lily while I was still living with her, and that – during that time – they had been having sex. I tried to remember whether I'd noticed anything suspicious. It was unlikely I had. By that stage in our relationship I was on a kind of trust autopilot: Lily wouldn't do that because Lily was Lily, because I lived with Lily and loved Lily, and because Lily lived with me and loved me. (Almost, I was trusting in the fact that I trusted her – and that, because she knew I trusted her, she wouldn't betray that trust.) I was leaving myself open to being wounded, in the hope that the possibility of my being hurt would be enough to prevent her doing anything to cause me pain. Which is fine when you love someone and feel their hurt as your own. But it was clear that Lily had gone, at some point, beyond that – or ducked beneath it.

She was capable, in death, of causing me a great deal more distress than when alive. (Everything now was total – a fact would remain a fact, without apology. Unfaithfulness was eternal.) But it was clear that – even before she died – she had crossed over into not really caring about whatever pain she might cause me.

The one thing Alun had said that I believed totally was that

Lily had told him I was on the way out. There was nothing to do with logic in my acceptance of this. It just felt true – it was so painful that I couldn't believe it untrue.

And so now I had to accept, with almost total certainty, that Lily died no longer loving me – and although she might have been carrying our child, it could equally well have been that of another man – a man whom she *did* love – would choose, was choosing, had already chosen over me.

When she called me to invite me out to dinner, all the self-reliance I'd built up during those six weeks alone was torn through by the slashing spin of false hope – she wants me back, she wants to say she's sorry, she wants to plead forgiveness.

Even her phonecall, so clear in its statement of our emotional agenda, hadn't been able to prevent that damage.

Once she sees me, I thought, she'll say what she *really* means. She just doesn't want the reconciliation to take place on the phone.

Now all the falsity of that hope was left untenable. I had proof: I had had the other man in front of me.

When Anne-Marie called to suggest she come round, I said I wasn't feeling too well. Tomorrow night, we agreed, would be better.

That night was the worst since coming out of the coma. All I'd feared was upon me, and there seemed little else left for me to hope for. I felt immensely humiliated – despite the fact that no-one was present to witness my humiliation. How could they be? It was in my version of a private past that the really important events were taking place. The only people who existed in this imaginary realm were Lily and myself.

When I fell asleep, I dreamt my way back into our flat. Actual scenes replayed themselves, all truth gone – nothing but surface and parody. Other scenes, ones at which I hadn't been present, appeared, in false flashback: Lily kissing Alun and coming straight home and kissing me; Lily buying two bottles of Alun's favourite vodka, ready for his next visit to the flat.

When I woke up, it was into a real present no less disturbed than the invented past. Lily had died no longer loving me.

It felt as if someone were pulling a heavy cowl of cold sweat up my back and over my head.

Perhaps I deserved what had happened – deserved it for laughing at Lily as she died.

Now, in my made-up scenes of her, she was always laughing, with Alun, at me. In the moment of her death, I'd been guilty of something that – in the dark of my bedroom – seemed almost as bad as pulling the trigger. But because of what I'd learnt about Lily's own guilt, I felt almost glad that I'd laughed. Now, if I could have travelled back to that moment, laugh at her is almost certainly what I would have chosen to have done.

And then I felt a further guilt overtake me: that, even out of some instinct of impossible retrospective revenge, I was wishing such things. It was disgusting that I should desire further punishment for Lily, dead as she was – deadly as her punishment had been.

There seemed only one way out of these nightmare convolutions, and that was to forgive equally both Lily and myself. But that was impossible – I still loved her, I still hated myself.

40

Saturday.

In the morning, I went to the gym and worked on my legs. They were probably stronger now than they'd ever been before I got shot. Back then, I'd never taken any exercise. But, despite my new-found fitness, forcing myself out of the wheelchair was a bit like trying to persuade a kid that they're too old for the pushchair. For some things, like moving around my flat, watching TV, playing computer games, the chair was really cushy. And it had already proven useful at certain moments, emotionally speaking. Alun Grey, in particular, seemed susceptible, in a typically weepy Welsh way, to the Adventures of Wheelchair Boy. And admittedly, the crutches were still useful for going upstairs – where I tended to lose my balance. But overall I was probably fitter than before – though about eight metres of colon were away and gone up the hospital incinerator chimney. I wasn't awake to say I'd like to keep them, jar them, display them.

Anne-Marie came round in the late afternoon and I took her straight to bed.

Afterwards, her face went all serious.

'Conrad, I think we should talk.'

She sat cross-legged on the floor. I sat back on the sofa.

'Don't you think, maybe, that this has all happened a bit too fast? With us, I mean. We were both very emotional and –'

'I'm glad it happened.'

'Well, so am I. Really.'

'You're just what I need.'

'But everything's so mixed up with Lily and Will and –'

'It feels great to me.'

'And to me, but –'

'What's really bothering you?'

'I hate to whine.'

'Is it something I can help with?'

'It's my job. You don't want to hear this.'

'Really, I do.'

Anne-Marie wasn't worried about how quickly we'd got into bed together. She just wanted to know that she didn't have to be Ms Happy with me all the time. I let her grumble on for an hour or so, then we fucked again.

Sunday.

Happy. So happy. Happier than I'd been, since.

I even half-decided to give up my ludicrous investigation. I was bad at this, very bad. Really, I couldn't take myself seriously. I just wanted people to tell me the truth. My badge and go home. The only person I'd handled properly was Asif.

And there my weakness lay. Because even if I didn't find out about the baby right now, I knew that – inevitably, eventually – I would want to, at some time in the future. And if that future were an 'our' future – Anne-Marie's and mine, for example – then that ignorance, that non-investigation, would begin to cause serious problems.

It was better as soon as possible to know, or to know that I would never know.

On Sunday evening, after Anne-Marie had gone home to get ready for the coming week, I thought over what I had discovered so far about Lily and her death.

It was clear that Alun and Dorothy knew much more than they had said. I would have to put pressure on them.

One way was obvious: threaten to go to the press with the

story of Alun's affair with Lily. They'd know that would do their Sunday-supplement status no good.

But then I thought of a more direct and a more infuriating way to go about it.

I got on the phone, first to the Barbican box office and then to a load of other booking agencies: I would be attending every evening performance of *Macbeth* for the next fortnight. The production wasn't exactly a sell-out, so I was able to choose where I wanted to sit almost every evening. I didn't go for one seat or area – sometimes I was up in the gods, sometimes the front row. I booked under several variations of my name, misspelling it a couple of times.

This would be fun.

41

Monday.

Vicky arrived on my doorstep just before lunch. She wasn't in any mood for chit-chat.

'Conrad, I really must insist that you stop pursuing your own investigations. We've just had a particularly distressing visit from Alun Grey. He says you went to see him at the theatre and told him Lily was pregnant – by him.'

'Oh, did I?'

'He demanded to know if he was the father.'

'I hope you didn't tell him.'

'Of course not.'

'Well, it's nice to see you're playing fair by both the candidates. Or should that be *all* the candidates? I think there might be others.'

'My main point is quite simple: if you continue to try on your own to find out who wanted Lily dead, you will severely hamper the police's own investigation. And even if you don't hamper it completely, you may reduce the possibility of a satisfactory conclusion once the case comes to trial.'

'Do you think I want this person – whoever they are – to go safely to prison, where I can't get at them? The hitman himself is sitting in some comfy cell –'

'I can assure you, his cell is far from comfy.'

'You're not trying hard enough. I can do better than you. And I will.'

'Conrad, we can stop you, quite easily. I'm only asking nicely because —'

'That's your job. Fobbing people like me off with excuses for delay. Well, if you threaten me with restraining orders and stuff like that, I'll go straight to the papers with the story of Brandy's baby. Now, I'd like to ask you a very simple question.'

'This discussion is over.'

We were still on the doorstep.

'Why haven't I received the inventory I asked for — the one of items taken from Lily's flat?'

'You haven't?' said Vicky, obviously a little stunned.

'No, I haven't.'

'But I asked them to.'

'And the inventory for my flat, as well.'

'Both of them,' she said. 'Honestly. I put in a request.'

I believed her.

'I'll try and find out what's happened to them,' she said. 'As soon as I get back. I wish they wouldn't keep doing this to me.'

'Who?' I said.

'Everyone,' she said, looking to the side.

I was in danger of starting to feel sympathy for her. To cut this possibility off, I launched into sarcasm: 'Well, thank you for that, Vicky. How is the investigation going? Any progress since the last time we spoke?'

'The investigation is progressing very satisfactorily.'

'You sound like a school report.'

'Just wait. Give us some time. God, we're trying to fucking help you.'

Now it was my turn to pause.

'Fucking help me,' I said. 'I wonder which counselling course they taught you *that* on.'

'After all the things you've said to me . . .'

'I think this is getting personal. Can I have another Victim Support Counsellor, please?'

'No,' she said. 'Conrad, I realize that you're very hurt and angry, and that you're just taking all your hurt and anger out on me.'

'Please don't flatter yourself,' I said. 'I'm finding plenty of other uses for them.'

'I think you should resume your counselling.'

'No *fucking* way – I'm working this through, and not by sitting at home in a wheelchair I don't need any more.'

'I hope that doesn't mean what I think it means.'

'You remind me a lot of Lily, do you know that? How old are you?'

'Conrad, grow up.'

Off down the path and into her car.

42

Monday afternoon.

I made a call to UCH to check that Asif was on shift, then took a taxi down there.

I was wearing my scruffiest clothes, and had bought myself some cigarettes and a lighter. I was getting into the part – I was a seedy tabloid journalist. (For this meeting, of course, the wheelchair was not required.)

Hospital Security, as I'd guessed, was almost non-existent. The closer I got to Pathology, the easier it became. (It's babies that get abducted, not corpses.) When stopped and questioned I merely asked where I could find my friend Asif.

To my surprise Pathology wasn't – as in films and on TV – down in the dark dungeons of the hospital building. In fact, it was on the uppermost floor – about as far, I thought, from the incineration tower as could be. It had natural light which came in through large windows. Seagulls could look in at unspeakable things on gurneys and stainless-steel tables then wheel away, keening. The pathologists weren't at all cadaverous – some were as ruddy as butchers. (Which worried me, obviously.)

Into Pathology, which I didn't really want to see.

I asked for Asif.

They beeped him.

I waited, looking up and down the long corridors.

This hospital had been more than home to me for six months: it had been my mother – had made my heart beat, had kept my lungs pumping. On a less symbolic level, I'd got to know a large number of the staff here. Luckily, I hadn't been recognized on my way up.

A gingery-haired young man in a white coat walked up to us. The receptionist nodded at him, then flicked her head in my direction.

'Are you that journalist?' he asked.

'Who are you?' I said.

'Asif,' he said.

When I didn't move, still looking him in the pasty white face, he said: 'I'm adopted, okay? My mother chose the name.'

'Hi,' I said.

We shook hands, me trying hard not to think of where his hand had just been and what it had just been doing.

The receptionist was still looking at us. The word *journalist* had alerted her.

'Isn't that fairly rare?' I asked, temporarily off track. 'Being adopted by –'

'This way,' said Asif, not wanting to discuss his upbringing.

I followed him down a side-corridor and then into a small white office. He sat behind a desk. There was no chair for me. This wasn't a consulting room. Pathologists don't consult.

Asif didn't seem particularly weird – apart from the fact he had ginger hair but spoke with a trace of his mother's Asian accent. There were half-moons of raw pinkness under both his eyes. His fingernails were even more bitten down than my own. This was a permanently worried man.

'As far as I'm concerned,' he said, 'and also as far as the hospital is concerned, this matter is closed. I don't see you have any business coming here to bother me.'

I brought out the cigarettes.

'Fag?' I said, offering him one.

He hesitated – to give him credit – for at least two seconds.

'Look, Asif,' I said, when we'd both sparked up. 'Let me be perfectly honest with you: this story of yours, it'll run, it's a decent

153

enough story. You know how people have this preconceived notion of what pathologists are like? You're flesh-cutters, you see. Ghouls. You do the stuff we don't want to have to even think about. And you spend so much time with dead bodies that you end up juggling with testicles and playing table football with eyeballs and shit like that. So, people are going to believe whatever I write – and whatever you say won't make a blind bit of difference. The only thing that really livens this story up is the fact that it was a minor –' (I enjoyed calling Lily 'minor') '– celebrity's mobile that you used. Otherwise, we wouldn't be interested – or only from a health service stroke police incompetence angle. Put all of that to one side for a minute. Remembering that I *will* run it if I don't get anything else. And then admit what we both know: that there's a much bigger story here which – for some reason – no-one wants to talk about.'

He looked at me as he took another drag.

'When she died, Lilian Irish was several weeks pregnant. I guess you were at the autopsy, or you wouldn't have phoned your mum to let her know you'd be late home. I want you to tell me about it. I want you to get me all the information you have about it.'

'No,' he said.

'Hear me out,' I said.

He shifted in his chair.

'If you help me, I won't print the mobile-phone story – and I'll make sure this doesn't get traced back to you.'

Like fuck I will. I was even telling the tabloid lies.

'You can't promise me that. It'll be so flaming obvious to anyone –'

'The truth is, I'm not especially interested in dead babies. What I *am* interested in is the fact that the father may have been another minor celebrity. What I really want is proof that they were having an affair.'

154

'You know,' Asif said, stubbing out his fag 'your job really is a fuck of a lot more disgusting than mine.'

'Now,' I said, 'I know you did DNA tests on the baby –'

'It was an embryo,' he said. 'Not a baby and not a foetus.'

'Meaning what?'

'Meaning it was less than ten weeks old.'

'You could tell that?'

'Anyone trained could tell that.'

'How?'

'All its organs and everything were in place. It was getting ready to do some serious growing.'

'About ten weeks, you reckon.'

'Nine or ten.'

Casually – as casually as I could, I said: 'Boy or girl?'

'I thought you said you weren't interested in that?'

'It's just the question you ask, isn't it? Like when they're born.'

'I should go,' he said, beginning to stand up.

'My guess is – you did the DNA test here, but the police took it away to look at the results. So, although I'm asking as if you *know*, actually you don't. And even if someone here *does* know, I'm wasting my time with you because you're not senior enough. They let you do a bit of cutting, but not any of that serious analytic business.'

'You couldn't understand the information even if I told you. A DNA fingerprint isn't much use to anyone except the police. And it's not like I memorize them for fun. It would be like memorizing every number-plate in that car-park down there.'

He was on his feet.

'So, I'm assuming that the police were fairly surprised to hear that she was pregnant – and that they ordered testing almost immediately.'

'Assume away, it won't do you any good.'

'Oh, it already has. You don't think I really expected you to

155

just toddle off and photocopy some confidential files? You've been more than helpful.'

He became confused.

'What?'

'Thank you very much,' I said. 'I think I can find my way out.'

'You've got nothing you can print,' he said.

'I'll just go and talk to my friends in the police. The ones that tipped me off about the mobile phone. Hopefully, they'll be able to give me what I need.'

I opened the door and walked out into the corridor. He dodged out behind me.

'But I won't be involved.'

'What would be the point in that?' I said. 'No-one's interested in you. They want to know about Brandy's Baby – or Embryo. God, I don't think we could print that. It might have to be Baby, and offend the purists.'

I concentrated on mundane things. The long corridor. The antiseptic smell. The red numbers above the stainless-steel doors of the lift. Chatting. Chatting easily. I wasn't going to permit myself to break down. Casually, I asked: 'Is it easy to tell their sex at that age?'

'If you know where to look.'

'Hah,' I said. 'Some things never change.'

We stood waiting for the lift.

'Come on,' I whispered. 'You can tell me – boy or girl? I'm just curious.'

I held the fags out to him.

Asif had a shifty look round, then said: 'Put it this way – I didn't fancy her much.'

Bullet #4

*The fourth bullet skids across the skin of my chest and hits me in the upper
left arm, the biceps brachii. The impact feels a little like the prod of a
particularly bullying schoolteacher. Nothing more. The bullet first makes
contact with me right in the middle of my sternum. It passes, half-in half-out,
down and across, making some little contact with the sternocostal pectoralis.
As it is heading roughly in the same direction as the muscle fibres, it does
less damage than it might otherwise. A bright white scar will be left across
my sternum. Passing through my arm, the bullet misses the median nerve by
about five millimetres and the humerus bone by about two millimetres.*

Later, I couldn't believe it had happened this way. The thing was a
phoney Hollywood injury. The kind of winging flesh-wound that allows the
hero to strap on an improvised tourniquet and go on fighting, bloodied but
unbowed. This was the maximum amount of damage that a movie star could
be seen to sustain. This, maybe, and a scar on whichever cheek emphasized
their best side.

Even as the shooting was taking place I was aware that it was something
for which I had been thoroughly prepared. I liked this kind of thing — this
was the video I'd rent, if Lily didn't insist on something girlie. And if
someone needed to get shot to get the plot going, then I wasn't going to
complain. I was deep into the by proxy guilt of genre already. By now all of
us have seen so many on-screen gun-killings that we judge whatever we see
against a very rigid pre-existent canon.

There are the stills: the apple spewing itself out around a brass bullet,
Capa's hand-grenade thrower during the Spanish civil war, Capone's oil-slick
sidewalk aftermaths. There are the black and white classics: going over the
top and performing Chaplinesque pratfalls at Passchendaele and the Somme.

There is the documentary: President John F. Kennedy succumbing to the magic of a bullet, that screw-faced Vietcong POW getting it side-on in the head, the US Congressman eating his gun at a press conference. There is the fictional: Straw Dogs, Bonnie and Clyde, The Godfather, Reservoir Dogs.

'Oh, that wasn't a very good one,' I thought, after the first bullet went into Lily. 'That wasn't at all realistic.'

In the end, this wound didn't really inconvenience me. By the time I came round out of my coma, it had mostly healed.

Sometimes, when the weather is about to change, it aches.

43

I got into the lift, forgetting even to press the button to another floor. I was on the top floor so there was no way but down. Someone called the lift. The doors closed. They opened again on the second floor. 'I'm going up,' said the nurse. I didn't reply. We went back up to the fifth floor. The nurse got out. Someone called the lift down to the basement. They got out on the first floor. Then someone on the third floor called it, and got out on the ground floor. I followed them – seeing the exit door, daylight, parked cars: a single taxi, waiting.

'Mortlake,' I told the cab-driver.

I was the never-to-be father of a never-to-be daughter. Lily had landed another blow upon me. It made me wonder whether Lily had known the baby's sex – almost certainly not.

'Are you alright, mate?' the cab-driver asked.

'Mortlake,' I said.

How many times would I have to feel this grief? And not the same grief every time – it seemed to come back renewed, empowered, having changed shape. I had mourned Lily, then a possible child, then a definite daughter – and I had found, on each occasion, that none of them were truly mine to mourn. I was a long long way from being the right person. I was no longer anything like the person I had been when Lily died. With each decrease in my ignorance came an increase in my confusion. This last expansion, to be honest, left me more shocked than shattered. I wanted this – whatever it was – to stop. I wanted to be at the very end of it.

Circumstances, cruel as they were, forced me to consider whether my reaction would have been different had the embryo been male. Terrible to admit, but its being female meant that I minded slightly less. What had been lost was, I felt, being of the opposite sex, just a little less intimately to do with myself.

However, the thing that had died inside Lily was not only a possible human being but also my own version of what my life would have been. That version had been ailing and dying ever since Lily kicked me out.

The version went like this: We would carry on living together. We might even have had children. We talked about children. I'd wanted them. She'd always put them off, on the grounds that she couldn't afford to take time out at such a crucial point in her career. (For Lily, every point in her career was crucial.)

And now I knew that she had definitely been prepared to sacrifice another human life – even if only a possible human female life – for that career.

The taxi dropped me off. The driver gave me his card.

'Any time, mate,' he said. 'I live local.'

I remembered that I had something I had to do: I had to be at the Barbican theatre that evening by seven o'clock.

I asked the taxi-driver if he could pick me up around six.

'Sure.'

'I'll have a wheelchair.'

'No problem.'

44

The first night, Monday, I'd booked a seat right in the middle of the front row. Alun and Dorothy must notice me, they must come to associate me with certain noises, they must start to get really pissed off.

For this production to have its full intended effect, it was necessary that the audience be cowed into total silence during certain key scenes. The actors had to feel they could create at will these precious pin-drop moments. Soliloquies . . . were . . . the most obvious . . . place. But there were other crucial moments of quiet: Banquo's ghost, Birnam Wood. Having once already endured the performance, I knew where these significant silences were most required. My plan was simple: sit there and insert a loud, tension-destroying cough into every single one of Alun and Dorothy's precious pin-drop moments.

This being the RSC, there was plenty of competition between actors to see who could produce the greatest number of silences. Which of them – we were implicitly asked to judge – really had their foot on the accelerator? And who the brake? Was it Alun or Dorothy, Macbeth or Lady Macbeth?

This first night of my plan, I improvised. Whenever a silence seemed to be looming, I put in a preparatory hack and then tried to pitch a good throat-rasper in more accurately.

At the same time I made a mental note where the hack *should go*, were it to be perfectly placed.

Part of the plan required my cough to be particularly unmistakable: I therefore put on my Scottish spinster hack – half-hiccup, half-apology-in-advance.

It was hard to tell how soon Alun and Dorothy noticed, but by the end I was certain they knew and were disconcerted.

As I don't wish to have to make too many more verbal visits to the Barbican, I will collect them all together.

Here is my Cough Diary.

Tuesday A good solid performance. Alun, I notice, is developing something of a facial tic. No doubt this is part characterization, but I have hopes that it is equal part persecution mania. I've also invented an important little marker: as the lights go down and the cast waits in the wings for the witches to do their business, I give a signature cough – just to make sure Alun and Dorothy know I'm in for the night.

Wednesday Lost it a little today. They are trying to break up the rhythms of the production, and shorten the silences. As a result, the play has (through my indirect intervention) improved. I limited myself to unmissably sharp surgical strikes. I also began coughing on top of crucial words. As I'm no longer scared of the huge acoustic of the place, my volume is becoming quite impressive.

Thursday Since yesterday a notice has appeared asking patrons to please refrain from making any unnecessary noise during the performance. An usherette had obviously been detailed to watch over me, to see how the man in the wheelchair behaved. I stayed silent throughout the whole of the first half. You could see Alun relaxing, getting into the flow. After the interval, the usherette had gone – and I launched in without mercy.

(I have to say, this hasn't been easy on me – the production is driving me mad. By now there's not a single self-satisfied detail I miss nor a piece of smug improvisation that eludes me. It took real strength of character to force myself down to the theatre this evening. I'm glad I did, though. It was one of my best performances.)

Alun and Dorothy are reacting quite differently. Alun, his head hanging, sullen unscripted silences punctuating his entire interpretation, has almost admitted defeat; Dorothy, on the other hand, merely becomes more and more hysterical.

The rest of the cast has obviously been informed of my hate campaign.

Friday For reasons that will become clear, I was forced to miss Friday. But this was all part of my plan: that Alun and Dorothy's performances should be disrupted – if not ruined, for them, in terms of satisfaction – even if I *weren't* there to do the destroying. Approaching every significant pause, there would be fear in their minds as to whether *this* was the one that was about to be shattered.

Saturday Before the performance, the manager had a quiet word. He'd obviously been told to 'stop the man in the wheelchair'. Luckily, there were another three men in wheelchairs – and he couldn't stop all of us. Tomorrow, I guess, he will check tickets booked under my name – and see I've been six days straight (plus one). Therefore I will phone up to cancel my remaining tickets and – surprise surprise – go on my feet and buy them at the door or queue for returns and pay cash. That'll confuse them.

Sunday Alun actually stopped dead, turned and peered out into the auditorium this evening. I was limited in my attacks, as someone turned round and told me to shhh after only my third sally. Life without the victimology of the wheelchair-bound (whom no-one dare shhh) is quite a different, difficult thing. I rationed myself to six coughs (three each for Alun and Dorothy), but apologized loudly after every one.

When the performance was over, I sent a note round to Alun

and Dorothy's dressing room along with a large bunch of white lilies. The note read: 'I can go on doing this for ever. I wonder if you can?' My phone number followed.

45

Tuesday.

The printout of Lily's phone bill arrived in the first post.

The most important calls, obviously, were those she'd made to Alun. Using my fluorescent marker-pens, I traced back all her calls to him. To my distress, I found that they occurred fairly constantly from around the end of *The Ghost Sonata* until almost the day she died.

In fact, just before that tour was the exact moment that Lily had decided to get a mobile phone. It looked as if her mobile, like so many, had been a means of conducting an affair. Or more than one.

Alun, it seemed, had been lying about the length and seriousness of his involvement with Lily. And also about his reason for becoming involved – that Lily had told him I was on my way out.

I wondered if Dorothy had been lying knowingly as well – or was she merely repeating the lie that Alun had told her, and the police. But the police, I remembered, had the printout as well. In which case, it was far more likely that the lie was to me alone – for the police would have seen through it in a moment. So, either Dorothy was protecting her husband by maintaining a lie – a lie that would be exposed as soon as we went to court – or Alun had managed to get the police to cover up for his affair. Neither explanation seemed any more or less likely than the other. Maybe they just didn't want to tell me the truth. Maybe they were just playing for more time.

And then I noticed something else: many of Lily's calls to Alun were in the evening. The reason for this seemed simple – Dorothy must have been safely out of the house.

A call to her agent, pretending to be a casting director for a film, gave me a rough c.v. of her past year's performances. A couple more calls to the RSC and other theatres firmed up the dates.

Then I had a thought – shouldn't I check when Alun had been working as well: strengthen my case by confirming that the evening phonecalls only came when Dorothy was off working and he was free to take them at home?

So, I repeated the casting charade with Alun's agent, then with the film companies he'd worked with.

The result was unexpected: on almost every occasion that Lily had called Alun and Dorothy's number in the evening, *neither* of them had been around.

For three weeks, during which there were five phonecalls, Alun had actually been off in North America and Asia touring a production of *King Lear*. At the same time Dorothy had been in Stratford as a miscast Mistress Quickly.

The calls, lasting ten or twenty minutes or more, had been made to Alun and Dorothy's house but not to them. Lily had been calling someone else, someone at their house.

There was only one person I could think of who it might have been: their fifteen-year-old son, Laurence.

46

When I came back from the Barbican on Tuesday evening, I found that someone had up-ended my dustbin on to the porch.

Stepping over the mess, I opened the front door. There was an envelope. It was charred around the edges and had singed some of the mat. Inside, I could see, without even opening it, was shit.

I tidied up, wondering who would want to do such a thing.

It was only after I'd cleared up the dustbin mess that I checked my answerphone. There was the usual message from my mother. There was a message from Anne-Marie. And then there was a message from the rough voice. It was very simple, it went: 'We know where you live.'

Immediately, I started to dial Vicky's number. But then I realized I would have to tell her that I'd been pursuing my own investigation via Lily's mobile-phone bill. I would have to confess to dialling up all those numbers.

I put the phone down.

How had they found out where I lived? And who were *they* anyway? Why did they want to frighten me? And why had Lily been making calls to them the day she died?

No serious damage had been done. I guessed it was quite easy to find out where someone lived from their phone number. Anyone could discover the area by dialling directory inquiries.

After I'd had time to sit down with a drink, I began to reason myself out of my fears. It was – as the phrase always goes – probably just kids fooling around. 'We know where you live' was too much of a cliché to have actually come from someone wanting to scare me. But the voice itself had something unmistakably real about it. It got to me, and part of how it did this was by sounding so confident in the knowledge that it *would* get to me. The rough voice wasn't merely terrifying, it was professionally terrifying. Terror (in the voice, in other people) was something its owner could turn on or off at will. Unfortunately, try as I might, I couldn't do the same. My terror stayed with me all night.

When I called Anne-Marie, though, I didn't mention it.

47

Wednesday. Nothing much to do.

I went to the local library and looked up a few articles on Alun and Dorothy.

Anne-Marie came round in the afternoon. She wanted to talk. From her handbag, she brought out a large chunk of dope. After lightering, crumbling, tobaccoing and rolling it, she started to smoke it. Immediately, her shoulders relaxed and her eyes went moist.

'I hate my job.'

'Then quit.'

'Oh, Conrad, I can't. The models need me.'

'I'm sure they'd survive.'

'Most of them are far worse than Lily ever was.'

'Wow,' I said, finding it difficult to imagine.

'Oh yeah. They have everything: bulimia, drugs, shitty boy-friends.'

For a moment I thought of asking Anne-Marie if Lily hadn't had everything, too. (Including the shitty boyfriends.) But she was already off on to another topic.

'What are you going to do? Go back to ... whatever it was. I never really understood it. Television.'

'No,' I said. 'Definitely not. I think I'll probably dig out an old idea I had for a screenplay. See if I might not be able to make a go of it. I don't have to work for a year or two, if I live off what Lily left me. And I can always sell her flat.'

'She left you her flat?'

'It was in the last will she made before she died.'

'Wow. How do you feel about that?'

'About as guilty as you'd expect.'

Anne-Marie looked at me as if to say sorry-for-asking.

'It's a nice flat,' she said. 'I always liked it.'

'I've been back a couple of times. It wasn't easy.'

'I'd like to see it again.'

'One day.'

I asked if I could have some of her dope.

'Sure,' she said. 'Keep it all.'

I had an idea it might come in handy.

'Tell me about your film.'

I made something up.

Then I told her I had to go out, and she left.

48

It was on my Wednesday-evening visit to the Barbican that I first began to suspect I was being followed. If I hadn't received the shitty parcel and heard the rough voice, I probably wouldn't have been looking out quite so alertly.

When my regular taxi-driver arrived, I carried my wheelchair out and put it into the back of his cab – looking up and down the road. Just as I was slamming the door behind me as I got in, I heard a large car-engine start up. I glanced back round just in time to see a Ford Mondeo pull out about twenty yards away.

When I checked a couple of minutes later, it was still there – one car behind us.

When that car turned off, I got a clearer view of the Mondeo. I couldn't see much of the two men inside it, except that one of them was black and the other seemed to have very white hair. He didn't look all that old, though. As to the car, there was something suspiciously null about it – no individual personality had been allowed to imprint itself. Although the number-plate revealed it to be a couple of years old, it still looked exactly as it would have done in the catalogue. Everything about the Mondeo – when put together with the fact that it was following me – screamed unmarked police car. But if these were police, following and watching me, then why hadn't they done anything about my shit-parcel visitors last night?

One explanation was that they'd only just started following me. Another, that they'd decided it would be a laugh (or to their advantage) for me to have the shit scared out of me. Perhaps they'd done it (the shit) themselves.

Of course, I wanted to see how my followers would cope once we got to the theatre. If they were really prepared, they would have tickets already – and that would make it even likelier they were the police.

The taxi drew up outside the front of the Barbican.

I didn't get out immediately, pretending to be fumbling for my change whilst actually looking out for the Ford Mondeo.

Disappointingly, it sped past and on round a corner.

I waited a few seconds more, arranging with the driver to be picked up afterwards, but the Mondeo didn't return.

After the performance I spotted the Mondeo again as we were crossing the river. It followed us all the way to Mortlake, although hanging further back than previously – probably because it wasn't hard to guess where we were going, and if they lost us they could easily catch up. Just to test this, I asked the taxi-driver to take me to a service station, so I could buy some cigarettes.

When we pulled up into the service-station forecourt, the Mondeo carried on past and parked, facing out, in a side-road.

'Thanks,' I said as I got back in, softpack in my hand.

'It's no smoking in the back there,' said the taxi-driver as we drove off.

'Home, James,' I said, stowing the cigarettes.

'James is actually my name,' said the driver, laughing.

'God, you must get sick of that joke.'

'Nah, course not.'

We laughed.

'I won't tell it again.'

'No problem.'

James drove me home.

'Same time tomorrow?' I said.

'Sure,' James replied.

The Mondeo returned to its parking space just as I was closing the front door behind me.

I felt more exposed than I had since childhood. When I was a boy, I was in a permanent state of battle-readiness. I knew that Germans could be waiting round the next corner or Japanese hiding in the next shadow. I armed myself with pieces of wood nailed together to resemble the guns of Polish partisans. I carried a bowie knife strapped to my snake-belt. I studied survivalist manuals. But I had been preparing for the wrong war. The Germans never wanted to invade Milton Keynes – not in my lifetime, anyway. And this obscurely disappointed me. I wanted to die firing at the enemy's incoming, arrogant, marching troops as they turned the bend down Amplewick Close. I wanted to splatter their blood on the Ford Cortinas and watch them dive for cover behind the birdbaths.

Scared, I wanted to go to the police and ask for their protection. And not just this following-me-around-in-unmarked-cars business. But it seemed to me that there was no way I could do that – not without giving up on everything: the investigation, my revenge. Either I was out on my own, taking whatever risks were necessary, or I was made safe, unable to do anything but wait. Now that I'd come so far, I didn't want to just give up. Part of me – quite a lot, actually – was enjoying the various new freedoms that being outside the law allowed me. For once, I could do what I wanted: be offensive, be dangerous. If this meant that I was myself in danger, then I would for the moment have to live with that. In one way I wasn't afraid of anything specific they could do to me – the three bullets had taken away my fear of physical harm. Anything else would either be less than that, in which case I could handle it, or more than that, in which case I wouldn't be around to have to handle it.

One practical thought occurred. Maybe I should start making some serious attempts to get hold of a gun.

I didn't sleep very well.

49

Thursday.

Yes, it was gun time.

From what I'd heard, it wasn't that difficult to get hold of a gun. All you needed to do was go to the right pub in South-east London and get talking to the right bloke. But I knew that I'd never been very good at getting talking to the right bloke. (Once, I'd come away from Brixton having completely failed to score some dope.) And I didn't want to waste too much time sitting in the wrong pub. What I needed was someone who could point me in the right direction – tell me the name of the pub and the name of the bloke.

I wasn't sure where to start, until I remembered something from the articles on Alun and Dorothy I'd looked up in the local library. Sub Overdale, the director of their production of *Macbeth*, had insisted on a great deal of pre-rehearsal research. Alun and Dorothy had gone on prison visits to meet real murderers. One of the articles also hinted that they'd spent time around some more glamorous, less caged criminals.

All of this had been set up with the assistance of the stand-up comedian Tony Smart.

As you probably know, Tony Smart is most famous for having done three years for armed robbery – and then for turning his life around, starting with a well-received appearance headlining the Her Majesty's Prison Wandsworth Xmas Party. After this success, he was allowed to travel to other prisons to do other gigs. By the time of his early release, he'd already been taken on by an agent. Within two years, he'd headlined at comedy venues all over London and had supported a couple of more famous comedians on their national tours. By the time I became interested in him, his first video, *Criminally Funny*, was featuring heavily on the shelves of WH Smith. And he was all over the telly.

A lot of Tony Smart's material relied upon an implicit threat to the audience. He'd never had much trouble with hecklers. He dressed like a nouveau spiv – flash bespoke tailoring, alligator shoes, gold chains. This, the less imaginative critics said, was 'post-Tarantino stand-up'. In a shoulder holster, he carried a replica of the gun he'd used during his armed robberies – resprayed in ironic leopardskin. In a way, when he was onstage, he was actually playing an ironic replica version of himself. He was safe. He was disarmingly disarmed. The money he'd once been unable to get enough of directly (from terrified cashiers), he now picked up in wads (from satisfied punters) through the box office. Which didn't mean he no longer got in trouble with the law – he'd been done twice in recent years: once for drunk-driving after a friend's wedding and once for assault at a post-gig party. Both incidents had upped his profile and provided him with some new material (the impending Back Behind Bars tour).

At the moment he was starring in TV adverts for a new brand of toilet cleaner – shaped like a powerful under-rim-shooting gun – with the tag-line: 'Protect your home from scum like me.' Various Watchdogs were aroused, which meant more publicity for both him and the product. Toilet-ducks had never been dangerous to anything but all-known-germs before. There were even some questions asked as to whether Mr Smart, as an ex-criminal, should be allowed to profit either directly or indirectly from his crimes. Even *he* wouldn't deny that much of his success (and all of his material) was reliant upon the idea that he was a hard man who'd once been even harder. The prospect of a challenge in the courts was something that had him spending a lot more time with lawyers than ever before.

He had it all, and he didn't want to lose it – the house in Islington, the E-type Jag, the ex-air-hostess wife; mates in top-ten bands and the England football squad; journalists on his doorstep.

For a boy from a dodgy area of Luton, he'd come a long way – via Brixton, via Wandsworth. And as a good working-class lad done good, he was giving-some-of-it-back: donating sequencers and samplers to a Luton music college, supporting meetings between the victims of crimes and their perpetrators, sponsoring a boxing club.

A recent documentary had shown him – flash suit, E-type – revisiting the tower block in which he'd grown up. There had been a lot of laughter, but you could see his eyes jumping from side to side – wanting to work out where *it* was going to hit him from next: the panic of someone who has left the street, and therefore isn't quite sure what *it* is any more – a new piece of street slang, perhaps, that he doesn't want to appear not to know. But Tony had made it through – the winks went tic-crazy, the pats on the back rained down like clubs, the jokes about lend-us-a-tenner were received with the implication that Tony found them *so* hilariously funny he might just have to work them into his next act. Uncredited, of course. Ha ha.

The really unique position that Tony Smart held, though, was that of the only 'real' (although admittedly minor) criminal that anyone famous in London knew – apart from their pimps and coke dealers. Tony was the one who sparkled with the glamour of violence done and violence understood. The fact that he said he'd given up – and as a now-recognizable personality he'd probably had to – didn't affect the straights at parties and on chat shows who wanted to know *what it felt like* to point a gun at someone's head.

It was most likely because of this side of his reputation, the reputation of a man who knew about crime from a street level, that Sub Overdale – Alun and Dorothy's socially militant director

– had contacted Tony Smart. There was also a snazzy PR angle: RSC luvvies sit at feet of gangland gag-meister.

Going the most direct route, I called Sub Overdale at the Barbican – in the hope I'd catch him in his office.

Sub was well known for attending every single night of his shows, and giving all the cast members notes the following day – down to the most insignificant extra. In the business he was called a 'challenging' director to work with, as in 'a total fucking nightmare'.

Luckily, I got him.

Once through, I explained that I was a great admirer of him and his methodology (I used that word) – and that, as a struggling young director (by now he wanted me off the phone as fast as he could) about to direct a student production (off!) of *Crime and Punishment* (off! off!) in Portsmouth (off! off! off!) I wanted to consult Tony Smart.

'Oh,' said Sub. 'I can't give you his home number. He's very touchy about that.'

'How about his agent then?' I decided to cut my losses and try to save myself another trip to the library.

'But I've got his mobile.'

He gave me it.

I thanked him again and again, doing my best to appear desperate to want to continue speaking to my guru – until he put the phone down on my gushing gratitude.

Part of me wanted to try the same story on Tony himself. But another part realized that I might do better with something a lot closer to the truth.

''Lo,' he said.

'Hello. Tony Smart? You-don't-know-me-but-I-got-your-number-off-Sub-Overdale. My name is Conrad Redman. You may remember – I was shot, along with Brandy, that is Lilian Irish, in the Le Corbusier restaurant on Fr–'

'Good restaurant that.'

'I'm now writing a book about the experience, and the police aren't being very helpful. I need to know about guns and hits and things like that.'

He was on-track by now.

'Gotcha.'

'I was hoping you could put me in touch with a few people.'

'You was goin' out with her, right? From the ads on the telly – *her*.'

'Yes, I was.'

'I'm doing a surprise appearance at the Comedy Store tomorrow evening, nine. Try out some new material, y'know. Speak to me afterwards.'

I would have to miss that evening's *Macbeth*, but I didn't care too much about that: it would just keep Alun and Dorothy on their toes. They might relax a little after the interval, but never completely. And, if I were lucky, there might even be a stand-in cougher at Friday evening's performance – who, of course, they'd take to be me.

It also meant I would be able to fit in something else that I'd been meaning to do – pay a visit to Alun and Dorothy's home whilst they were both definitely away. If I was lucky, their son Laurence would be in. I needed to talk to him.

50

Friday.

At six o'clock James's taxi drew up in Belsize Park.

We had passed through street after street of tall pale buildings divided up into six or eight flats. But Alun and Dorothy's, when we came to it, was in a more modern 1930s block.

The doorbell had both Grey and Pale written on it. I held it down for a couple of seconds – Laurence was bound to have something on too loud. He was fifteen, his parents were out.

'Yes?' he said.

'I'm a friend of Lily's.'

'Yes? And?'

'Her boyfriend. The one who was shot.'

'What do you want?'

He wasn't being as hospitable as I'd hoped. But I was prepared.

'I'd like to talk to you about her . . . and incidentally I've got some really good dope on me.'

After a comedy-pause that Tony would've been proud of, the buzzer went.

Alun and Dorothy's apartment was the sort of place that featured regularly in interior-decoration magazines. They had attempted to mix the very modern with the antique by making the antique showy and the very modern minimalist. (A very modern thing to try and do.) Thus Bridget Riley would hang happily (or so the theory went) above Louis Quatorze. The apartment, on the top floor, had more than its fair share of light and space – both of which seemed Scandinavian rather than

English. Stripped-pine floors and whitewashed walls – very Lily. A large Whistler-grey entrance hall, decked with yellow roses, led out into the main living area – off which bedrooms, bathrooms and storage space occurred. Square petals round an oblong flower. At one end was an open-plan kitchen – Dorothy 'loved to entertain'. (It had been afforded by Alun's first, belated trip to Hollywood (1974), to play the villain in a schlock-horror movie. His facial hair – handlebar moustache and muttonchop sideburns – was the most terrifying thing in the entire film.) All of which décor was ruined by some overelaborate curtains – draped, tied, ruffled, pummelled – which simply screamed 'menopause'. Someone in the apartment, you could tell, was straining away from received upper-middle taste and yearning towards a kind of mollifying Middle English Country comfort. Dorothy was showing signs of wanting to become a grand Tory lady, with huge amber rings and the hairstyle of a 1950s Bayreuth Brünnhilde. She was turning her environment into one vast sea-anemone-type labia-fest – frills and pink prettiness. How far was Dorothy from the Pekingese on one cushion and the soft-centred chocolates on another, I wondered.

Laurence's room, when I entered it, was painted black – an obvious rebellion against the rest of the apartment's levity. There was a large ultraviolet lamp, stack speakers in all four corners, and Day-Glo stars and UFOs stuck to the black ceiling. On the wall was a single black-framed poster, a black and white photograph:

KURT COBAIN
1967–1994

The dead singer, guitarist and lyricist of the second group to call themselves Nirvana. Below the poster was a black Fender Telecaster guitar.

The carpet was black, the bedsheets, the furniture – everything in the room, it seemed, apart from Laurence's pasty adolescent face.

Laurence was skinny, slouching, sullen and very sexy. He looked as if he'd stumbled out of a heroin-chic fashion shoot. His skin was bad, but he had that fuck-you-I'm-gorgeous attitude. His fingernails were painted sludge-green – perhaps he'd got bored with black. There were the inevitable body-modifications – but more restrained than one might have expected: a black-etched tattoo on his shoulder and a single spike coming through the middle of his lower lip. This made me feel like I was talking to a rhinoceros or a spiky tropical fish – it did enough to confirm what it was meant to confirm: that I was talking to a member of another, younger, wilder generation.

In Laurence's room, I was an old person – even though I knew every one of the aesthetic moves it was trying to pull on me.

In the corner facing the black-covered futon was the multimedia centre: TV, stereo, PC, CD-rom, Sega and Nintendo. It looked as though Laurence was a serious nerd.

I decided it was worth wasting some time proving that even though I was a member of an older generation, I could still waste time with the kids.

'*Tekken II*,' I said. 'One joint a game.'

Laurence nodded and loaded it up. He was pretty cocky – little did he know.

I thrashed him – I dragon-kicked him, I leg-swept him, I headbutted him, I kakaekomihijiuchied him. I did everything the pre-programmed moves allowed me – that is, everything short of disembowelling him and making him eat his own kidneys.

We lay back on the futon. Almost an hour had passed.

He looked at me, nodding, acknowledging that some respect – at least – was due.

'Tell me about your coma,' he said.

Like all adolescents, he had a fascination with any state of total obliteration.

I told him all about my coma. It seemed a strong point of communication between us – but not as strong as the dope that we fried, crumbled, rolled into Rizlas and passed back and forth.

Anne-Marie's was some pretty devastating shit – I doubted he'd ever been quite so blown away by the rabbit droppings he and his friends were likely to have scored off reassuring Rastas.

More respect was due.

He lay back on the black, bringing up the subject as if he, not me, was the one who wanted to talk about it.

'I liked Lily a lot. She used to call me, when she knew my parents were out. We used to talk.'

Well, there was my main question gone.

'What about?'

'Oh, everything, you know – shit and stuff. What was happening with me and with her. Life-stuff.'

'You're at college, right?'

'Now, yeah. But back then I was still at school.'

On the floor I noticed a number of copies of the *Stage*; they were open on the Artists Wanted columns. Some of the ads were ringed in black marker.

'Interested in what?' I asked. 'Acting?'

'Yeah,' he said. 'I'm going to college next year. I have an agent already. And I'm in Spotlight. I've done a couple of things, nothing great. It's a laugh. I like films most of all. Action movies. But there's never any decent parts for anyone my age. I'd like to play a villain: a real psycho. That'd be cool.'

'Did you talk about me when you were with Lily?'

I was doing my best not to inhale without looking like I wasn't inhaling.

'Oh' – he had the stoner smile on by now – 'I know *all* about you.' He giggled. 'She used to tell me everything. Ev-ry-thing.'

'For example.'

'Sex,' he said, with more giggling.

'Ah,' I said.

182

'Or not sex,' he said. 'Sometimes.'

I smiled. I managed a smile.

'How did you meet her?' I asked.

'It was the summer holidays. I went on tour with Strindberg for a few weeks.' He made Strindberg sound like a deathmetal band. 'Everyone else was just so *old* and serious. Not Lily – she was up for anything. Sometimes she went onstage just ripped to the fucking tits. It was really funny to see, up in Scarborough or Somewhere-on-the-Sea. You-know-what-I-mean. But Strindberg was off his head most of the time as well, wasn't he? We used to hang out during the days – trying to find something to do in these fucking awful one-dog towns. If you looked hard enough, there was usually something. You-know-what-I-mean. We'd go fuck up tea dances and bingo sessions. I love bingo. But scoring was a fucking nightmare, whatever you say.' For a moment I thought he meant scoring bingo games. Then I realized he meant drugs. 'They'd have the stuff, they just wouldn't sell it to you. 'Cos you sounded like you came from down South and were middle class.' He rhymed the word with gas. 'They'd sell to Lily, though. You-know-what-I-mean. Everyone would sell fucking anything to Lily. It was mega.'

I-knew-what-he-meant.

'She did a lot of drugs on that tour?'

'All the fucking time.'

'Who do you think shot her?'

Laurence sat up, unsteadily – he was deep in the slow-space of dope, right where I wanted him.

'I dunno.'

'Did your mum and dad tell you she was pregnant when she died?'

He hunched over on the side of the bed.

'Yeah – well, I heard them arguing about it a few days ago. They came back from the show and just the next two hours . . . I wasn't supposed to hear.'

'So you know who might be the father?'

'You.'

'Yes.'

'And Dad . . . That's what they were arguing about, you know. Saying, "You fucked her, didn't you? It's yours!" My mum's a bitch when she gets mad.'

'I told them about it. I went to see them at the theatre.'

'Everyone here's been so fucking arsey ever since.'

'Lily started seeing your dad on that tour, didn't she?'

'I dunno. Maybe.'

'Your dad went to the police after I'd told him. He wanted to find out if they'd done any testing – if they knew for definite he was the father.'

'They didn't tell him anything.'

'Have they taken blood samples off him before?'

'Yes. Months ago. They didn't say why. They're not telling anyone anything.'

I checked my watch. It was time to set off.

'I'm going to see Tony Smart this evening, you know.'

'Oh yeah,' said Laurence. 'He's cool.'

'Here,' I said, chucking Laurence the small clingfilmed chunk of dope.

'Thanks,' he said.

'We should meet up sometime,' I said.

'Yeah,' he said, and lazily we shook.

'I can find my way out,' I said. 'Can I use the phone to call a taxi?'

'Sure. It's in the kitchen. The number's on the board.'

This was good: I wanted as much of a look-round the apartment as I could manage without exciting Laurence's suspicion. But from the wacked-out expression on his face, it was going to be several hours at least before he became excited about anything. I left him in his black bedroom, lying back and sniffing the dope.

51

Back in the central living space, I wasn't sure where to start. Scanning the whole room once again I didn't notice anything I hadn't before. But what was I expecting? Something that would tell me, for definite, that Alun had been the father? A test-tube full of stealable sperm? Or maybe some cross-referenceable DNA printouts?

Out of habit I looked at the titles of their books – a slightly more literate selection than I'd expected from actors. Then I checked their videos, where there were a couple of work-out routines called things like Fat-Burner and Butt-Buster.

This was a public space, though. I needed to see where things were hidden.

Quietly, I looked into a couple of rooms. If Laurence caught me I'd tell him I was searching for the toilet. I found the master bedroom third door I tried. Just as I was sliding my way in, Laurence's music slammed on.

The track was 'Rape Me' by Nirvana, from their album *In Utero*.

Over the top I heard Laurence giggling – then he started to play along not badly on his Telecaster.

More time for me in Alun and Dorothy's bedroom.

It was a large but cosified space – not a pine futon on the floor but a black steel four-poster, not clothes rails but two vast walk-in closets. The tasteless tide of Dorothy's menopause had reached the flowery sheets and the frilly valence. On the wall above the 1930s-style tiled fireplace was Man Ray's photograph of a woman's back with cello-holes cut into her.

The guitar continued, slightly quieter. This was exciting. I wasn't meant to be here.

There were two bedside tables – it wasn't hard to work out whose was whose: Dorothy's was untidily piled with self-help books going back a couple of years, each generation of further knowledge piled on top of the half-read last – a sedimentary accumulation of shysterism: *Mars and Venus in the Bedroom* over-topped *Further along the Road Less Travelled* which rested upon *Toxic Parents* which surmounted *People of the Lie*. At the very bottom of the pile, side by side, twin foundations, bearing all the others were *I'm OK – You're OK* and *My Mother My Self*. Resting beside these was a bowl full of pill-popper packets – I glanced through: HRT, Nurofen, Ibuprofen, seriously bug-eyed sleeping tablets, Morning Primrose Oil, Starflower Oil, Anti-oxidant Complex, Aloe Vera, Vitamin Supplements, Calcium Tablets, Minerals, Magnesium-OK, Confiance, Ginseng. It was surprising that green chemical froth didn't come out of Dorothy's mouth every time she opened it. Alun's bedside table was much more –

Suddenly, the music stopped, and I could hear the phone ringing in the kitchen. Laurence would assume I had made my call and left.

I went to stand behind the bedroom door, trying to peek through the jamb and listen in on his conversation. Luckily for me the phone was a cordless – and the moment Laurence knew who was on the other end, he walked over to the living-room sofa, picked up the remote and started flicking through all the TV channels but with the sound off.

The first words I caught were: 'I *know* you told me. Look, Mummy, I *know* you told me, okay? I *know*. Do you hear? I know.'

He listened to Dorothy. She must be phoning out during one of her times off-stage. It was about seven-fifteen. About now she'd be preparing for . . . I couldn't tell. It was still fairly early on. Perhaps she hadn't even been on stage yet.

'Look, I handled it, you know. Yes, he's gone, now. And it

would have been much more suspicious if I hadn't let him in. And I didn't tell him anything he didn't know already.'

More Dorothy, who from where I was standing was almost audible in a tinny cartoon kind of way.

'No, he *didn't* ask that. I don't think he has any idea . . . Well, I lied. I told him Lily and me were just good friends. Look, I handled it. Stop treating me like a fucking spazz.'

Dorothy.

'What *is* your problem with that?'

Dorothy.

'No, I have a great vocabulary, a stupendous vocabulary, a fantastic, outlandish, enormous, explicit vocabulary . . .' Here he started to giggle. 'Of course I haven't been at your stash . . . He left about half an hour ago. No, he wasn't in a wheelchair! I don't know. He said he was going to see Tony Smart . . . Well, don't go all mental. What's wrong with that? He's a funny guy . . . I think he was just going to catch the act . . . Mum, why are you losing it so badly? He won't come back . . . Look, I handled it . . . Jesus . . . Okay . . . Okay, I won't . . . Have a good one . . . Okay, bye.'

Laurence threw the handset down on the sofa and slouched off back to the bedroom, muttering rather accurate impressions of his mother: 'You let him in, idiot! How could you! How could you let him in! Why did you let him in! Didn't we tell you *not* to let anyone in! He knows about you and Lily! He knows about Tony Smart!'

His door slammed. His stereo started up again. His guitar.

Alun's bedside table was much more organized. There were three books – a mushy old *Concise English Dictionary*, a brand new *Color Atlas of Embryology* and a large textbook called *Genetics*, 3rd edition. Each had pages marked with little slips of paper.

Alun had obviously been telling the truth about not knowing if he was the father – and the books looked new enough to have been bought shortly after I broke the news to him.

It was clear I would have to forget about calling a taxi.

As Laurence's music continued, I tiptoed my way across to the hall. When he'd slouched back into his room, Laurence had left the TV on. It was the Channel 4 news. Jon Snow was sitting there in a lovely silk tie in front of the photo of Lily that they'd always used – the one she really hated, of her as a dementedly grinning Brandy. Jon's head moved from side to side, quite jauntily: he was concentrating on an issue, not a tragedy (for that he tended to remain still) – but then the picture cut to a view outside the hospital.

A man in a lab coat was talking into several microphones. The caption came up: 'Ernest Calcutt, Head Pathologist, UCH'. He finished speaking, surrounded by hospital security men, and then Asif stepped forward, wearing a suit. He read from a folded-up piece of paper – a very short statement. The microphones flicked away from him, picking up the interviewers' shouted questions. Asif was overwhelmed. He said something easy to lip-read: 'I'm sorry.' His eyes had gone misty in the flashbulbs and arc lights. The microphones flicked again, more randomly this time. Asif was about to say something when Calcutt put his arm round him and turned him away. The footage cut off as they walked back to the hospital foyer, pursued by a couple of photographers.

Back to Jon Snow in the studio, some of the jauntiness gone. He turned to the screen on his left, on which was displayed a woman I recognized. When the picture went full-screen with a caption I saw that it was the Health Minister.

I'd been standing there for at least two minutes, completely open to discovery. Slowly, I turned round – only to see Laurence in his bedroom doorway, looking at the TV. In his hand was the end of a long black telephone-connection lead. He was obviously heading to the kitchen to plug it in – I guessed for his modem.

'You didn't see me,' I said. 'I wasn't here.'

'Why didn't you turn the sound up?' he said.

'See you later,' I said.

For a moment he thought about trying to attack me. But then I think he thought *What's the fucking point?* He wasn't going to kill me. At most, he might be able to take me hostage – tie me up and wait till his parents got home, ask them what to do. (Not likely.) His mistake (not seeing me out the door) was already long past. He made a dipping movement with one shoulder, as if about to pick something up off the floor. The lead was still in his hand.

'If it's any consolation,' I said. 'I didn't hear anything I didn't know already.'

'Shit,' he said. 'You *heard*.'

'I wasn't spying,' I said. 'I was . . . snooping.'

'Find anything?' he asked.

'Not a lot,' I said. 'Why? What should I have been looking for?'

'That's the door,' he said, and pointed. 'This time don't miss it, okay?'

I stood there for a moment. He went over to the phone socket and plugged in the connection.

'Why aren't you gone?' he said.

He watched me as I slowly backed out through the hall. Stepping out on to the landing, I pulled the front door shut behind me. The locks clicked.

For a moment I crouched down and listened. I heard his bare feet pad over. The locks rattled as he checked them. Then he padded off again.

52

The cab drew up outside the Comedy Store. I was only fifteen minutes late for the show.

I got myself a beer and had a look round. The Comedy Store, off Leicester Square, was low-ceilinged, black-walled, overheated and cramped. Everything in the room seemed to be sweating.

I got to my seat without being taken for a heckler or an upstager or any other kind of comedy-fodder.

The comic on stage was a nondescript bloke, wearing a collarless cheesecloth shirt, faded blue jeans and desert boots. He looked like about 50 per cent of the male audience (and about 5 per cent of the women) – although he did have considerably less hair than anyone else in the room.

He was slowly dying. Punch-lines thudded out into a soggy semi-silence. It was like watching porridge cook – occasionally, a bubble would blurp to the surface and the steam would hiss semi-silently out. There would be a guffaw over here, a snigger over there – but they would never amount to anything that you'd call actual laughter. The bloke was clinging white-knuckled to the mike stand. The symptoms of imminent death were there for all to behold: pallor, clamminess, dilated pupils, lack of sensitivity to pain.

A drop of sweat ran down the thin bridge of his nose and swung for a moment at the tip. By chance, the drop fell off just as he'd delivered the punch-line to what he obviously felt was his best gag. It involved a housewife and a washer-dryer trying to decide where to go on their first date. The droplet of sweat hit the microphone, giving out a mini-thud of its own. A few of the audience who had been caught up in the drama of it's-going-to-fall-no-it's-not laughed with relief and recognition. The bloke, who hadn't noticed what was going on with his sweat, looked round the room with a delighted smile.

'I've been Henderson McIntyre, thanks for listening.'

There was a forgiving round of applause as Henderson jogged off.

The compère came on – and made observations about wall-paper patterns for a couple of minutes.

'And now a big surprise, the moment you haven't all been waiting for, into the Roman arena of the open mike to preach to the lions and eat the Christians – the ker-rimin'lly funny *Mister* . . . Tony . . . *Smart*!'

The microphone was crunched back on to the stand. The lights went down, leaving only a single spot. Tony, carrying his trademark replica gun, came out to loud but measured applause. He still had to prove himself here. This wasn't *his* audience. Yet.

Tony's act was mostly to do with the comedy of violence. He was getting laughs from stories of hard men shooting their own bollocks off. (Not from me, he wasn't.) The highlight came when he re-enacted an armed robbery in the style of anyone whose name the audience shouted out. This routine went on for about ten minutes as more and more suggested characters were introduced: robber (the Home Secretary), cashier (Godzilla), copper (Ronnie Kray), getaway driver (Stevie Wonder), have-a-go hero (Marcel Marceau), underworld boss (Yoda). The audience were killing themselves. Tony was in the sweet eye of the comedic hurricane, calm surrounded by whirling chaos. There he stood, unable to deliver his next line over the screamingly hysterical reaction to his last.

Finally, Tony bowed, fired a couple of imaginary rounds off into the crowd with his replica gun and was gone.

This time the audience was abandoned in its applause. They wanted him back, but he didn't come.

I went up to the bar. Henderson McIntyre was there, staring into the abyss of a pint. I stood as far away from him as possible. I'd had more than enough of the dead.

As I waited for Tony, I thought about how clear it was why he'd become successful. He was one of those men who quickly rise in their chosen profession (usually the arts) because they so physically intimidate their critics that they get great notices from day one. Tony was known to be mightily 'connected' – and though most critics spend all day sitting on their arses, they are still – as a class – known to value their kneecaps.

Tony surfed in on a minty-crisp wave of freshly applied aftershave. He'd changed his shirt (yellow to orange), but was wearing the same blue suit and alligator loafers that he'd had on on stage.

'Let's go' was all he said, after I'd attracted his attention and he'd shimmied up to me.

There were people definitely hovering. If Tony didn't leave soon he'd be giving in-depth comedy-career advice to a queue of bald men in cheesecloth shirts. He'd already given his advice – I'd read it in a dozen interviews. Tony always said something like, *Give up. You're never going to be good enough. If you've got something else, do it. But if you're a failure even at giving it up, then you might be in with a chance. Just don't come asking Tony Smart for advice.*

As we passed Henderson McIntyre, Tony gave him a big pat on the back.

'Happens to the best of us, mate.'

Henderson wanted to say something but couldn't.

'What doesn't kill you, eh?' said Tony, winking.

Henderson almost managed a smile.

We set off again, fast – and so did Tony's mouth.

'You see, I am motivated solely by hatred and jealousy. Other people, I see how well they are doing and want to do better. D'you understand me? This isn't about bringing joy to the masses;

this is about bringing masses of dosh and wonga and moolah to my bank account for me to spend in any way I see fit. These are the quotes. I hope you're getting them down. This *is* an interview, isn't it? What are you? *Time Out* again?'

'No,' I said.

The flow halted. He looked at me with all the implied violence I'd been expecting, then moved off again.

'Oh, right,' he said.

He didn't bother with the stage door. He was quite happy to be recognized and adulated while moving along at about near-jogging pace. Men, he cruised straight past; women – especially the bigger-breasted ones – caused small stutters in his stride.

Ritual farewells were exchanged with the Comedy Store box office: 'You could hear a fucking pin drop in there,' and 'Fuck off, you tight cunts,' and 'Bring your pyjamas next time, big boy,' and 'I'm never working this shithole again.'

And then we were out into the cool dark crowded street.

'Follow me,' said Tony. 'Can't you keep up or something?'

'Um, actually, I've only been off crutches a couple of days.'

'Oh shit.' Tony halted, remembering more clearly who I was. 'You all right?' Suddenly I'd turned into his infirm grandmother. 'Take your time. Sorry, mate, I'm just so fucking buzzed when I've come off, you know. I mean, did you see that? Did you fucking hear that? All new material that was. Haven't used one word of it before. And I fucking killed. I had the whole fucking room. It wasn't the greatest, mind. You need more for that. You need something . . . transcendental. But they were dead in there, weren't they? Fucking slain.'

He was speeding up again, surfing the gone moment, pulling 360s on the recollection, tubing down the barrel of joy. He was also, I realized, like all stage-people, desiring something more – a positive response, confirmation, praise – from me. If it would add sweep to his self-surf, he wanted to know what I thought, but if it would beach his being-belief, he wanted none of my opinions.

There was no need for me to lie –

'You killed,' I said.

Tony grinned gurningly, and led me across Leicester Square, along an alley beside the Wyndhams Theatre and down some narrow steps into something called the Koha Bar.

'It's Albanian-owned,' he said, as we walked in.

The barman was the kind of handsome that you'd call chiselled – particularly when you caught sight of the scar that had been left on his right temple. He recognized Tony and served him before two other men who had been waiting. Without asking, Tony ordered me a Budvar.

A low table was free in the far corner. We took it – this was how Tony's life went: working-class hero, friend to the Albanian people, obstacles clearing themselves from his path, goodwill springing up like plastic flowers all around.

'My grandmother's half-Albanian,' said Tony. 'The other half could've been fucking anything. She used to live in Portsmouth.'

I nodded, as if that explained everything – which, in retrospect, it did.

Our Budvar bottles tipped together, up towards the white-washed brickwork of the ceiling.

'What do you want?' said Tony, wiping his mouth with an orange handkerchief.

'Questions,' I said. 'Answers.'

'Uh-huh,' he grunted, going into right-man-in-right-pub mode.

Before I got on to my more specific questions, I decided to ask around the subject – see how much of Tony's hardness was real and how much image. What I really wanted to know now was his connection with Alun and Dorothy.

'What do you know about me being shot?'

'Nothing much,' shrug, sip – i.e., *You've got to ask the right questions before I give you the right answers.*

194

'I'll tell you what I think. Please interrupt and correct me if I go wrong. Someone wanted Lily killed – and whoever was with her at the time, as well. Now, if they were an amateur – like I am – they'd have to have found someone to help them. Someone like you –'

'Nah,' he said.

'– like you would have been a few years ago.'

'Guns, yes. Killing people, no.'

'Look, the guy who shot us had a flash bike, flash clothes –'

'And a pretty fucking flash gun.'

'Really,' I said, realizing that I'd have to dumb myself down even further to get what I wanted out of Tony.

'Most guns used in armed robberies are stuff left over from the Second World War, or Farmer Giles' old shotgun, or something your mad uncle Frank's built in his shed. As I understand it, what we're talking about was a Gruber & Litvak – practically brand-new. If you want my opinion, the guy who shot you is a real expert. He's been well paid in the past. He's able to demand exactly the gear he wants. Fantasy stuff. He gets paid vast amounts of cash to do something he's very good at.'

'If he was so good, why did he get caught?' I asked. 'And why am I still alive?'

'Bad luck – or, in your case, good luck. Happens to everyone.'

'Well, he hasn't told the police anything.'

'He wouldn't. He's a professional. He'll do his time, keep shtum, come out and collect a nice little bonus.'

Two men walked down the stairs and into the bar. One of them was very white and one of them was very black. They were wearing identical charcoal suits, identical down to the very folds. Also, identical dark glasses, black shirts, blue ties, black loafers. Both of them were carrying mobile phones in their right hands. I recognized them: these were the undercover policemen who'd followed me in the unmarked Mondeo. Together, they removed their dark glasses. The bar was so dingy that the albino had no need to squint – but his eternal squint lines were there, raw and pinkly etched into his skin, like nappy rash, all around his eyes. I thought of baby chicklets before they get their feathers. Everyone turned to look at them, then turned away so as not to get caught looking again. In my experience, the albinos I'd met had always been fairly irascible – one might say ratty – individuals. This one seemed no exception. His every movement was a tetch or a twitch. The black man was a picture of stillness and calm. The two of them went up to the bar – ordered drinks – came over – sat down at the table next to ours. So strong were their don't-look-at-us vibes that people kept involuntarily turning to look, not at them, but at the vibes. I could feel the curiosity of others reflecting off them and on to us: were we being so obvious as to stare?

'If I wanted to get hold of a Gruber & Litvak,' I said, 'where would I go?'

'Well . . .' said Tony, glancing over towards the albino. There was the merest glint of eye contact.

'Germany,' Tony said, as if that were what he'd originally been going to say. 'They're manufactured in Germany.'

'So, they're very hard to get hold of in London?'

The albino and the black man started talking about football: QPR and Wimbledon, Arsenal and Spurs. Just in case I was wrong about them being policemen, I listened closely to their talk – neither of them had the rough voice.

'Almost impossible,' said Tony. He finished his Budvar.

'Can I get you another?'

'Uh-uh-uh,' Tony was freaking out completely – clammy and stuttering, like a stand-up virgin. He hated the police. 'Okay, then, you know, right . . .'

Once at the bar I did my best not to get served, leaving Tony alone with the two policemen, to see if there'd be any further contact.

There wasn't, at least none that I saw. The police obviously knew that their mere presence — each of them was about as present as anyone I'd ever seen — would be enough to keep Tony in line.

An idea occurred to me — a very naughty one — as I carried the two beers back to the table.

'Cheers,' I said, loud enough for Tony to know the police could hear. 'Thanks for your help. I don't think I've got any more questions. I'll just follow up on everything you've said.'

Tony looked terrified.

'But,' he stammered, 'but I haven't told you anything.'

'No, really. You've given me more than enough — I didn't expect you to be anything like so helpful.'

He looked at me, jacklighted. His explaining would have to come later — elsewhere.

I was sure the idea of talking to the police, of risking his wonderful life, was what had got him panicked. If I'd been him, I would have panicked, too. But then again, if I'd been him, I wouldn't have gone round giving free advice on crime and criminals to anyone who came asking.

The police were still talking about football. Not a word of what we'd said had registered, externally. But if possible they were both even more intensely present than before. They seemed the very embodiment of the law: whole long lines of corridors and holding cells and courtrooms and prison cells — all stretching out into the behind-them distance.

We drank up, in silence, untasting, quickly.

Tony was sulking. He was in the weaker position, probably because he was more clearly aware what his position was. I had outsmarted him. (No pun.) This wasn't something he was used to. As I glowed with beginner's luck, he glowered with expert's pique. Or maybe it was something else: this being just another step up for him, further off street-level, less in touch with the necessary instincts.

Perhaps he'd have to make another visit back to Luton, this

time without a documentary crew behind his shoulder. Perhaps it was a fitting moment to touch base with a few of the homeboys again, try to descend, try not to look like an ignorant cunt who has lost at least as much as he's gained.

'Think I'll be off,' I said, then stood up and held out my hand.

Tony took it and shook. He couldn't leave with me now – he'd have to stay or appear weak.

'Thanks again,' I said.

Just before I got to the bottom of the stairs, I snuck a glance at Tony. He was looking, one-eyed, straight down the neck of his bottled beer, as if he expected to see another eye looking back at him.

I saw the black policemen start to stand up.

When I next looked round, half-way down the stairs into Leicester Square underground station, the black man was following me, speaking into his mobile phone.

My stiff legs meant I was a little slow down the stairs and couldn't risk a move on the escalators. I decided there was no point trying to lose him – plus, he was supposedly there for my protection, anyway.

During the Tube journey, the black man stood opposite me, about ten feet away, beside one of the doors.

He followed me out of Hammersmith station.

It took me ten minutes to get a cab. I almost offered the black man a lift.

Bullet #5

The fifth bullet missed me completely.

53

As the taxi pulled up outside my house I noticed that the front door was glistening strangely, as if it were wet. The Mondeo was already parked in its usual spot, a little further up the road.

After I'd paid off the driver and got out of the cab, I saw what had happened – someone had thrown bright red paint all over the door to my flat.

Walking slowly up to the door, I tried to take in the full falsely bloody image. I wiped the paint off the area around the keyhole with my handkerchief. The paint was very slidy and wet. I glanced across at the Mondeo, wondering.

Closing the door behind me, I checked to see whether any more delights had been posted through the letter-box. There was a single white envelope, long and slim, heavily laid paper. A little of the red paint had seeped under the front door and into the edges of the hall carpet. I took off my shoes to avoid treading it into the rest of the flat. Then I carried the letter through into my kitchen and carefully slit it open with a kitchen knife. It contained a single piece of foolscap, of the same quality as the envelope. The message had been printed out from a laser printer in Times Roman. The words were clear enough:

Leave it alone.

I went to bed strangely excited: I was getting somewhere, annoying someone. I was on to the right 'it' because 'it' was important enough and secret enough for that someone to want me to leave 'it' alone. But there was no chance of that.

Instead of deterring, as they were meant to, these scare tactics served only to encourage me. The closer I was to danger, the nearer I came to the truth. If it were a truth that was important enough to make someone want to kill me, then it was probably the truth that had caused Lily to be killed.

For several hours I lay awake. Outside, I could hear cars driving along roads, jets descending towards Heathrow and cats making whoopee.

When I opened my eyes I could see the curtains glowing lighter and lighter the more I looked at them. (Not morning coming, not that, not yet, just an illusion of the dark.) And when I closed them, my retinas were painted bright blazing blood red.

54

Saturday morning.

Asif was all over the tabloids. Most of them – and I bought them all – carried photographs from the previous night's hasty press conference, the one I'd seen on the TV in Dorothy and Alun's apartment. The majority of the picture editors had chosen shots of him lit harshly, from way down below his knees, so that he appeared haggard and ghoulish. But some brighter spark on the *Mirror* had gone digging, and had managed to excavate a photo from a medical-student revue Asif had taken part in four years previously. Here, he was dressed as a Victorian undertaker – stovepipe hat and long black tails, plastic vampire teeth and wild staring eyes. There was no shortage of puns from the headline and caption writers: Asif was Doctor Death, the Grim Bleeper, a Slab Assistant. The journalists' actual copy served only to finish him off: Asif's job was *a grisly trade*, he was known for making *cutting remarks*, there was *a deathly silence* surrounding the case. This wasn't the man I'd met. This was a media creation, already many-times-spun, a doctored doctor (though he wasn't really even *that*) – a man of whom one could believe any heinousness one liked. They'd used all the demonizing tricks on him. Asif had become, almost, a cartoon.

The *Mirror* also carried a photograph of Asif's mother. She was much as I'd imagined her: small, sweet-looking, dressed in her best sari, trying to close the front door against an advancing bristle of lenses and microphones.

I was sorry to see this happen to them, but I was more worried that Asif would think it was *me* who had tipped everyone off. Of course, my name wouldn't appear as a byline to any of the stories. But then, even whilst I was playing a journalist, I'd been careful not to give Asif even a false name to check.

I thought about calling his mother to commiserate, but I doubted the family were taking any calls. Any denial on my part at this point was likely to be taken as further confirmation of my guilt. Trusting journalists was not something Asif was likely to do again.

As far as I was concerned all this press attention would have one important result: the police would be forced to explain what they had been doing recently and why there seemed to have been so little progress. The press weren't looking for the same thing I was: I wanted the person who hired the hitman – the person who originally wanted Lily dead. All they were after was a quick trial of the hitman – and hopefully more revelations about Brandy. The police's attitude of wait-and-see immediately suggested to the press that there *would* be more to see. That was likely to be the story for tomorrow, though. Saturday's story was hospital incompetence, health-service cuts, greater regulation and phone polls: Should Asif be Sacked?

I had to decide what to do myself. A couple of calls from journalists came through to the phone in my flat. I had no idea how they got the number. When I asked, they wouldn't tell me. After a couple more calls, I got fed up of being coy. I wasn't putting any more pressure on Asif if I could help it. But I *was* going to try and focus more attention on the police. I spoke to about twenty journalists, some from as far away as Australia and Texas.

The average interview went something like:

'Mr Redman, what was your reaction to the news that Asif Prakash had used your girlfriend's mobile phone after she died?'

'I was deeply distressed,' I said, putting the inverted commas round deeply distressed even before they did. Even though it was almost the truth.

'Do you think Asif should be sacked?'

'Certainly not. I'm sure his kind of work is done under a great deal of pressure. It was a mistake – an error of judgement. Asif's paying for it simply by being the focus of all this attention. His life's probably been ruined. Leave him alone.'

'But surely you don't condone this sort of behaviour?'

'It was the wrong thing to do. But I'm sure Asif regrets it at least as much as I do.'

'Do you blame cuts in the health service?'

'Yes.'

'Do you think the Health Minister should resign?'

'Oh, yes. Her position is no longer tenable.'

'What do you think Lily would have thought about Asif using her phone?'

'I don't think she'd have minded very much. But I'm sure she'd have wanted the Health Minister to resign.'

'Do you have anything else you want to say?'

'Yes – I think the investigation of Lily's murder has been incompetently handled, in every aspect, from the moment it began. The police seem to have put it on the back burner. My own insights into the case have been completely ignored. Make no mistake – the man in prison isn't the only guilty person in this case. Someone wanted Lily dead. Someone hired that hitman to kill her. The police should be trying to find that someone a lot harder than they are. Lily may only have been my ex-girlfriend, but I still loved her deeply. I cannot let this matter rest until it has been settled to my own personal satisfaction.'

55

It was the last but one journalist, a woman from the *Mirror*, who started the real trouble:

'Is it true that you went to UCH and met Asif?'

'Excuse me?'

'He tells us that someone very closely fitting your description did.'

'He does . . .'

'He's told us quite a lot.'

'Really?'

I put the phone down and didn't pick up when instantly it rang again.

From that brief conversation I guessed that the *Mirror* had signed some sort of exclusivity deal with Asif and had whisked him (and his mother, too, probably) off somewhere the other papers couldn't get at them – some Caribbean island paradise. In tomorrow's *Sunday Mirror*, Asif would probably be pictured sitting in a beach bar, sipping a pina colada, and quoted as saying, *I blame health-service cuts. Junior doctors are put under so much pressure. Sometimes they crack. I suppose I cracked.*

I wondered whether he'd tell them about Lily's pregnancy, and if he did whether they'd be able to print it – or whether that was currently *sub judice*. For the moment, however, Asif had been satisfied with merely dumping me in the shit.

Within half an hour, I'd had two more calls asking the same questions: Had I met Asif? Why had I met Asif? How had I found out about Asif?

Foolishly, I'd arranged to have a handyman come round and clean the red paint off the door. He had just started working on it when the journalist from the *Mirror* arrived. A photographer had come with her in the same car, and he started taking shots immediately. I could hear his camera whirring on and on – on to the front page of tomorrow's *Mirror*. The handyman was working with the front door half open. After the photographer had got what he needed (not much), with and without the handyman in view, the journalist started asking him questions about what he was doing. Why was there blood-red paint on my door? When had the paint appeared? Was the paint still wet? Was Mr Redman at home?

'Yes, he is,' I said, and pulled the handyman inside.

I locked the front door behind us.

'Into the living room,' I said.

Cocky, he walked through.

'Right, please go home now. I'll pay you for the full job if you don't say another word to that journalist. I'll probably want you to come back and finish the thing once she's gone away. But if you talk to her, I'll use someone else.'

'Okay,' he said. I knew he was lying but there wasn't much else I could do. I gave him the money and let him out the front door again.

The *Mirror* reporter shouted in a question at me. ('Asif might be fired. What do you think of that?') Then she turned her attention to the handyman. Despite having my money in his pocket, he merely beckoned her a few steps down the road before starting to tell her all he knew. As I stood behind the front door listening, I could hear him saying, 'You'll be using the photos with me in 'em, won't you?' And the *Mirror* reporter was reassuring him and giving him a load of flannel about *Yes, it's better to have a photo with someone in than no-one at all so we'll probably end up using the ones with you in unless we can get some of Mr Redman himself.*

The journalist found out what she could. When had I called

about the paint? Had I sounded distressed? Had I given any indication as to who might have done such a thing? (Here the handyman lied outright and said I'd mentioned having 'enemies'!) Who did *he* think had done it? (As if *his* opinion counted for shit.)

After the handyman left, I heard the journalist knocking at my next-door neighbours'. They answered without hesitation – their only decorum so far having been to peer out at proceedings through their net curtains rather than standing blatant on their doorsteps. These people were lower-middle, not working class.

At this point, I knew what was going to happen. I was about to become 'a loner who keeps himself to himself'. Maybe if I'd invited the whole street in for crumpets and cocoa every evening for a year, I could have avoided this fate. But as it was, I was on my way to becoming a creature capable of any indecency. The tabloids, care of my next-door neighbours, were setting me up. By tomorrow evening they'd probably know that I'd once picked my nose during biology class – and by the following evening their readers would know as well.

('A bit of a loner, is he? Keeps himself to himself, you say?')

I felt: annoyance, anger, rage, fury.

It wasn't my fault that someone had leaked the story of the morgue phonecalls to the press. That had probably been a policeman, wanting a bit of easy cash to help re-Tarmac his drive. But how had they made the connection between Asif's anonymous journalist visitor and myself?

Most likely Asif was far more forthcoming with the *Mirror* – over his pina colada – than he'd been standing beside Doctor Calcutt on the hospital steps. At the mention of a mysterious visitor asking questions – and claiming to be a journalist – the real journalists would have set off immediately to find out who it had been. I imagined photos being faxed down to a small sub-post-office in the Caribbean. Pina coladas were by now pouring like pink waterfalls. Asif raises his drunken head and points an unsteady finger. 'Thassim. Thah-one vere.' Thunk –

down the head crashes again. Off scurries the still-very-sober journalist. They'd worked pretty fast, if that was how it had been.

Once she'd finished with my neighbours, the journalist came back to my front door and started ringing on the bell. This kind of press attention had only happened to me once before. There had been a ludicrous (or so I thought at the time) story in one of the tabloids about how Brandy and Cyril were having a torrid on-screen off-screen affair. The doorstepping had gone on for a couple of days before something more important came along – someone slightly more famous was discovered to have been having a torrid on-screen off-screen affair. But that experience hadn't really taught me anything about how to deal with door-stepping. If people really want to bother you, then they can. Unless you can afford bouncers and getaway limos, there isn't much you can do.

The phone rang again and I waited until the answerphone picked up. It was the *Mirror* journalist phoning from outside, even as she rang the doorbell. I could hear the doorbell coming down the phone with a few milliseconds delay on it – synthesized, digitized and de-digitized. The journalist shouted into the phone as she shouted through the letter-box. This was becoming unbearable.

I did what I could: I pulled the nicotine-brown plastic box off the doorbell and unscrewed the bell.

The moment she heard the bell go dead, the journalist started knocking instead.

I turned the volume all the way down on the answerphone. I put on a Nirvana CD very loud. I lay on the sofa with a cushion over both ears and yelled *blah-blah-blah*.

My next-door neighbours – both of them – started to bang on the walls. Perhaps I was no longer a suspiciously quiet loner who keeps himself to himself. Perhaps I was becoming a bloody nuisance with all that racket.

I watched – engulfed in noise – as the message-counter on my answerphone went up and up.

The album came to an end. I put it on again and made a cup of tea.

Then I went and did something I hadn't done before – sat in the garden. It was rankly overgrown with thigh-high grass and neck-high weeds. Through this green sea I waded to the far end, where I found something I'd forgotten: a shed.

When I opened it up, it wasn't too bad inside – dry and dusty and completely empty apart from a bucket and mop, some coils of rope and a defunct lawnmower. After first removing the mop, I turned the bucket over and sat down on it.

For one long moment I felt a sort of deep mischievous calm coming over me. I sat there like a just-crowned king – mop in one hand and cup of tea in the other – reigning over the garden shed, and with the fourth estate pleading for admittance at the outer walls of my castle.

The only shame was, I didn't have a crown. But maybe I did. I took out my handkerchief, knotted it at the four corners and put it on my head. Now the picture was complete – except I'd drunk half the tea.

Quite clearly, regally, I watched as a decision was made in my head: I would go to the theatre that night, and the following night, whatever happened, whatever intervened. This would draw some attention to Alun and Dorothy – attention which I doubted they'd appreciate. (If the journalists managed to get in to one of the performances, it would merely be an added disturbance on top of my Cough Campaign.) I might be able to use this intrusive attention somewhat to my own ends after all.

I was about to go back inside to call and book James's taxi for the evening when I heard a police siren coming down our street and saw the flashing blue light reflecting down off the television aerials above the houses.

It wasn't Vicky. Not yet. I had been expecting her from the moment it became public knowledge that I'd been to see Asif.

More private investigations? More illegitimate delving? Vicky would turn up eventually. But this, when I opened the front door a slight slit, was nothing more than two ordinary policemen sent out because:

'We've had several complaints about the noise, sir.'

They stood between me and the photographer – although he jumped back and forth to try and get an angle.

'Come inside,' I said.

I'd already turned the stereo off.

In the hall I explained to the policemen what was happening. They were not impressed by the fact that I might be of sufficient importance to have a journalist outside my house. What *did* impress them was the possibility that the journalist outside my house might just be interested in *them* – if they went and had a chat to her.

'What can you do to stop it?' I asked.

They looked at each other.

'If they're not breaking the law, not a lot.'

'But isn't it harassment or something?'

'Why did you say she was interested in you?'

It just wasn't worth trying to explain again.

'Okay, I'll keep the music down from now on. But the neighbours didn't complain about the noise of me having a journalist bashing down my door.'

'We'll have a word with her,' said the policeman. 'Please don't force us to have to caution you.'

I smiled and promised and let them out.

For fifteen minutes there was no knocking – and then it resumed, slightly less passionately.

I called James. Then I called Anne-Marie, to inform her of what was happening. She offered to come round, but I told her that it would be better for her to stay away. I didn't want her getting involved. And, to be honest, I was quite looking forward to having a break from her.

56

James and his taxi turned up on time. I'd explained the situation to him on the phone. He beeped his horn three times as he was coming down the road. After grabbing the folded-up wheelchair, I squeezed out the front door, locked it behind me and crashed on into the passenger seat of the cab – the door of which James had leant over to open for me.

The photographer, who had been reading a copy of a rival paper, took a couple of strides to catch up – but then was pecking away at me with the flash. The journalist dashed for her car, which luckily for me was facing the wrong way down our street.

The flash kept exploding in the left side of my face as James promptly drove off.

When the photographer could no longer keep up, he turned back to get into the journalist's car.

Because of this double delay, and a bit of shading the speed limit along Mortlake High Street – plus a double-back – we easily escaped.

'You're very good at that,' I said to James. 'It looks like you've done it before.'

'Once or twice,' he said, with a glance in the rear-view. 'Angry husbands, that sort of thing.'

'Really,' I said, feeling our easy-natured chat lurch as it hit turbulence.

'Not on my own account, of course,' said James, steadying the conversational controls.

We laughed.

'So, who did your front door?' James asked.

'Dunno.'

'And what were that lot after you for? Have you just signed for Chelsea or something?'

I laughed, and tried to explain: Asif, the hospital.

'There may be a few more quick getaways to make,' I said. 'Could –'

'No problem,' said James. 'If I'm around, you've got me. And I'm around a lot of the time these days. My gaffer hasn't hardly called anything decent in for me in weeks. But I don't quite understand – when I picked you up at the hospital, you'd just been in to talk to this Asif bloke about what?'

It was a relief to have someone to talk to who wasn't directly involved. I told him the whole story from beginning to end – including the visits with Robert, Josephine, Alun and Dorothy, Asif and Tony Smart. The telling of it took most of the journey. James nodded and yessed and ahhed, but didn't interject much. Occasionally he said, 'Pardon?' and I had to speak up. He was a very good listener.

Just as we were about to pull over in front of the Barbican, I asked him directly:

'Do you think I've been doing the right thing?'

'Oh, I don't know,' he said. 'Sometimes it's best to just see how things go. I know the police aren't the greatest thing in the world, and they make my life hell by spending their whole time chasing me for touching a pavement rather than getting after the real villains. But if you believe that they're really doing nothing, then I suppose you might as well do something for yourself. You're not going to be able to arrest anyone, though. You'll have to call them in for that.'

I didn't tell him that the only call that was going to be necessary was for an ambulance – and that I was pretty certain someone else would be making that one for me.

We arranged for James to be outside the back of the theatre

212

after the show, just in case the *Mirror*-mobile had somehow managed to catch up with us.

As it turned out, I didn't see another journalist until we drew up again outside my house. Unfortunately, now that I saw one, I saw more than one – I saw about ten. Plus ten or more photographers.

'You sure you want to go in?' said James. 'I could take you to a hotel.'

'They'd be banging on my door all night,' I said. 'No, I'll try this – see how it goes. Same routine tomorrow?'

'They may try to block the road.'

'We'll be too fast for them,' I said – shouted, actually. I had to raise my voice to be heard above the thumping on the window and the screamed questions.

I tried opening the door on the pavement side, but they were all standing too close – deliberately, I suppose. I got out on to the road and walked around the back of the car. I ignored the questions, did not shield my eyes from the flash bulbs and made my way slowly up to the front door. As James drove off, I could hear someone shouting at him, 'Where did you take him?'

As I got the key into the door, a surge from the journalists smashed me up against it. Luckily, the red paint was now dry and didn't stick, blood-like (for the cameras), to my coat.

I tumbled through the door, flinging it shut behind me, and fell down on the hall carpet in tears.

57

Sunday morning, and the journalists turned up early. One or two of the younger ones had spent the night in their cars. The phonecalls had started around seven – the red light flashing, the beep, the quiet crackle as the message was recorded. The message counter clocked up – 24, 25, 26 – until the memory was full. That had never happened before. I was interested to see how the answerphone coped. But nothing exciting happened: it merely played the outgoing message and then neglected to record the incoming. The journalists started knocking on my door around eight. But the knocks were intermittent and came without much conviction. A couple of photographers tried to peek in through the front curtains. All of it only served to make me want a gun even more intensely. Not to use, just to have – to know I had.

Around nine, I sat down at the answerphone with a cup of tea and pressed Play. Most of the messages followed the same escalation: from ingratiating to wheedling, from cajoling to threatening. These, I deleted, often half-way through the first sentence. I got to recognize the voices and phrases – the most persistent one being *This is Sheila Burroughs of the Mirror*.

Only a couple of messages were of any interest. My mother had rung, saying she was going to come round at eleven to see that I was alright. Vicky was also there, also announcing an eleven o'clock visit.

'I think we need to have a talk,' Vicky said.

I called my mother back immediately. The only way this situation could become even more embarrassing would be if my mother were to give an impromptu press conference on my front steps. I had no doubt that she'd speak out long and loud on the subject of my virtues – and then longer and louder on my defects. On the phone, I managed to persuade her that yes I was fine and no it wasn't a good idea for her to come round and really from now on I'd call her at least once a day, promise.

'Have you seen the papers?' she asked.

'No,' I said.

This was a problem. I solved it the only way I could think of – by phoning James and asking if he could buy me copies of all the Sundays, bring them to my door and post them through my letter-box.

'I'll pay you for the lot this evening,' I said.

'We still on for that?' James said.

'Sure.'

'You must really like that play,' he said.

'Fucking love it,' I said.

He was round within half an hour. There was some banter between him and the journalists as he fed the thick-folded wodges of paper through on to my hall carpet. I felt the urge to stick my hand out through the letter-box, just to touch some friendly flesh.

'Oh,' someone said, 'he'll *read* us but he won't actually talk to us.'

There were unconvincingly amused guffaws.

I carried the paper stack through into the dark-curtained living room.

I couldn't help but be reminded of Lily. The weekend after one of her openings was always dominated by dangerous supplements. Lily would sit on the sofa, anatomizing every single one of her reviews – and their reviewers. Confidential information about him – it was usually him – would be disclosed: how this one regularly didn't turn up until the third act (and even then he was pissed), how this one always gave rave reviews to bottle blondes (his mother had been a bottle blonde), how this other one hated all women (because he'd lost a testicle doing National Service). Sometimes Lily would get into one of her ultra-rages. Breakable objects would be thrown, and some of them would hit their intended (fast-moving) target – me. Suicide threats would be made, pill bottles grabbed and fought over and grabbed back, over-dosages estimated. The downstairs neighbours would phone up and complain about the screaming and banging. Lily would tell them to fuck off or she'd fucking kill them.

To try and calm her down I'd suggest we go for a walk or a swim.

'What do *you* know?' she'd say. 'You've never put yourself up on that stage for people to come along and stare at! You've never tried to create anything! With you it's all excuses for why you haven't *actually* got around to getting off your arse and doing something. So, don't criticize *me* for over-reacting. You have no idea what it feels like!'

To suggest we go for a walk or a swim was, in the logic of Lily's rage, to criticize her for over-reacting.

Thing was, her reviews were usually excellent. Quite a few even scraped ecstatic. But if the belated, blonde-besotted, bollockless reviewer even glanced at a caveat – be it lighting or costume – it was taken as a direct attack on Lily's very integrity.

Review days usually ended with Lily laid out upon the sofa, surrounded by crumpled pages, dead-faced, intoning, 'Nobody loves me. I want to die.'

Well, now I *had* put myself up on that stage for people to stare at – unwittingly, it has to be said.

Only one of the Sunday tabloids, the *News of the World*, led with the story – and that was only because it was a good excuse to print some videographs from Lily's made-for-TV murder-mystery shower scene on pages four and five. (Lily naked, Lily wet, Lily screaming, Lily dead.) The other papers buried it in the home news. Other issues of greater import or titillation were already taking over. If things continued like this, my doorstep would probably be clear in a couple of days. Asif's revelations continued in the *Sunday Mirror*. As I'd thought, he was photographed on a beach. But he wasn't in the Caribbean, only the Isle of Wight. And the pina colada was nowhere to be seen. Instead, there was a large pot of tea. 'My mother's always wanted to come here,' he was quoted as saying. 'She's always loved Tennyson.' I was relieved to see that he didn't seem to have mentioned the pregnancy. Instead, he had progressed to a more general revelation of goings-on in the UCH Pathology Department – the sick jokes, the cuts. My behaviour was explained as stemming either from distraught grief or impatience at police delay. A Met spokesperson (Chief Inspector Hetherington) was quoted as saying that my actions *might damage the eventual chances of a successful prosecution*. All of this was much as I'd expected.

But the small article I found on one of the inner pages of the *Sunday Sport* came as a very nasty shock:

> **Ex-con turned top stand-up comic, Tony Smart, 32, was badly beaten up yesterday night outside his Islington mansion. The unknown assailants, who are believed to have used knuckledusters, made off without stealing anything from him. Smart was quoted as saying: 'I've been in more pain – watching West Ham play at home.' Police are investigating.**

This gave me something to think about until Vicky turned up.

One major possibility seemed to be raised: that the black man and the albino who constantly followed me around weren't policemen at all, but were – in fact – the unknown assailants who had beaten Tony up – and perhaps twice vandalized my house.

In trying playfully to scare Tony by giving them the impression that he'd seriously helped me out, I'd unwittingly ended by getting him beaten up. If so, then I must be in some real danger myself. They hadn't attacked me, yet. Perhaps they were waiting for me to find out something I shouldn't.

Vicky arrived just after eleven.

I left her outside the door with the question-screaming pack for just a few seconds longer than was necessary. It was a small opportunity to make her suffer the discomforts of impatience.

'How are you?' asked Vicky, as we turned to go into the living room – as if she were really being civil.

'It would be nice to have a couple of policemen outside my door, to stop them knocking on my door and shouting through the letter-box. Apart from that, I'm very well thank you. How are you?'

'Oh, I'm okay.'

She didn't look it.

'This is supposed to be my weekend, you know.'

I offered her a seat on the sofa which, after some hesitation, she took.

'You've caused us a huge amount of trouble,' she said. 'I don't think you have any idea how much. I mean, you seem to be doing your utmost to make us seem stupid and incompetent.'

She was finding it hard to cover up her sadness and depression.

'It's unfair of them to expect you to stop me,' I said. 'If I were put under house arrest by a squad of armed guards, *then* I might sit round doing nothing.'

'Conrad,' she said. 'I'm sorry that I can't tell you what we've found out. But – believe me – if you knew, you'd be acting very differently. Wait until the trial. Everything will be in the open then. It's not particularly simple. I shouldn't even be telling you this, you know.'

'Is there anything new that you can tell me?'

'We're setting a date for the trial – in about six months. The Old Bailey.'

'Fantastic.'

'Perhaps you should take a nice long holiday – or go and live somewhere else.'

'How's Tony Smart?' I asked.

'Scared,' said Vicky, then realized it had been a trick question. 'Oh shit,' she said.

'So far,' I said, 'have I actually broken the law?'

'No, I don't think so.'

'What do you know about whoever tipped red paint all over my front door? I think I'd like to report it.'

'You've caused us so much trouble, I wouldn't be surprised if it wasn't a couple of disgruntled coppers.'

'So, you knew it had happened?'

'There were pictures in the paper.'

'I think I might need protection. Whoever beat up Tony Smart could come after me.'

'You'll be perfectly safe if you go away somewhere.'

'Will I find out at the trial who the father of the baby was?'

'I can't prejudice the prosecution by telling you what evidence they may or may not choose to introduce.'

'Be a little imaginative. You want me to stop, you give me what I want. Tell me if the baby was mine. Tell me who wanted Lily dead. Or if not that, then at least tell me that whoever wanted Lily dead is going to be properly punished.'

'I don't know about the first two, but the last – yes.'

She looked embarrassed, as if she'd said too much.

'Look, Conrad, I'm under real pressure. There's people who

think that if a man were doing my job he'd keep you under control. Every time you go off limits, I take the blame. No-one touches you. Just because you've been in a bit of a coma and got shot. It's so fucking unfair. I wish someone would just shoot me. I'm sure it's a lot easier.'

'Would you like a cup of tea?' I asked.

'Please,' said Vicky. 'For me. Stop.'

She was genuinely getting tears in her eyes.

'Look,' I said, 'can't we just dump all this sexual-tension-being-nasty-to-each-other stuff? Really, we just fancy the pants off each other. Why can't we just go to bed and fuck?'

Vicky looked at me – even more hurt, if possible.

'Well,' I said, 'it was worth a try.'

'What sort of perverted little wank-fantasy do you live in, Conrad? This isn't the letters page in some nudie mag – this is reality, yours and mine.'

'But wouldn't it feel good to have sex with the national press outside, not knowing what was going on? Wouldn't that give you a feeling of power and control? Wouldn't it feel exceptionally naughty?'

'I think, yes, I'm *sure* you've just managed to destroy my last few kind feelings towards you. If you continue trying to investigate this case on your own, I will have you arrested.'

'You can only do that if I break the law.'

'Don't count on it. That hasn't stopped us before.'

'Just a blow-job,' I said. 'Not full sexual intercourse – how about that? Go on.'

'You're disgusting,' said Vicky.

'Everyone is disgusting,' I said. 'That's not the point. Sex happens when two disgustingnesses coincide. I was just checking whether or not ours did.'

Vicky stood up, picking up her cheapo work-handbag.

'I'm going to try and get you a man to deal with, next time.'

'Okay, then, goodbye.'

We walked to the door and I let her out.

'Oh,' I said, 'and I still want those inventories. Remember?'

Her look told me *exactly* where to go, and *just* what to do when I got there.

She *No commented* her way through the press. Good girl.

58

Next, I gave Anne-Marie a call.

She was flattered that Hitler was calling her live and direct from his besieged bunker. This was pant-wetting stuff.

'What's it like?' she asked, meaning press intrusion.

'Oh,' I said. 'You know. It's a bit of a pain. I wish they'd go away. I'd really like to see you, but they're going to follow me everywhere I go – and you can't come round here and see me.'

'I could,' she said – as I'd known she would.

'Really,' I replied. 'You don't know what that would mean. By the end of the day, they'd have interviewed relatives you didn't even know you had. I'm not even sure they're not bugging my phonecalls.'

'Don't get paranoid.'

'I miss you and I want to lie next to you and hold you close.'

'Soon,' she said.

'Yeah, they'll lose interest in a couple of days.'

'Conrad' – Anne-Marie had changed her tone – 'why did you go and see Asif?'

'You don't want to know,' I said.

'I do,' she said.

We exchanged a few more endearments before I hung up. The thought occurred, not for the first time, that Anne-Marie might herself be investigating me. But I wondered whether I shouldn't suspect her a little more and trust her a little less.

All that remained to do that day was the Cough Campaign. This time the paparazzi on their motorbikes were able to keep up with us as we drove into town. James made no especial attempts to elude them – there was no point. Plus, I *wanted* them to find out where we were going. This extra pressure on Alun and Dorothy – even if it were only perceptible to themselves – might be just enough to get them to crack. I decided to send them a card saying: I can go on doing this for ever. I wonder if you can? They would hopefully panic at the indirect press attention, and contact me.

I'd had another thought, earlier in the day: perhaps I'd be able to direct some press attention towards the black man and the albino in the Mondeo. But when I snuck a look out of the front window, up and down the street, they were no longer around. Obviously they felt my movements were being traced efficiently enough. Or perhaps they feared that they might be spotted and questioned. I doubted they could pass as journalists, even though now was the most inconspicuous time of all for them to be sitting in a car outside my front door. It seemed as though attending a very bad performance of *Macbeth* was the furthest my press management could go.

Although I didn't know it at that moment, this was the last very bad performance I was going to have to attend.

The call came last thing Sunday evening.

Alun held the receiver, though I could sense Dorothy near by. She was the one in control – deciding what he should and should not say.

'We want to know,' said Alun, 'what it will take for you to stop disrupting our performances.'

This was the point we reached eventually, after Alun had called me a *bastard* and a *fucking cunting bastard* a few dozen times.

'What I want – all I want – is the truth.'

'You must agree to go nowhere near this theatre, or our flat, or our *son*.'

'But we were getting on so well. And I just love the play.'

'Those are our terms.'

'Well, then, I'll be at tomorrow night's performance. With the national press. They may become a little more suspicious when they realize I'm going to see the same play *every* night – a play starring someone who has been widely rumoured to have had an affair with a woman who was later murdered. I wouldn't be surprised if some of them weren't on to that already. Had any phonecalls?'

Alun's hesitation gave them away – yes, they definitely had.

'I will contact you when I can,' I said. 'I don't expect they'll be all that interested in me for *that* much longer.'

Dorothy must have grabbed the phone.

'And don't you dare come near us until you're completely sure you're on your own.'

'Hello, Dorothy,' I said. 'I think your performance has really improved in the last couple of weeks. You're probably the best Lady Macbeth I've ever seen.'

So obvious.

'There's a real depth to it – an understanding – an empathy.'

'Thank you – I'm glad you –'

'Do you think it might be the guilt?'

Crunch.

I put the phone down immediately. After a minute or so, it rang – but I didn't answer.

Dorothy didn't leave a message on the answerphone, but I could hear her distress hissing – like tears falling into a deep-fat fryer.

59

Monday.

The only reporter left that morning was loyal, persistent Sheila Burroughs of the *Mirror* – and even she had been deserted by her photographer. Her picture editor had obviously decided that another shot of me in front of a red-paint-stained door wasn't going to sell any copies.

James brought round another load of papers. Asif was still there – clinging on to coverage. More interestingly I learnt that Tony Smart, even before he was beaten up, had been intending to leave the country. The *Sun* reported that, just the week before, he'd asked his agent to book him in for a two-month residency aboard a Caribbean cruise liner – rest and recuperation, easy audiences, selling out. 'I wanted some peace and quiet,' Tony was quoted as saying. 'Keeping quiet is very important to me at the moment.' But the passport office, for some reason, hadn't wanted to let him out of the country.

According to the report, Tony got off quite lightly with his beating. There was a picture of him. Both his eyes had been blackened; he had a ring-cut down one cheek and another across the bridge of his nose; his lip was split and flattened. He looked more handsome, and even more criminal, than before.

Sitting there, reading about Tony Smart, the one thing I didn't expect was for the phone to ring and for it to be him.

'You saw what they did to me?' he asked.

'Pretty bad.'

'I hope you have some idea of how *gently* they treated me. I mean, these men were practically breast-feeding me compared to what they're likely to do to you. At the moment, you're protected by invisible forces. But they won't always be around to guard you. You managed to drop me in some serious shit – which, by the way, I myself don't forgive you for. But let that pass: me and my baseball bat are the least of your worries. You're lucky that I was able to convince those two gentlemen that I really *hadn't* talked to either you or the police or anyone about any substantive issues – if you know what I mean. If I hadn't, you'd have had my death on your conscience; along with however many others you have right now. So, accept a little advice: rent some porno videos, stay home, whack off. Go to the local supermarket and buy yourself some full-fat ice-cream. Take up sky-diving or bull-fighting or Russian roulette. But if you want to have yourself a long and happy life, forget this going-round-asking-people-questions business. Don't ask a stranger on the Underground for the time. Don't ask a policeman for directions. Don't ask for ketchup in McDonald's. Don't even ask for world peace in your prayers at night. Be a good boy and then, one day, you'll be able to be a good man and then, another day, you'll be a good old man. Because otherwise you're going to become the action movie to my little trailer. This was apprentice work – a little first-out-of-the-gate stuff. If you want to see some masters at work, close up, really fucking close up, you just carry on doing what you're doing. And, believe me, there's nothing I'd like better than to see you back with your bandaged buddies in intensive care. Did you like it there? Did you?'

I put the phone down on him, excited. I was getting close to something.

Around eleven, Sheila Burroughs knelt down at the letter-box and shouted through, 'It's okay, I'm leaving. You can come out now.'

'See you,' I shouted back. 'Don't forget to write.'

Ten minutes later, I checked to see that she hadn't been lying

– but it was true: the street was back to full-on suburbanity.

Excellent.

I called up James and got him to drive me further east – Brixton, Clapham, Bermondsey. Here, I chose a cruddy-looking pub (one with cages over the windows and a nationalistic name on the sign) and arranged for him to pick me up a few hours later. I went in in my wheelchair, as it was more to my purpose to look fucked. I was wearing dodgy clothes: sweatshirt, tracksuit bottoms and trainers. I hadn't shaved or washed my hair.

Once inside the pub, I ordered my pint and – as I'd hoped – some friendly soul passed it down for me off the bar.

After this introduction, me and the kindly soul got talking. We found a table to sit at. Soon enough, he was asking me about the wheelchair and I was telling him something not too far from the truth. I changed the venue, the motive, the company. But I kept the gun, the coma, the outcome.

Other friendly souls started to listen in.

'Cunts,' one friendly soul said. 'Fuck off.'

They didn't.

Somewhere along the line, I started talking about guns, guns generally, their rarity, their availability . . .

On the first day, I met a great deal of knowingness but very little actual knowledge.

'Oh yes,' said one of the kindly souls. 'You can have anything you want – easy – for a price.'

The second day followed much the same pattern. But then, on the third day, in the cruddiest, most easterly pub I'd dared enter – one where they'd had to carry me and my wheelchair backwards over the threshold – I got talking to a man who wasn't boasting or bullshitting.

Once it became clear I wasn't bullshitting either, we began to make some tentative arrangements.

'End of the week, mate,' I was told. 'It'll be coming in the country end of the week. We'll have it for you Sunday, no problem.'

My gun-contact gave me his mobile number and we shook hands. In my excitement, I almost stood up out of the wheelchair.

When I got home that first unsuccessful day there was a message on my answerphone from Anne-Marie.

'Hello? Conrad? Are you there? Oh, god, I'm – oh, shit. Look, can you come round? I really need to see you. I'm at my flat. But only if you can, you know. Is it any better? With them outside? Something's happened and. You don't have to, you know, but, you know, I'd really like it, okay. And. Oh god. Bye.'

As James had only just driven off down the road, I decided to call another cab company to take me there. I didn't want to become too dependent. I was over to Anne-Marie's in half an hour.

Anne-Marie lived in Chelsea. I knew the address, though I'd never been there before. It was a basement flat in a tall Georgian building. I rang the aluminium doorbell.

Anne-Marie came to the door. She looked ugly. Her face was very red. She'd been crying. 'Come in,' she said.

'What is it?' I asked.

Anne-Marie led me through into her living room. It was done out in defiantly cheerful colours. The green cushions didn't match the orange sofa and the orange sofa didn't match the red walls and, somehow, the brown carpet managed not to match anything else at all. Anne-Marie was a little more composed than she'd been on the answerphone.

'They sacked me,' she said, and started crying again. 'This morning I walked in and they just gave me the sack.'

'Oh, no,' I said, weakly.

'Sorry, I shouldn't have demanded you just come round like that. You must have other things –'

'Nonsense,' I said. 'I'm –'

'You are,' said Anne-Marie, as if I'd said exactly the word she'd wanted. 'And you've been through so *so* much worse.'

'Look, I wasn't really what you'd call *around* for a lot of it,' I said. 'Did they give any reason for sacking you?'

'I'm too old,' she said.

'How old are you?'

'Thirty. Unless you make it far enough up the ladder by the time you're thirty, they fire you. They say it freaks the models out to be working with *old* people. What the agency wants is young women, just slightly smaller and puffier and less neurotic than the models.'

'That's stupid,' I said, whilst seeing the pure logic.

'That's the fashion industry. All they want is young bodies – they haven't got any use for anything else.'

I knew it was sympathy not suggestions that Anne-Marie was after at this point. We could talk about what she was actually going to *do* a little later. I'd seen Lily like this, seen her like this often – her career was a career of Doubt. Every audition, every part, every rehearsal, every scene, word, line – Doubt. Plus, Doubt overall. *Should I be doing this? Aren't I wasting my time? Everybody's time?* But, from the outside, I could see that Lily's periods of greatest Doubt were always those of her greatest advancement. What felt to her like floundering and drowning appeared – to the observer, to the outsider, to *me* – as a perfectly poised freestyle. The questions she addressed to me were always and only prompts. What I was meant to do was ask her the exact same questions back, so that she could dismiss them as my own stupid misinterpretations of the truth.

Lily needed to broadcast her insecurity, then have it beamed back to her – so she could sit in front of the TV of her personality and slag off every single thing that appeared on it.

All this gave me some idea of how to deal with Anne-Marie. Although Anne-Marie was a far less extreme case than Lily had ever been. Her flat, as far as I could see, was still intact: plates and windows were as yet unbroken. That wouldn't have been the way with Lily. And Anne-Marie didn't seem to have hurt herself, not physically. Whereas Lily would definitely have had the razor-blades out by now. Always careful, of course, not to cut anywhere that would affect her chances in a casting session. Lily's breasts were flickered over with scars – pale tracings in seemingly random directions. I used to kiss these thin white ridges, as if I could kiss them better – mend them – unzip them. She used the blade from a safety razor. Not mine. She would buy it herself. Quite premeditatedly. The cuts were long and clean and she would dress them in the bathroom afterwards. I used to find the red-streaked cotton wool in the bin. Lily's bras, going into the washer-dryer (I always did all the laundry) would have little dashes of blood smudged on the inside of the cups. Sometimes, from the timing, I knew that she must have done this to herself before an audition, in the theatre or studio toilets. There she would have been, reciting the lines of some new washing-powder commercial or vicars-and-knickers farce, wanting that shitty part so badly that she was bleeding to get it.

Once, she shaved off her pubic hair – and I almost died from the thought of what else she might have done with the razor.

There was nothing I could say to her about this. Lily didn't mind me knowing, but she did mind me mentioning. The trauma was something I had to accept as part of the person she was – the person she couldn't help but be. If I did mention it, I would immediately hit 'Don't!' If I pursued it, I would face a week of sullenness and no sex.

That Lily could be happy like this – happy bleeding – was one of the hardest things to deal with. 'It's not as if women aren't used to a little blood,' she'd say. 'A little pain.'

Until the inquest, however, the only people to know about Lily's razorblades were myself and however many lovers she had had. Alun would have known. Cyril would have found out.

In comparison, Anne-Marie's skin was perfect. Her life, really, wasn't looking all that bad, either. However, I let her dictate whether or not it was appropriate for us to use going-to-bed as a way of healing her particular wounds. It was inevitable, I felt. We weren't yet intimate enough for me to achieve her consolation by words alone. She took me by the hand and, wordlessly, led me into her bedroom.

In a way, I might have objected: there was a sense in which Anne-Marie – though she might deny this out loud – was suggesting that her pain (at losing her job) and mine (at losing my life) were equivalent and equal. They weren't comparable at all – a point I wanted to make clear. Some other time, though.

We had gentle-sex – sex that was loving in everything but love. If there had been more love between us, the sex might have been more honest, less gentle. Our bodies were saying not *I love you* but *I might one day love you*. Each kiss was promissory and each caress borrowed from the future.

When Anne-Marie came she was making sobbing noises, new ones, ones that I hadn't heard her make before. They didn't stop as dutifully she went down on me – dropping tears into my pubic hair and lifting her head up to take gasps in between sucks and licks. I was cruel enough to enjoy the novelty of this, and didn't ask her to stop.

Afterwards, we got out of bed, ordered pizza and watched a weepie that Anne-Marie owned on video. It was all for her – that evening. There was no way I was going to deflect it towards a more shared enjoyment. I took pleasure out of guiding her towards the soft warm centre of her chosen comfort zone (clichéd as it was), just as I took pleasure tonguing her to orgasm.

Thank you was all she said for much of the second half of the evening. *Thank you* emerging from under the neck of her sloppy cashmere sweater. *For being here. For being you. For being lovely.*

When the moment seemed right, I put my idea to her: 'I may have some work for you, just while you're looking for something else.'

'What kind of work?'

'Well, you know I told you I had this idea for a film . . .'

'Where's the script?' she said. 'Can I read it?'

'I'm afraid it's mostly in my head at the moment,' I replied. 'I'm going to get some of it down on paper. Then what I'd like to do is audition some actors – you know, get them to read through a couple of scenes. And then I can work with them on getting the script into some kind of final shape. Fancy helping out?'

'Love to,' said Anne-Marie, perking up. 'I've always wanted to move into film production. This could be perfect.'

'I don't want to see more than three or four of the best chances for each part. We can weed out the no-hopers early on.'

'I understand.'

'I'll pay you,' I said. 'But you'll have to do exactly what I say.'

'Exactly,' said Anne-Marie, with sexy irony – mimicking me exactly. She was a very good mimic. Not as good as Lily, but still pretty good.

'It wouldn't take much – placing a few ads, looking through the replies.'

'Really, I'd love to. It would be just like booking, wouldn't it? – looking through all the hideous photos.'

Together we drafted the four ads. This was how the most important one read:

WANTED: boy actor/young man. 16–18 for lead villain in no-budget short. You will be slim, dark, good-looking. No previous acting experience required. Please write enclosing CV and b/w photograph to Lazarus Productions.

And then we gave the address of Anne-Marie's flat. (We'd agreed that putting mine might just draw unwanted press attention.)

Anne-Marie said she would place the ads the following day in the major trade papers: *Stage and Screen*, the *Stage*.

It was late by the time we finished, so I stayed over.

I didn't sleep very well, and neither did Anne-Marie. She was made restless by my presence in her bed, and I was made restless by her restlessness.

I remembered sleeping with Lily – the long perfect sleeps of Saturday and Sunday morning, where when it started to get light we'd wake up just enough to tell each other to go back to sleep. But I also remembered being out at sea with Lily's tempestuous nightmares – how the mattress would twist and buck with her flailings – how I'd have to grab her, slap her, calm her down.

Everything with Anne-Marie was returning me to Lily – I don't think she had any idea of how much history I was regaining access to. It was like opening a forgotten folder on a computer and finding a hundred more forgotten files within it.

Lily had created the pattern of my relations with women, probably for the rest of my life. Never again would the most important things be new, stunning, incomparable.

Lily had left her scars everywhere.

60

Tuesday.

I left early in the morning, guilty at how much I'd been thinking of Lily and how little of Anne-Marie. It sickened me to think how much Lily still dominated my life, my dream-life.

For the first time I realized that I was never going to be able to reduce the amount of time I'd spent with her. It frustrated me – I wanted to phone her up and tell her to stop bothering me. She seemed constantly to be scattering images of our life into places where I would glimpse them. She was guilty of always pushing her presence forwards in my mind. I was full of a childish feeling of *It's not fair, it's not fair, go away and leave me alone.* I was being stalked by her and by her memory: I felt like accusing her of harassment, getting a restraining order.

Anne-Marie had said she was going to spend the day job-hunting. I hoped she'd find something, and I hoped the something would take her somewhere far away from London. I wanted an end to this relationship, but an end for which I wouldn't have to take any responsibility. Anne-Marie was becoming annoying. She wanted me to be present for her the whole time. All I'd wanted from her was the chance, for a few hours, to disappear completely from my own view. Anne-Marie couldn't help but be a reminder of all she wasn't, all she could never be, all that Lily had been. I'd begun to pity her, and that surely was telling me that it was time to end it. Something must come along that would allow me to look good even as I was dumping Anne-Marie. A job in New York or LA would be particularly convenient. I'd be able to make my speeches of pained splitting devotion. I would appear noble and bereft. She'd cry; it'd be over; I'd be free. But, of course, I still needed her around for the moment.

Back in Mortlake the post and the papers were awaiting me on the mat.

Ever since I'd begun appearing in the tabloids, the amount of junk mail I received had at least trebled. Every charity to which I'd ever made a donation now wrote me a begging letter. This post contained an invitation from a group formed to campaign for Healthcare Reform. They wanted me to become their spokesperson.

There were other slightly more personal communications – old friends getting back in touch: hasty postcards with change-of-addresses on, long letters containing page-after-page of self-recrimination.

I took all of it through into the kitchen and dumped it in my permanently-open-on-the-floor black bin-bag.

I checked that day's *Mirror*. Asif had ducked beneath their horizon of interest completely. A couple of days' NHS bleating was all they'd been able to take.

I phoned UCH, the Pathology Department.

'Is Asif back from the Isle of Wight?'

'I'm afraid we can't give out details regarding hospital staff.'

I tried phoning his mother, but she'd obviously had her number changed.

It seemed I'd reached a temporary dead-end so far as finding out whether I was the father of Lily's child.

However, now that the journalists had left me alone, I could arrange my meeting with Alun and Dorothy.

I called them at home. Laurence picked up, and I had a bit of a chat with him. Soon, though, Dorothy must have realized who it was. With a shrill cry, she grabbed the phone out of his hands.

'Leave him alone,' she said.

'Mum,' I heard Laurence whine.

It took a few minutes to persuade her that I would now be able to go out without my retinue of followers and admirers.

We arranged to meet on Hampstead Heath at three o'clock the following afternoon. It would have been nice to have been able to choose somewhere to put them less at their ease – like the Chamber of Horrors at Madame Tussaud's, the Royal College of Surgeons Museum or even Highgate Cemetery, right beside Lily's grave. But Dorothy made it clear that it was only *there* and only *then* that they would deign to meet me.

So, there it was going to be . . .

After sorting that out, I had a doing-stuff day.

I was going to need a load of cash quickly, to buy the gun, so I phoned the bank and got all that arranged. Lily had left me the contents of her deposit account, but I needed to be able to get hold of the money at short notice.

I called her solicitor, the greyly efficient man who'd sat at my bedside during my convalescence.

'I'm afraid, Mr Redman, that you've rung at a rather inopportune moment. This is, in fact, my last day at work. I'm about to hand over all my current clients to a very capable colleague of mine. You see, I have a cancer of the terminal variety.'

I offered my sympathy.

'No, no, that's quite all right. Good innings and so on. If you'll just let me put you through.'

I spoke with the colleague. He agreed to transfer Lily's substantial bank balance into my current account as soon as possible.

'I was sorry to hear about –'

'Yes, we're all going to miss him terribly.'

'He was Robert's solicitor as well, wasn't he?'

'Almost thirty years.'

'Do you know if there was ever any mention of contesting Lily's will?'

'I'm afraid I can't disclose another client's business to you.'

236

I wasn't going to get anything here.

As Lily's flat might come in handy later, I phoned up and had the utilities turned back on. I also had the phone reconnected to Lily's old number.

In the afternoon, James took me and my wheelchair to visit the pubs of South-east London.

Anne-Marie came round in the evening.

'I've placed the ads,' she said. 'They'll go in this week. Thursday.'

'That's good,' I said.

'Not much else on at the moment. Plenty of advertising space. Easy . . .'

'Good.'

I had nothing more to say to her.

61

Wednesday.

It was time to get ready to go and meet Alun and Dorothy. I wore tough clothes, somehow fantasizing my way into a kidnap scenario – with Alun sticking a Balaclava over my head and Dorothy roping my hands up too tight.

James drove me up to Hampstead Heath. We talked about the way the newspapers had treated me. He sympathized.

I don't know whether they took pleasure in being late; leaving me to be cruised once every couple of minutes. Certainly when they arrived they didn't apologize.

Alun, wearing a battered greatcoat, was every inch the windswept Welshman; Dorothy, sporting brightly coloured Afro-patterns, was Menopause Ethnic personified.

As we started to walk along, furtively talking, I knew that Alun and Dorothy knew that passersby would take me for their son. This pleased me: it was something they hadn't thought of. Anyone seeing us might guess that I'd brought them here to tell them that I was gay, and that this was where I met my friends, and that they would just have to accept me for who I was.

It was a delight to me that no-one ever seemed to recognize Alun and Dorothy. Life with Lily had involved a certain amount of standing to one side whilst she gave her autograph. But even though Alun and Dorothy had been on posters all over London for the past two months, no-one gave a toss about them. They were theatre; Lily had been TV. They were everything Lily had wanted to become – and, most people, they were nothing.

'Let's get this over with as quickly as possible, shall we?' said Dorothy, as much to Alun as to me.

Take charge, she was implying. *Be a man. Be the man I thought I was marrying when I married you. Be windswept.*

'What do you want to know?' asked Alun, weakly.

'When you arranged to see Lily that evening, what did you think you were meeting to talk about?'

'What do you think?' said Dorothy, waspishly.

'. . . about us,' said Alun.

'But you cancelled. You told her that it was over.' I said.

'It was,' said Dorothy.

'Alun?'

'As far as I was concerned, it was.'

'But Lily?'

'. . . was a little harder to convince.'

'Tell me, Alun, had you lied to Dorothy before – told her you were going to stop seeing Lily but carried on?'

'That's none of your business.'

'Okay, another question: Did the police DNA-test you?'

'Yes,' he replied. 'They took a sample of blood when they first questioned me.'

'Were you the father of Lily's child?'

'They haven't told me the results. But I've been subpoenaed to appear at the trial, and told not to leave the country without informing the police.'

'We've had to cancel a Canadian tour,' said Dorothy.

'Have you been subpoenaed as well?' I asked her. Her mouth went soft round the edges – like a false-toothed woman's.

'Yes,' she said, mumbled.

I asked her directly: 'You had something to do with Lily and me getting shot, didn't you?'

Alun began answering, 'That's not true. What –'

I continued to attack Dorothy. 'It was about Laurence, wasn't

239

it? Lily was either having, or about to start having, an affair with him, wasn't she? You couldn't stand it.'

'That isn't true,' wailed Dorothy. 'I thought it was true but it wasn't. I asked him – *we* asked him – confronted him – and he swore it wasn't true and we believed him. He doesn't lie to us, not when we ask him a direct question.'

'What do the police know?'

'We've told them everything,' said Dorothy.

'Everything you haven't told me?' I asked.

'You'll hear at the trial,' she said.

'What will I hear about?' I said to Dorothy. 'Will I hear about how Sub Overdale introduced you both to Tony Smart? How he wanted you to meet some real murderers? How you did? How you, Dorothy, got carried away? How, out of jealousy and fear, you arranged a real hit? How something went wrong? How Alun found out and cancelled the date, so he wouldn't get killed? Or how you got scared and told him to cancel, leaving Lily to get shot with whoever she happened to invite along in Alun's place?'

'That is the most ludicrous thing I've ever heard,' said Dorothy.

'But you have to admit,' I said, 'someone wanted *both* of the people at that table shot: Lily and whoever was with Lily. And if that person was meant to be Alun, then the only person I can think of who *might* have wanted that is you.'

'Do you think I'd want my husband killed?'

'Yes, at a certain point in time, I think you did.'

'Lies, complete lies,' said Dorothy. 'It was a coincidence, that's all. Alun cancelled the date. Lily arranged something else. How do you know they didn't want to kill her *and* you.'

'Only Alun and Lily knew they were going to meet in that restaurant at that time. If Lily didn't tell anyone, then that leaves only one person who knew. You.'

The wind had got up a bit. Thunder was introducing itself diffidently, mildly, just over the horizon.

'Come on,' said Dorothy to Alun. 'We're going.'

'What are you going to do?' asked Alun.

'Just keep quiet,' said Dorothy. 'He can't *prove* anything.'

Alun put his arm around Dorothy.

'I know this may sound bizarre,' he said, 'but I'm very grateful to my wife for doing what she did.'

'Stop!' said Dorothy, but he went on. For once he was windswept.

'My relationship with Lily was foolish and immature and wrong and dangerous. Someone would have ended up getting hurt – more than just emotionally. Lily wasn't stable: you of all people should know that. Sometimes she just lost control. She was madly jealous. In fact, I was caught between two jealousies – but one was the jealousy of love, the other of possession. Lily couldn't stand to lose me, and certainly not to my wife. It was more than her pride could take. You know the kind of things she was capable of. She terrified me, sometimes – the way she would hurt herself to hurt other people. Everything with her was a declaration or an ultimatum. Nothing existed on a sensible, domestic level. And that's where I live: I save the fireworks for the stage. You don't really need them – not when you can be mad in Shakespeare, anguished in Chekhov. Most actors and actresses live very quiet, suburban lives. But Lily couldn't stand that. Dorothy realized what was happening – and Dorothy saved me. She gambled. The stakes were high. She won. Lily lost. But that was what Lily wanted all along – impersonal tragedy wasn't enough for her, she needed it all to herself. She wanted to be the victim that no-one could deny. Really, Dorothy was just helping her fulfil her vocation. But now I think we've told you all we know, and can. The police have taken extensive statements from both of us. We're innocent – and so are you. Just get on with your life. Stop living in the past.'

Dorothy took him roughly by the arm and hustled him off down the hill. I could hear her, chiding him for giving so much away.

241

Now, I had my final version: Alun had arranged the dinner meeting with Lily; Dorothy had found out; Dorothy had gone into a mad rage, everything coming together at once – jealousy, hate, fear, anger; Dorothy had arranged to have a hitman put on Lily and the man with her; the hitman had known what she looked like anyway – from the TV; Dorothy had then told Alun not to go; Dorothy had told him that if he did, he would die; Alun had believed her; Alun had cancelled with Lily; Alun hadn't told Lily about the hit, he'd just told her not to go to the restaurant; Lily, stubborn and piqued, had kept the booking; Lily had invited me along as the only person she could get that late on a Friday evening; for some reason, the hit still went ahead . . .

A stupid mistake, but Dorothy was still the one who had caused Lily's death to occur.

I felt very calm as I walked away from the meeting with Alun and Dorothy. But slowly the crackling white noise of hatred began to interfere with the smooth transmission of my thoughts.

Dorothy was stupid – a stupid woman: self-pitying, self-justifying, self-centred. I would have hated her anyway, on principle, even if I'd had hardly anything to do with her. But the stupidity of her actions; her lack of remorse; her continued and continuous and continual attempts to excuse what she'd done; the ignorance of her own real motives – jealousy of Lily's beauty and success. Everything more I learnt about Dorothy made me hate her more.

Alun I didn't despise – him I merely pitied. He was a weak man; weaker even than I'd thought. But I could see that – along with myself – he had genuinely been in love with Lily. Enough in love, I believed, to have given her up to save her life. Enough to have lied to Dorothy about stopping seeing her. Once, twice – my guess was he'd done it a number of times before.

This threatened contract killing had been the act of a woman who no longer knew what to do. Dorothy had obviously tried every other way she could think of to keep Alun away from Lily. Some of the likelier methods it disgusted me even to think of. But she'd also been ingenious: persuading Alun to accept a tour away from London. And then getting him to star alongside her in *Macbeth* – so she could keep an eye on him every evening. She'd been planning ahead, but it hadn't worked. Lily's hold over Alun was too strong. From what I could see, that hold seemed to have been broken now, by Lily's death. Alun was a guilty man, a man full of regret, but he didn't appear to be a man in mourning. Dorothy really *had* managed to have her way and win him back. The price had been – incidentally or accidentally – Lily's death and my near-fatal wounding.

Though I hated to admit it, I almost had to admire her for this. Stupidity has its advantages: it sometimes gets what it wants by doing completely the wrong thing but by doing it so remorselessly that *something* at least happens – and when something happens, due to the unpredictability of events and people, the outcome may accidentally be what was initially desired. It was the worst and final thing: that out of all this mess, stupid Dorothy had stupidly managed to achieve her stupid aims. Alun was with her again, enslaved – like the member of some totally unconvincing (to outsiders) cult. Dorothy's terror at being unloved – unlovable, probably – was there for all others to see: Alun, however, now saw only the fake fact – the fact Dorothy wanted to impose upon him – the fact that she *deserved* to be loved. In every moment they were together she was abusing him more and more. Alun was a docile beast – his only stubbornness had come out of an intense desire: Lily had been something he truly wanted.

A very nasty thought came to me, which – at the time – I dismissed almost immediately: if Lily had reached Dorothy's age, she might well have become very like Dorothy. They both had their ways: their rages, their selfishness. No doubt part of Dorothy's behind-the-scenes domination of Alun was, like Lily's, a feigned bleating helplessness: 'I'm useless – I'm awful – no-one loves me

– everybody hates me.' Alun's life (as had been mine) was a matter of reassurance and more reassurance. He was the foundation-repairer of Dorothy's built-upon-sand monument (to herself).

A second even worse thought came: if Lily had lived, and I had got back together with her, and we had – as a couple – reached Alun and Dorothy's age, would I have become as weak, as pathetic as Alun?

62

That evening I called Anne-Marie and she came round with two large bags of healthy food.

'You're not eating well enough,' she said.

She took over the kitchen.

'Wild mushroom risotto,' she said.

'Great,' I replied.

'With asparagus,' she added.

'Mmm,' I said.

'I never used to have time to cook, but now I do. I'm going to get really fat.'

For once, I really wanted to make an effort to listen to her. I was ready to pay great attention to everything she said. But everything she said, or so it seemed at the time, was hardly worth paying any great attention to.

'I'm quite enjoying being unemployed,' she prattled. 'I've started watching daytime TV.'

A few hours later, as we lay in bed eating strawberries, a brick smashed through the front window – crashing into my bedroom, landing on the record-player.

Two feet to the right, and it would have been Anne-Marie's head; three feet, it would have been mine.

Wearing only pants and a T-shirt, I loped out the front door and into the street.

A car was driving off rapidly towards Mortlake High Street. I couldn't see what make it was. All I could discern were the red squares of the tail-lights.

Back inside, Anne-Marie seemed to be calmer than I was. Her first instinct had been to start picking up broken things – the triangular fragments of vinyl. She turned the overhead light on (we'd been in candlelight) and looked at the smashed turntable. The deck was deeply dented. Anne-Marie carried the waste-paper bin over and started picking up pieces of the splintered record with her fingertips. She left the brick for me – as if the mere fact that it had been thrown through *my* window gave me sole ownership of it. It frustrated me that she didn't touch it: Lily would have been over beside it in a second – examining it passionately, closely, empathetically, as she examined all things to which violence had occurred: smashed-up cars, roadkill, boxers, women in supermarkets.

The brick had one simple word chalked on it: CUNT. This wasn't good enough – I'd expected at least a letter, Sellotaped or rubber-banded to the brick's body.

I felt ludicrous, walking over to the bookshelf and placing the brick there – as if it were just another hardback volume, quarto or folio.

Going back over to Anne-Marie I tried to stop her tidying up. 'Aren't you scared?' I said. 'It almost hit you.'

Anne-Marie looked up at me incredulously. 'But it *didn't*.'

She went back to the pieces of the stereo.

'I suppose this has been happening quite a lot – since you were in the papers.'

'Some things, you know – the paint.'

'I'm glad I'm here. Are you alright?'

'I'm fine.'

'Are you sure you're alright?'

I realized that I was shaking. Everything inside me suddenly felt liquid. I sprinted to the toilet not knowing whether I was going to shit or puke. I solved the dilemma by doing both, extravagantly, at the same time.

I hadn't had time to lock the door, but Anne-Marie decently stayed outside. I could hear her there, though she didn't say anything. It made me feel a little better and a little worse to know she was listening to me, too.

The brick itself wasn't what had set me off: it was the bang it had made smashing through the window. For the first time since the shooting, I was getting the kind of clichéd flashback that my counselling had warned me of: I was shell-shocked.

I felt ashamed of myself, of my own psychology, for being so bloody obvious. In a way, I felt that some characteristic of mine – of intelligence, sophistication, wit – should have excluded me from trauma. Shouldn't someone as self-aware as I was have been able to side-step all that? I was stronger than other people, wasn't I? My whole psychology was less fucking obvious. Counselling was for people so stupid that, first session in, they had to have the concept of counselling explained to them. Maybe I should have listened a bit more, back in the hospital. For the first time I began to realize that being in denial means not just denying you're in denial but also denying that you're denying that you're in denial. And so on. There was no arguing (psychoanalytically, intellectually, wittily) with my bowels: this was me, here, shitting myself. I might not like it – I might not approve – but here I was; and I was me; and me wasn't as cool as I'd always hoped.

When I emerged from the toilet, I felt myself to be less of a man – less than a man. Anne-Marie was all consolation. I'd thought that because of this, I would be less attractive to her. Again, I was wrong. This at least gave her something to do – she became my nurse. Taking my soiled pants and T-shirt and putting them in the sink to soak. Tucking me up in bed. Disinfecting the toilet floor and the toilet seat, and giving the toilet a clean for good measure. And then lying down beside me and listening to all my weakness flowing out – my weakness, my confessions of weakness, my confessions of the vanity of my belief in my own strength. And then, suddenly, I stopped speaking. Now I was underwater, fallen through the ice, freezing, drowning. She jumped in after me and swam down to me and grabbed hold of me. For a while we were underwater together – looking up at the ceiling of my room as if it were the underside of the ice. And for some reason we didn't drown or freeze. We were surviving because our hearts had slowed and stopped. We lay there, looking up at the ceiling and watching where the bubbles trickled along the dark grey-blue underside of the ice. We were hoping for some of them to lead us back to the hole we'd fallen in through, to the way out, to air and life. And when we surfaced it was with horror and gasping.

I'd fallen asleep, into a dream of the whole thing happening again.

The night was quite warm, but the air moving through the fractured window made it seem chill.

Anne-Marie was close beside me, comforting, giving me words of advice that at any other time I would have mocked. This was talkshow territory. I was being dragged into the world of Dorothy's bedside table. I was feeling the fear and doing it anyway.

Anne-Marie put the overhead light on, brought in some more candles, put on one of my Sinatra tapes. (I'd mentioned to her my belief in the-healing-power-of-Easy.) Slowly, she reassured me; recomposed me; reconstructed me.

She was my angel of the obvious – I couldn't have made it without her.

63

Thursday.

In the morning, Anne-Marie told me that the only things I'd said, all night, were 'She's dead' and 'My baby.' I would move the words around. 'She's my dead baby.' Repeat them in different combinations. 'My baby she's dead.' But I never altered them. 'Dead baby dead.'

'Weren't you scared?' I asked her. 'Didn't you think I'd gone mad?'

'In a way,' she said, 'I was more worried that you *wouldn't* go mad. I couldn't see how you were going to cope, otherwise. Going mad almost seemed the safest option.'

I felt much better: purged.

When she was sure I was all right, and when she had arranged for a glazier to come round, Anne-Marie went out to buy a copy of the *Stage*. I asked her to buy the rest of the papers, as well.

We'd obviously missed something. Last night, while we were under the ice, Tony Smart, despite his battered face and bruised body, had appeared on a TV chatshow.

From what I could gather, he'd come on like a serious gangster (dark glasses and even darker hints). And despite the studio audience understanding even less of what he said than usual, his reception had been uproarious. Crime had simultaneously been seen to pay and not to pay. He'd made the reconnection with the street that he'd so desperately needed. Folk-hero status was beckoning. His broken face was on every tabloid – and every tabloid had sent along women with very large breasts and even larger smiles to comfort him. His appearances at the Comedy Store were all sold out – people wanted to make it along whilst the bruises still showed.

'Here they are,' said Anne-Marie.

She unfolded the *Stage* and pointed out our ads.

'No typos?' I said.

'Aren't you excited?' she asked.

'Of course.'

'You seem more interested in that other paper.'

'No, I'm excited,' I said.

'When am I going to get to read this famous script then?'

'Soon, very soon.'

Anne-Marie was annoying, but she was right. It was time to get my script into shape.

I did, in fact, have about fifty pages of something I'd attempted and abandoned a couple of years earlier. I'd written it just after meeting Lily, back before disparagement had replaced encouragement – back when she might even, for a few months, have believed in me. The idea was to make a spy-thriller set in London's clubworld (I used to go to clubs, back then) – the drug barons would be the spymasters, the DJs the double agents. I'd even come up with a title, *Spaced Out*. It sounded contemporary, low-budget, sexy, believably filmable. This was the project that attempting to work with screenwriters had driven me to.

Re-reading it now, I was appalled to see that the work I'd done with the screenwriters had actually been a lot, lot better.

The dialogue in *Spaced Out* was attempted-hilarious. There was, as far as I could see, no plot. My characters were cardboard cut-outs jump-cutting their flimsy way through a two-dimensional world. One of them (I blush), the love-interest, Nina, was a direct steal from Lily; another, Adam, the hero, was a flattering self-portrait – a version of myself that looked good with six o'clock shadow, lit other people's cigarettes unthinkingly, could escape Rottweilers by scaling brick walls full-stop.

One of the younger characters was a clubber called Johnny. I hadn't really defined him to any great extent – at the time, all I'd known about him was that he was going to end up dumped in the Thames with a Cellophane bag of self-raising flour stuffed back up his arse. (Not sure how I was going to film *that*.)

It didn't take much to change the script round and introduce the scene that I was going to require.

Anne-Marie got very excited to see me tapping away at the laptop, and kept interrupting me with offers of tea – as if that was going to help 'with my inspiration'.

64

Friday.

Vicky came round unexpectedly in the morning, which was rather awkward. I introduced her to Anne-Marie. They were obviously checking each other out. My vanity saw jealousy but my sense saw curiosity.

'How have you been?' Vicky asked.

'I didn't enjoy the attention very much, if that's what you're getting at.'

'That surprises me.'

'How about your lot? Cope with the pressure?'

'Oh, yes. We can take a lot worse than that. The journos can stand around outside the police station, getting themselves into a lather whenever anyone goes in or out – doesn't bother us. They need us for the next story, and the story after that, and the story after that. They have to give the appearance of pursuing us – if only to themselves. In actual fact, the pressure's been more off than on recently.'

'You seem to have calmed down a little.'

'Oh, I've calmed down a lot. Two weeks from now, and I'm moving on. You'll have Victim Support Counsellor Mike Hughes to deal with. I think you'll like him. He takes a different approach.'

'Washing your hands of me?'

'Just scraping the last bits out from under my nails.'

Anne-Marie, who had been watching, horrified, now chose this moment to offer Vicky a cup of tea.

'We enjoy it *really*,' I said.

'Do we?' asked Vicky. 'Speak for yourself. He's made my life hell this last couple of weeks.'

'Really?' said Anne-Marie.

Somehow they agreed to go off into the kitchen together for a private and extended discussion of my faults.

I turned on the TV.

Suddenly it hit me: Anne-Marie was going to blab something about the film script. It was very unlikely that Vicky would draw any correct kind of inference – but, still, I didn't want her to know about my plans.

I strolled casually into the kitchen, and the conversation stopped.

'Everything okay?' Anne-Marie asked.

'Fine,' I said.

'We'll bring it through,' Vicky said.

And – as little wanted as that – I fucked off back to the TV. I kept the volume low in an attempt to eavesdrop on them.

Occasionally, I would catch Anne-Marie's voice ascending some peak of indignation or abseiling some cliff of disbelief. 'He didn't!?' They were really enjoying this – I could tell.

It reminded me of when I'd just started to come out of the coma – how furious it had made me to have my limbs moved around as if I had nothing to do with the matter. I could grunt, by then. I was seeing blurry patches of light and starting to understand whole sentences. But the thing that annoyed me most happened a week or so later, when I asked – politely if a little slurredly – whether they could change my catheter. It had been leaky for ever, probably since they put it in. Now that I was conscious, though, it was starting to cause me some serious discomfort. I'd wake up, four in the morning, the rubberized undersheet forming a shallow bowl of urine around my buttocks. Slowly, it would go cold. When I shouted for a nurse to come and do something, they'd close the door on me.

Having Vicky and Anne-Marie discuss me in the other room

was like hearing the nurses laughing and chatting down the far end of the ward, always just on the frayed edge of audibility – so I'd never been sure if it was their distance or my brain-damage that was keeping me from understanding them.

The nurses would be discussing my *ways* – using gossip as a means of getting to the end of their shifts. And I would hear their casual tone, and would be tortured by it – tortured by the absence of it in anyone's exchanges with me. For as soon as one nurse went off shift, and the other came in to have a look at me, the tone would be gone. Instead, I'd be condescended to: 'Change your catheter – you should count yourself lucky to be alive.'

My mother – that almost constant presence, of TV-movie-scale devotion – was no better.

'Do what the nurses say,' she'd add. 'They know best.'

But they're not reclining in a trough of their own stale urine, are they? And neither are you. If only they'd change the catheter there wouldn't be this problem – they wouldn't have to mop up after me the whole time.

(Which came out as grunt-grunt-snort-grunt.)

'I'm sure they know what they're doing.'

When Anne-Marie and Vicky came back in with a tray (matching teapot, tea-cups and saucers; tea-strainer; biscuits layered like armadillo scales on a matching plate) there was a terrible female knowledge in their eyes. I had been weighed in the balance and found wanting – oh yes. But, so far as I could tell, Anne-Marie hadn't yet mentioned the script. I could either now – as I had in the hospital – give my testosterone-asserting moan-and-groan (which never got me anywhere) or I could lie back and allow them to baby me (which – in hospital – at least got my buttocks dry for a couple of hours). There was no choice. If I let Anne-Marie control the conversation, there was now even more chance she'd give me away. All the better reason to keep them on the safe subject: my impossibility. I decided to spill some tea on the carpet – just to illustrate what a mess-monster I was.

'Look at you,' said Vicky.

And they both did. Then they each of them looked at the other. Then they laughed.

'I need a laugh,' said Anne-Marie. 'I've just lost my job.'

'Oh, what did you used to do?' Vicky asked.

Anne-Marie explained. 'But it wasn't really as glamorous as you'd think.'

And then Vicky, incredibly, said: 'Have you ever considered joining the police?'

After that, there was no stopping them. By the time Vicky left, they had exchanged phone numbers.

'Now you *behave*,' said Vicky, speaking to me directly for the first time in half an hour.

'Don't worry,' said Anne-Marie on the doorstep. 'I'll make sure he does.'

If I hadn't needed her help to arrange the auditions, I would probably have dumped Anne-Marie that very moment. I had one mother already, thank-you-very-much; I didn't need some kind of übermother, too.

I spent most of the rest of the day refining or pretending to refine my script.

On Saturday, Anne-Marie and I did couple-things: shopping, cinema, meal, sex. Anne-Marie kept talking about the prices of two-bedroom flats. I made sure to stop off at the bank and make a large cash withdrawal. Anne-Marie was erecting a future, I was destroying one.

65

Sunday afternoon.

I told Anne-Marie that I was going to collect some things I wanted from Lily's flat. She offered to come, but I told her I'd prefer to go alone. I set off to South-east London, to collect my gun. I'd already phoned ahead to check that everything was okay.

It was the first time in a couple of days that I'd seen James.

'I was starting to think something had happened to you,' he said. 'Thought you'd done a runner.'

I told him about the brick through the window.

'Are you going to report it?'

'What's the point?'

'Fair enough,' he said.

My gun-contact was waiting for me in the public bar. He was a very small man who smelt strongly of cheap aftershave. At his feet was a zip-up sports bag so blatantly criminal that its logo might as well have been a sawn-off shotgun.

'Nice to see you,' he said.

We went together into the Gents, him passing a few nods telling his mates to keep it Out Of Order for the next few minutes. Burly men stepped across in our wake, ensuring that our transaction would pass uninterrupted.

I was carrying the cash down the front of my underpants.

'Safe,' he said, as we stepped into the cubicle.

The toilet was seatless, paperless, but definitely not odourless – a sonic hum of alcoholic urine rent the upper air, a base boom of shit took care of the lower registers. If there were such a thing as the sound-barrier for smells, this toilet broke it and then some. It wasn't the sort of place where business was likely to be conducted in a leisurely fashion.

The guy unzipped his bag, carefully perching it on his knee, not letting it touch the piss-sodden floor. Reverently, he pulled the gun out. It was swaddled in bubble-wrap which took him a few moments to unwind. I stood impatiently to one side – the father, useless at the birth. The gun emerged: finished in silver and blue. When he passed it to me, he did so with both hands – cradling it. Oh, it was so small and so heavy and so beautiful and so deadly. Come to daddy, baby. For several long moments I was happy just to gaze, but then I took hold of it properly. Baby.

The guy took the gun out of my hands and gave me a quick demonstration of its functions – the three different kinds of safety; loading; cocking for the first shot but automatic thereafter.

After seeing the gun, handling it, I'd've wanted it even if I hadn't needed to do anything with it. The gun was an art-object, worthy of the Design Museum – like a Porsche or a Leica. All its metal movements and intermeshings were Germanically smooth. And yet, at the same time, I found it difficult to reconcile this clinical machine with the passionate dying flesh of Lily.

'Excuse me,' I said, almost swooning.

The combination was too much: the smell (reminding me of the moment when the nurse used to unhook my catheter – meaty, male, testosteroney piss-whiff) and the sight (a gleam of efficient metal drawing me towards a similarly efficient revenge).

As I handed over the bundle of notes, I couldn't believe I was getting away with such a con: all the cruel perfection of *this* for *those* cabbagey pieces of paper? It seemed for a moment that I'd have to kill him to get away with such a thing; but he seemed happy enough with his wad of notes. He gave me the bullets, the maker's manual and the catalogue; he even threw in the sports bag – just so I'd feel like a proper armed-robber.

Now that the deal was done, he became lascivious in his praise of the gun – kept wanting to take it back off me to show me yet more felicitous features. He wanted me to take him for a connoisseur, but he was for ever trapped on the other side of the counter; I gave him money, yes, that was a necessity – but, in comparison with him, I was an angel of pure *use*. He had had custody (for a short time) of the commodity; I had taken full possession of the thing itself. He had thwarted its vocation, cramped its style, held it back; I would give it total liberation.

Half-way through a discourse on the relative merits of rapid-fire settings as opposed to a straightforward single-shot action, he remembered his grubby self.

'Nobody can trace it,' he said. 'It's completely clean. No history.'

(Telling me it was clean – the purest object I had ever handled!)

James asked me no questions when I came out of the South-east London pub carrying a newly acquired sports bag. I'd had a lie prepared, if he'd asked: a camcorder. But he knew that I hadn't come down here for something I could buy in any high street. We talked about other things completely – of football, of politics. But we talked more as men than before. Did I sense a new respect in his use of the indicator? Maybe. Admiration, even, in the crispness of his cornering? Perhaps.

Back outside my flat, I overtipped him.

When she asked me what was in the bag, I told Anne-Marie it was just some stuff from Lily's old flat.

'Diaries. Photographs she wouldn't let me have when we split,' I lied. 'That kind of thing.'

Anne-Marie looked disappointed that I still cared about my past – about another woman in my past. (And that I wasn't going to show her the photographs, read her the diaries.)

'I want to sort through it – decide what to keep and what to throw away.'

Her smile returned.

I stowed the sports bag in the bottom of the wardrobe. Anne-Marie knew (I think, on some level) that it didn't contain 'stuff'. As I was putting it into the back of the wardrobe, she saw me swing it back a couple of inches too far. I was slamming the 'stuff' around not as neutral material but as something I had to demonstrate (as much to myself as to her) that I felt neutral towards. I was too smug in the pretended unsecrecy with which I surrounded it: it had a halo of false insouciance. Yet Anne-Marie was wise enough to let me think I'd got away with this. She wasn't going to go sneaking a look in the bag. Instead, she would wait, letting her awareness slowly weigh upon and become a burden to me. If I was worth being with at all, I would come to feel it – she needed me, at least, to be *that* sensitive.

However, wise as she was, she did miss the central fact: that I'd myself changed. And this was just the most recent alteration. Anne-Marie's inability to see this was hardly surprising – she hadn't known me well enough *before* to judge me against how I was now: and, of course, in between my before and my now came an event of such alteration that even the most intimate foreknowledge would have been next to useless. Even Lily, after all her life-hours with me, having passed through the breakfasts and arguments, inhabited the undersheet world of whispered sophistry and babytalk, known me both bawling and crowing – even Lily, alive, would not have been able to say for definite anything about me. I had become someone unpredictable – even to myself. There were things I was doing, and thinking about doing, that would never have got further with me before than flash-fantasies: *in-my-way-on-the-escalator-die-fucker-die*; *won't-look-at-me-you-gorgeous-fucking-bitch-die*.

We went through into the living room.

'Tea?' I said.

'Lovely,' she said.

I made it, in the kitchen, in silence.

'Here,' I said.

'Thanks,' she said.

I got the terrible feeling we were running out of things to say to each other. But that was because I wasn't being completely truthful; I was avoiding the only subject that, for me, held any emotional truth at all: killing.

66

Monday.

I wanted to find out more about Lily's pregnancy. Asif would be no help – I was already aware of that. It looked as though there was no way I could get anything more out of the police. Not on my own, anyway: with the assistance of the tabloids, I might just be able to force a statement. But that, of course, would have Sheila Burroughs et al doorstepping me again. I decided that I needed to remain a private citizen for a little longer. Josephine, the person who probably knew the most, wouldn't talk to me. That left only one person who might know anything. I would have to go and see The Mistake.

I knew that if I tried to make an appointment, I would never get in to see him. The best thing, or so I guessed, was to turn up distraught – emotion would melt the prophylactic secretary.

The Mistake's offices were in the City – a small brick building amidst the glass towers of corporations. Everything about it said 'We own this land. We value it at more than mere money. We're here and we're staying here.' Here was trustworthy un-Real Estate.

And The Mistake's room, when I'd blubbed and blabbed my way in, was similarly trustworthy-looking: small and cramped, with a framed photograph of the queen up above the second filing cabinet (N–Z). Yet space had somehow been found for two deep leather club chairs and a low glass table – the early evening snifter was a tradition resolutely to be upheld.

I had moderated my distress the moment I gained entry to

the inner sanctum. There was no need to make the situation immediately uncomfortable.

After minutely shuffling some papers, The Mistake came out from behind his desk, shook my hand, guided me into one of the club chairs, sat down opposite me and then gallantly did his utmost to give the impression that my popping in was the highlight of his day so far, and that – such was the tedium of his life – it was also likely to prove the highlight overall.

He stretched his legs, as if we were relaxing in the boss's office whilst the 'real' boss was away – although *he*, in fact, was the boss, the bosses' boss. I glimpsed his sock-suspenders, framing oblongs of waxy white flesh.

We chatted for a few moments about his filing cabinets, which I'd admired on my one previous visit (Lily, lunch, embarrassment, escape): they were a dark blue, ex-Navy. The Mistake had rescued them from a frigate about to be scrapped. They had some special mechanism inside them (which he'd told me about before – but didn't hesitate to tell me about again) to prevent them from toppling over in stormy seas.

The idea of this appealed to me: storm-proof Navy filing-cabinets in a financier's office in a Georgian terrace in the Square Mile.

But it was time we got on to our real subject: I made a short speech, then waited for The Mistake's response. It didn't come.

'Did you hear what I said?'

'Oh yes,' said The Mistake. 'I heard.'

He looked down into the black pockmarked shine of his brogues – then reached down and, with his forefinger, flicked off a dusty piece of fluff.

I asked again: 'Did Josephine tell you anything during your reconciliation?'

He winced – either at my mention of that or at his own memories of it.

'You will understand that it wasn't a subject easily approached.'

Dead end.

'I wondered if you might have known – if you might have used some of your influence to find out . . .'

I tried to allow him the opportunity to decide whether or not to take the inference. By such half-clues, our conversations had always previously advanced – little leaps, tiny sidesteps. This time, however, we were having to follow the dance steps numbered out upon a sheet of paper on the floor. One by one, no short cuts. It was the tango or nothing.

'I think you overestimate my importance, Conrad.'

'Did you try to find out who the father was? Because it might be my – that might be me. I think it was – but I don't know, and I need to find out.'

'Sometimes one overestimates one's own importance, too.'

It took me a moment to realize that what he'd just said had been intended as further self-depreciation rather than a direct insult to myself.

'Does that mean you tried and failed?'

'I have been told, quite firmly, that I will have to wait until the trial – like *everybody* else.'

This was as close as The Mistake was going to come to saying yes; he'd tried and he'd failed.

'Right,' I said. 'But I would like to think that if you did manage to find out before then, you *would* tell me. I hope you can imagine what it's like for me – not knowing: guessing, but not knowing. The uncertainty –'

The Mistake looked as nearly human as I had ever seen.

'I had to identify the body, you know,' he said. 'Josephine was off somewhere with one of her men-friends. Cornwall, I believe. The police couldn't locate her, so they called me. It's not the sort of sight a chap forgets in a hurry. In a way, I was glad I spared Josephine that. Lord knows, I've done her enough services over the years. I don't think she appreciates it, though – quite how awful it was; and that's part of the service, don't you see? –

protecting her from the knowledge of just how bad the thing was from which she needed protecting.'

'I think I'll be going,' I said.

'So you see, I couldn't really discuss the thing with Josephine.'

'I hope . . ' I said, 'I hope you don't blame me too much.'

'Blame you?' said The Mistake, hearing me properly for the first time in minutes. 'No, I don't – I blame God.'

At this, I couldn't stop myself from staring at him. It was as if in my relations with him I'd constantly been dropping pebbles into a well, waiting to hear a far-down splash, and hearing every time nothing, nothing, nothing. Suddenly, though, by throwing a larger pebble or waiting a little longer, I'd heard it – a small, sodden plop of metaphysical resentment. Only now did I realize *quite* how much The Mistake resented being who he was. It had never occurred to me that I hadn't been telling him anything new, in my earlier callow cruelty, by revealing the nickname that Lily and I had given him. From what I now saw, The Mistake had come to that realization himself – he'd always known that he was The Mistake. Probably since before he even met Josephine. But The Mistake hadn't been his ex-wife's; not as far as he was concerned. He blamed a far more august being.

When I left that office I thought of him – for the first time, really, since we'd nicknamed him – by his Christian name, Robert.

As I walked away from the low Georgian building, I was convinced that I knew – at every moment – what Robert was doing: buzzing his secretary; telling her in an even voice to hold his calls for fifteen minutes – no, half an hour; sitting back down behind his desk; glancing at the framed photograph of himself, Josephine and Lily – all falsely ecstatic with the squint-into-the-sun expressions of holiday snaps; weeping as I had never had cause to weep (not self-pityingly, but for himself – for the entirety of himself).

Although the day was hot, I felt as if I'd just strolled into a meat-freezer – and that someone had locked the door behind me. I realized in a terrible instant that Robert was the loneliest man I'd ever met.

And another chilling thought immediately overcame me: that although Lily had always denied any similarity between her and her father, she had – in fact – equally as much in common with him as with her mother. Lily's mother was essentially gregarious: she didn't actually believe in her own emotions until they were projected on to, and reflected back by, others; Lily's father, in contrast, was a solipsist: he couldn't really believe that anyone other than himself *had* emotions – and certainly couldn't bring himself to hold the putative emotions of others as of any value. He therefore undervalued communication – believing all conversation inferior to talking to himself. Lily lined up beside her father in this – this terrible unwillingness to reach out, this terrible (when seen from outside) unreachability – and also, now I thought about it, in any number of other things.

On the surface, they were very different: he, dull; she, brilliant. But – and it was only now I saw that this was possible (as well as how it *could* be possible) – the very things which made Lily's father unattractive were those which had made Lily attractive: his hardness, his self-reliance, his style.

Even to allow myself to think this was, I felt, to betray Lily's memory – or worse still, her very essence. It was as if I were altering (by my perceptions) not only what I now thought of her but what, back then, she'd actually been – back then, when, cold as she was, and lovely, my love might have meant something to her.

I let it drop – I had gone too far with this: Lily's posthumous appearances had already done enough to alter what I'd thought of her. Something, at least, of the original should be preserved. Lily should remain as Lily had been because that was how Lily had been. Lily had been the Lily I had known – and lived with – and loved; the Lily that, for a while at least, had loved me back. I didn't want to rewrite my history of her too much – if I did, it might take away too many of my current reasons for living.

67

To try and fix my preferred version of Lily, I paid my delayed second visit to Highgate Cemetery. This sunny afternoon, we both needed something: she needed re-interring; I needed to allow my memories of her to fuse with the new facts I'd found out about her. Lily, or at least my previous version of her, was the person I'd set out intending to revenge. Paying her a visit was something I might not be able to do for some little while afterwards, if things went to plan.

I walked up the wide crunchy path, past Karl Marx's tomb, towards the area of newer graves.

There was a slender female figure standing over the pile of rotting flowers that were Lily's, that were lilies. For one uncanny moment, I thought that it was Lily herself. The figure was wearing a dress I recognized as identical to one that had belonged to Lily. Then, of course, I realized: it was Josephine.

I wondered why she would be there on this particular day – then I remembered that she didn't need a reason: this was her dead daughter; she probably came here every day.

There was a bunch of fresh flowers, red roses, on the top of the decaying, spread-out pile.

I walked more heavily than necessary upon the gravel of the graveyard path, hoping Josephine would hear, glance up and take the chance to recompose herself before I came close enough to speak. But she was oblivious to all forms of tact. I'd seemingly come upon her during a renewed grief or a relapse into the worst of the old.

When I stepped up beside her she turned her head as little as possible, taking in – as far as I could tell – my shoes and my trouser-legs. Even so, through the tears, she was able to identify me.

'Oh Conrad,' she said. 'You've come as well.'

Josephine stepped aside, allowing me to stand at the foot of the grave. Something in her movement made me realize that she expected me – as had she – to have brought fresh flowers. That I hadn't became a sudden and awful embarrassment. The social forms were what had carried Josephine through – but they were also what she employed to make a public display of her grief. As far as she was concerned, it had been my duty to bring flowers. I felt ashamed even as I realized how ludicrous was the basis for my shame. As if the depth of one's feelings should be measured by the number of trips one made to the florist.

When Josephine realized (from my immobility) that I hadn't brought the apt tribute, she flinched away slightly – as if my failure had caused her real physical pain.

This was the son-in-law I would have made. (I don't think she realized quite how far from becoming her son-in-law I'd always been. Marriage had always been the M-word, as far as Lily was concerned.)

Kindly, she saw that my grief needed to be acknowledged in some unfloral way – in words; and so she gave me the opportunity to speak my tribute:

'Life just isn't the same without her, is it?'

'You can say that again.'

This was how I envisaged Josephine at the funeral: as honestly distraught as she had ever been, yet maintaining all the usual social forms. I didn't know the forms as well; they had been invented and disposed of by earlier generations. My repetition of them was guessy and hollow. This made me feel childish – as if Josephine were my mother: my mother, specifically, when dealing with calamity. *This is what being adult is about*, my mother always seemed to be saying. *You're starting to learn – but, really, as yet, there's no basis for us to communicate.*

What I'd just said wasn't enough. I tried for more – at the same time avoiding any variants upon, *We'll never see her like again* – although that's what I really felt like saying; along with, half of me at least, *And thank God for that*.

'I feel as if I won't be able to mourn her properly until I've worked certain things through – until I've found out just who she really was.'

Josephine looked at me sideways, head down. It was a shyer and far more girlish movement than I'd ever seen her make before.

'I suppose you mean the baby.'

For a moment I couldn't speak: cliché but true.

'They buried it here, did they? Along with her.'

Josephine nodded.

'Will they put its name on the headstone?'

'The ground here is unconsecrated – we can do whatever we like, really.'

'Have you given it a name?'

Josephine flinched away from the grave.

'How can one?' she wailed. 'I mean, how can one?'

'*She* not *it*,' I muttered to myself.

'I've finished here,' said Josephine. 'I'll leave you alone.'

'No,' I said. 'I don't want to hang around. I just wanted to – you know – to see her.'

'I *know*,' said Josephine, as if I'd said something very tactless – as if I'd denied she was Lily's mother.

Things were starting to go really wrong; I needed to say something, and quickly. Josephine got in before me:

'You know, this whole experience – I suppose you might call it an experience – has brought me back to religion.' I remembered Lily's Christmas Catholicism. 'I had to convert to marry Robert. That should have been the first sign, shouldn't it? Of what he

269

was really like. You'd think I would have noticed something as big as that. But, at the time, I just thought it would mean a bigger, more exotic wedding. And I went along to see the priest and everything – learn the catechism. But I never thought that it would actually mean anything to me. I've been going back to see that same priest, you know. He's still there, in the same smelly flat. And half the comfort, I'm sure, is that *nothing* in his flat has changed at all. I mean, I'd swear in a court of law that he's wearing the exact same slippers he wore thirty years ago. (I got to know them quite well, you know: I spent most of our sessions staring at them to avoid his eyes. Virgin birth, all that.) And that seems to symbolize for me the continuity, the very staying-there-ness of the Church.' (I could see this was becoming a speech; there was no way I could stop it.) 'I think it started coming back to me during the funeral. I'd always resented the fact that the Church used these big ceremonial occasions – christenings, marriages, funerals – to get their mental claws into you. It seemed a bit sneaky. But now, I think, I understand, and even agree that it's right. Because those are the points – don't you see – when people reassess their lives. The Church is just there to give them an opportunity, through its rituals, to think and – perhaps – to change. And I have taken that opportunity. You may think I'm speaking of it rather lightly, even perhaps a little blasphemously. But I wouldn't have made it through without it. I do feel a bit of a cheat – what with the Christian religion being one of suffering and martyrdom; and I ignored it for so long, until I myself was suffering.' (I expected her to acknowledge her own martyrdom as well.) 'But there's no resentment from the Church about that. They've been around for a while; it's what they expect – what they prepare for. And, in a way, over all those years of ignoring them, they do prepare *you* for it, also. It's them you're ignoring, specifically – not anyone else. Not the Protestants. You're ignoring priests and mass and the Virgin Mary. When I went back, I was surprised how much of the catechism I still knew by heart; and I must only have thought of it it eight or nine times in all those years.'

I could see already that Josephine Irish's next novel was going to be unbearable – and, probably, unbearably successful. She had a hook now (grief) to go along with her line (long and lilting) and her sinker (the dying fall at the end of each long and lilting line). If she didn't end up writing educational literature for the Jesuits, she seemed doomed to a future of tearful talkshows and pathetic phone-ins.

I realized that I'd been silent for so long that Josephine would feel no qualm about continuing.

'It surprised me that I was able to keep on writing, through it all. But, you know . . .'

The weather that afternoon was unfairly colluding with Josephine's frogmarching me towards pathos. Mayflies were transporting their sunshine halos around the cow-parsley. The ivy was gently trying to shake off its winterdust. It was enough to turn any two walkers-together into friends, lovers or – at the very least – co-reminiscers. This was the weather of childhood photographs – before the blonde hair turns mousy, before the clear skin is prinked by spots. This was the weather in the photograph on Robert's desk. I didn't believe in it. I wanted absurdist weather to suit my absurdist emotions: hailstorms at 90°F, sub-zero horizontal rain. But the afternoon was on Josephine's side, not mine. She was terribly suited to this moment of light; it warmed and softened her face, smoothing out the lines. I could see Lily in her, just as I'd seen Lily in Robert – but this was more lyrical, more sexual.

She was talking on and on, but I think she could tell I wasn't listening. Instead, she took the opportunity to make certain flattering expressions, to turn her face towards and away from the shadows. I felt as if I were being wooed – something Lily had never done; she'd never felt the need to ask me to come to her. I was always half-way there well before she'd even started to think of it – if she ever had.

It seemed natural, at the time, however abhorrent afterwards, to take Josephine's hand. It seemed inevitable to stop and turn and face each other, in tears. It seemed, before we even kissed, that we'd already kissed, kissed many times, kissed through kissing Lily.

Josephine's mouth was very soft, granny-soft. I knew she had dentures, and – even in the soft-focus haze of our coming together – I tried to see if I could tell the difference between them and real teeth – Lily's, say. The edges where they met the gums seemed a little thicker and cruder, but that was all.

Most of my mind was off and away – thinking how odd it was that this was happening; thinking – already – of possible excuses Josephine (and I) might be forced to use afterwards: *ridiculous, the moment, grief, something.*

I was infuriated by the thought that Anne-Marie was at my flat in Mortlake, and that I couldn't take Josephine there.

This is silly, I almost said. *We know exactly what we're doing – and we're still doing it.*

I reached up to brush a lock of hair out of Josephine's eyes, then remembered how many times I'd made this same attempted-tender gesture with Lily. I deflected it (at the same moment, almost deflecting the entire encounter).

Josephine was choked, more exposed than I was.

'Where were you going to go?'

'I *was* going to go home,' I said.

'Can we go there?'

'No, that wouldn't be a good idea.'

'Alright,' she said, softly. 'Mine. I have a car.'

For my own sanity (later), I needed to say something prevent-ative: 'You're sure?'

But Josephine's pathos prevailed.

'What's the point in being sure?' she said.

She took my hand, kissed it, and led me to her Volvo.

68

Josephine's body – in preparation for the old lady's body it was soon to become – had begun to swathe itself in fragrant powders. When I got close enough to kiss it, which I did (it must be admitted) more than a few times, I began coughing frantically. The powders, no doubt, were intended to be anti-offensive rather than offensive; but they served to warn me off from approaching too closely – in any sense. Josephine's house, too, was a collocation of powders and other desiccated things: dust, mainly; little display bottles full of coloured sands, collected from various deserts and beaches; a myriad of potpourri; jars of rice, beans and pulses. Even Snafu and Glitch seemed dehydrated, making the milk Josephine poured out for them bubble with their furious tongues. (Josephine took some pleasure in pointing out that the cats didn't seem in any way to recognize me.)

I'd been to her house before, of course – but never alone, always strainedly accompanying Lily.

From the photographs of her beautiful self (none including The Mistake) that I saw around the living room, Josephine – unlike Lily – had once been full-fleshed. I'd seen the images of Lily here before: Lily had always been stalky-stringy, even as a baby.

The lines of Josephine's figure were crisp now rather than curvaceous. The bone-structure of her face was so delicate that one felt if one blew on it too roughly one would alter its basic structure. Her pubic hair was dusty – like tumbleweed on a soft grey desert. At the time, the density of my desire for her had bent the usual coordinates of my sexual universe sufficiently out of shape for me not to find all of this repulsive and motherly.

Yes, I spent a great deal of (mental) energy trying *not* to think of my mother. Not crying out to her. Not fucking her.

Josephine, or so it seemed to me at first, was something (an object) I had to treat with extreme care. Her skeleton was more than immanent within her – it was a presence very close to the surface, rising. But she obviously felt herself to be more resilient, and more in need of mistreating.

'Don't be gentle,' she said, during. 'I can't stand gentleness. I'm sick of it. I didn't bring you here for that.'

I couldn't help but think of Robert – had this been her way with him? And had he, ever the gentleman, refused not to treat her gently – in a gentlemanly way?

I flashed disgustingly back to a honeymoon not my own. Was this her great disappointment?

Occasionally, when Lily and I were together, I used to get the feeling that, once upon a time, Lily's father had done something terrible to her – and that that was the real reason Josephine had left him. This would certainly have explained Lily's resentment of him. But now I tended to think that this resentment could be explained by the fact that he hadn't abused her, and had thereby deprived her of any obvious, immediate, clear reason for being as completely fucked up as she was. (I had no doubt that Lily blamed her father totally for fucking her up, whatever he had or had not, really or in her fantasies, done.)

What a terrible involvement in Lily's pre-psychohistory this was. It felt like incest: taboo was half its attraction. The other half, I suppose, was healthy perversity: I didn't *want* to be doing this, and so I was doing it. The perversity of choice – the exercise of choice over desire: that was what was being proven here.

Josephine's fingers progressed rakingly down my back.

I had started to let some of my hate of her and my resentment of her livingness, her daughter's deadness, come through into the style of my fucking her. And she seemed to appreciate this expression. It was what she'd wanted, been referring to.

No longer were we thumping in such sweet congress; jazzy, I set up counter-rhythms – trying to anticipate her clenchings and frustrate them; trying to forestall her easy-early orgasm.

'Better,' she said. 'Much better.'

Josephine's self-hatred was finding its expression in having my unwanted cock slamming up towards her infertile womb.

The bones of my pelvis mashed against hers, slowly becoming slickly lubricated. The easier it became, the harder I fought against its becoming easy.

The forms and folds of Josephine's body, now it had gone slack, reminded me more and more of Lily, when she had sex-relaxed. It was more difficult to maintain this illusion (and my erection) with my eyes closed: with my eyes closed, Josephine's old-lady perfume came to dominate everything, and I imagined myself the Beast Boy raping a whimpering pensioner. And so I kept my eyes open, staring at the narrow Y-shape that her arms made at the armpit. This was the thing about her most like Lily.

Whilst we were fucking, Lily had always wanted me to pull her hair back, scratch her, dig my fingernails into her buttocks, slap her face, pinch her nipples, draw blood somehow.

'It helps,' she used to say, by way of explanation.

It disturbed me that Josephine was the same.

Where had Lily picked this up? In some archetypal childhood sex-interruption scene? If so, had her mother been with The Mistake or with some stranger? Or had she and her mother simply discussed the specifics of sex (gone into what they were into)? Or was it coded out somewhere in her genes?

Josephine and I were learning things about each other – things so obscene that, I felt, there was no way we would be able to meet again. The dinner table would be an abhorrence. A glance across the street would be blushing and cries for a taxi. The mere memory would be knees hitting the toilet floor and hands clutching the sides of the bowl. But that was for the future we were struggling against each other to deny.

Our bodies were rubbing themselves raw at every point of contact. Our pubic hair was brillo-padding the skin down hard against our pubic bones.

Josephine was on her way – over and out. All she needed was more of the same, more of the same, more of the same. And I needed to finish this – I needed to slay her totally. This wasn't enough.

I thought of Dorothy – of how easily this could have been her I was fucking. But I wanted to send bullets up inside her, not slops of spunk. Velocity was required: hardness, mass, heat – all the damage-causers. Bullet-headed, my cock was a poor parody of the real fucking that *somebody* was going to get.

In sixes, I counted my thrusts.

Frustratingly, Josephine began to come on a three and a half. I kept going till the six, and the next, and the next, were complete.

Then I pulled out of her, climbed up her and started to wank off over her face. I was going to put an end to these powders; liquid was coming her way – unexpected face-cream, good for the complexion; give her back some of her youth.

But Josephine (perhaps deliberately) misunderstood me. Not wanting the facial, her mouth went round my cock, her fingers cupped my balls, and when I came it was into the roof of her mouth. This was the oyster of her disgust, and she knocked it back without hesitation. Whatever was allotted to her, whatever she had self-imposed, whatever internal baulks and hesitations there might be, the performance would pass uninterrupted.

I, on the other hand, pulled away from her immediately. There was no way I was going relax, treat this as anything even half-way towards domestic, towards relationship. Even a glass of water would have been hospitality accepted, indebtedness hinted at, reciprocation begun. Already I was off the bed, looking for my trousers.

'What is it?' asked Josephine, wiping her mouth unnecessarily: she knew that it had all gone in.

Being slutty, lying naked on the destroyed bed, gave her an air of whorish possession; and I was her punter, spent, embarrassed, rushing back out to the stability of his life; sweating, guilty. If I had had a realistic amount, say £100 cash, I think I might even have left it for Josephine on her bedside table, tucked under the magenta edge of the porcelain lamp.

I stumbled about, trying to get one foot and then the other into my underpants. For some reason I resented the idea of having to sit or lean on anything for support whilst I dressed. I wanted to get out of there without incurring any further debt – however minuscule.

'Where are you going?' said Josephine. 'Is anything wrong?'

'I have to be home,' I said, then added unnecessarily, 'I'm moving back into Lily's old flat soon.'

Josephine reached over for the pack of low-tar cigarettes on the bedside table.

'Won't that be a little difficult?' The understatement of post-coital camaraderie.

'Just because it's difficult doesn't mean I shouldn't do it. I have my reasons.'

Josephine lit up and lay back.

'I still can't see what Lily saw in you – it obviously wasn't sex.'

Struggling into a white cotton T-shirt, no answer to this insult came to me. Josephine was being underhand. Perhaps this had been her reason for going to bed with me (more correctly – taking me to bed): to gain power over me, to be more able to hurt me. As if I needed to be hurt. As if I deserved more. If so, it was a very adult way of going about things. Sex for motives other than sex. (How very unadult adult movies are.)

The fact that I'd kept Lily's flat had clearly meant a great deal to her.

Suddenly, all our carefully contrived soft-focus was gone. Our Director of Photography had fallen out of love with our skins – with human skin altogether. The thing came up hard and cruelly lit: pores like holes in a greasy colander, areas of outlaw hair, bulges-to-be-politely-ignored, the silver snail-tracks of Josephine's stretch-marks.

A few more thumps and bumps and I was into my socks and shoes.

Josephine watched calmly from the bed, letting her low-tar smoke rise up to the ceiling.

There was no way I could compete with Josephine: I was up against knowledge and knowledge of knowledge, knowingness. In my mind I had become the thirsty child, sleepless, in search of a glass of water, who meets the alcoholic dinner-guest in secret quest of the cooking sherry. We could whisper together for a while in the darkened kitchen. But as she tottered off – her breath smelling heavy-thick like flu and sweet like cherry-drops – her every stagger was in an idiom, a language, that she knew I didn't speak: shame. I wasn't ashamed, and so I hadn't fallen into that degree of adulthood: mine were not yet the pained pleasures of grown-ups; I had still to suffer the disintoxication of all intoxication. I was being breathily included in a secret shame, and the very fact that I was being included proved just how far from true incorporation I really was. Maybe I could run upstairs with my water glass leaving silver splotches behind me on the hall carpet – and maybe I would go to bed big with the excitement of a shared lie and a humiliation not yet understood. But I would wake up the following morning a shameless child.

'I'll call,' I said, last thing before I left.

'Do,' emphasized Josephine.

I got out of the house, not even asking her to call me a taxi.

And so I had to wander around St John's Wood for half an hour before an amber-lighted black cab stopped.

One car, which I thought at one time might be an illegal taxi, seemed to be following me. It was not a Mondeo. It was a Mercedes.

69

It was late afternoon by the time I got away from Josephine. Anne-Marie had been in my flat all day. I'd trusted her. I'd left the sports bag in the bottom of the wardrobe. Part of me was worrying about whether she'd snuck a look. But the greater part was dreading the return home. So far, we'd had sex every night we'd been together. Tonight, she'd expect it. Tonight, she might not get it.

I hadn't really been unfaithful, I kept telling myself. Anne-Marie and I were a contingent fact: nothing had been settled upon, everything was goodwill and implication. Now, for me, the goodwill had deflated and the implication was already becoming suffocating: I wasn't responsible enough, at the moment, for a real relationship. Fuck, I was on the rebound from Lily's death and my own near-death – bouncing at high velocity towards the death of two other people. I didn't want the excuse of therapeutic workings-out: I needed a bit of straight-time, not this double-back bendy-straw stuff.

Anne-Marie would have to take whatever peripheral pain was going round. I wasn't going to tell her about it, but if she found out I wasn't going to deny it. I was about to kill people: no-one should tell me how to behave; I was likely to spend the rest of my life in jail; no-one had the right to deny me the maximum amount of sex available. Perhaps I should ask the taxi-driver to drop me off at a brothel.

'Excuse me, mate,' he said, 'but you're not mucking around with me, are you?'

I thought he somehow knew the inside of my head.

'It's just,' he said, 'that car behind us seems to have some friends of yours in it – they've been following us ever since I picked you up. I don't like people playing silly-buggers with me.'

I looked round. It was the two again, the albino and the black man.

'They're not my friends,' I said.

'Do you want me to stop, anyway?' he asked.

'No. Keep going.'

The car followed us all the way back to Mortlake. As I got out, they got out; as I walked to my front door, they followed me – faster – catching up.

'Excuse me,' said the albino.

'Don't make any trouble,' said the black man.

'Come with us.'

'We're going for a little drive.'

All of a sudden it felt as if someone were mixing low-grade cement in my bowels.

Although the curtains were drawn in the front room, I could see that some of the lights were on. Music was playing: the *Amadeus* soundtrack. Anne-Marie was inside – only a few feet away. It was even possible that she'd heard my footsteps on the garden path. She might look out between the curtains or come to the front door.

I thought about shouting, making a run for it. But the two would have caught me up in seconds – displeased, more likely to be violent.

Instead, as I turned round, I put my hand behind my back and gently tossed my keys towards the front door. (Hopefully, Anne-Marie would find them the following morning. If she did, she would know that something had happened to me. Something bad.) A moment later, I gave a loud cough – intended to cover up the chink the keys would make hitting the concrete.

It didn't work.

'Oi,' said the albino.

'Nice try,' said the black man, smiling.

'Now, pick them up.'

The two escorted me back to their car. It smelt of cigarette ash. On getting in, they both lit up immediately. I didn't ask them not to.

The black man drove.

'Aren't you going to blindfold me?' I said.

'We're not going anywhere,' said the black man.

'We're just driving,' said the albino.

'We thought we'd take you on a little tour,' said the black man. 'Sites of local interest.'

And so they did.

One by one they drove me past a number of very unrandomly chosen places – and the two took turns in saying:

'This is a graveyard.'

'This is a hospital.'

'This is a funeral parlour.'

'This is the river.'

'This is the dump.'

'This is the police station.'

After about six of these, the albino turned round to me and said, 'Getting the idea, are you?'

Fear crackled in the back of my throat like electricity.

And so it continued:

'This is another hospital.'

'This is another graveyard. Nicer than the other one, don't you think? Less crowded.'

We drove. We just drove. We drove east. Crossed the river. Drove further east.

'You realize,' said the black man, 'that we can do this any time we like – take you for a little drive – take you anywhere we want: to a lake, to a building site. And if your maths is up to scratch, you'll notice that there's two of us whereas there's only one of you.'

I didn't react. Not outside, anyway. Inside, it felt as if my vital organs had just launched into the hokey-cokey.

'We could have taken Tony out for a *long* drive, but we didn't. We decided to leave him where he was. Somebody wanted Tony taken care of – but gently. And Somebody wants you to know that anything can happen – anything at all. You have been a minor irritation, so far; but you're becoming irksome. Buying guns is not a good idea.'

I didn't bother denying it.

'You've been attracting too much attention to yourself. Now, this Somebody I'm speaking of, he's a man who doesn't like attention. He's quite happy to see the law take its course. It saddened him to learn that you survived the shooting: that didn't do his reputation very much good. He has a very good reputation. He'd chosen the right man for the job: he was a bit of a nutter – and maybe Somebody didn't *really* mind that the nutter got caught. But Somebody did want to see the job done properly. So, you see, you're really a blot on Somebody's copy-book. And the more you make him remember you, the more likely it is he's going to have you scratched out. What you must do from now on is let things happen as they are going to happen. Let the trial go ahead. Identify the man who shot you. Feel happy when he is convicted. Don't open your mouth. Don't mention us. Don't push it any further. It's not worth your while – it's very not worth your while. Please let me emphasize: the Somebody I mention isn't worried on his own behalf. If he's guilty of anything, it's of introducing one person to another. Of trying to help. One person who might be useful to another. That's all. Nothing more than that. This may, in retrospect, have been a trifle ill-considered. But he really isn't guilty of anything at all.'

'Here,' said the albino, turning round in his seat.

I thought at first he was going to hit me but he looked straight over my shoulder.

'Someone's on us,' he said.

The black man checked his rear-view.

'You see what I mean,' he said to me. 'This is unpleasant. I hope you understood what I just said. Now, when I stop the car, I want you to get out.'

He accelerated round the corner and did an emergency stop. I wasn't wearing my seat-belt, so was thrown forwards against the back of the passenger seat.

'Get out!' the black man shouted, showing real anger for the first time.

I fumbled around the handle.

'Shit,' the black man said, and accelerated off again.

I looked out the back window. The car following us was a Mercedes.

For a couple of minutes the black man did his best to lose it, but he couldn't manage – the rush-hour traffic was too syrupy.

'Have you got the handle this time?' the albino said. 'You pull it towards you – down under the ashtray.'

I tried it, and the door popped out.

Immediately, the car did an emergency-stop. The door was flung forwards by the force. I was surprised it didn't snap off.

'Go!' they both shouted.

Without hesitation, I jumped – and the moment I was out they were accelerating away.

The Mercedes slowed as it drove past. I had time to see a couple of men, one of them looking towards me inquiringly – seeing if I was still in one piece. Then they sped after the other two.

To my astonishment, a third car (a Rover) – also containing two men – roared past, paying a lot less attention to me.

I'd been dumped somewhere in the East End. I didn't know my way round at all. I found a main road and then a phonebox.

At least, I thought, I would now be able to give Anne-Marie a decent excuse as to why I was late and and why I didn't – for the first time – feel like having sex with her. When I called, Anne-Marie picked up before the second ring.

'Do you have enough cash to pay for a long taxi ride?' I asked.

'Where are you? I've been worried.'

'Do you?'

She said she did.

'I've been for a ride with some friends,' I said – slipping easily into thuggy understatement. 'I'll be home as soon as I can: have the money ready.'

It took me another half an hour to find a cab willing to go south of the river. I'd walked a couple of miles by then, trying to think of what had been happening to me: who had the people following me been? Surely one lot were the police: the guardian angels that Tony Smart had mentioned. But who were the others?

Paradoxically, I felt safer now that I'd been warned off. I wasn't going to make any more inquiries into the case: all I was after now was my revenge.

It worried me that 'Somebody' knew I had the gun. I'd hoped to keep that a secret: I'd wanted Dorothy to be the first person to know, looking up the barrel of it, realizing her stupidity – about to die, about to disintegrate, in the full consciousness of it. Bang.

But Somebody *did* know about it. And if this man – whoever he was – knew I'd got hold of a gun, then he probably knew I wanted to use it; and he must have a fairly good idea of who I wanted to use it on. Yet he hadn't warned me off that – just off himself.

I assumed that Somebody was one of the men who Tony had put Dorothy and Alun in touch with, when they were assiduously researching how to be murderers. If so, then he knew that Dorothy was behind Lily's killing. Must know.

And if I'd been followed even only part of the time, he also knew that I'd found out what she'd done.

He didn't have to be a criminal mastermind (though maybe he was) to work out my intentions . . .

But maybe he didn't care about my intentions: maybe they slotted in quite well with his other plans, whatever they were.

And so the warning-off had the opposite effect to that intended. It was quite clear that, if I left things to go their own way, if I allowed the police their day in court, if I *behaved*, then the hitman would get sent down – and nothing at all would happen to Alun and Dorothy. For some reason, the police were leaving them alone.

The hitman had kept his mouth shut, and with good reason. It wasn't going to be worth his while – in prison – to ditch some East End crime supremo in the shit. As things went, he was probably cushdy for the next ten years. If he kept quiet.

70

Anne-Marie was very relieved to see me back – and I spent most of the first half of the evening lying to her about where I'd been and who I'd been with. The threatening drive now lasted three or four hours, and its route took in most of London. I omitted all mention of Highgate Cemetery and, of course, of Josephine.

I had a bath first thing after I came through the door; getting rid of all residual powder-smells – though my fear-sweat had probably covered them anyway.

Anne-Marie brought me a glass of red wine, and sat on the loo whilst I soaked. She wanted to hear what real criminals were like.

'Do you think they had anything to do with that brick through the window?' she asked.

It was something I'd been thinking about myself.

'It seems a bit crude,' I said. 'So it probably *was* them.'

After we'd eaten some of Anne-Marie's leaden pasta, she fetched all the responses we'd so far received to the *Stage* advert. I didn't want to look at them. I was knackered. But I knew we had to do it as soon as possible.

We talked through the actors' applications: grinning colour photographs (grinning glossies – 5″ × 7″), all the different genres of actorly appearance – intense but chummy, lyrical but tough. About two hundred had replied.

The problem, if I really *had* been casting, was that all of them – without exception – looked like actors (and not ordinary human beings).

Lily had been artificial, too: but, I think, she had been aware of this. The world in which she appeared to be most at home was the world of her six cereal ads. Not on the actual set: there – when I had once or twice visited – she seemed constrained by the fact that she was subject to very uneven levels of attention. Sometimes, when she was in front of the cameras, it seemed as if everyone on set was completely ignoring her – her as *her* – and concentrating on the one subdivided aspect of her that had immediate importance for them: her lighting, sound-level, make-up; her as compositional element. Sometimes, it seemed that everybody was all at once attempting to touch her, alter her. Sometimes, she would be in a one-on-one huddle with the director. Sometimes, she rewarded the crew with flirtatiousness – the suggestion that she really *would* meet them in the pub afterwards. But when this was all resolved: edited down and tweaked and made as saleable as possible, Lily seemed to have found a greater and more satisfied form of existence.

It hurt me to see how far away from her I was in all this: the process by which I might join her was so excruciatingly long – and I didn't even have the beginnings of it. I didn't have the looks, the skin, the talent, the desire: the terrible wanting that – destined for success or obscurity – shone like a bottle tan from each of these actor's glossies. Even the falsest of them had something I hadn't – and any one of them could have met Lily in that artificial world which she now never left.

There was one piece of video with both of us on: a spoof of the cereal ad from the joke-reel a friendly director had put together after wrapping the sixth cereal ad. In it, I was a dead piece of light: embarrassing to other people even more than to myself. It was like shooting a ninety-year-old's eyes in extreme close-up; you felt there should be a law against it, winced away.

We worked through the three supporting rôles, and then came to the star. I picked out, from the photos, anyone who looked vaguely like Laurence.

'This is a possible,' I'd said.

Then I glimpsed his glossy, sticking out half-way down a pile. Impatiently, I waited for him to come through: delighted he'd bitten. But then Anne-Marie picked him out all by herself.

'This one looks good,' she said.

'Hmm.'

'He's the right age.'

'Experience?'

'Not a lot.'

'We'll put him in. Maybe get him out of the way early.'

It amused me to think how differently this conversation would have gone had Anne-Marie flicked quickly past his photo.

We narrowed it down to twenty, ten, then six. Anne-Marie was able to persuade me round to having a look at Laurence. But not without some difficulty.

'Okay, we'll forget the others for the moment – start with the male lead.'

'Good idea.'

'Could you phone them up and arrange for them to come round on Friday? Your flat, alright? I don't want to do it here. In case the press –'

'Fine.'

'And in . . . this order.'

'Yep.'

Laurence was last.

'What I'm going to do is get them to do a really difficult scene, one where they really have to act. Make them really give it loads. Here's the speech I thought I might use.'

Anne-Marie read it through.

'It's great,' she said. 'Really convincing.'

I hadn't expected anything less.

71

In the morning I waited until Anne-Marie had gone back home before having James take me into town.

First, I went shopping: to a cycle-equipment place just south of Sloane Square. Inside, it smelt freshly and wonderfully of rubber. Without wasting any time, I bought myself a very expensive bike – a Trek Death-Raider. (Everything was to be fitting: Synecdoche City.) I also bought a cycling top, shorts and shoes that were as close to the hitman's as possible, mirrored shades, a Day-Glo helmet, a pack of three pollution masks and a large courier bag.

In the shop's covered-in-decals changing room, I tried all of it on. When I looked at myself in the mirror, I was – for the first time in months – delighted with what I saw. The thing I liked most about these clothes was how modern and efficient they made me feel. Lycra. Nylon. Viscose. None of these fabrics had existed before this century. Christ, even bikes had hardly been invented back then.

I couldn't help comparing my half-wasted legs to the solid bike-powering machines of the hitman. But that didn't matter. By assuming this costume, I was drawing closer to something: closer to the man who had turned me into what I had become. He'd done this almost entirely, but not single-handedly. Really, it had been a team effort: Lily in life and death had contributed just as much: Lily and her deadborn, deathborn baby.

Looking at myself, I felt the kind of power that the hitman must have felt – sexing himself up for the kill.

His plan was obvious now. He could become just one among a dozen bike couriers, nipping between film companies in Soho. He would blend in, morph out, kill someone, kill another person, morph back in again, blend.

His plan – his failed plan.

After getting changed back into my normal clothes, I went up to the counter and paid. I put it all on my credit card. Next month's bill was going to be fun. Not my problem, though – by then I intended to be living on the state: prison food, prison wages. Either that or dead.

'Don't you want a bike lock?' the grungy assistant said.

'Nah,' I said. 'Don't need one.'

I left the bike behind. I would pick it up on Friday, the day I needed it. They'd have it ready, fine-tuned.

From a phonebox, I called the *Mirror* and asked for Sheila Burroughs. With Asif, Robert and Josephine all ruled out, the press was my last chance to find out about Lily's pregnancy. When I got through, Sheila was – to say the very least – surprised to hear from me.

'What's up? Have you decided to talk?'

'Maybe,' I said.

'What about?'

'Something.'

'I'm interested,' she said. 'In anything.'

We arranged to meet in an hour.

Next, I took a cab to Le Corbusier and made the booking for Friday evening – in person. Nothing substantial had changed: nothing that would destroy the symmetry of my revenge. The layout of the tables was identical. The maître d' wasn't around, but my favourite waiter was.

'You remember,' I said. 'I wanted a booking.'

'Of course,' Michael said. 'How are you?'

'A lot better, thanks.'

'When for?'

'Friday evening. Eight o'clock. And I'd like . . . my usual table.'

'The reservation . . .'

'Isn't in my name. It's Pale, Dorothy Pale.'

I wasn't risking Alun's name: and Dorothy was the one I wanted the police to identify, straight off. Dorothy was to make the first editions and the mid-evening news.

'For two?'

'For two.'

'She's the actress, isn't she?' Michael asked.

'Yes.' I said. 'A close friend.'

As he wrote her name in the reservations book, I was conscious of his being unusually conscious of me. An idea occurred: he might be useful. I decided to chance it.

'I'm busy for the next couple of days, but how would you like to go out sometime – for a drink?'

He looked at me – our relationship changing in a way he seemed to have hoped for. His eyes were twinkling and his voice went up a couple of notes.

'That'd be lovely.'

'I'll give you a call.'

'Okay.'

He pulled a card out of his back pocket and gave it to me. Beneath his name was the single word ACTOR.

'See ya soon.'

I hated being cruel. It had just been an experiment. After it all went down, he'd probably understand.

Ah, his little face!

I felt like a very minor celebrity, hitting on groupies – obvious but sometimes fun. And, god, the guy had seen me being shot. He'd been around for the blood. In fact, actually, he'd saved my life. I owed him a drink if nothing else.

I spent a few minutes looking over the back entrance to Le Corbusier. Nothing special. It would do.

72

Sheila Burroughs and I met up in Pâtisserie Valerie, Soho, as arranged. I walked in the door, squeezing between the glass shelves full of cakes and the customers waiting to pay. Sheila was there early, and had secured one of their rare tables for two. She recognized me, waving me over the moment I came in. She offered to pay for coffee, cake, whatever I wanted – a cappuccino was all. I felt like I'd drunk a couple of quintuple espressos already.

Sheila was a frowzy blonde woman, with stained teeth and the general atmosphere of knowing how if not to dominate then at least to exist alongside men. She had been submerged in a tobacco cloud of masculinity for so long that her arms and legs had thickened, her voice deepened, her manner altered, her values adapted. Her earrings were as unfeminizing as those of a female body builder. She wore too many large gold rings upon her fingers – suggesting a sentimentality that might come in handy when interviewing the bereaved. Even at a supposedly left-wing paper like the *Mirror* these working-class talismans (like a lucky-charm bracelet clinking up against the Queen's white satin gloves) would hold her back: she needed to minimalize her lifestyle to maximalize her potential. A career adviser would have told her these things. (A career adviser would probably have warned her off the news desk.)

Sheila looked harassed but was trying to suppress any hint of impatience. She was clearly angry with me for not having chosen to speak to her at a time when the story was hot. Now that I'd changed my mind, she was flattered that I'd chosen her. (Even though, in print, the *Mirror* had offered me the chance to put my side of the story – blank cheque.) She was, however, or so I thought, angry at herself for even being flattered. She wanted to be hard and neutral, but couldn't: this was *her* story – she'd been first to arrive on my doorstep and last to leave. Righteously did she deserve it; passionately (though not too deeply) did she desire it.

The waitress brought our orders. Sheila had capitulated in the face of Irish coffee and a large Danish.

A Dictaphone sat on the table between us, half-covered by a copy of the *Sun*.

'How much are you thinking of?'

I hadn't thought of money at all. However, the grander gesture, of not taking any or giving it all to charity, *did* – on the moment – appeal.

'This isn't an interview,' I said. 'You can quote me on it – but only on Monday. If you don't agree to that, we stop talking now.'

'I need to know what *it* is first.' She offered me a cigarette; lit one for herself; ash flew over her Danish; she tutted; hips-lips, lips-hips.

'It's a story – a new story. A new spin on an old story.'

'Listening,' she said.

And I told her as directly as possible: 'When Lily was killed, she was six or seven weeks pregnant.'

'Oh my god.' She bit down upon her thumbnail.

'I found this out from Asif. He didn't tell you, which surprises me: I guess he thought there was still a chance he could keep his job.'

'He's lost it now, you know. From what I've heard he was very pissed off with you.'

'I wonder, do pathologists have to respect confidentiality – no disclosure of what passed between doctor and corpse?'

'Anyway,' she said, smiling now she knew there was a story.

'I wanted to find out if I was the father. It was a boy. You

294

would want to know, wouldn't you? Anyway, I don't think Asif knows: the DNA stuff was done by the police forensic people. So the police *do* know – and they won't tell me. I think a bit of pressure from you might speed them up.'

'Well . . .' Sheila said. 'Don't overestimate –'

'I just want to know who to mourn, whether to mourn.'

'You say you want to know who the father was. But why? Isn't it certain it was you?'

'No,' I said, neutrally. 'It's not.'

'I see.'

'Lily was having an affair – several.'

'With who?'

'Alun Grey, and several more. But he's the only real possibility – I've checked the others.'

'Who's he?'

Yes! Not tabloid-famous now, but he would be – soon.

'The actor – Shakespeare.'

'The one you kept going to see at the theatre?'

'Uh-huh.'

'Damn,' she bit hard on her thumb. 'I knew I should have checked that whole thing out. I suppose you were turning up just to piss him off?'

'You could say that.'

'Are you sure I can't quote you?'

'Not till after the weekend.'

'Why not?'

'Do you think you'll be able to find anything out?'

'The Met can be a bit leaky, now and again. At worse, we might be able to force a press conference out of them – make them look shitty and mean. You might need to do a bit of crying for the cameras. If you really want to play the victim, that is.'

'I don't want to have to do anything. That's your job.'

'We'll be back on your doorstep.'

'I'll only speak to you, Sheila.'

She opened her handbag and pulled out a crumpled contract.

'Sign this,' she said.

'In the politest possible way, *fuck off.*'

'It was worth a try.'

I took a sip of my cappuccino, then asked: 'Where do you think you'll start?'

'Asif. The hospital. Then try and get the Met to spring a leak. Then I'll publish.'

'When?'

'If no-one else gets it . . . this Thursday.'

'Don't worry, contract or not I won't talk to anyone else.'

'Thank you,' she said, about to start flirting, but giving up the attempt as she wouldn't have done a few years earlier. Now the next question came blankly, almost without interest: 'Why me?'

'Because you're a woman,' I said. 'And I didn't see too many more of those outside my door.'

'Right.'

'Have you ever been pregnant?' I asked.

'I had an abortion about ten years ago.' Courageously matter-of-fact.

'Then you know how I feel. Oh, Lily was going to have the thing aborted anyway – but don't print that.'

'Wow,' Sheila said. 'Are you alright? You don't look too well.'

'You're the first person I've told.'

'Don't worry,' she smiled. 'I won't tell anyone.'

We stood up together.

'Aren't you going to have that?' I asked, pointing to her untouched Danish.

'No,' she said. 'Not hungry any more.'

73

By the time I finished all my errands, it was early evening – grey and smoggy. As a change, I took the Underground home. For the first time in months, I was returning home with the rush-hour commuters. Even when I'd been editing sharks at the Discovery Channel, this had been a fairly rare occurrence. Usually, back then, I either finished early or worked late. There was always either too much work or too little – deadline or deadtime.

As I stood there, holding on to a rail of stainless steel, I expected to feel some sort of connection with the people around me. All of us had gone out to do a day's work, all of us were returning home more slowly and uncomfortably than we would have wished. Instead, I felt an almost total separation from, and – I have to say it – superiority to, every single person in the carriage. They merely had jobs; I had a mission.

For the first time, I realized how real criminals felt. (Strict in my definition, I felt that I would only become a real criminal myself after I'd shot Dorothy. Buying the gun wasn't enough.) It wasn't just the fact they committed crimes – took something without paying for it, left someone permanently injured. It was also that they walked around, day to day, with the quiet knowledge of what they'd done. Of course, given this knowledge, they were always going to feel superior to all the tax-paying, law-abiding John and Jane Dohs surrounding them. Those with the knowledge were different. They had something extra. They had seen beneath the surface. They knew how the thing really worked. They were outlaws. And so was I.

Standing there, among the dead-faced strap-hangers, I thought about my beautiful gun – and I couldn't stop myself from smiling.

Something made me panic the moment I saw my front door – still covered in blood-red paint. I'd been planning to move out the following day. But now that I'd told Sheila about the baby, it was only a matter of time before the paparazzi were back on my door-step. That was a rationalization, however. What really decided me was the paint. I couldn't stay another night in this flat.

Anne-Marie was in the living room, watching TV.

'Pack up,' I said. 'We're moving out.'

'I've phoned all the actors,' she said.

'We've got to go.'

'Didn't you hear what I said?'

'You phoned all of them?'

'Yes. They're coming at the times you wanted.'

'Great. Get packed.'

'Where are we going?' she asked.

'I'll tell you when we get in the car,' I said.

She didn't oppose me – nurse-humouring a fractious patient. Of course, because she didn't live with me, she hardly had any stuff to get together. And all I cared about was my gun.

Still, packing up took me about an hour. I finished with a suitcase full of clothes, many of which I might never wear again. There were the other usual holiday things: alarm clock, shaving kit, medicines. I also fetched a length of good strong rope from the garden shed. Anything else I didn't have but needed I would buy.

We carried the bags out and stowed them in the boot of Anne-Marie's car.

Anne-Marie got in the driver's seat.

As I walked back towards the flat, I looked around for any of the familiar following-me cars. They weren't there – not on my way.

I locked the front door.

'Before we drive off,' I said, after I'd sat down in the passenger seat, 'I want to tell you that I think we're going to be followed – and you're going to have to get rid of them.'

Anne-Marie looked round as obviously as any person could.

'Don't!' I said.

'Please don't patronize me,' she said. 'What do you want me to do, then?'

'Just drive off. We'll see first.'

It was nine o'clock already. One last time, I tried to think of anything I might have forgotten, anything I might have left behind. But there was nothing.

'Okay,' I said. 'Let's go.'

I was slightly disappointed not to see any of the parked cars pull out behind us.

'Keep going,' I said.

'What else am I going to do?'

Our tail joined us on Mortlake High Street.

'Go left here,' I said, to confirm – and confirmed it was.

'That Mercedes is the one following us,' I said.

'No-it-isn't,' said Anne-Marie.

'Try driving in circles for a bit,' I said.

Anne-Marie went twice round the next big roundabout. The Mercedes followed us all the way. Anne-Marie was convinced.

'Who are they?' she asked.

'Friends of my friends from yesterday afternoon,' I said. 'Or the police. Or journalists. I don't know any more – and I'm almost certain it doesn't make any real difference. Now, do you think you can get rid of them?'

'Where are we going?'

'Notting Hill. Lily's old flat.'

Anne-Marie smiled. She liked the idea of being able to get in amongst all Lily's old stuff.

'Come on,' I said.

She tried a few tentative manœuvres – accelerating away from traffic lights, stopping to fill up on petrol. Nothing seemed to work. Then she said, 'Who do you think they're following, the car or you?'

'Me, I'd say.'

'I'll drop you at the next Underground. Give me a ring on my mobile when you get to the flat, and I'll come over.'

'What if they keep following you?'

'I'll just go home – you can still phone me.'

I almost loved her, then.

At the next Tube station, Anne-Marie slowed the car. I got out and rushed in. I didn't look back.

Later, Anne-Marie told me that, at the exact moment I bolted, the Mercedes had been unsighted by a bus. The men in the Merc (who she described as 'thugs'), didn't notice that I was gone until a couple of hundred yards later – by which time I was safely on a Tube train.

However, although I was in no immediate physical danger, my anxiety levels increased. I'd escaped, but would Anne-Marie?

She still had all my stuff in the back of her car – including, oh god, the bag with the gun.

I couldn't spend too much time worrying about that – things would either happen or they wouldn't. Instead, I concentrated on making my way surreptitiously to Lily's. As it was clear that no-one had followed me on to the Underground, I took the most direct route to Notting Hill. But once there, I approached the flat in a very indirect and cautious manner. When I was sure that I wasn't being watched, I snuck in the front door.

After a quick look round to make sure everything was alright, I called Anne-Marie.

'It's fine,' she said. 'I lost them.'

'How?' I asked.

'Don't keep underestimating me.'

This episode seemed to have changed her slightly – she was more in control: of me, of us.

'You can come over,' I said. 'If you like.'

'Oh, thank you,' said Anne-Marie.

She arrived half an hour later, and we carried my stuff in and up.

'You must feel a bit weird being here,' she said, looking round the living room.

I explained that most of the weirdness had occurred during my previous visit.

Anne-Marie examined the kitchen just as if she were flat-hunting.

'You know,' she said. 'I never got much sense of Lily from this place. It still doesn't seem very – you know – *her*.'

I resented this observation all the more for recognizing its truth. Lily's tastes had always come off-the-peg. Whatever was 'in' that month, that's what ended up in our flat. Her flat. It scared me that Anne-Marie could be so perceptive.

'Lily was very busy,' I said. 'She didn't have much time for home-making.'

'*Busy* isn't exactly the description I was looking for. I know she was busy.'

We went through into the bedroom.

I lay back on the bed in the hope that Anne-Marie would join me, simplifying things. She didn't. Instead, she pulled open one of the closet doors.

'God,' she said. 'All her clothes.'

For a moment or two she flicked hanger and thumbed fabric, emitting the occasional hum of approval or whistle of envy. Then Anne-Marie turned round and, looking at me very directly, said: 'Are you still in love with her?'

All the questions.

I tried to calculate the risks of admitting out loud that I was (crying, losing control, pissing Anne-Marie off); and my moment of calculation gave me away – gave Anne-Marie time to take advantage.

'It's okay,' she said, sitting down non-sexually on the edge of the bed. 'It's not as if I can't see for myself.'

(Non-sexually. This was about as unsexy as it gets – telling an almost-girlfriend about a dead ex-girlfriend.)

'Lily was . . .'

Anne-Marie waited. I knew what she was thinking: I might have loved Lily (might *still* do), but I'd never come close to knowing her. If I had known her, I could have talked about her – and, as I talked, it would have seemed as if Lily were only in the next room; that we could hear her feet squeaking and creaking on the polished pine; smell the sweet smoke of her just-lit cigarette; hear her humming, monotonously, as always. But, in that flat, at that moment, Lily was a completely dead thing – a dead thing dying again – dying through my inability to make her even partially live.

Suddenly, superstitiously, I leapt up off the bed, strode over to one of the wall-closets. Something in me was convinced that behind its blank white door I would find Lily's upright skeleton – not mouldering or clad with flesh-remnants, but clean and fresh as an anatomical model.

I pulled open the closet door.

The smell of Lily was instantly around and about me: half-alive, half-dead. All of a sudden, Lily was present – present in all her selfishness. (Lily's selfishness had been her skeleton: it had held all that beautiful flesh in place. If her cheekbones were a photographer's dream, it was the nightmare below the surface that defined them.) She was present for Anne-Marie, as well; showing up through my distress like bones on an X-ray. Being skeletal had always been Lily's one true ambition – and now it was doubly achieved: here, in our minds; there, in her grave.

When I turned round, Anne-Marie was looking at me with real concern. I needed to say something, to explain my mad leap.

'Why don't you try something on?' I suggested, as casually as I could.

Anne-Marie got up from the bed and came over to where I was standing.

'Can I?' she said childishly.

I hadn't expected her to want to put on Lily's clothes.

'Really?' I asked.

'What would *you* like me to wear?'

If I was going to be sick, I might as well projectile vomit: I picked out the ghost dress.

'Put this on,' I said, picking the hanger out.

'This?' said Anne-Marie, obviously delighted that I'd started with one of the designer frocks.

'Yes,' I said.

'Right,' she said.

'Fine,' I said.

'Out,' she said.

The hard floors and bare walls of the bedroom were turning our talk to minimalistic monosyllables.

I went out into the living room, then through into the kitchen for a glass of water. It was a cup of tea I really wanted, but I knew there was a chance that Anne-Marie would want sex in Lily's old clothes. The thought of a cup of tea going cold whilst we fucked was somehow unbearable.

I tried to work out why I was doing this, having this done; partly, it seemed to me, for the chance – once again – of humiliating Anne-Marie. I knew, from the way her hips felt in my hands, from her heaviness against and on top of me, that she was several sizes larger than Lily. But if humiliation were my main motive, I should have gone for a frock from Lily's modelling period. That was when she'd been skinniest. (Most of the weight had been lost down the toilet bowl, but a few pounds had dissolved into the swimming pool.) The ghost dress was loose. It would accommodate and perhaps even flatter Anne-Marie's curves.

'Ready!' Anne-Marie shouted.

I wanted longer to work out how I felt. My emotions were so complicated that I seemed to spend most of my time just spooling through them on fast-forward – checking to see what was on the tape; intending to go back later and watch the whole thing properly.

As I entered, Anne-Marie was inspecting herself modellishly in the full-length mirror.

'Ta-dah!' she exclaimed, spinning round to strike a pose: one of her arms up, ostrich fashion; the other punching her hip.

I looked at her, trying to put my face into some sort of unhorrified shape.

There was the sound of thinly stitched seams unpicking. The arm was tearing out at the armpit; a rip was forming a couple of inches beneath Anne-Marie's left breast, exposing flesh.

I'd miscalculated.

At that exact moment, Anne-Marie looked so pathetic I almost loved her. (That she was prepared to make herself appear this grotesque, and all for me.) She wasn't a model, never could have been – no-one knew that better than her; she, who'd sat watching nervous schoolgirls turn into psychotic world-famous stick insects. I knew, too: I'd lived with a model. I knew how models related to clothes – how they dived into them as casually as into a hotel swimming-pool; how the fabric swished, watery, into the right shapes – flowing over the hollows they have where most of us have bulges.

Anne-Marie held the pose; held the smile. She had to. Where she was standing (submerged in a dress where Lily once floated), there was no oxygen. She had to hold the smile, the breath. To breathe out would be to bring drowning that little bit closer. And, more practically, breathing out might risk another rip under her other breast.

By default I had become Anne-Marie's life-guard: either I rescued her, or she would turn blue-lipped and lose the irises of her eyes in the dead heavens of her skull.

I dived in, putting my fingers into the small tear – feeling Anne-Marie's pitiful white skin against my knuckles – and I pulled the swimming-pool surface apart: giving her room to breathe, allowing her body out into a world of space that wouldn't satirize it, pulling myself under, pulling her out.

'Agh!' she cried. 'Don't!'

'Why not?'

She'd taken her bra and pants off.

There was now a shingle-size tear around Anne-Marie's middle. The fabric was getting tight and ropey as we pulled against it. It would only rip in one direction – sideways; and we'd done all the sideways ripping we could. To rip more, we needed scissors – or risked bruising and crushed nipples and you-hurt-me recriminations. I paused: a final rescue needed. I pulled my T-shirt off over my head – allowing her to copy. The top half of the dress came off, leaving her semi-bruised by her own struggling fists; as if she'd been fighting or woken up puffy out of nightmare-sleep. As she started to pull the bottom half down, I saw a tear appear around her belly – I pulled it, and – mercifully – we had our first modellish, physical luck in the whole dress scene: it started to peel away in a diagonal downwards strip.

'Turn around,' I said.

Anne-Marie started the wrong way but almost immediately corrected herself. I pulled at the dress, extracting it into an uneven four-inch strip – until I reached the harder-stitched hem at the bottom; and Anne-Marie had to step out into my sarcastic arms.

We were laughing, for want of any better or more socially approved response. To tell the truth, we were lost – caught in a moral white-out. There was so much guilt in what we'd been doing, and so much innocence – it was hard to tell which predominated. The whole scene felt so much like the very very end of childhood and the earliest beginnings of middle age (dressing up, fancy dress).

This was the moment we both knew our relationship couldn't

last – but because of the difficulty and pain we'd gone through together to gain that knowledge, we felt a sudden tenderness for each other.

On coming into the flat we had known we were going to have sex but we hadn't known what sort of sex it was going to be. Now, we knew: we were going to have the sex of pathos, of anticipated regret.

When we finally fell asleep, it was with our backs to each other – frankly separate.

74

The next morning I took the Tube to Victoria station, then a coach out into the country. After getting off in the most rural-looking town, I took another bus out to a small village. For half an hour, I tried to find somewhere obscure and secluded. Eventually I discovered quite a thick little copse of grid-planted fir trees.

I took the gun out of the sports bag for the first time since buying it. She was more beautiful than ever – a thing of pure brutal accomplishment. It still amazed me that there were men whose minds were constantly employed in trying to improve the design of machines intended to kill other men – and no-one arrested these designers, or called them murderers.

Handling the weapon made me feel like an art terrorist/theorist, convinced that I and I alone had discovered the perfect painting implement. This metal device was a creator of massive blood-flowers (a flesh-gardener) – huge gorgeous gory blooms, thrown up on walls and mirrors. This was the non-brush that Jackson Pollock spent his whole life in quest of – creating an instant composition of red and grey: all the Great Art Themes of Life and Death; controversy over the manner of the art's making (dripping/triggering); the randomizing element (loss of control but control over loss of control); the collaborative nature of any true bullet art. (Dot. Dot. Dot.) And I was about to go and collaborate on a couple of specific deaths – painting them all over Le Corbusier's shattered mirrors. This was going to be a hell of a grand opening: of heads, of arteries. Paint no longer a buried metaphor for blood. This would be authentic impasto – the real Real Thing: Death. Perhaps I should put a call through to *ArtForum* first; have them send a couple of critics along. Get some restaurant critics in there, too.

I loaded the clip up into the handle, butting it in with my wrist – the force was unnecessary – it slid in like good, wanted sex. I clicked off the safeties, turning the machine dangerous.

Just as the gun-contact had shown me, I cocked the firing mechanism: this was necessary for the first shot. After that, the pressure generated by the bullet just fired re-cocked the gun automatically.

I pointed the gun at the exposed trunk of one of the fir trees. I wanted to pull the trigger but couldn't: I wanted to know how loud the gun would be before I fired it. I thought of different bangs, snaps, cracks, pops.

The day was sunny but too windy for comfort. Sounds might carry unexpected distances in unexpected directions. There were farms close by, and I couldn't guarantee that no-one would hear the shots. But maybe that didn't matter. Perhaps they'd just think it was someone disposing of rabbits or ramblers or something. I had no choice, really. I had to test the gun, and here was the safest place I'd managed to find.

I went off into some kind of daze – and when I came round I found myself stood there with the barrel of the gun pointing into the side of my head.

Never before had I knowingly been so close to suicide. There had been low times, back in the hospital. But when the urge had been there, the means hadn't – and vice versa.

For a couple of instants I let myself feel the possibility of remorse: maybe the best thing for everyone was to kill myself right here.

Then I saw Dorothy, onstage, flailing her way through Lady Macbeth's hand-washing, and I knew that this was a woman incapable of truly acknowledging the depth of her guilt.

Maybe in the instant between me firing the gun and it splatting her brains out, she would dive into the knowledge – slow-motion.

Suddenly, I felt something rip down through me – as if I were a newspaper and someone were tearing off a strip. I felt: anger, resentment, hatred.

If there was a final moment of decision to go ahead, then this was it.

Fuck Alun. Fuck Dorothy.

I pulled the trigger.

The bang was much quieter than I'd expected and the recoil far more gentle.

Ah, I thought, *those Germans*.

No longer worried about interruption, I walked up to the tree to examine the hole where Dorothy's imaginary head had been.

At the point of impact there should have been a chunk ripped out at least as big as my fist.

Going slightly closer, I saw the bullet lodged in the tree's outer bark. A single touch was enough to make it fall.

I didn't need to test it, but I did – I stepped back a couple of paces and fired off three rounds into the tree, point-blank.

Nothing. No destruction. No penetration.

I'd been sold blanks.

I pulled the clip out and looked at one of the bullets, suddenly so much less beautiful. But, from what my untrained eye could see, there was no way of telling that this wasn't a real bullet.

Distraught, I got the bus back to the village and the coach back to London.

It couldn't all be for nothing – not my plans and lies and adaptations. I wasn't going to allow this to thwart me. Everything had to be done in a particular order. This had to be corrected. Otherwise the order would be destroyed. I would correct this.

75

From Victoria coach station, I called my gun-contact's mobile number. Doing my best not to sound too pissed off, I arranged to meet him in our usual pub. He said that he could be there in half an hour. I took a cab down to South-east London. When I walked into the grotty public bar, my contact was there – chatting to the landlord, ready to do business.

'Toilet,' I said.

He followed me in and locked the door behind us.

'You sold me fucking blanks,' I said.

I held out a few of them in my hand.

'Never seen these before in my life,' he said. 'Honest.'

'They don't work.'

'You remember – the ones I sold you were gold at the end, these are silver. Look.'

I had a vague memory.

'Someone must have switched them,' he said. 'Nicked them. Who's had hold of the gun since you got it? Been out of your sight, has it?'

Oh most definitely.

I remembered Anne-Marie's curiosity about the contents of my sports bag. Was it possible that the one person I'd thought I could trust had started deceiving me? It was a mad thought: where would she have been able to get hold of blank ammunition? One answer was all I could think of: she'd phoned up Vicky, she'd told the police. That meant not only that Anne-Marie suspected but that the police *knew* what I was intending. In which case, why hadn't they arrested me? I didn't have time right now to think of that.

'I want live ones – ones that'll do some serious fucking damage.'

'Give me ten minutes,' he said.

'How do I know I'll see you again?'

'I'm not going to skip the country just 'cos of this, now am I?'

'No,' I said. 'But I need them today.'

'You'll get them –'

'And this time I want to test them.'

He held back. 'Tricky-dicky,' he said.

'But not impossible.'

He looked at the pissy floor, his shoes. 'No.'

I waited for him in the bar while he disappeared off down the street. This was one of the worst moments. I truly believed I'd never see him again. But half an hour later, he came back and – after a quick word with the landlord – beckoned me to follow him.

A door was pulled open in the floor behind the bar. Down a steep ladder and we were in a large, dark cellar.

Aluminium casks lining the walls; plastic shrink-wrapped lemonade bottles; a slightly wet concrete floor; a musty smell – half beer, half rats.

'Come along here,' he said.

I followed.

Someone had come down into the cellar after us: I recognized him – a burly barman.

Nods, back and forth.

'The jukebox will play a little louder upstairs,' he said. 'And Paul's going to shift some barrels. That's the best we can do. You get one shot only.'

He pulled out a fresh box of bullets, held one up for my inspection.

'Gold. Live.'

Then he loaded up.

There was a pile of smelly old mattresses in the corner. In front of them was the old-oak circle of a broken table-top. My gun-contact aimed at it.

'Shoot into that,' he said.

He gave the nod to Paul, who started shifting barrels around. The report of when they hit the floor fired off like gunshots. Upstairs, the music began to thud louder and deeper.

'Quickly,' he said.

I took aim, tried to coincide with one of Paul's crashes, squeezed the trigger.

Greater recoil, louder noise – and a hole the size of a golf ball left in the circle of wood.

'Satisfied?' he asked.

'The same number of bullets,' I said.

'Minus that one.' He pointed at the hole.

'Satisfied,' I said.

We shook on it.

'Can I keep the blanks?' I asked.

He didn't let go.

'What use are they to me?' he said.

He still had hold of my hand, firmly.

'You can count this as a freebie. I wouldn't do it for all my customers, but seeing how you paid well over the odds for that gun . . .'

He smiled and finally let go.

'You can stop now,' he said to Paul as we walked by.

We shook hands again in the public bar. The music had again been turned down. Everyone was too sensible to look too closely at the two men who might or might not just have fired a gun in the cellar.

I paid for a couple of drinks with a fifty and told the landlord to keep the change. I didn't expect gratitude, which was lucky, because I got none.

Carrying the same suspicious sports bag, I walked out of the pub – as close to being one of the lads as I'd ever been. But still pretty far off at that.

The question immediately came up of what to do now. Could I trust Anne-Marie not to pull the same trick again? What could she have told the police? Not everything. Had she mentioned the script? The audition? Laurence? No, that connection she couldn't have made.

My first instinct was to confront her. Then I thought better of it. If she didn't know – but how? – then my every question would be self-incriminating. *What did you do with my bullets? What have you said to the police?* I decided to act as normally as possible – whilst no longer trusting her.

Of course, I'd still have to leave her alone for periods. But she wouldn't have the gun or the bullets to fool around with. Those I could leave somewhere safe. However, the only place I could think of to stow them was in the garden shed at my old address in Mortlake. It was far from ideal. I was pretty sure I'd be able to get there unobserved today. But on Friday, after Sheila's story had gone in? I would have to gamble that the paparazzi would have discovered (from my delightfully helpful neighbours) that I hadn't been home for several days.

I took a black cab direct to Mortlake.

I could tell something was wrong as soon as we rounded the corner and began to drive down my street. Something was wrong in the composition of the place. Something, I realized, was missing. But it was only when we drew up half-way along the street, just as I'd told the cabbie, that I saw – or rather didn't see – what it was that was missing. It was my house, my flat. Instead, where it had once been, there stood a charred black mass haphazardly cordoned off with blue-and-white police crime-scene tape.

'This it?' asked the cabbie, after I'd sat silent and motionless for a minute or so.

I nodded.

'Yes,' I said weakly. 'I used to live here.'

He turned round to look at me.

'Lucky you moved out then, isn't it?'

I checked again, looking at the doors of the houses to the left and right – hoping that I'd made a mistake, and that I'd see (welcome this time) the blood-red paint-sloshed porch. But everything I'd taken in at first glance was confirmed.

Through the black gape of the front door, I could see all the way down the ruined hall and out into the back garden. The shed, as far as I could make out, was still intact. I didn't need a key to get at it. But then, neither did anyone else.

'Are you alright, mate?' the cabbie asked.

It was only then I realized that I'd started to cry. I thought back to my pathetic bonfire of everything-to-do-with-Lily. The arsonists, whoever they were, had merely completed the job. I should have felt thankful towards them. I had supposedly left everything behind already. Up until this point in my life, most of my valued possessions had been made out of paper: favourite books, diaries. A few years ago, plastic had made its entrance: videos, cassettes, Polaroids, CDs. Only now (with the gun) had metal become a matter of sentiment. Really, I'd no longer had any need of anything that had been destroyed. The burning of it all, however, was something I myself would have put off – perhaps for the rest of my life; and perhaps the putting off would have been the ruining of my life. No person should become the archivist of their past loves. Not to the exclusion of future ones, certainly. But I couldn't help feeling bereft. In my head, I played back the now-destroyed tape of Lily's cereal adverts. The image had already deteriorated. She jumped from expression to expression, costume to costume. Now she was in the shower being stabbed; now she was standing beside me in the spoofed ad.

'I'm sorry, mate,' said the cabbie. 'But the meter *is* still running.'

I couldn't face becoming a modern genre-piece for some imaginary CNN news crew – picking stoically through the ashes of my gone home.

'Notting Hill,' I said.

I'd decided to return to Lily's flat and hide the gun under the floorboards – in the secret place where Lily used to stash her drugs and diaries.

'Are you sure you're alright, mate?' asked the cabbie.

'Notting Hill,' I said.

The cab pulled off.

I couldn't stop myself looking back at the house. The wood of the door-frame was black streaked with white, just like Dorothy's hair. I turned to face forwards.

The escalation was almost complete, I thought: from rubbish-tipping through brick-tossing to building-torching. The only thing left was a direct assault upon my body: injury then fatality then desecration.

It was only as we turned out of my road that the thought occurred: Who did this?

76

When I told Anne-Marie about the fire, she took my hand and led me into Lily's bedroom. We lay down.

'I thought, what if you'd been been inside,' I said. 'I thought, what if you were dead.'

She consoled me and I consoled her.

'Just think if we'd been staying there,' she said.

'Yes,' I agreed.

After a while, I asked if she could go to the shops and get me some painkillers. When she said she had a huge stash of Nurofen in her handbag, I insisted on another brand. Reluctantly, she went out.

As soon as she was gone, I called Sheila at the *Mirror* office. She picked up.

'Sheila,' she said.

The sound of typing in the background.

'I know about the fire,' I said.

'Phew,' she said. 'I thought I was going to have to break the news to you.'

'Why should that scare you? It's your job: standing on the doorsteps of bereaved mothers, asking them how they feel about government policy on this issue.'

'I can see you're a little upset.'

'It was a horrible flat.'

'We'll have to mention it in the story.'

'I never liked it.'

Sheila paused, then tried to get the conversation back on track.

'The story's going in for tomorrow. Front page, I think – unless something stronger comes in. Where will you be, if I need to contact you?'

'I'll be out of contact.'

'A phone number.'

'No, you can trace those.'

'Please.'

'Here's my mother's.' And I gave it to her. 'What did Alun say when you asked him?'

'He said, "No comment" and shut the front door.'

'Did he sound upset?'

'Why are you so interested?'

'I think he knows whether or not it was his kid.'

'You mean someone's told him?'

'I mean, he knows when he last fucked Lily.'

Sheila spent a moment taking this in.

'We've got some nice pictures of her,' she said. 'Looking maternal.'

'You have to protect me from the rest of the press,' I said. 'Keep them away from me.'

'Only if you go exclusive.'

'No, this has got to be a complete feeding-frenzy.'

'You're on your own, then.'

I thought of Anne-Marie's betrayal.

'I am that already.'

Sheila let this go by.

'Who do you think torched your flat?'

'Believe me, Sheila, it could be any number of people.'

End of conversation.

Anne-Marie came back from the shops and handed me the painkillers. The look she gave me was enough to make me want to swallow the whole pack.

'Are you okay?' she asked.

'I'm fine,' I said. 'What did you do about the actors?'

317

'Don't you remember?' she said. 'I told you.'

'What did you do?'

'I phoned them all,' she said.

'All of them?'

'Yes. They're all coming.'

'You're certain?'

'Conrad, what is it? Talk to me.'

I took two of the painkillers.

77

Thursday.

In the morning I went out to the newsagent's to buy the papers.

The headline was BRANDY'S BABY.

A Mirror Exclusive.

Byline: Sheila Burroughs.

My photograph had not been put on the cover of the *Mirror* – that had been saved for a shot of the maternal-looking Lily juxtaposed with a shot of Alun in his greatcoat – walking fast and looking at the pavement.

Yes!

I flicked through the other tabloids. A couple of unresearched spoilers had got in, but no-one had scooped Sheila. I went back to the *Mirror*. There Sheila's picture was, beside the byline: all working-class perm and grinning aspirations. Perfect, and not like Sheila at all. I turned to the inner pages: a retread, from cuttings, of Lily's shooting; a slightly bitter going-over of Asif's articles (why, if he knew, didn't he tell us about the baby?). As promised, I was sympathetically portrayed and not directly quoted.

'It's a terrible thing,' said the newsagent. 'Terrible.'

'Yes,' I said. 'It was.'

'Such a young girl, and so beautiful.'

'Well . . .'

'You were a very lucky young man.'

I didn't want to start an argument.

Sheila had overplayed the pregnancy and underplayed the

fatherhood issue, as far as she'd been able. They would be getting at Alun tomorrow, just as they'd got at Asif. Thankfully, she'd slanted the whole thing towards making the police look bad. The story ended with a demand that they declare who the baby's father was. In the public interest.

To change my appearance slightly, I went into the nearest barber's and had a crew cut. I decided I wouldn't shave.

A copy of the *Mirror* was open on the glass table behind the cutting chairs. The barber didn't say anything but I was terribly aware of his nonchalance.

As well as the tabloids, I guessed that the police would be quite seriously interested in tracking me down and talking to me about the torching. It would be, I guessed, highly suspicious if I didn't come forward. They might even start thinking that I'd done it myself.

When Vicky and Anne-Marie met, they had talked for quite a while. I couldn't be sure what had and hadn't been said. It seemed likely, though, that Vicky would be able to find Anne-Marie – either through the phonebook or the modelling agency. I wondered how long this would take, once Vicky found out I'd disappeared.

Back from the barber's, I showed Anne-Marie the front page of the *Mirror*.

'Why've you had your hair shaved off?'

'I was just fed up with it.'

Anne-Marie took in the headline.

'Shit,' she said. 'How long have you known?'

'A while.'

'Why didn't you tell me?' she wailed. 'Why don't you ever tell me anything?'

'It wasn't important.'

She wasn't listening. Slowly, she sat down upon the sofa – reading all the stories from beginning to end.

For the next couple of minutes I got nothing out of her but the sound of pages turning.

The phone started to ring. She moved.

'Don't answer it,' I said. 'It's bad enough that the thing's connected.'

'But it could be anyone.'

'If you pick it up, they'll know we're here – that someone's here – and we won't be able to come back for at least a week.'

'What do you mean?'

'The paparazzi – press and photographers. It'll be open season on me now.'

'You don't seem very upset.'

'I wanted this.'

'This is all going wrong,' she said.

The phone stopped ringing, then started again. Anne-Marie got to it before I did.

'Hello,' she said, then held it out. 'It's for you.'

'Who is it?' I whispered.

'Who is it?' Anne-Marie asked.

I heard the phone answer, 'Josephine Irish.'

Taking the receiver from Anne-Marie, I said: 'I'm sorry, Josephine, I really can't speak now.'

'I want to see you,' she said. 'I have something to tell you.'

'I'm very busy.'

'It's about Alun.'

That halted me. 'I'll call you.'

'You said that last time.'

'I will. I'll call you.'

I put the phone down, eyeing Anne-Marie. She knew better than to ask me any questions. It was now clear to her that I'd been doing a great deal behind her back. A phonecall from Lily's mother, particularly on the day that Lily was back in the papers, wasn't going to add too much more to her suspicions.

'That was a very stupid thing to do,' I said.

'Don't call me stupid.'

The phone started ringing again.

'We'll have to go to yours,' I said. 'We can't stay here.'

She sulked but moved.

78

As far as I could tell, no-one followed us during the drive from Notting Hill to Chelsea. Anne-Marie remained silent most of the way. It was important for me to try and persuade her that I still trusted her. I wanted to explain why I'd, at least in her eyes, over-reacted.

'Look,' I said. 'You've never been doorstepped. You don't know what it's like.'

'Of course I do,' she said. 'Some of my models used to spend their entire lives dodging the press – and who do you think helped them make it through? Who ordered the taxis and brought over the cigarettes and went in the decoy car? You can't tell me anything I don't already know.'

'I'm sorry. I forgot.'

'Well, remember a bit more, why don't you?'

No more conversation after that.

For a while, I thought that Anne-Marie was going to make me sleep on the sofa. But when we got to her flat all my stuff went straight through into her bedroom. I stowed the sports bag on top of her pink-painted wardrobe.

As soon as I could, I turned the TV on for the twelve o'clock news bulletin. There was no mention of Brandy's Baby, no statement from the Met.

From the bathroom came the sound of heavy running water.

'Can I use the phone?' I asked.

'So, I can't touch *your* phone,' Anne-Marie shouted back, 'but *you* can use *mine* whenever you like!'

'Can I?'

'Oh, alright.'

I waited until Anne-Marie was installed – the watersounds now reduced to feminine lappings.

Josephine answered within two rings.

'Meeting up could be difficult,' I said.

'How can I make it easier?' she asked, sarcastically.

'You can drive over to near where I am.'

'Where are you?'

I wanted somewhere we were unlikely to be seen. The best place seemed to be Josephine's car.

'Pick me up outside McDonald's on the King's Road.'

'When?'

'Tomorrow,' I said. 'One o'clock.'

'Alright.'

Before Anne-Marie got out of the bath I transferred the gun and bullets into my courier bag. From now on, I would take it with me wherever I went.

I cooked dinner. I made jokes. And by the end of the evening, Anne-Marie had almost forgiven me everything.

79

Friday.

It was one of those bright, brisk days when the sky seems a couple of layers thinner, and space just that little bit closer.

As I walked along the King's Road, the cold air made my lungs feel huge and healthy. The gun in the courier bag banged against my hip like a kid punching me to try and get my attention.

McDonald's. One o'clock. Josephine was on time. I got into the Volvo.

The air in the overheated car was choked with Josephine's perfume: Poison.

'What is it?' I asked.

'Let me at least park somewhere,' she said.

We drove into a side-street of white stucco houses.

'Okay,' I said, after she'd switched the engine off.

As she turned to face me, I saw that the lower rims of Josephine's eyes were moist and pinkly red.

'This isn't very easy for me,' she said.

'You said on the phone it was to do with Alun.'

'Before I say anything, I just want to remind you what you said about the flat.'

'What did I say?'

'You said that you might not want to keep it.'

'And you still want it?' I asked, unnecessarily.

'Of course I do. It's very important to me.'

'I'll bear that in mind.'

Josephine ran her hands up and down, in semicircles, round

both sides of the steering-wheel. I started pulling at the Velcro of the courier bag – thinking how cool it would feel to pull the gun on her.

'I knew all about Alun,' she began. 'Lily told me she was seeing him. She told me quite early on. Just after it started, I think. They even came round to my flat for dinner. It was charming – to see them playing at being a couple. To be honest, I thought Alun would be far better for her than you ever would. He's a proper man. But it was obvious enough that he was never going to leave his wife. Lily couldn't see that. She believed anything and everything he said. He lied to her constantly.'

'Like a proper man,' I said.

'When Alun came along to the funeral, I could see that he was feeling terribly guilty.'

'He was at the funeral?'

This was news to me.

'He hung around at the back, but, yes, he was there.'

'Did *you* invite him?'

'No.'

'Dorothy wasn't there, was she?'

'Of course not. Anyway, I went up to him and told him that if he ever wanted to talk, he could call me.'

The air in Josephine's car was becoming oppressively cloying.

'And he called,' I said.

'It didn't take him long. We've talked quite a lot, since then. Dorothy doesn't know about it. There are quite a few things that Dorothy doesn't know.' Josephine smiled a disgustingly prim little smile.

'Such as?'

'Will you at least *sell* me the flat?' she said.

I looked at her. It seemed as though she'd been rejuvenated by something, since the last time I saw her.

'I'll put it on the market. I'll tell you when.'

These were meaningless promises. I could promise to give her the flat, and it wouldn't make any real difference. I didn't know where I was going to be, come tomorrow evening. And between then and now, I certainly wasn't paying a visit to my solicitor.

Josephine breathed deeply, in and out, in and out, for what seemed like a long time. I noticed that she was gripping the steering-wheel to stop her hands from trembling quite so obviously.

'Thank you,' she said, after a pause.

'Well?' I said. 'Go on.'

'Alun was feeling guilty that he hadn't told Dorothy about Lily being pregnant. He genuinely doesn't know whether you or he was the father. But Lily did tell him that she was pregnant. He spoke to her, once more, one last time. This was after they were meant never to speak again, after he'd promised Dorothy. He spoke to her on the phone. That was when Lily told him about the baby. It was Thursday evening, the day before she died. He described her to me as *totally deranged*. He said it scared him. Because of this, he told her he couldn't ever see her again. Until that point, he'd been thinking of carrying on behind Dorothy's back. He did love Lily. But, in the end, her weirdness scared him off.'

I felt as if my insides were about to burst out, like a television exploding – sparks and dust.

If Josephine was telling the truth, Alun had managed to keep Dorothy ignorant of Lily's pregnancy right up until the moment I wheeled my way into their dressing room at the Barbican. Everything he'd done after that had been acting: his immediate response, the books on his bedside table. Bizarrely, I admired him for this. And I'd thought I was the one his performance had been for. In a way, he must have been very grateful to me for telling Dorothy first – before the trial. I couldn't really see what he'd had to gain by not telling her. Then I remembered how Vicky had come round to mine to tell me off after a supposedly distraught Alun had visited her. Perhaps that performance, too, had been for Dorothy's benefit. Surely he'd already told the police about speaking to Lily one final time? Probably he, and they, were only upset because I'd found out.

'Who did Lily think the baby belonged to?' I asked.

'She wanted it to be Alun. She hoped it was Alun.'

'When did she tell you all this?'

'She phoned me up, the morning she died.'

I remembered the call from the phone bill.

'Well,' I said. 'That isn't very much. That's hardly worth a flat.'

'I don't know how to say this. The last time I spoke to her, Lily seemed to be very fatalistic. Everything in her life seemed to have come to an end. She'd thrown you out, and good riddance. She'd finally decided to give up the cereal advertisements. She knew she wasn't going to have this baby. Alun had said that he couldn't see her again, so she thought that was over. Plus, at the very end of our final conversation, she was talking about having a new will made. One in which I was beneficiary, in which I got the flat.'

'That doesn't prove anything.'

'The more I think about it, the more I'm sure she knew what was coming.'

'Rubbish,' I said.

'She blamed you. She said that if she hadn't been pregnant, Alun would have kept on seeing her.'

'That's not logical.'

'Well, that's the way she saw it. He'd said goodbye for ever just after she told him about being pregnant. That's when she must have made the connection.'

'He said she sounded deranged.'

'But she was very calm the next day when she spoke to me. Calmer, in some ways, than I'd ever heard her.'

I dismissed my memory of Lily's manner at Le Corbusier.

Josephine continued: 'Her exact words were, "I'm not going to have the little bastard. It's caused me enough trouble already."'

328

Bastard. Bastard. Bastard.

'Drive me home,' I said, quickly.

'I think Lily was glad to be killed. I think, somehow, she knew what was going to happen in the restaurant. I think Dorothy's little plan backfired. I think Alun told her about it, and by the time she spoke to me she had decided to turn up anyway.'

'You know all about Dorothy?' I said, stunned.

'Yes,' said Josephine.

'How?'

'Some of it Alun told me, some of it I worked out for myself.'

'Why didn't you tell the police?'

'I did.'

'You did.'

'Yes.'

'What did they do?'

'Not a lot, so far as I can see. They said the investigation was ongoing.'

Josephine tried to take my hand.

'Look, Conrad, Lily wanted to die.'

'I don't want to hear any more.'

'Let me finish: I think she invited you along deliberately. As far as she was concerned, what was going to happen would solve all her problems at once.'

I got out of the car and walked away.

Behind me, I could hear Josephine starting to sob.

I wasn't going to listen to that kind of madness.

80

Our first audition was due to take place at four. We were giving the actors half an hour each. I hoped to be able to get rid of them faster than that. The scene they were to play was simple enough. Their character, Johnny, had been kidnapped. The kidnappers made Johnny phone his parents and tell them to do whatever they (the kidnappers) said. It was a scene comprising maximum emotion and minimum subtlety. But it did – even though I say so myself – have a certain *truth* to it.

A couple of the earlier actors did a passable impression of terror. I enjoyed torturing them. Importantly, Anne-Marie got used to the whole set-up: the threats, the screaming; the way I tied them up to help get them into the rôle. With each of the actors, I did a little improvisation: I made them – as an exercise – pretend they were talking to their own mother. Most of them were delighted with this.

Everything was set.

Laurence, due at six, arrived five minutes early. Anne-Marie answered the door and led him in, just as she had with all the others. Anne-Marie was behaving very well. Laurence was wearing black.

'You?' he said, surprised.

He shook my hand, gripping it slightly too tightly and for a moment too long.

'You know each other?' asked Anne-Marie.

'We've met,' I said.

'Why didn't you say?' she said.

'I didn't want to sway you either way,' I said. 'We'll talk about this later.'

'You should see it at our house,' Laurence said. 'It's mad – photographers everywhere. My parents almost didn't let me out. But I lied. I told them I was –'

'What is this?' said Anne-Marie, sharply.

'Shall we get on?' I said.

Laurence sat down on the sofa and I gave him a couple of pages of script to read through.

I was seated opposite, in one of the two non-matching arm-chairs. In between us, on the brown carpet, was a low glass coffee-table stacked with fashion magazines. Underneath this was the courier bag, which now contained the Gruber & Litvak, the live bullets, the pollution masks and the rope.

Anne-Marie perched herself dubiously on the left arm of the other armchair. She wasn't happy with this new situation, but that didn't matter so long as she behaved.

'Hmm,' Laurence said, not even half-way down the page. 'This is good.'

'I think it could do with some improvement,' I said. 'Let's do a read-through, just for the words. No emotion.'

He did it. Raving, really.

'This time,' I said, 'try it with this blindfold on. Loosen up. Try to go completely over the top.'

He went. All the way.

Anne-Marie looked a little uneasy, even though she'd seen this with all the others. She was watching me almost as closely as she was watching Laurence.

After he had finished his run-through, I sat back for a moment or two – as if to ponder, in a directorial-dilemma kind of way.

Eventually, I managed to drag something up from the depths.

'How do you think we could change it to make it more *real*? What would *you* say to *your* parents?'

'Well,' he said, 'I call my mother *mummy*.'

'Really?'

'Yes.'

'And is that what you'd call her if you had a gun pointed at your head?'

'I guess so.'

'And your father?'

'I just call him dad.'

'Let's try it,' I said. 'But hang on.'

I took the blindfold off, then got the rope and tied his hands together behind his back.

I pointed two gun-fingers at him.

'Mummy? Hello ... Mummy ... Mummy, listen – I've been kidnapped. No, this isn't a joke. They've got me here: they're here right now – pointing a gun at my head. Please! Agh! Don't! Alright. I'm trying. Mummy, you've got to do exactly what they say, do you get it? Exactly. You must not call the police. Or anyone. Just do what they say.'

'Okay,' I said. 'Stop.'

I picked up the phone, shielded the number, dialled Alun and Dorothy's.

Hope they're in. Hope they're in.

But where else are they likely to be, with the nation's press on their doorstep?

And didn't Laurence just say they were at home when he set off?

It began to ring.

'Hello,' said the phone.

They're in.

I reached into the courier bag and pulled out the gun.

'Mummy?' said Laurence.

I pointed the gun at Laurence's head. I shoved the receiver into his face.

'Once again,' I said. 'With feeling.'

Laurence began the speech.

'Conrad,' said Anne-Marie, 'what the fuck do you think you're doing?'

'Exactly what I planned to do; exactly what you helped me do. Now shut up.'

'That isn't a real gun,' Anne-Marie said. 'It can't be a real gun.'

'What?' said Laurence, breaking the script.

I could see he was thinking of attacking me, even though his hands were tied behind his back.

'Don't move,' I said to Laurence. 'Keep going.'

Laurence kept going.

I pointed the gun at Anne-Marie's belly.

'This is a real gun with real bullets. No thanks to you.'

'What?' she said.

'Sit down,' I said. 'Next to him.'

Anne-Marie edged her way round the coffee-table and sat down beside Laurence on the sofa.

Laurence finished his speech.

'Much better,' I said.

'Mummy, please,' said Laurence. 'It's Conrad. He's got a gun.'

I tapped him sharply on the head with the receiver. '*That* wasn't in the script,' I said. 'Was it? Who said anything about improvisation?'

'Conrad?' said Dorothy.

'Oh my god,' said Anne-Marie, her eyes all of a sudden wide. 'It's a real gun.'

'Alright, Dorothy,' I said. 'Let me tell you what you're going to do, and – more importantly – what you're not going to do . . .'

For once, Dorothy listened.

After I'd made it quite clear what she had to do to see her son alive again, I put the phone down on her in mid-sentence – a minor pleasure, but sweet.

'Conrad,' said Anne-Marie, 'what are you going to do?'

'I have big plans.'

'Oh shit – that gun's really loaded.'

'Yes.'

'Please don't point it at me.'

'Never should have trusted you, should I?'

'What's going on?' said Laurence. 'Is Mummy in on it? Is Mummy part of the audition?'

'Yes,' I said. 'Mummy's part of the audition.'

'It's a great script.'

'Stop creeping, you little shit. There's only a minor part in it for you – unless I do some seriously major damage to your head.'

'Leave him alone,' shouted Anne-Marie.

I aimed the gun at her eyes.

'Oh shit,' she said. Then she started laughing, although it was obvious that laughing was something she didn't want to be doing. Each ha ha ha convulsed her upper body like a sob. Her eyes watered up, but these were physical not emotional tears.

'Please don't point it at me,' she finally said.

'Lie down on the floor.'

Like a hard slap, this killed her laughter.

'I'm lying down now,' she said.

And she was.

'Put your hands behind your back.'

'I'm doing everything you say.'

Now she was behaving like the perfect little hostage.

'You know I'll kill you if you try to stop me.'

'I believe you, Conrad.'

Speaking my name – calmly, gently, reassuringly.

With the rest of the rope I tied her hands and feet together.

'That's not too tight, is it?' I asked.

'No,' she said.

I tightened it some more.

'That's better,' she said.

'I'm going to gag you. In a moment or two. Not right now.'

She didn't respond to this.

I stepped over Anne-Marie's hog-tied body so that I stood in front of my other hostage.

'Open wide, Laurence,' I said, nudging the gun barrel against his lips. He opened up: total cock-mouth.

'Nod once for *yes*, twice for *no*. Did you ever fuck Lily?'

He nodded once.

'God!' said Anne-Marie.

'You did?' I asked.

Once.

'When? When you were on the Strindberg tour?'

Once.

'What about afterwards? Back in London?'

Twice.

'And just before she died? Are you sure you didn't fuck her then?'

Twice.

I got closer, staring into Laurence's dilated pupils. He could still be lying, I thought. Probably not about having had sex with Lily. This was no time for adolescent bravado. But he might still be reluctant to admit the possibility of fatherhood. Maybe he thought I'd blow the back of his head off if he said he'd made Lily pregnant.

'Did you know that your father fucked her?'

Once.

'So it wasn't just the tabloids?' said Anne-Marie. 'He really did?'

'Lots,' I said. 'Lots and lots.'

Laurence was choking: on the barrel and on his fear of the barrel. I didn't want to get too much saliva on the gun, so I pulled it out – lightly tapping his teeth. He coughed a little, as if he'd half-swallowed a pube.

'My dad doesn't love my mummy,' he said.

'What a shame.'

'Conrad,' said Anne-Marie. 'What are you doing?'

'Gagging you,' I said, turning round.

From the courier bag I took out the three pollution masks I'd bought in the bike shop. They should work perfectly – no choking to death, no shouting for help.

For the first time Anne-Marie looked totally afraid.

'Trust me,' she said. 'I'll help you. I love you.'

'Hold still.'

Her mask went on first, easy. I fastened it tight. Her eyes bulged as she deprived herself of air by fighting for it too hard.

'Deep slow breaths,' I said.

She gave me one of her don't-patronize-me looks.

I strolled back to Laurence, got right up close.

He whimpered, shaking little shakes. Snot had started to run from his nose down on to his black long-sleeved T-shirt. The band, I noticed for the first time, was called Slayer. He'd had his sixteenth birthday only a month or so before. Poor darling. Poor . . .

I smelt something.

Poor baby-darling.

Something rich, round, brown.

'You'll be sitting in that for the next few hours,' I said.

Laurence looked down at the carpet, ashamed.

I slipped the mask over his head, fastened it, tightened it.

'I'm just going to be up in town,' I said. 'Killing your parents.'

In his frustration at not being able to get at me, he toppled over. There he lay on the sofa: bum in the air, writhing – as if I were about to anally rape him.

I knelt down and looked him in the eye, spoke gently to him, motherly, fatherly.

'Your mummy arranged to have me and Lily shot. She was trying to stop your daddy – and you – fucking Lily. Unfortunately, I survived. I'm sure you'd be doing the same thing if you were me. I've got nothing against you. For some reason, Lily liked you.'

I fetched a couple of high-backed chairs from the dining area, put them back to back. Then I dragged Laurence over to them, made him sit. His trousers squelched. The air ripened.

'Don't move,' I ordered.

I dragged Anne-Marie over, as well.

From the kitchen, I fetched a large roll of clingfilm – and I wrapped it around the two of them from ankles to necks.

Just for fun, I checked Laurence's bag – I found a diary, which I flicked through: it was only for this year. Nothing Lily-related. I went over to him, holding the diary.

'The stars in the top left-hand corner,' I said, pointing them out. 'That how many times you wanked?'

Once. Yes.

'You should be careful,' I said. I put the blindfold on him. 'That damages your eyesight.'

Before I put on Anne-Marie's blindfold, I looked her right in the eye.

'I thought I could trust you,' I said. 'Well . . . anyway . . . I couldn't.'

I was just moving towards the phone, the cord of which I intended to cut, when it started – more violently than usual, I felt – to ring.

Anne-Marie and Laurence tensed up, hoping already for rescue.

Six rings.

Click.

'Hi, this is Anne-Marie. I'm sorry I can't get to the phone right now . . .'

Come on, come on.

Don't be my mother.

'. . . but if you leave a message I'll call you back.'

Beep.

'Anne-Marie? Anne-Marie, this is Clare. You know, from Conrad. He calls me Vicky. Anyway, if you're there, please pick up . . . Please . . . I really need to speak to you. It's about Conrad.

337

Is he there with you? We need to know where he is. I suppose you've seen he's all over the papers again today. Well, some of them, anyway. The rags. Guess that's why you're hiding out, as well. Look, it's – There's people here who really need to speak to him. His house got burnt down, you know. They've arrested someone in connection. Anyway, are you there? Look, when you get in – What?'

The line went muffled. Vicky was talking to someone the other end. I thought I heard her say *fucking hell*.

'Look, call me when you get in. As soon as you get in. Bye-bye.' Shit.

My hand was on the receiver. I was so tempted to pick up. The moment she said they'd arrested someone for torching my flat. It felt like I was holding back every instinct I had.

Some time soon, Vicky would have to tell 'the other people' who were looking for me where I might be. I supposed Anne-Marie having given over her phone number as a private thing might hold her back for a while. But she'd be forced to give it up eventually. Perhaps she'd already told the person who interrupted the call.

I couldn't now turn off the answerphone; the police would phone first (probably), and would know something was up if they didn't get the same response Vicky had.

A line-not-working signal would have them straight round. (I'd tried my old burnt-flat number, just for the hell, and that's what I'd got.)

I realized that I was verging on late, though I'd left plenty of time.

I went into the kitchen and fetched Anne-Marie's portable breakfast radio. I turned it on to Capital FM.

Let them endure the punishment of quarter-hourly traffic reports whilst bound to a chair.

It was the news. At the risk of being delayed again, I stopped to listen.

There it was, right at the bottom.

'The Metropolitan police have denied insensitivity in their handling of the shooting of Lilian Irish, better known as Brandy. Revelations in yesterday's *Mirror* newspaper suggest that Brandy may have been pregnant at the time of her death. The whereabouts of her boyfriend, film producer Conrad Redman, also shot in the original incident, are currently unknown. A Met spokesperson confirmed Redman had been given comprehensive counselling. Redman's house was burnt down in suspicious circumstances two days ago. An arrest has been made in connection with the arson attack.'

I closed the curtains, turned the lights out and went through into Anne-Marie's bedroom.

In front of her full-length but a-little-too-narrow mirror, I got changed into my killing gear. I was intending to walk the short distance to the cycle shop, where I would collect my beautiful new bike. However, looking at myself now, I realized that I would seem terribly out of place: a bike courier, without a bike, in genteel Chelsea, in the early evening. The fact that I was wearing a brand-new Day-Glo outfit wouldn't help a lot, either. For a moment I thought about risking it. I felt I was travelling so fast that suspicion would only catch up with me afterwards – after I had accomplished what I meant to accomplish. From now on, in one way, perhaps, the more witnesses the better. But I had to be cautious. Another bright glance convinced me: I put my jeans and T-shirt on over the stretch Lycra. The bike shoes, I put into the courier bag – along with the Gruber & Litvak, the live bullets, and all the rest of my equipment, including a copy of the *A–Z*. (I wasn't going to allow getting lost or anything as obvious as that to frustrate me.)

I went back into the living room and for a moment just stood there – looking at what I'd achieved so far (with a little help from my gun): Anne-Marie and Laurence, clingfilmed together, like some piece of crappy avant-garde theatre. The thought of this made me laugh out loud.

Laurence flinched away, as if the fact I was laughing made it more likely I was going to shoot him.

'I know you can both hear me,' I said. 'I'm leaving now. I wish I had something big and significant to say, but I don't.'

81

Out the front door.

As I turned left at the top of the steps, a familiar car pulled out: the Mercedes. Inside it were the two men that Anne-Marie had described as 'thugs'.

How the fuck had they managed to find me, when the journalists and the paparazzi hadn't?

Then I remembered: this had been the car that followed us when we left to drive from Mortlake to Notting Hill. After I escaped on to the Tube, Anne-Marie had been trailed all the way home.

Since I'd now gone missing from both Lily's flat and my own, it was obvious they would come looking for me here.

But who were they? They weren't from the tabloids, otherwise they'd be taking photographs.

When they'd followed us before, I hadn't really had much idea who they were. I'd thought perhaps they were the police. The last thing I wanted was to be arrested just outside the door.

I quickened my pace.

Just as I was coming out of Anne-Marie's side-street on to a larger road, the Mondeo appeared out of nowhere.

I glanced inside, and saw the two familiar figures.

The Mondeo screeched out in front of the Mercedes, then all of a sudden slowed down to walking pace.

With parked cars on either side of the road, there was no way that the Mercedes could overtake.

I walked quickly, glancing now and again over my shoulder.

But nothing changed: the two-car convoy trailed me all the way to the cycle shop.

It was a relief to get in the door.

Looking out through the spokes of one of the bikes in the window, I could see that both cars had parked up.

Not only that, both the thugs had got out and were shouting at the albino and the black man through the Mondeo's side windows.

The grungy assistant recognized me. My Trek Death-Raider was ready: tyres pumped, seat adjusted.

I asked if I could use the shop's changing room.

'Sure,' the assistant said.

Once inside, I took off my T-shirt, shoes and jeans then wrapped them in a bundle.

Nervously, I checked once again that the Gruber & Litvak was in the courier bag.

I needn't have worried. There it lay, looking devastating. As gorgeous as Lily. As sexy as revenge.

I put on the gloves, crash helmet and mirrored shades.

I checked my watch: seven o'clock.

I had an hour to get to Soho – easy.

Back in the main body of the shop, I took possession of the bike. The assistant held the door open as I wheeled it out on to the street.

Opposite me, the thugs had got back into their Mercedes and driven forwards so they were touching the Mondeo's bumper.

I dumped my no-longer-wanted clothes in a bin outside the cycle shop, and pulled the pollution mask down over my mouth.

I saw the albino point me out to the black man.

The Mondeo's engine started.

I mounted up and took off, back the way I'd come.

The Mondeo pulled a U-ey. The Mercedes copied it, ten yards behind.

I cycled along Pimlico Road and turned up Lower Sloane Street. The two cars followed.

Now that I was sure they weren't going to try and stop me, I started to relax.

I hadn't ridden a bike in years, and the simplicity of this rediscovered pleasure delighted me.

For a while, the enjoyment of this was enough. But, eventually, I began to think of what Josephine had told me that afternoon.

I cycled up Sloane Street, crossed Knightsbridge – the two cars right behind me all the way.

All the rest of the afternoon, I'd managed to block her words out of my mind. By making preparations for the auditions. By checking my equipment. By watching and listening to the news. But now, everything she'd said about Lily seemed to come back to me.

What was going to happen would solve all her problems at once.

I couldn't let myself think about this.

My vision started to get blurry.

Just then I came out opposite Hyde Park.

To distract myself, I cut dangerously across the traffic on Knightsbridge.

Once over to the other side of the road, I cycled into the park. It was pedestrianized. The cars couldn't follow me here.

One of the thugs got out and ran after me for twenty yards or so but soon gave up and went back to the Mercedes.

I rode along Rotten Row, parallel to the road, dodging between walkers and rollerbladers. The gravel of the path roared beneath my tyres.

I was getting used to wearing the shades. The pollution mask made my deeper, sped-up breathing come loudly to my ears. (I thought of myself, back in UCH, intubated, respirated. I thought of Anne-Marie and Laurence back in her flat, breathing through their masks – always short of air.) The helmet was becoming a little sweaty inside. The gloves against the black-foam-rubber handlebars gave me some kind of super-grip. All my equipment felt right.

The two cars picked me up again at Hyde Park Corner.

I waved back at them.

Only a bit of fun, lads.

The Mercedes had overtaken the Mondeo.

Up Piccadilly.

It had only taken me fifteen minutes to get this far.

Shaftesbury Avenue was busy with theatre-goers getting out of taxis for seven-thirty curtains.

I was preparing to make a simple left on to Frith Street when I saw them: two identical vans parked, one after the other, at the end of the road.

I cycled past without looking too closely or obviously at them.

(Maybe it was just a coincidence.)

I doubled back, attempting to approach Frith Street down Old Compton Street.

Crowds outside *Les Miserables*.

I was watching now for anything unusual – and the unmarked vans were definitely that.

I felt disguised, in my bike-courier's outfit – face and everything covered – though its newness suddenly struck me as a dead giveaway: I should have done some dust-bathing – rolled around in the garden, kicked the bike about a bit.

On to Greek Street, riding parallel to Frith.

This was where the back entrance of Le Corbusier let out.

I decided to risk one sortie past the door.

It was enough: the maître d' was standing on the steps talking to a man I knew I should recognize. He was wearing a black uniform, covered over with lots of oblong pouches. It took a moment, but – James, my taxi-driver!

James, a policeman? I couldn't believe it. That must mean . . . I wanted to work out exactly what it meant, but I didn't have time.

The police knew what I was up to, alright. Perhaps they'd already discovered my hostages and pieced it together; perhaps ratty Alun and Dorothy had called them.

The two cars were managing to keep up.

James caught sight of the Mondeo and jerked straight round, staring – he'd recognized it.

He watched the Mercedes go by with some interest.

I turned away, cycling anonymously, I hoped, but not before he'd spotted me looking back.

'Hey,' he shouted. 'Hey!'

I sped off.

I had no time – no time. South down Greek Street. Down towards the Thames. Left on Shaftesbury Avenue. Thinking. Thinking. Right on to Charing Cross Road. What to do? I kept going, on towards Trafalgar Square.

I heard the Mondeo run a light behind me.

Just by chance, I saw the alley down which Tony Smart had led me. The Koha Bar.

I hopped on to the pavement and cycled past the pub tables.

I stopped my bike outside, then remembered that I hadn't bothered to buy a bike lock. At the time there didn't seem to be any point.

Oh fuck.

I just left the thing on the street. I needed a moment or two to think. Plan again.

The Koha Bar was almost empty. Just a barman and a few thirtysomethings nodding along to some very low-tempo music. A DJ in NHS specs stood behind the turntables. One or two people took a glance at me, then turned coolly away.

I checked the time again: seven thirty-two.

Just then, the black man walked down the stairs and into the bar.

'Don't worry,' he said. 'My mate's looking after your bike.'

'Why are you following me?' I whispered, through the pollution mask.

'Let's just say that the situation has very recently changed. Somebody has decided that he sympathizes with your aims.'

'What aims?'

He took a step closer to me. I pulled the mask off my face, let it hang round my neck.

'We know what you have in that bag. We know what you intend to do with it.'

'What's in the bag?' I asked.

He named the Bermondsey pub in which I'd bought it.

'Let's just say, we have friends there.'

I beckoned him over to a vacant table.

He looked cautiously around the room before sitting down.

'Supposing you *do* know,' I said. 'I'm fucked anyway. There's police all over the place.'

'Don't worry. We can help you with them.'

'Who are the guys in the other car?'

'Unsympathetic parties.'

'Meaning?'

He looked at me sideways, as if to say *Do I have to explain everything?*

'They'd like to see you fail. It would be advantageous to them.'

'Why?'

He was about to reply when a gunshot sounded outside.

In an instant, the black man was out of his seat and half-way up the stairs.

I ran after him, fast as I could.

When I emerged into the alley-way, I saw the albino lying on the pavement.

Women at the pub tables further along were standing up, screaming, hands over their mouths.

The albino was curled up in a foetal position. Blood was pulsing out of where his umbilical cord would have been.

The black man was cradling the albino's head.

I looked all around. My bike was gone.

'They stole it,' the albino gasped. 'Tried to stop them.'

'Shit,' said the black man.

'It's not too bad,' replied the albino to a question no-one had asked. When he spoke, I could hear the sound of something wet slapping back and forth.

'Don't fucking die,' said the black man. 'Please don't fucking die.'

Then he looked up at me. 'Sorry, mate,' he said. 'You're on your own.'

In St Martin's Court, a group of people had gathered – attracted by the gunshot and the screaming. They were looking towards the bleeding figure on the ground. They'd seen me, connected me with the incident.

The police would be here soon. I had to get away.

I ran across St Martin's Court and up St Martin's Lane. I crossed over and continued up Monmouth Street, then headed for Charing Cross Road via West Street.

On the corner of the street was the theatre where *The Mousetrap* was always showing.

I could hear a police siren starting up. Or maybe an ambulance.

On Charing Cross Road, I found an empty telephone box. I had one last chance, I guessed.

From my courier bag, I pulled out my wallet. From it, I extracted Michael's card. His address was Old Compton Street. He was due on shift at Le Corbusier. Either way, he should be in the area.

I dialled his mobile number.

Two rings.

He answered.

'Hi,' I said, trying not to sound out of breath. 'It's Conrad.'

'Oh, hi,' he said.

'How are you?'

'Fine,' he said. 'In fact, more than fine. I've just been given the evening off.'

'Why?'

'No idea. All these strange men started arriving. Then they just told me to go home.'

'Look,' I said, 'I'm just in Soho. How about we go for a drink?'

'Well,' Michael said, 'I guess I'm free.'

'Why don't I meet you at Le Corbusier, at the back door?'

'Mmm, my favourite place,' he said.

'We can go somewhere and talk.'

'Lovely.'

'Five minutes?'

'At least give me time to get changed. I've only just got in.'

'Ten.'

'See you.'

I put the phone down, guilty about using him this way.

Checking up and down the street for police, I stepped out of the phonebox.

Just then, I caught sight of the two thugs – they were trying (without much success) to shove my brand-new bike into the back of their Mercedes.

'Come on,' one of them said. 'Twist the handlebars round.'

They were right outside the window of Murder One, the specialist crime-and-mystery bookshop. I doubted that they'd have appreciated the irony.

I could easily walk from here to Le Corbusier in ten minutes. Should I just leave it alone? Let them keep the bike? Avoid any further trouble?

Something inside me said no. I'd been burgled twice, and was all for kneecapping the bastards. For once I was faced with the very people who had stolen something from me. I was armed, and I was fucking angry.

I ran towards them, reaching into my courier bag.

One of them spotted me and alerted the other.

I pulled out my Gruber & Litvak, cocked it.

'Give me my bike back,' I said.

They looked at each other. One of them had a gun, I knew – the gun with which they'd shot the albino. But that gun was currently in its owner's pocket, where it was absolutely useless; mine was sweeping over them, deadly.

'Okay,' one of them said. 'Okay.'

The other pulled my bike out of the back of the car, then let it fall on to the road.

I didn't want to risk reaching down for it, taking my eyes off them, giving them a chance to attack.

Passers-by had stopped to stare, but not as many as I'd expected. There was an ambulance loudly arriving further down the street for the shot albino – most eyes were on that.

'Pick the bike up,' I said.

They did, together.

'Give me your guns,' I said.

They reached into their pockets, again together.

'*One* at a time,' I said. 'You first.'

The thug flinched away as the gun chose him to aim at.

'Okay,' he said.

Gently, he took his gun out and dangled it.

The gun, I noticed, was an old service revolver: crude, black. Nowhere near as nice a gun as mine.

'Drop it,' I ordered.

The revolver hit the pavement.

I went through the same routine with the other thug.

His gun – also a revolver – was equally old, equally ugly.

'Now get in your car and drive away,' I said.

One of them looked like he was about to have a go.

I felt very calm.

Part of me was worrying that Michael wouldn't wait, the rest knew that he would.

The two thugs got slowly into their Mercedes then drove quickly away.

I picked the revolvers up and put them in my bag, along with the Gruber & Litvak.

There was a small round of applause.

'We're just rehearsing for a film,' I told the crowd.

The bike seemed okay when I picked it up. They hadn't slashed the tyres or anything.

I mounted up and cycled back down Charing Cross Road, up Old Compton Street.

Picking up as much speed as I could, I cycled round on to Greek Street – where the fire escape to Le Corbusier emerged.

Michael was standing there, alone, smoking a cigarette, a little rucksack on his back, right beside a large pile of bin bags. He was wearing a tight baby-blue top and navy-blue combats. He smiled shyly as he saw me riding up.

'Nice outfit,' he said.

Just then a man stuck his head out the back door of Le Corbusier. It was James. I heard the crackle of his police radio.

'Clear off, gayboy!' he said to Michael, then he saw me. 'Shit,' he said.

I was off the bike by now, dumping it in the road.

I reached into my courier bag and pulled out a gun – the wrong gun. It was one of the dirty old revolvers that I'd stolen from the thugs. No time to worry about that now. I grabbed Michael round the neck and held the gun against his temple.

James was still looking at me.

'Sorry about this,' I said to Michael. 'But you have to help me get inside.'

'What's going on?' he said. 'Is this some kind of joke?'

'Do what I say, or I *will* shoot you.'

I wasn't sure if this gun would work if I pulled the trigger. Because it was a revolver, it had a completely different mechanism to the Gruber & Litvak.

For all I knew, its safety was on. If James was a trained policeman, he might be able to spot that the gun was deactivated. If so, he'd be able to attack me with impunity.

I needed to know that the revolver was working. There was only one way to find out. I pointed it into the pile of black bin bags and pulled the trigger.

The bang terrified Michael, made James wince, made me smile.

'Okay,' Michael said. 'Okay – okay.'

James was about to disappear inside.

'What's that?' said his radio.

'Out into the street,' I ordered.

He came, slowly, hands behind his head, like he'd have made me come if he were arresting me.

'Cross all the way over to the other side of the road,' I said.

He did.

Michael and I backed in through the fire door.

There was no-one immediately inside.

When the door was safely closed behind us, I made Michael tie it shut with his belt.

'Look,' I said to him, 'you're not going to get hurt. I just need you to help me get through to the upstairs dining room. Take me there, and I'll let you go.'

'Are you going to shoot them?'

'Who?'

'The people you booked for. Are you going to shoot them?'

'Are they here?'

'Of course they are.'

'I'll shoot who I have to.'

'The place is full of police.'

'I know – why didn't you tell me?'

'They said not to tell anyone.'

'I'm not just anyone.'

'Shit,' he said. 'Shit shit shit. I'm so stupid.'

351

We walked up an industrial metal stairway, clanking. Another fire door at the top.

'Hold on,' I said, reaching into the bag and pulling out the Gruber & Litvak with my left hand.

I kept the revolver in my right hand, pointed at Michael.

'They'll be expecting us now,' I said. 'You first.'

Michael opened the door.

We walked into the kitchen, strip-lit steel. But there were no chefs or commis chefs. There was none of the usual culinary cacophony of plates and swearing. Instead, radios crisply fuzzing on and off. Instead, six policemen pointing guns of various calibre at my head.

'Police,' they all shouted. 'Put the gun down!'

'Shh,' said one older than the others. 'Conrad, put the gun down. We can sort this out.'

I pointed the revolver into Michael's head, moving round to the right.

'Let me through,' I said.

'The gun won't work,' the senior officer said. 'It's not live ammunition.'

I pointed the thug's revolver at his grey-haired head.

'Well,' I said. 'What about this one? Does this one work? Shall we find out? Shall we?'

'Christ,' he said. 'Where did you get that?'

'You will all put your guns down,' I said.

I was half-way round the room now. Immediately to my left was a large stainless-steel deep-fat fryer, full of dirty-golden oil.

'You will put your guns in *that*.' I pointed at the fryer with the barrel of the Gruber.

They looked at it with disbelief and distaste.

There was a big red button on the fryer's control panel. I edged Michael round so that I was close enough to push it. Click. The oil began to heat. Then I backed away, keeping the gun always to Michael's temple.

'One by one,' I said. 'Or I demonstrate just how live this ammunition is.'

They lined up – each giving me a real I'm-going-to-fucking-get-you-for-this look.

'First into the batter,' I said.

Each of them dipped his weapon in the thick white liquid before dropping-plopping it into the now-warming oil.

As they did, the grey-haired one spoke: 'Conrad, we know what you think – we know you think we've been doing nothing. But, really, we've been very busy – working on many levels. We've been trying to bring the right people to justice – all of them. And Dorothy Pale and Alun Grey aren't the only right people. There are others. You don't know the full story yet. If you put the guns down, I'm sure you'll come to see it's the right thing. Believe me. Trust me.'

'I don't even know you,' I said.

'I'm Chief Inspector –' he started to say.

'I don't want to know you,' I said.

'– Hetherington,' he said.

'I want you to leave. Out the fire door. And I don't want to see you again. Not until I'm done. Then you can arrest me.'

For a moment we all stood still. I could hear the guns, starting to deep-fry.

I pointed the revolver a few inches to the right of the Chief Inspector's head and fired.

Everyone ducked, apart from me.

'Now,' I said. 'Out.'

They walked round the far wall, up to the fire door, opened it, filed quietly out.

I kept both guns pointed at Michael.

'That dustbin,' I said. 'Move it so it blocks the door.'

He obeyed. His fear of death had matured. It had now become a kind of total listlessness. His skin had turned pale grey. His eyelids hung low. He hardly had the strength to move. (Don't shoot me, I'm already dead.)

'And the other,' I said.

Zombie-like, he walked it over.

I grabbed him round the neck again.

'We're going into the upstairs dining room,' I said, giving him a push to set him off.

Through the double swing-doors, emerging near the top of the stairs, beside the till – where the maître d' usually stood.

At first I thought the only people in the room were armed policemen. Of these, there were about ten – all aiming their weapons directly at me. But then I saw the top of someone's head sticking out over the curve of a table. And when I looked in the mirrors of the far wall, I saw a couple of dark shapes crouching behind chairs.

'Everybody up,' I said. 'In my sight.'

More radios fuzzing.

The maître d' appeared first, only a few paces away from me. He'd been hiding in front of his usual station at the till.

'Get back,' I said, letting him stare for a moment up through the gun barrel and into death.

He almost fell over as he stumbled, cowering, away, slamming against the wall.

I was pleased to see Alun and Dorothy getting into their chairs, over at the table I'd booked for them.

'Conrad,' said a familiar voice.

It was Vicky, seating herself at the table beside *the* table.

'Will you listen to me?' she asked.

'You said he wasn't going to get through,' stage-whispered Dorothy. 'You said we'd be completely safe.'

'Now,' I said, 'I want all the police to throw their guns on to the floor – down there – in the middle – now.'

Guns were thrown, metal slamming on to wood.

'And I want you all to sit down normally at the tables, as if you were just here for an evening meal.'

The policemen hesitated.

'Do what he says,' hissed Vicky.

In a moment or two, half the seats in the place were occupied by men in heavy black uniforms.

'Now, pick up the knives and forks.'

Gingerly, they picked them up.

'And now, pretend to be eating.'

I pushed Michael forwards until we were about ten feet away from Alun and Dorothy's table.

'Conrad,' said Vicky.

'Where is our son?' said Alun, manfully.

'Let me handle this,' said Vicky to Alun.

I was getting very annoyed.

'Alun, please change places with Dorothy. She must be sitting with her back to the mirror.'

They glared at each other.

'Dorothy is going to be Lily and you are going to be me.'

'Oh God,' said Dorothy, starting to cry.

'Do it!' I screamed.

They moved round.

Wonderful.

I heard a giant imaginary click – this was it: everything was now in order.

All that remained . . .

'Give me five minutes, Conrad,' said Vicky. 'No-one will move. The SO16 officers will stay *exactly* where they are. Is that clear?'

Someone mumbled their assent.

'Conrad, I can explain. You see, Dorothy and Alun aren't the ones you should be angry with.'

'No?' I said. 'I can't think of anyone better.'

'Christ,' said Alun, looking up the barrel of the revolver. 'I think he's really going to do it.'

My revenge was no longer going to be perfect: same time, same table, same weapon, same number of bullets. I still wanted to use the Gruber, but I was now almost certain that the bullets it contained wouldn't be capable of the killing I intended. Plus, there was no food upon Alun and Dorothy's table – despite the fact that earlier, on the phone, I'd dictated the exact order they were to make. (Chardonnay. Veal and asparagus. Plaice and puffball. I even got Dorothy to repeat it.) My revenge wasn't going to be perfect, but it was going to be close enough.

I aimed for Dorothy's heart, two inches beneath her left breast.

'It was Lily,' said Vicky. 'Lily wanted you dead.'

'It's true,' shrieked Dorothy. 'It was her, not me.'

'Shut up!' said Vicky and I, at the same time – her whispering it aside, me screaming it straight out.

'I don't want to hear,' I said. 'I know enough – I know who put me here.'

'Who did?' asked Vicky. 'Go on – who?'

'They did.' My gun-sights waved over Alun and Dorothy's faces – aghast.

'No,' said Vicky. 'They had something to do with it, both of them. Dorothy hired the hitman but it was to –'

'Yes,' I said. 'Yes. I know.'

Michael wriggled under my arm.

'Stay still,' I said.

'But I can't breathe,' he wheezed.

I relaxed my grip on him, slightly. 'Don't put me off my aim,' I said to Michael. 'This is important.'

'Dorothy confronted Alun,' Vicky continued. 'She told him about the hitman – that he'd die if –'

'I know all that,' I said. 'It's enough.'

'Lily rearranged the hit. She called the hitman up, pretended to be Dorothy.'

'Yes,' shrieked Dorothy. 'Listen to her.'

'It was suicide, Conrad. Lily committed suicide. It was only murder if you'd died.'

'No,' I said.

'She wanted you dead and she wanted herself dead.'

'She didn't.'

'And she wanted Dorothy punished. And she wanted Alun to feel guilty.'

'This is wrong,' I said.

'And she wanted the baby dead.'

'No,' I said.

'The baby that she'd convinced herself was keeping her apart from Alun.'

I couldn't speak any more.

'*Your* baby,' said Vicky.

My vision was blurring.

'It was your baby, Conrad – your daughter.'

Unable to sob, I coughed.

'Lily wasn't well. She was ill.'

'My baby,' I managed to say.

'Yes, Conrad,' said Vicky.

'It was yours,' said Alun.

'My daughter,' I said.

'And it *died*,' said Dorothy. 'She wanted it dead.'

'No!' shouted Vicky, knowing what was coming.

I knew what was coming, too – I knew it in my body.

'You stupid woman,' I said.

I aimed at Dorothy's absent heart, two inches beneath her left breast.

I pulled the trigger – slowly, slowly, slowly.

Bullet #6

The sixth bullet is the one that does the most damage to me directly. By this time I am lying back — suspended on two chair-legs, reclining as if in a hammock — my feet are caught under the lip of the table — flying, I am flying. The bullet, therefore, enters my belly at a very oblique angle. It penetrates my right side and rips through my lower intestine — going slightly front to back.

As it passes through, avoiding most large bones, it goes directly into the area where my womb would have been had I been a woman. If I'd been carrying a baby myself, I would have lost it.

My rectus abdominus muscle is split, rent up the middle like Velcro being pulled apart.

Mostly I encounter these things not as the drama of their happening but through the aches and pains of their aftermath: I am well acquainted now with the word chronic.

Adulthood, I realize, is a relationship with this word: coming to know first it and then, later, its younger brother terminal.

The sixth bullet, meeting mainly soft flesh, passes fairly cleanly through — compared to what it might have done. I am lucky. I am having a narrow escape. I should thank my lucky stars. It comes close to some important arteries (superior and inferior mesenteric) and nerves (lumbar plexus and superior gluteal).

I do lose some sensitivity around my midriff. Not much — not that I'll really miss.

My penis is fairly far from harm, thank the Lord. And my spine — my spine isn't as endangered as it might be.

Where I lose out is in the guts, the digesting area. The front bits go —

those more peripheral and less protected by the body's self-defensive evolution.

We, as humans, are sea-creatures — liquid, eminently squishable. If you examine enough photos of gunshot wounds, there is one easy conclusion: the human body is not made of hard things like bone and tough things like muscle, it is made of fifty-five jellyfish, all piled on top of each other, waiting to meet a bullet and become overt. All human insides are longing to fulfil their jellyfish vocation and get into the open air.

82

After I'd shot Dorothy, I stood and watched as she crumpled up. She did this in a completely unstagey way – there was no affectation to it, she simply folded herself over until she was as small as she could be. She didn't make much sound, only a low repetitive grunting as she tried to breathe. At the time I suppose I noticed there was no blood spurting out of her. (The police, on top of all their less successful precautions, had equipped both Alun and Dorothy with bulletproof vests.) But I thought she was dead, anyway. Later, I learnt that the impact of that first bullet against her ribcage had sent Dorothy's heart into arrhythmia. While I stood there, deciding whether or not I could be bothered to keep shooting, whether it wasn't already finished, Dorothy had gone into cardiac arrest. I wanted to keep shooting. Really, I did. The second bullet, I knew, had to be aimed at her forehead. The third, at her belly. Then I had to start on Alun: heart, head, belly; four, five, six; chest, miss, guts. But Dorothy's face was down, now – her head, resting on an empty white plate. All I could see of her was her hair. The only sound in the room was her grunting-breathing.

In the next moment, Alun had put his arms around her and blocked her out of my view completely.

He called her name.

And as I stood there, all vengefulness gone, all interest in life gone, one of the policemen lunged at me.

Yes, I had disarmed them. Their weapons still lay in a rough pile on the floor. But, silly me, I'd told them to pick up the knives and forks. And this one brave policeman had decided to improvise.

He jumped up from his table and grabbed me from behind. With his right arm, he pulled the revolver away from Alun and Dorothy; with his left hand, he stabbed me in the guts with a fork.

The pain was minimal. But I had nothing left to do. This was the easiest way out.

I let go of Michael, dropped both guns and fell to the floor.

The rest of the police were on me in seconds.

83

Ha ha ha.

They took Dorothy and me to University College Hospital in the same ambulance.

84

Afterwards, when she visited me at UCH, but nowhere near as clearly and directly as this that follows, Vicky said:

'Dorothy was foolish. Sub Overdale put her in touch with Tony Smart. Through Tony she met up with some minor villains. Through them, she was introduced to some seriously nasty people. She arranged everything with them, weeks in advance. She never met the actual hitman. All she was waiting for was an opportunity. When she found out that Alun and Lily were going out to dinner, she called the contact number she'd been given. It was a mobile phone. Stolen. She spoke to a man. She says she doesn't know who it was. We're almost certain it was the hitman. She told him where he'd find Lily and Alun. Le Corbusier. Eight o'clock. "Kill them," she said. The price was far above the going rate. She was being swizzed. And then she went to Alun and told him, "I've arranged to have you killed – you know I can do it: we know the right people, now. The very next time you see Lily – and you're intending to see her tomorrow evening, I know – the very next time, you will be gunned down. Even if you cancel this date, and see her again some other time, I'll have you killed then. Both of you – or just her – I don't know." And so Alun got scared. He wanted Dorothy to tell him it was all a joke, all empty threats. So she played him a tape she'd made of some of the phonecalls she'd made to the hitman. Everything's on the tapes. But Alun still didn't believe it was really happening. He thought Dorothy had got some actor to do a scary East End voice down the phone. So then Dorothy hands him the phone and tells him *Dial this number*. The hitman answers. All it needed was for him to hear that voice, the same as on the tape. He tries to put the hitman off, but Dorothy grabs the phone from him. They get into a big fight, tearing at each other. Eventually, Alun starts crying. He promises never to see Lily again. This is all taking place in their flat, by the way. Dorothy gets Alun to phone Lily up – to tell her that it is all over, for ever. She is listening as he says it. Alun doesn't say why, he just says that it's over. "I've got to see you," Lily says. "I have something to tell you." Dorothy screams into the phone. "You're never going to see him again! He's mine!" She slams the phone down. Dorothy is satisfied. She phones the hitman to cancel the hit. She agrees to pay him a quarter of the promised money for his trouble. Then she goes off to the theatre. She was in a play by Ibsen. Alun remained at home. Dorothy thought she could trust him. She thought that he was all hers again. That she'd won him back. But as soon as she's out the door, Alun phones Lily. He tells Lily that the thing he wants most in the world is to carry on seeing her. But he can't. He tells her that Dorothy is going mad. That she's arranged to have them killed. Lily doesn't believe it. She wants to see Alun again. He says it's impossible. Lily insists. She tells Alun she loves him. She tells him that she's pregnant with his child. He doesn't believe her. She tells him again. She says she'll kill herself if she can't be with him. He panics. He says it really is over. Even if Dorothy hadn't done this, it would be over. Alun puts the phone down on her. Next morning, Friday, Lily calls Laurence. His is the disconnected number on Lily's bill. 09.15. Remember? At that point he had a phone-socket in his room. It was a birthday present, so he could plug in his modem. He only got a phone later – which was why Lily used to call him on his parent's number. After all this happened, his parents had the line disconnected. So, anyway, Lily calls Laurence and they talk about what's been going on. He's pissed off because Dorothy's told him that *he* can never see Lily again either. No explanation. All he knows is that his parents had a real big argument the night before. Lily asks where they are. Laurence says they're in rehearsal. They don't know he's home. He's bunking off school. Lily says she's coming round. When she arrives, Laurence has something to show her. After the argument the night before, he saw his mother putting some tapes in the dustbin. When she's not looking, he gets them out, takes them to his room and plays them. Not only that, he plays one of them down the phone – so that the recording of the touch-tone automatically dials the number. At the same time, the number is displayed on the handset. He writes the number down. He hears the voice on the tape. When Lily comes round, he shows her the number. She, of course, commits it to memory. They talk for a while and then she goes. It is about eleven o'clock in the morning. She gets a taxi and calls the hitman's number from her mobile. When the hitman answers, she starts to talk to him as if she were Dorothy. You know how good she was at impressions. Well, she has Dorothy down to a T. She tells the hitman that things are to go ahead exactly as planned. Last night, she says, she had a bit of a wobble. But now she's certain that she wants it done. And to prove it, she'll pay twice as much as she was going to before. The hitman is a bit dubious, but he accepts this. Lily ends the phonecall. She is, I imagine, very pleased. She is going to achieve everything she wants: she will be dead, you will be dead, Alun will be grief-stricken and Dorothy will have both the police and the hitman after her for the rest of her life. And so Lily, knowing now that she is going to die that evening, goes ahead and arranges things. She has her hair done. She buys a new dress – the same dress she wore to her last date with Alun. She phones you and arranges for you to come to the restaurant. You're the easy part. She knows that you're still in love with her and would cancel anything to see her again. She phones her mother to tell her about the baby and the abortion. She phones her solicitor to ask about changing her will. She doesn't want the money and the flat left to you, as they were originally. Nor does she want to die intestate, and have her possessions divided equally between her parents. What she wants is to ensure that everything goes to her mother. But there isn't time for that. So, she just has to let it slide. If both you and her are going to be dead, it doesn't really matter anyway. You're the one she blames for all of this. You made her pregnant. You made Alun leave her. She hates you. You've ruined everything. She phones your answerphone. I'll play you the tape.'

85

Lily says:

'It's all your fault, he won't – Alun won't – have me any more and it's all because of you and your fucking baby, which I'm no way going to have, you know: I'm not even going to fucking be alive in an hour's time, bastard. What did you think was going to happen? I don't care if they hear this. We were crap, you know. I never loved you. Not like I love Alun. I want someone to know that. Hello?! *When you hear this.* Ahem, of course you're not going to hear it, Conrad. Because you're going to be fucking dead. You're going to be dead with me – and it's all going to come back to Dorothy. But it's all you, really. I want you to die. I just hope I get to see you die. Cunt. Cunt. Cunt. That's what I think of you. You talentless little fucking shit-shit. Oh, what's the point. Conrad, you cunt –'

86

Vicky continued:

'And so, in the evening, Lily turns up at the restaurant – looking wonderful. You're full of hope that this is the reconciliation. You go to the table. And, as arranged, the hitman comes in and gives you three shots each. Lily dies, you don't. Next thing Alun and Dorothy hear is that Lily has been shot – and you, too. They read about it in the paper. Imagine how Dorothy feels: she'd arranged this thing; she'd cancelled it; but it had somehow gone ahead. She's a murderer. And imagine how Alun feels: he spoke to Lily again, after promising Dorothy he wouldn't. He suspects what happened. He suspects Lily rearranged the hit. And what about Laurence? He knows from the tapes all about what his mother had planned. He also knows that Lily came round that morning and that he gave her the hitman's number. The police have already caught the hitman, but he tells us nothing. He's just some hotshot – wanting to show that he can get away with anything, wanting to earn a reputation. Eventually, we get to Alun and Dorothy. We bring them in for questioning. They tell us everything. Alun tries to cover up for himself. Neither of them knows about Laurence. But we already know that Dorothy isn't really responsible. We have the message that Lily left on your answerphone. The one you've just heard. We have Lily's diaries – which tell the whole story. (The sniffer dogs found them in her secret hiding-place. They also found her drug stash.) We've talked to Lily's parents. We already know that Lily rearranged the whole thing. But if we arrest and charge Dorothy, we fuck everything else up. You see, what we're really interested in is the people that Tony Smart helped put Dorothy in touch with. The real villains. Technically, Dorothy isn't even a murderer. It was conspiracy to, but even *then* she called it off. Lily was guilty of plotting your murder. We can't charge her. We have the hitman himself. He's going down. But we know that the whole thing was a set-up from the start. The hitman's boss thought he had a dangerous one on his hands. So he let him go along with Dorothy's mad plan for shooting someone in the middle of a crowded restaurant. He knew the stupid idiot would get caught. He wanted him banged up in prison. He was too much of a liability outside. And all this time, while you were trying to put the blame on someone other than Lily, we've been trying to get to *him*. The boss. And we were almost there. All we needed was for Dorothy to agree to drop him in it. She was keeping quiet. She was terrified of him. It was only when you kidnapped Laurence that she agreed to help. In the end, you helped us. That was one of the reasons we didn't arrest you. But that was a whole other mess. No-one was telling me anything. I didn't know about James. I certainly didn't know that they were selling you guns and blank bullets. That was a completely different operation. They were desperate to keep you quiet. You see, if you made any noise, then we'd have to arrest Dorothy – and that would be her gone as a witness. They thought the best way to do that was to watch you discreetly, via James. They were so close to getting to the hitman's boss. Days away from having enough to arrest him. Then, when they noticed that his men, the albino and the other guy, were following you, they thought that might be a useful connection. But then some rival gang got wise and started following them (and you) around. They were hoping to fuck the whole thing up and get the boss arrested. That would be him out of the way and them home free. It was the albino and the other guy who chucked the paint on your door and the brick through your window. It was them that did Tony. But as soon as their boss knew we had Dorothy, he was on your side. He'd had Dorothy closely watched the whole time. It was Asif who torched your flat. He was so fucking pissed off at losing his job, he wanted to do something to get back at you. I sympathize with him, really. Though all this has actually been rather good for my career. *Grace under pressure*, that's what the Chief Inspector called it. So, anyway, there you are – running round, causing all this chaos. Half the time you're really useful to us – because you're putting the wind up Dorothy and bringing her nearer to helping us; half the time you're a real pain in the arse – buying guns, buying bullets. But there were guys at the station who've been after this boss practically their whole careers. He was their school. And they were prepared to do almost *anything* to get him. So, when James found out what you were after, they set up the bloke in the pub. You got the gun you wanted, with blanks. Then you found out they were blanks, so they sold you some more. It was all going to work out fine, until you managed – completely by accident – to get hold of that real revolver. Before then, of course, you'd disappeared from view. That was my fault. I didn't tell anyone about Anne-Marie until late on. I couldn't believe she'd be stupid enough to go on seeing you. Then there was the business with the bike. Your friend the albino died, you know. Right there on the street. You could have ended up in serious trouble if we hadn't known what we were about: the ballistics of the gun you used to shoot Dorothy exactly matched those of the gun used in the shooting of the albino – and in several other unrelated incidents. Some also fatal. Anyway, then you went off and used Michael to get into the restaurant. We didn't know you knew him. And then you shot Dorothy. You stupid idiot! If we hadn't put her in a bulletproof vest, she would have died. Luckily for you, she didn't. She won't be able to act again, though. You completely fucked her ribcage. But at least she's around to speak at the various trials that are going to be happening. As will I. As will my new best friend Anne-Marie. As will you. Unfortunately. With Dorothy's testimony, together with Tony's and Laurence's, and a whole lot of circumstantial stuff, we now have enough to bring the hitman's boss to trial – and to have him convicted. That's what we were waiting for all along: the evidence needed to make a complete case. It's what they call *corpus delicti*.'

87

A couple of weeks into my second stay at UCH, I got one of the nurses to bring me a phone. From my hospital bed, with the curtains drawn all around me, without really knowing what I was intending to say, I called Lily's flat. After listening to my own voice on the answerphone ('I'm sorry no-one's here at the moment please leave a message and we'll get back to you . . .') I began to speak. Not exactly to Lily. Not exactly to myself. But not exactly to anyone else either. This, or something like it, is the message I left:

'It's probably a bit mad, but I know you're still really there. I've been trying to work out whether, in all this time, you haven't been more alive than me. In some ways, at least. You certainly changed more than I did – than I allowed myself to. As far as I can see, you're a completely different person to the one I thought I knew. Almost, anyway. And even her, I didn't know very well. That's partly because you spent most of the time we were together lying to me and partly because I've spent most of the time since then lying to myself. I think I knew. Really, in most ways, I think I knew the whole thing. But there I was, just going on with it – letting you work out your revenge on me, through me. I feel like I've been chasing – I don't know what I feel like I've been chasing. A ghost, I suppose. I don't like that word. It's not vicious enough for what you are. You're something else. You're more like, what? A bullet. Harmless enough by itself, held in the palm. But when following its trajectory, as you continued following yours, it's pretty fucking lethal. Just by not being alive, you've done so much damage. I wasn't going to say I hate you. That seems so obvious. Of course I hate you – how could I not hate you? But, now I think about it, I think I probably hated you all along. It wasn't you doing all this to me, I was doing it to myself. You might say that you knew that was going to happen, but you didn't. You wanted me dead. The people that you wanted merely punished have been – or will be, pretty soon. But I'm still here, you know. I'm still here . . . Oh, fuck it . . . I'm bored with this.'

Even before I put the phone down I was already in hysterics.

88

That's what I remember saying.

But it may not be completely accurate because when I went along to Lily's flat a few weeks later to start clearing all her stuff out, the message hadn't been properly recorded.

When I tried to play it back, all I could hear was the cackle-crackle of far-off static.

Acknowledgements

Invaluable in the writing of this book were: Vincent J. M. Di Maio's *Gunshot Wounds: Practical aspects of firearms, ballistics and forensic techniques*; Ulrich Drews' *Color Atlas of Embryology*; R. M. H. McMinn, R. T. Hutchings, J. Pegington and P. H. Abrahams' *Color Atlas of Human Anatomy*; Elisabeth Bronfen's *Over Her Dead Body: Death, femininity and the aesthetic*; Philippe Ariès' *The Hour of Our Death*; and J. G. Ballard's *Crash*. Also, the exhibitions *Doctor Death: Medicine at the end of life* (Wellcome Institute for the History of Medicine) and *The Quick and the Dead: Artists and anatomy* (National Touring Exhibitions).

The author would like to thank Simon Prosser; Lesley Shaw; Sarah Day; Harriet Braun; Mic Cheetham, Oliver Cheetham; Alex O'Connell; Dominic Hill; Lucy Till; Anica Alvarez; Julian, Caroline, Maisie; Georgina and Charlotte.